DAISY'S WARS

Meg Henderson was born in Glasgow. She is a journalist and the author of the bestselling memoir, *Finding Peggy*. She has also written many well-loved novels, including *The Holy City*, *Bloody Mary*, *Chasing Angels*, *The Last Wanderer* and *Second Sight*.

Visit www.AuthorTracker.co.uk for exclusive information on Meg Henderson.

DAISY'S WARS

Meg Henderson

HarperCollins*Publishers*

HarperCollins*Publishers*
77–85 Fulham Palace Road,
Hammersmith, London W6 8JB

www.harpercollins.co.uk

This paperback edition 2006
1 3 5 7 9 10 8 6 4 2

First published in Great Britain by
HarperCollins*Publishers* 2005

ISBN-13 978 0 00 655246 8
ISBN-10 0 0 00 655246 3

Typeset in Bembo by Palimpsest Book Production Limited,
Polmont, Stirlingshire

Printed and bound in Great Britain by
Clays Ltd, St Ives plc

*For Pip Beck Brimson and all the girls and women
who served as WAAFs in World War Two*

I

If there was one thing wireless operator Daisy Sheridan had learned it was never relax in the tower. You sat there as the boys went off, cheered on by every female on the base, looking forward to the end of your shift and hoping that by then all the boys would have made it back safely, though you knew they wouldn't. But even when losses were confirmed and the stragglers rolled in, if you were smart some instinct kept you alert. Now here it was, the unexpected, as sure as eggs is eggs.

'Daisy, I'm not going to make it back,' the voice said. 'The old kite's in bits, the crew are dead and I've taken one in the head. Something wrong with my eyes, can't see much, and my chute's useless.'

'Oh, here we go,' she replied tartly, 'another one trying for the sympathy vote.'

The boy at the other end of the line laughed quietly. 'Have I got it?' he asked. 'The sympathy vote, I mean?'

From the moment the boy's voice had come over the radio Daisy was aware that the atmosphere in the Langar tower had suddenly become still and silent as the others listened to the conversation, willing him to make it home. It was always like that, on a wing and a prayer, as they said.

'No, you haven't!' she said archly into her mike. 'Do you think you're the first Fly Boy who's tried that line on me, sunshine?'

He laughed quietly again. 'Daisy, will you write to my mother?' he asked.

'You really are determined to carry on with this, aren't you?' she sighed. 'What makes you think I write to mothers anyway, sunshine?'

'We all know that you do, Daisy,' he said softly. 'Promise me? Tell her I was a good, clean-living boy!'

'Now I *know* this is a joke!' Daisy snorted. 'Stop fooling around and get back here. We've got you, we can see you. Just put less effort into trying to chat me up and more into flying and you'll make it.'

There was no reply for a moment, save a crackling on the line. 'If I do make it back,' he said eventually, 'will you marry me, Daisy?'

'Now we've got to it!' she said sceptically. 'Are you a million-aire by any chance?'

'How did you guess?' the boy laughed. 'You know I wouldn't have dared ask if I hadn't been!'

'Then of course I'll marry you. So get your arse back here in one piece,' Daisy replied, 'and no excuses, I've got witnesses.'

'Daisy?'

'Yes, fiancé of mine?'

'Talk to me.'

'And what do you think I've been doing?' she demanded. 'I have pilots out there in *real* trouble to deal with and I'm on the line to a chancer like you. I'll be on a charge over this, y'know! And another thing, it would be polite to discuss the ring now that we're betrothed, don't you think? Will it be a nice, big, flashy family heirloom?'

For a moment the line crackled again as she listened to the sound of breathing, the noise of a sick engine in the background, then nothing. For a long moment there was silence, then Daisy felt a collective sigh as the entire tower let out the breath it had been holding. Another one gone, another boy lost, and he hadn't been that far away either. Almost imperceptibly Daisy lowered her head for an instant to steady herself. 'Any chance of a brew?' she asked calmly, already turning to the next call.

The Control Officer bent over her and said quietly into her ear, 'I wouldn't log that last one,' and Daisy nodded wordlessly without looking up. Everyone knew that eyebrows were raised from time to time over her conversations with pilots in trouble as they tried desperately to make it home after a raid. The rule was that only official jargon should be used and every word had to be logged, but everyone also knew that Daisy handled situations like this with ease, effortlessly performed several tasks at once, was never out of her depth and didn't blub – who could ask for more? That's what they said, anyway, she knew that, Daisy always coped – in an unmilitary manner it was true, but she coped. The stragglers were still coming home from the raid, those who would come home that was, and the names of those who wouldn't were already being wiped off the blackboard, though you never really gave up hope till you had to.

Without looking up, Daisy wondered which of the names being wiped off at that moment was his and what kind of chap the boy had been. Her mind was already turning to the letter she would send to his mother telling her what a good, clean-living boy he had been, how they had all loved him and would miss him terribly. Then she tossed her head slightly and went back to work.

At the end of the shift the other WAAFs waited for her.

'You go on,' she said, 'you'll be lighting up gaspers as usual and I prefer clean air, thanks.' Every time she said something of the sort she was taken back to her childhood and living with a mother who had had to fight for every breath she took, turning anyone with a lit cigarette or pipe into an enemy. Her mother was gone now too, but Daisy still hated tobacco smoke. It made her cough for her mother's sake, she always thought, rather than her own.

She quickly turned her thoughts away. She didn't want to think about Kathleen, she just wanted some space so that the sound of the boy's voice would leave her mind, but she had thought in the wrong direction if she was looking for a diversion. She left the tower to walk alone in the cool morning air, smiling to herself as she wondered why the others didn't ask her how the smell of aircraft fuel and burning didn't offend her 'clean air' demands – burning flesh too, often enough.

She gave another shake of the head. 'Daisy Sheridan copes!' she told herself quietly. 'Behave yourself, girl!'

She did cope, it was true, but sometimes she needed a little time alone to file the latest incident in her mind, to commit it to where thoughts of her mother already lay, in the care of 'the real Daisy Sheridan', rather than the one people saw, the one she seemed to be on the outside. They were all there, the people and events she didn't want to think about, at some time or other, like ghosts inhabiting her mind, all being cared for by 'the real Daisy Sheridan' until she had time to deal with them properly. During this long war there were so many ghosts that she often wondered if there would be enough time left in her life when the fighting was over to think about them properly.

'When the war is over' – that was what everyone said. They had said it so long already that it had lost its meaning; nobody could really look ahead and visualise a war-free time. For five bleak years everyone with someone in the Forces, and that meant almost every family in the entire country, lived in dread of receiving a telegram from the War Office that started '*I regret to inform you* . . .'.

The war had become a habit, that was the truth. There were children who had been born and gone to school knowing nothing but drabness, rationing and fear, knowing their fathers through photos and tales told by mothers who had no way of telling if they might ever see them in the flesh. Funny to think she had ever been a child like that herself, and not too many years ago either; but, on the other hand, she had never really been a child like that, when she came to think of it. Neither of the Sheridan girls could ever be described as like other children.

When she thought of Kay a picture came into her mind of her older sister on the stage in one of Newcastle's Hibernian clubs. It wasn't her first memory, but it was the one seared into her brain, probably because it was so perfect. Daisy had been about seven years old, so Kay must have been about nine, her delicate, heart-shaped face with the big, bright blue eyes framed by her hair, a cascade of dark red waves that ended at her waist, a child of truly exquisite beauty. As Kay stood, her small feet slightly hen-toed, on the worn wood of the floorboards, bathed in a single cheap spotlight, the colour of her eyes had been intensified by a puff-sleeved dress in a satiny, shiny material of the same vivid blue. The colour complemented her colouring perfectly and the dress was strewn with sequins that shone like diamonds, sequins her mother and Daisy had sewn on by hand. To complete the false glamour that was Little Kay Sheridan, a big matching bow held her hair back from her face as she sang of emotions she didn't understand and probably never would.

'I'll Take You Home Again, Kathleen', she had sung that night, always her big closing number, their father Michael's favourite song in honour of their mother, Kathleen — and judging by the Irish Geordie audience, a favourite of theirs too. Kay sang to them in her clear, strong voice, evoking nostalgic thoughts and memories of Ireland, the country where they still felt they belonged, and she sang with such feeling that tears always ran down the cheeks of people who were three or four generations removed from Ireland, but still regarded the green, green land across the sea as 'home'.

In the corner of the stage, Kathleen Sheridan sat on a shaky wooden chair, her eyes gleaming, her cheeks two bright red circles as her lips silently moved in time with her daughter's, her face reflecting the feelings on Kay's innocent face in this well-rehearsed routine.

Even then, though she was two years younger than Kay, Daisy had been amazed at how easily the audience had been fooled by what sounded like emotion in her sister's voice. She was a great turn in the Irish clubs, Little Kay Sheridan, just as her mother had been before her, but one day Little Kay would be a great star. That's what everyone said, wiping their tears away after Kathleen had been safely taken home once more, and not least because of her wonderful voice. They loved to cry, that's what Daisy had learned. People liked nothing more than sentiment, real or imaginary, it didn't seem to matter, especially to the Irish, but then she had already half-understood that. They had never been welcome in Newcastle: even those born and bred in the city were regarded as foreigners. Having an Irish name was a handicap that made sure you didn't belong in what was, what had become, your own home in your own country, the only one you'd ever known.

The Sheridans had fared no worse than others, better than

6

many, but they were still Irish and that meant Catholic and Fenian. You carried it with you like an ugly scar, so that you were only really at ease among similarly disfigured people. That scar was what held the exiled Irish together.

'Your great-grandfather Bernard was just a boy from a poor farming family,' Daisy's father would tell his own. 'He had to leave a home in a beautiful land where he was loved and come to a hostile place like this just to stay alive.'

He would shake his head mournfully at this point, as he did at various points throughout the tale, and Daisy wasn't very old before she knew in advance where each shake would come.

'Those who could afford it went to America,' Michael continued, 'but the really poor like Bernard had to go wherever work was to be found, to big cities like this damnable place.' Another sad shake of the head followed.

Newcastle had been rich in industry in the early 1800s, with chemical works, shipbuilding, engineering, coal mining and, at just that time, the invention of the railways. Most of the new arrivals became navvies, building railroads and viaducts, camping beside the newly built lines, surviving cheaply, saving what they could to one day afford to bring their wives and families or their sweethearts over to Newcastle.

'All they wanted was to be able to earn enough to look after their own, to have normal family lives,' Michael continued, 'but the only work they'd give the Irish was the hardest and worst paid, so they could only afford the dirtiest and cheapest lodgings. Bernard was going to work on the railways, he had family working as navvies who had spoken up for him, and he would've joined them if it hadn't been for Lord Londonderry.' Another shake.

In 1844, Lord Londonderry, who owned coal mines in Seaham in nearby County Durham, was in dispute with his workers, so he threw them out of their jobs and tied homes and brought in 150 Irishmen to do the work instead – for lower wages, of course. Bernard had jumped at the chance. His earnings wouldn't be as high as those of the miner he was replacing, but they were considerably better than he could have earned for equally back-breaking work building the railways. If the Geordie miners didn't want it, he and another 149 did.

'He landed at Whitehaven and had to walk over miles of moorland to get to Seaham, but he didn't care. He knew he could earn good money sinking shafts for new mines and that if he worked hard he could afford to bring the lovely Niamh over from the ould country.'

'The lovely Niamh.' That was how Michael always described his grandmother, making Daisy feel that she had a special relationship with the old woman she had no memory of. Daisy had entered the world as 'the lovely Niamh' had been taking her leave of it, but they shared a bond.

What Bernard and the others didn't know then, and, in their circumstances, probably wouldn't have cared about if they had, was that the incident would become another weapon against every Irishman or woman in the Newcastle area for all time. They became known as 'the Seaham Scabs', though local myth would transform the numbers from 150 to thousands, and the stigma of the Irish Blacklegs would encompass anyone with an Irish name for generations to come. Even fifty years later, when work was slack, miners of Irish descent like Daisy's father were laid off first from pits where they had worked for three generations longer than the English miners who were kept on.

'Was it fair that my grandfather and the others took the jobs and homes of other men?' Michael Sheridan would ask with a shrug when he recounted the old tales. 'Probably not. We wouldn't have liked it much if it had happened to us, now, would we? But when people are starving the first things out of the window are principles. Besides,' he would say with a note of bitterness, reaching for the bottle once again, 'I think we've been punished enough by this city for the sins of our grandfathers, don't you?'

Listening to him, Daisy would nod firmly because that was what her father wanted, but she didn't really feel as he did. She understood the hurt, but she didn't *feel* it, nor the melancholy. That was mainly a male thing, though she sympathised with Michael's feelings over the treatment of generations of Irish Geordies. Sometimes, in the retelling of the old stories, she would glance at Kay, trying to gauge her sister's reaction, but there was no expression there, save the one she always had, beautiful but blank.

'Their only crime had been to be starved into taking any work they could get and to love Ireland!' Michael's voice would rise in a kind of crescendo at this point. 'And God knows, the one they lived in didn't want them.' And here his voice would crack completely.

And, Daisy knew, it lost few chances to let them know they would never be accepted, no matter how long they were there, which in turn made them keep to themselves, living, working and socialising only with each other, keeping alive a vision of the green place across the sea that they had left, never to set foot on again.

Daisy understood that, but she didn't understand why generations who had never seen Ireland seemed to remember it even more strongly and lovingly than those who had. Somehow she didn't feel part of their maudlin, defeated attitude that all too often led to the bottle. That, she began to understand as she grew older, was part of the problem. What it did to her was make her determined that she wouldn't be there any longer than necessary. It gave her the will to move on from Newcastle and from the way the Irish all too often dealt with the city. She didn't know where or when she would achieve this, but she did know that she didn't belong to either side, and she didn't want to belong either. There was a world out there where all these ancient hurts, tiresome resentments and mindless animosities didn't matter, and that's where she belonged.

While Michael retold the old stories to his daughter, across the continent an odd-looking little Austrian was working himself into a simmering rage because Germany had lost WW1. Daisy had no way of knowing it, but it would take the little Austrian's ambitions to present her with that opportunity to move on when she was eighteen years old.

2

When Bernard Sheridan and the other 149 Seaham Scabs took over the forcibly vacated homes of English miners, his work would make him and his family itinerants, moving from colliery to colliery, wherever he was needed to open up a new pit. Sinkers dug through the earth to where unworked coal seams were to be found, creating new work for miners and increased profits for the owners. It was back-breaking and dangerous work, but there would never be a safe job as long as the mining industry existed, and in time he picked up the special skills needed from his fellow sinkers.

They worked in teams of up to six, digging the soft earth on the surface by hand to open up a hole measuring ten feet by fifteen. As they dug deeper, a reinforcing framework of wood was constructed to stop the walls of the trench falling inwards and burying them alive. Gradually the wood was replaced with brick and stone, and at the same time wooden shafts would be sunk through the soft earth to the rock beneath. To get through this layer, hammers, chisels and some-times explosives were used to clear a path to the coal seam below. The hole would run straight down for a hundred feet or more, with the men being lowered down to work and hauled back up by steam-powered sinking engines.

It went without saying that accidents were frequent. It was not a safety conscious era, and Lord Londonderry was no different from other mine owners in caring not a toss for his workers, as he had already proved. If some protested about the conditions, there were always others willing or desperate enough to take their place.

Danger came not just from the explosives they used, but from boulders falling down on the sinkers working below, and it wasn't unknown for a man to fall into a deepening pit. Other risks came from the earth itself, at a time when geology wasn't understood. Encountering a sudden rush of water not only weakened the sides of the dig, but risked drowning men before they could be hauled back up. Suddenly finding quicksand had the same effect, and, occasionally, they would hit gas, always a danger, even with ventilation shafts installed. The job of the sinker teams was a skilled one that took time to master, but it suited Bernard in one way, because he had been used to the open land all his life and the thought of being completely underground, huddled in a dark, wet, three-foot-high seam, hulking coal all day, scared him. In other ways it suited him less, precisely because he was a country boy and he hated the increasing darkness as he descended from ground level, the lack of space and air. But it was still better than that three-foot seam, and if you looked up you could see the sky above.

As a sinker he would work till the coal seam was reached, sink the shafts to support it, leave the actual coal-digging to others, then move on to the next village where his skills were needed. It wasn't uncommon for each child in a sinker's family to be born in a different village because home was wherever their father happened to be working at the time, with the boys going down the pits and the girls into service or to work on farms.

As fate would have it, though, Bernard would work in the Newcastle coalfields for only fourteen years, before an unlikely scenario brought his time to an end.

'I never knew my grandfather,' Michael would say, 'but I heard so much about him that to this day I can almost see him. He was a small, stocky man, well-muscled because of the work, with brown hair and grey eyes; quiet, so they say, and cheerful. He didn't draw attention to himself and his only ambition was to save enough to take his family back to Ireland one day, though he wasn't the only one who was doing that. He missed the open air and the space, and in his mind he thought he could go back home, buy a farm and start his life over again. He had to work as a sinker, but his heart wasn't in it, and when he had a few hours off, he walked.

'My father told me he would go off on one of his walks and just disappear for hours at a time, then come back and get ready for work again in his quiet way.'

Daisy could almost see Bernard through Michael's eyes, just as Michael saw him through his own father's, and she wondered if he was ever aware that he was describing Granda Paddy and himself as he talked about Bernard. She never tired of Michael's stories, even if she was never sure how true they were, because each time she heard them it was as if she was seeing her past a bit more clearly, and feeling a sense of herself that much stronger.

'He liked the sea, I think it was that space thing again. You know how you can stretch your eyes when you look across the sea?'

Daisy nodded.

'And it reminded him of Ireland, of course, because his home wasn't far from the sea and he was used to boats. He liked to spend time where fisherfolk were to be found, to walk by the riverside and down the lanes, Dark Chare, Blue Anchor Chare and Peppercorn Chare. And that's what he was doing on that October day in 1854,' Michael said with a sigh, 'walking along the Tyne by Guildford, looking at the fishing boats landing their catches and the wherries taking loads to bigger ships lying down river. Then there was the big explosion.'

A fire had started in a worsted factory in Hillsgate, Gateshead, and quickly spread through the cramped riverside buildings to a warehouse containing thousands of tons of sulphur, saltpetre, turpentine and naphtha. As it exploded, stones and bricks were thrown across the Tyne, starting fires on the other side, and fifty-three of the crowd that had gathered to watch were killed, including Bernard Sheridan.

'He'd been using explosives at work every day for years,' Michael said, 'and he died at the age of thirty-four in an explosion on his day off. Now isn't that just plain unfair? And they talk about the luck of the Irish,' he would finish bitterly, as though the whole world regularly conspired against them.

Bernard's wife, Niamh, left a widow at the age of thirty with six children to care for, briefly considered moving back to Ireland, an instinctive reaction to run for home in times of trouble. Niamh was made of sterner stuff, though, and she used the money Bernard had been saving 'to go back home' to rent a house in Byker, a working-class area far from the coalfields, and became a landlady. She was small, as all malnourished people were in that era, with dark blue eyes, her fine fairish hair in a bun that never quite contained the strands, and she had a bustling air about her. She was a feisty woman who had opinions and voiced them freely in a way that Bernard never would have. She resented the anti-Irish feeling she and her children faced every day, and remarks that blamed the Irish for being poor, uneducated and dirty.

Newcastle was a busy port and, like all ports, the constant traffic of foreigners brought diseases like typhus and cholera to the city, particularly when there were many people crammed into little space. The native Geordies always blamed this, as everything else, on 'the Irish'. Whenever she met with this kind of bias, Niamh would point out that if the Irish were kept in low-paid jobs they could only afford the worst housing. So it was from necessity, not choice, that they lived in over-populated tenements with no sewers or drains, and was it any wonder some of them drank out of despair and became even more maudlin about 'home'?

Secretly, though, Niamh disapproved of drink. She thought it a great failing of the Irish, particularly the males, and she had no time for the false sentiment it brought out in them, though she would never have admitted it outside her own four walls. Her own father in Ireland had been a case in point. He drank to escape his circumstances but he drank his wife and children out of any hopes they had of improving their situation.

Niamh had never forgotten that: it was partly why she had seen moving to Newcastle as a step away from that attitude all those years ago. She soon learned that it didn't matter where they lived, though. The Irish saw themselves as defeated victims wherever they were, and turning to the bottle was too often their only response to their problems. It wouldn't happen to her children, she decided. She would make sure they understood they had to help themselves, and the way to do that was through learning. 'Now, her I do remember, her I will never forget,' Michael said with a smile. 'My, now, there was a busy woman for you. No time for slackers, no time for complainers, she believed in getting on by helping herself. "Don't feel sorry for yourself," she used to say. "Make something of yourself instead." And all her children learned to read and write, including my father, her youngest. I don't know if you remember your Granda Paddy, Daisy, but he always had a book about him, didn't matter what it was or how many hands it had gone through before his had touched it. He always had a book.'

'Your Granny Niamh called him her "wee sponge", didn't she?' Daisy replied right on cue, knowing how her father liked to talk about his family.

Michael nodded, smiling at the memory. 'Because he read everything he could get his hands on, he just soaked every-thing up. She was a wonderful woman, you know. She fought for everything she had, every inch of progress her family made was down to her. And she only took in Irish lodgers, that was her way of fighting back.'

'Well, they were the most needy, weren't they?' Daisy said, like a response to the priest at Mass. 'If she didn't take them in and provide decent lodgings, who would?'

'Exactly,' Michael replied. 'She was helping men coming over from the ould country like her husband had, and keeping her family fed while she was doing it.'

So that's where the practical but helpful and straight-talking gene had come from, Daisy would think. Not from the Sheridans at all, but from Granny Niamh, who had named her Daisy.

The old woman hadn't been dying of any disease. She was simply worn out, and the newborn child had been taken to her on her deathbed, where Niamh had insisted on sitting up and holding her.

'My, look at that wee face,' the old woman had said as she looked at her new great-granddaughter, 'as bright and fresh as a daisy.'

Those were the last words Niamh ever spoke. Shortly after holding the newest arrival she lapsed into unconsciousness and died two days later, and so the child had been named Daisy Niamh in her honour.

If Daisy had chosen her own name it would've been something glamorous, like Kay, perhaps, who had been named for their mother, Kathleen; but as it had come from Great-Granny Niamh she had decided long ago that she could put up with it. The fact was that Kay suited her sister. It sounded feminine, bright and sparkling somehow, just as she was on stage. Or perhaps because of her act her name had been touched by an invisible magic wand that had left some sparkle dust behind. Kay was like Kathleen, so said Michael Sheridan – same dark red hair, bright blue eyes and beautiful voice – and Daisy would smile, though she couldn't imagine her mother ever looking like that.

Granda Paddy had had ambitions for his children, Michael always maintained. He'd wanted to keep them out of the pits just as much as his mother had her children. 'He was crushed at having to betray his mother,' Michael said, 'and he never got over it.' The fact was that the times were against great leaps forward by the Irish Geordies. In the late 1800s the Irish were still confined to the most menial jobs or the ones no one else wanted, even if 'native' Geordies did complain that the incomers were depriving them of work. And incomers they still were, though they had been born there. Old Niamh's sons had few opportunities in life, it was true, but what they did have were contacts in certain parts of the mining industry from previous generations, so that was where they found work. They became colliers in nearby Washington, in the solidly Irish-Catholic Usworth pit, where wet, dangerous conditions were acknowledged as among the worst in the industry. Even so, no Irish Catholic would have accepted a job in the better working environment of the equally solid Newcastle Protestant C Pit, even if one was ever offered, which it wasn't.

Michael always became sad when he talked of his father, who was, he said, a clever man.

'He had the heart and soul of a poet,' he would say, 'and always a thirst for learning; but he didn't have a chance, he spent his entire life digging coal. If ever there was an injustice,' and he'd shake his head and look away. 'I think it broke Granny Niamh's heart that he had to go down the mines.'

Daisy had never thought that. She knew instinctively without knowing how that Granny Niamh had been a realist, that she had been fully aware that it would take more than one generation for her family to get on, up and out. She looked after the exiled Irish who came to her door, and cared for them well, so there was no great fortune to be made out of her lodgers. What profit she made did no more than supplement the meagre wages of her children when they were old enough to work, keeping a roof over their heads, clothes on their backs, food in their bellies and – it was an important 'and' – enough to buy books and the will to do so.

Niamh was under no illusions. She knew the way out was through learning and she was giving them a respect for it, laying the foundations for those who would come after her and hoping they would be able to afford to continue to learn. Even as a small child Daisy knew her father didn't understand this. Indeed, there were times when she felt that she had been born older than him, and in many ways she probably was. She was coming to the conclusion that most men never really grew up and the Irish variety grew up least. Their childlike natures were part of their charm, but as she was exposed to it early she was immune to it, so having Michael as her father, exasperating as it often was, had been a bonus. Daisy had been cut from Niamh's side of the cloth, and she recognised in her father all the characteristics of the Irish: nostalgia, sentimentality and the childish fun that could turn to maudlin at the opening bars of a song from 'home', especially when accompanied by a drink or two. She would inwardly shake her own head as she listened to him. Much as she loved her father, she knew he was a man who lived on his emotions, heart over head every time, but it was a false heart, driven by that familiar and disabling melancholy. Ingrained in Michael, as in so many Irishmen, was the conviction that nothing would ever work out for him or his, simply because they were Irish. It was as though they were born to be losers.

With the First World War looming the pits had worked flat out in 1913, producing huge stockpiles of coal, only to be rewarded in 1914 with working only two or three days a fortnight; and the Irish, as usual, were first to be laid off. Unemployment was high when General Kitchener made his call in March 1914 for 100,000 men aged between nineteen and thirty years to join the army.

The miners, believing it would all be over by Christmas, decided to have a paid holiday on the state rather than see their families starve. The local regiments were the Northumberland Fusiliers, the Durham Light Infantry and the Green Howards, and, thinking the Howards was a Catholic regiment because of the 'Green' in the title, it became the target of the Irish. When they discovered their mistake they founded their own regiment, the Tyneside Irish, though most of them had been English for at least two generations by that time.

Michael Sheridan, being just over the upper age limit,

continued to toil in the mine while others marched off to years of conflict, if death didn't get them first. For some reason he felt aggrieved that he had been stopped from going to war, while maintaining that the whole thing had been fixed to ensure that there were more Irishmen fighting for the British Crown than Englishmen.

Even though she was a child as she listened to these stories, Daisy knew they were all the proof she needed that the average Irish male was, well, at best illogical. Michael's voice, usually lubricated by a drink or three, would soar with anger and indignation as he embellished this strange, double-edged example of bias, and Daisy would turn away so that he didn't notice her laughter.

Poor Granny Niamh, strong woman that she was – it couldn't have been easy to cope with all that, Daisy thought, sensing that her great-grandfather and her grandfather had been exactly the same as Michael and his brothers. It was a family trait, a *male* family trait. Michael blamed his inability to move up in the world, as he did everything in life, on anti-Irish prejudice, and his escape was in telling his stories, wonderful and entertaining as they were. His father, Paddy, had kept his nose in books as *his* escape, and Bernard had walked off into the distance on his own whenever he could, as a means of dealing with life, even if it had ironically brought him an early death. The Irish had been pre-destined not to be allowed to succeed; it wasn't their fault, it was the fault of the English, or the world, or maybe even the God they said their rosaries to. And if they were bound to be defeated then what was the point in trying?

Not that you could blame Granda Paddy too much. His adult life hadn't been any easier than his mother's had been, though she had dealt with her lot better then he did. His wife had died giving birth to Michael, so there was no adult woman to push him or the five older sons she left behind. And it was always the women who pushed, they were the backbone of every family.

Their daughter, Clare, was the eldest, so in the way of things in their culture she took over the running of the house and family at the age of twelve. The only help she ever got was from older women in the family, all of whom had more than enough work with their own families. Besides, she was a female and, in the eyes of others in the family, she was doing what she should and therefore she would cope. She wasn't the first child obliged to suddenly become an adult, after all.

Though she had never set eyes on her Aunt Clare, Daisy had a soft spot for her and longed to find her one day, when she was grown up. Clare had brought up her six brothers, cared for her father and run the home for more than twenty years, missing out on any life of her own; but though no one suspected it, Clare was making plans.

Michael, the youngest, was the last to marry and leave home, and the day after the wedding Clare had declared that now she had done her duty, she was off. Without saying a word to anyone she had already booked her passage on a boat to America, her packing was done, and when she left she said firmly that she would not be coming back.

There was general shock within the family. It was all very well to say Michael was off her hands, but she was the official mother figure and never likely now to have any children of her own, so she should take her part in looking after her brothers' offspring. Besides, there was her father – she couldn't leave him to fend for himself.

'Bugger my brothers' children,' Clare had replied with feeling, 'bugger my father and bugger the rest of you if you don't like it. I've done enough. I'm the wrong side of thirty and I've never had a life, it's my turn now.' And with that she left Newcastle forever.

Typically, rather than look after himself, Granda Paddy took his books and moved back in with his elderly mother.

Michael would tell this story in a shocked voice, hurt that any woman related to him could desert her duty. It brought disgrace on the entire family, especially as everyone in the community knew about it. The only person who did not criticise Clare in these old tales was, Daisy noted with pride, Old Niamh – and Daisy herself, of course. Every time her father recounted this terrible abandonment, Daisy cheered inside. As a small child she had been rifling through family pictures and papers in Granny Niamh's house, where Granda Paddy still lived, and she had found an envelope with an American address on the back. Inside was a picture of Aunt Clare taken in New York, dressed in the clothes of the time, long skirt, high-necked blouse and buttoned boots. On her head was a flat hat like a pancake with the merest hint of veil that had been firmly pushed out of the way, and she had a robust bag over one arm, and clutched in both hands an umbrella. The sepia snap was too dark to be able to see Clare's colouring, and her expression was so severe that it made Daisy laugh out loud. It was as though she was saying, 'Well, I'm here now, take it or leave it. If you choose to ignore this attempt to keep in touch, well, bugger you all again.' Though the truth was that taking a picture in those days took so long that even the most determined smile would die before being captured.

It was the only tangible link to Aunt Clare's existence and Daisy never discovered if anyone in the family had ever replied, but she always felt that it was significant that it had been sent to Granny Niamh and Granny Niamh had kept it. So Daisy took it and kept it too, never mentioning it to anyone. If there was one thing Daisy learned from her childhood it was that women were always the practical ones, the strong ones who were relied on so that the males could wallow in their feelings. Granda Paddy, Michael and all the rest avoided, in their own ways, trying to help themselves and so never achieved anything for their families, and so it was that in due course Michael and his brothers followed Paddy down the mines. If she and Kay had been boys, Daisy was sure that they, too, would have been expected to do the same, and, as it was, going into service was regarded as the highest they could achieve if it hadn't been for their mother, though that was accident rather than design.

When she was young, Kathleen Clancy had been a highly-regarded singer in their community, and though Michael had worshipped her from afar as a boy, he finally met her when her brother came to work beside him. The Clancys were a musical family, every one of them played an instrument or sang, but Kathleen was the youngest of seven and therefore benefited from the fact that there were many wages coming into the house as she was growing up, giving her the opportunity to develop her talent.

For Michael the Clancys were a revelation. 'Everywhere you turned in their house there was music,' he'd say. 'They were all gifted, touched by God.'

Daisy always let the last bit pass. Michael was her father, after all.

'And there was Kathleen, so beautiful and with that glorious voice,' he'd remember aloud, his eyes shining. 'How could any man not love her?'

Michael had pursued her for years, just as many other young men had, 'until she caught me,' he'd say with a grin, glancing at his wife. And watching the affectionate look that passed

23

between her parents, Daisy understood that her father still saw her mother as she had been, to him she hadn't changed at all.

After they married Kathleen had continued with her singing, but something had happened with their first child's arrival, or slightly before, though no one had been aware of it till afterwards. She had bloomed for the first six or seven months of her first pregnancy, then she seemed to weaken, but those last months were tiring for all women so no one worried. After the birth she never really returned to normal, though once again there were reasons: the birth had been long and punishing, besides, a new baby could exhaust anyone.

It was Daisy's birth two years later that had set the seal. Once again a weakness set in at six or seven months and from then on it seemed that Kathleen couldn't catch her breath and the slightest exertion had her gasping for air. One of the pictures of her mother Daisy would carry in her mind for the rest of her life was of Kathleen on wash day, bent over a washboard, rubbing her family's clothes up and down its corrugated metal strip, and suddenly stopping and resting her forehead on the wooden frame for support, breathless and sweating.

On each cheek Kathleen developed a round red spot, as though she had been wearing rouge, so that she always looked so healthy, if you discounted the fact that she couldn't breathe. It was down to some illness she had had as a child, a doctor had told Michael. It had affected her heart, and she shouldn't have any more children.

Michael couldn't understand why they blamed her heart when it was obviously her lungs – he was a miner, he knew about lungs. Despite what he had been told, Michael suspected that his wife was suffering from tuberculosis, the scourge of the working classes who were forced to live so tightly packed together. In an attempt to provide her with more space to effect a cure, he had managed to rent a terraced house in Guildford Place in Heaton, a mile from Byker, in a single row of houses facing onto the railway line. It was far too big for the family, having more bedrooms than they could decorate, heat or use, but that was how Michael was, he had no balance in anything he did or thought. Kay and Daisy shared a bedroom upstairs, a step or two above the separate toilet and inside bathroom, which was a luxury, and the others lay empty.

'I made sure,' Michael would say firmly, 'there would be no more children.' And Daisy would nod just as firmly, though she had no idea what he meant. It would be some years before she made any connection between her mother sleeping, indeed living, in the big room at the front downstairs, and her father sleeping in the one at the back.

There would be no more singing for Kathleen either and her brightness began to fade. She was like a candle burning down and slowly dimming, her life hovering around the last flickering of a wick, only just sustaining a glimmering of fire. The rouge-like stain stayed on her cheeks and, as her beautiful red hair lost its vibrant colour and became a dull, light brown, her lips took on a blue tinge that grew deeper the more she exerted herself.

No one had any clear idea of what was wrong with her. There was no money for doctors or medicine because every spare penny went to promoting Kay's career. Even if there had been, there was little any doctor of the time could have done for Kathleen anyway.

From those years came the sound Daisy would never forget, of her mother trying to breathe — a harsh, rasping sound that would haunt her dreams. With Michael working night shift down the pit, Daisy would creep into her mother's bedroom and ask if there was anything she could do, and Kathleen, weary-eyed, sweat glistening on her body and too breathless to reply, would give a slight shake of her head and close her eyes. Sometimes, decades after her mother was dead, Daisy would wake in the night, just as she had when she was a child, that picture in her mind as she waited in the darkness for her mother's next tortured breath, fearful that it might not come. Sometimes she was out of bed and on her way to her mother's bedroom again before she realised it was just a dream.

3

That Kay was blessed with her mother's looks and musical ability was a great joy to Kathleen. It gave her another chance to shine through her daughter, so that her talent had not been lost. It also gave her something to live for, which was no bad thing in itself as there was little that the medical world could have offered, and anyway, given the choice between financing Kay's future and her own present, Kathleen would undoubtedly have chosen the former.

From when Kay first started to sing, which was from birth if you believed her besotted parents, Kathleen had worked with her daughter as much as her health would allow. Even when she couldn't, there was the rest of the musical Clancy clan to help. Kay would be a star, she would claim the success that Kathleen had been destined for, but she would go one step further. Kay would one day sing not only for the local Irish community but for the world.

To enable the talented Kay to do this the entire family had to be behind her, and that meant every penny went towards her career. Michael, who was no realist himself, could refuse his wife nothing. He might not have understood his wife's illness, but on some level he seemed to accept that it was a one-way street, so what Kathleen wanted, Kathleen must have, and Kathleen wanted her daughter to be a star.

It was fortunate that when Daisy came along she proved to be not just plain and capable but without any sense of the music that flowed through her sister's veins; Kay could go on singing while Daisy coped, and so she found herself drafted into the family 'business'. It had been like that for as long as she could remember. Daisy learned to sew the dresses Kay would need for her stage work, a skill Kay herself couldn't be expected to learn because she had to perfect her gift. Likewise, Kay couldn't be of any help about the house or to her sick mother, because her music kept her too busy, and besides, artistes of her calibre did not have roughened hands.

So, as Kathleen's health gradually deteriorated, Daisy managed the household: buying groceries, cooking, washing, cleaning out and setting fires, much as Aunt Clare had done before her. Part of the burden she took on, though she never regretted it, was to nurse her mother, too, and the workload increased so gradually as she grew that she barely noticed how much she was doing. Even if she had noticed, it was just how life was. It was no one's fault, not Daisy's and certainly not Kay's, and she knew her sister had been given no more choice in these arrangements than she had herself. Their lives were, as the lives of all children were, driven by adults; they simply conformed.

Indeed, deep down Daisy felt sorry for her sister. She was far from sure that Kay got any pleasure from her music. The whole drive was to put her in a position to exploit it, and that didn't necessarily mean she should enjoy it. There wasn't a free moment, from piano lessons to singing lessons, rehearsals, auditions, dress fittings and performances. It was a life Daisy would never have wanted for herself and, if anything, she was awed by her sister's ability to stand before audiences, however adoring, and perform. Daisy knew she could never do that.

The money Little Kay's appearances brought in, plus Michael's earnings, went back into her career, so the family had little if anything left over. But when she heard Kay sing all Daisy's doubts disappeared. No one, she thought, could make such a beautiful sound with a voice if they didn't love doing it. Years later, when she looked back, she wondered about her sister, though. It was as if Kay had no personality and simply went along with whatever others planned for her, not once giving an opinion, never mind disagreeing. She simply smiled that innocent smile and complied. Sometimes, remembering her sister, Daisy would wonder if there had been something wrong with her and if she had been born like that or simply conditioned. How could it be possible for anyone to be so good-natured and obedient all of her life: no tantrums, no off-days, always perfect. Could it be normal to exist as a completely blank canvas for anyone and everyone to paint their dreams on? She had envied Kay's voice at times, but later she came to feel pity for her, because although she was there, in a way it was as if she had never actually lived.

Daisy would work in the house when she got up in the mornings, go to school when she could and return to more chores. Then she would have to accompany her sister to her next appearance, because as time passed Kathleen's condition worsened and she rarely moved from her bed, and Michael would be at work.

Daisy felt no resentment, just concern over what she hadn't had time to do because there weren't enough hours in the day, and anxiety about how Kathleen was when she was alone at home. She wasn't aware of it at the time but, looking back, she realised that deep in her mind had lurked the knowledge of

Aunt Clare's 'shameful' bolt for freedom. She would take out the secret photo and smile at the grim-looking woman clutching her umbrella as a shield, and somehow she didn't feel trapped for eternity.

It wasn't as if she was forced into a life of drudgery, playing Cinderella to her beautiful sister. Everyone just pitched in to forward Kay's career. There was always Dessie Doyle, for a start, there was no denying that, though Daisy wished she could.

Dessie was two years older than Kay, four older than Daisy, and was Kay's childhood sweetheart, the boy next door, the son Michael would never have, and Daisy had never liked him. He had been there as long as she could remember, just like many others in a community where neighbours were as close as family, but Dessie stood out because of his closeness to Kay. Wherever Kay was, there he was, too, sticking so close to her that she couldn't turn round and, more importantly, so no one else could get near her. He never took any notice of Daisy – she was just plain, quiet Daisy, the fetcher and carrier. Kay was the sole focus of his attention.

Not that Daisy objected – she was invisible to most people, especially when Kay was around – but there was something almost dismissive about Dessie's attitude to her, as though once he appeared her presence was no longer required. All through her childhood Daisy resented him, even if she couldn't quite work out why. After all, every male took over, there was nothing unusual in that. Like all males, too, Dessie was attracted to Kay, who was a local celebrity almost from the time she could walk onto a makeshift stage.

Daisy didn't trust him, that was what it was. It was that simple; even though he had never given her the slightest reason, it was just a feeling she had. Michael thought it was a simple case of jealousy, that Daisy resented her father's affection for the boy or the boy's attachment to Kay, but Daisy knew it wasn't. Her dislike of him was at gut level, an instinctive distrust for no reason she could think of. She had never felt other than suspicious of him; she felt uneasy when he was around and he was around increasingly as Kay grew into her teens. Daisy should have been grateful to have someone there to take on her duties as Kay's escort so that she could look after her mother, particularly with Kathleen's health deteriorating. It should be a relief to know that, no matter what, there was someone to take Kay safely to and from her appearances. She just wished it could be someone other than Dessie.

Even when Kathleen was too ill to watch her daughter perform, she was anxious to hear how the night had gone and couldn't settle till she heard Kay arriving home with Dessie. He was totally accepted as one of the family, but as he went with Kay to Kathleen's bedside, Daisy felt a kind of drawing back from the tall, dark boy. When they were children walking to school together, she would deliberately fall behind because she didn't want to walk in his company. Even then he was an intimidating force, at least to her: taller than all the other children, thin, dark, sallow-skinned and suspect, that was how she remembered him. He had greasy black hair falling across his forehead, giving him a shifty look as his dark eyes peered out at the world, those brown eyes so dark that they, too, looked black. At that time they were always on Kay, as most men's eyes were.

Dessie worked for Haggie R. Hood & Sons, a hemp and wire-rope manufacturers at Willington Quay on the Tyne, a step away from being a collier, and his ambition and application had taken him from the physical work of the factory to the office at nearby Akenside, so that in his late teens he was working as an order clerk. This impressed everyone else and, if he had been anyone else, it would have impressed Daisy, but he was Dessie Doyle and where others saw in him a determination to better himself, she saw only a man on the make. Whatever strides forward he had made, she guessed, they were at someone else's cost. There was no opportunity too small for Dessie to take advantage of it.

'I don't know why you can't be civil to him,' Kathleen chided Daisy, after Dessie had announced, shyly of course, another promotion.

It turned Daisy's stomach to see his modest performance, probably more than his 'I'll protect Kay' one.

'I don't know either,' Daisy admitted, tucking in the blankets around her mother and arranging a crocheted shawl across her shoulders. Kathleen was recovering, hopefully, from yet another bout of bronchitis. 'I think it's the way his eyes dart about to make sure everyone knows how modest he's being, to see if the act is going down well.'

'Daisy, that's terrible!' Kathleen replied huskily.

'But it's true,' Daisy laughed. 'I don't know how the rest of you miss it, he's like an animal lining up his next kill, a wolf or something.'

'You're just being nasty,' Kathleen retorted, already wheezing with the exertion of saying a few words. 'And he's got Kay a job in the office beside him, too, so she won't have to do rough work in a factory or go into service being somebody's skivvy.'

Daisy hardly paused, but in her mind she was thinking, *Like me, you mean, Mam, like me?*

They didn't mean to be unkind, of course. She knew that, but to her family that was her place in life – Daisy the skivvy – whereas Kay was destined for greater things, even if the career plan had faltered somewhat. Time had passed and by the age of fourteen Little Kay was no longer so little. When she sang she was no longer the sweet, innocent girl in the blue dress with puff sleeves, and, even if her voice was probably better, she was in that odd stage of being neither child nor woman. It was a hard enough time for any girl, but it left Kay in a professional hiatus with bookings dropping. There were always other sweet little girls around to take her limelight, though none with her talent, it was true.

It was a time when other girls in similar positions lost their confidence. Some never stepped in front of the spotlight again, but it had no effect on Kay, something that puzzled Daisy. It was part of the non-personality she had noticed before. Kay didn't exist as herself, only as whatever or whoever those around her wanted her to be. She seemed to have been born devoid of the ability to think for herself. Was that because she had never been allowed to, Daisy would wonder. Had she been conditioned to be compliant, or had the music simply taken over an empty space where something that should have been there was missing?

It was decided that during this temporary lull in Kay's progress to the top of the showbiz world, she would fill the gap by working. In an office. Beside Dessie. He was keeping her under his wing, Michael and Kathleen said, watching over her, though Daisy felt it was more than that. It was about control: he was making sure she didn't get away from him. And what was wrong with that? He had adored her all her life, hadn't he? Wouldn't he want to protect her? And all Daisy could think was, *Yes, but . . .*

Then it happened, the huge thing that had changed the universe forever. When she was fourteen, Daisy reached the optimum body weight of six stones and puberty assaulted her. All her life she would maintain that she had gone to bed one night as a flat-chested, plain, unremarkable child and wakened next morning inside an unknown sex-bomb's body. Everything was different; her centre of gravity had moved and her map of herself had altered in some strange way so that she bumped into things and knocked others down. It was almost like learning to walk all over again. There was just so, well, much of her in places where there hadn't been before, all of it moving in ways she didn't understand and couldn't control properly. And as for the lumps in the front, well, they just kind of got in the way all the time, so that she constantly tried to move them out of the way till her head got the message that they were stuck there and couldn't be moved. And her mousy, unremarkable features had gone as well, and in their place was this beautiful, sensual face with striking blue eyes, framed by luxurious golden tresses.

Sometimes when she looked in the mirror she would stop for a moment and stare at the unknown female looking back at her and try to find an explanation, a reason for the transformation, then she would shake her head. There was no explanation. With Kay, she knew, it had all been minimal and gradual. She had just seemed to grow taller and slightly curvier, becoming a beautiful adult version of the beautiful child she had been: even someone who hadn't seen her in years would still have recognised her as Kay. With Daisy the process had not only been overnight, but more extreme and, as she insisted, it bore all the hallmarks of a mistake by Mother Nature. Either that, she thought, or Mother Nature had been at the gin and turned mischievous, only there was no way of reversing the prank she had played. Out there, somewhere, was the rightful owner of the body Daisy now owned, someone who was used to its curves and could handle the shape, a female who would be aghast at what *she* had woken up with.

The first person to notice, apart from Daisy and her no

doubt equally horrified exchangee, was eighteen-year-old Dessie Doyle.

Dessie had never, in all the years they had grown up together, acknowledged her existence, which was fine because he gave her the creeps even when he didn't look at her. But once the new body – the new Daisy – arrived, he couldn't keep his eyes off her. At first she had felt so vindicated by his reaction that she could have screamed with happiness – now she knew why she had disliked him so much, he was indeed a creep – but shortly the joy of being right all along turned to disgust. He almost drooled when he saw her, and he made sure he saw her a great deal. His eyes never left her, following her around wherever she was in the house till she felt sick. She knew nothing about sex, but instinct told her what was in his mind, and at fourteen that frightened her, so that she wanted to run to her bed, pull the blankets over her head and hide.

For the first time, Dessie took to touching her. Nothing out of place, of course, just normal contact, but normal contact that had never happened before. A hand on her elbow as they passed each other in a doorway perhaps, but she was aware that he was passing her much more than he ever had before. And he would hold things out to her, so that she had to take them – a jacket, a bag perhaps – and in doing so he always ensured that his skin touched hers.

He began talking to her so that she had to make eye contact with him, and he held it that second too long for comfort. He began smiling at her, too, making her turn away and cringe, though he seemed to take her obvious unease as maidenly embarrassment. No one else noticed, which confused her, till she realised that to her family she was still Daisy – Background Daisy. Regardless of how she looked she would always be Background Daisy. Kay was still the focus of their attention.

Not that Dessie Doyle was the only male who changed the way he behaved towards the new Daisy, but he was in her own home, that was the difference. She would walk down the street, recoiling from the glances of males along the way, hunching her shoulders in an attempt to disguise the curves they looked at so longingly, while at the same time there was a kind of fury inside her that she should be made to feel that way. Unfortunately this heightened her colour so that her face glowed and her eyes sparkled, which enhanced the overall effect that her hunched shoulders tried to distract from.

Still, once inside the house she could close the door on all the other eyes, but Dessie had free passage any time of the day, or the night, too, if he had thought of it. He was regarded as family and therefore the door was never closed to him. And the propriety of the era made sure he had plenty of opportunity to be around Daisy. No one doubted that he and Kay would marry in due course and, though he was completely trusted by Michael and Kathleen, there was an unspoken understanding that the younger sister would act as unofficial chaperone, especially as the sisters shared a room. So there was no getting away from Dessie's leering eyes, and his hands, his entirely innocent hands, though the very thought of them coming near Daisy made her feel sick.

And that's when a new, even more assertive Daisy started speaking in her head; one who questioned everything and wondered if things should or could be different. It was part of her reaction to suddenly feeling vulnerable due to the way males treated her. To them she was an animal to be stalked, hunted, and inevitably, in their eyes, claimed as a prize. For a time she floundered, feeling helpless, before she realised that this game didn't necessarily have to be on other people's terms. She could make up her own rules, decide her own strategies.

She began to understand that she either spent her life running from the predators or she turned, faced them and took control. After all, if she had something they wanted, then she had power – it was there for the taking.

It took a lot of thinking out, but Daisy had plenty of time for thinking while she did the usual daily chores, and gradually a new persona took over the new shape, even if no one else noticed it at first. Daisy was becoming her own person.

4

When the time came for Daisy to start work, as her sister already had, Dessie, good old reliable Dessie, had stepped forward.

It was a normal evening in the Sheridan household. Dessie was always there or thereabouts, his arm around Kay, his possession, but his eyes on Daisy even with her back to him, as she sat at the table, concentrating determinedly on a newspaper laid out in front of her, her arms crossed over her chest for extra protection.

'I was thinking,' she heard him say to Michael and Kathleen, 'if you don't mind, if I'm not talking out of turn,' Daisy's face contorted with dislike, 'that I could put in a word for Daisy at the ropeworks.'

Daisy's eyes shot wide open with shock.

'My, Dessie,' her father said affectionately, 'that's a kind thought! Isn't he a good friend to this family, Kathleen?'

Kathleen didn't reply. More and more she had to conserve her breath, but Daisy sensed her mother nodding in agreement. She knew Kathleen would be just as delighted at Dessie's kindness as Michael was, but Daisy had other thoughts.

'Isn't that a kind thought, Daisy?' Michael persisted.

'Mm,' Daisy replied distantly, calmly turning a page of the newspaper on the table in front of her and quickly returning her arm to its position across her chest, trying to disguise her thoughts and her feelings, but already planning to halt Dessie's fantasy of setting up his own little harem. Sometimes necessity isn't the mother of invention, desperation can work just as well, and Daisy was desperate enough to think of ways out. Bright as she was, school 'had never really interested her, probably because she was always tired from her main preoccupation of running the house and looking after everyone in it, but she was certain of one thing: with or without Dessie Doyle's presence, she was bound for better than working in a rope factory.

As he left that night, basking in Kathleen and Michael's glowing admiration, he leaned over to where Daisy sat. If there was one thing more sickening than having to look him in the face, it was being trapped in a seated position as he leaned towards her, against her, from behind.

'We'll have fun together, Daisy,' he said brightly, and she knew exactly what he meant, even if the others didn't.

'Mm,' she repeated, pushing the chair backwards against him and getting up, getting away from him, and, for an instant, her elbow connected with his stomach. It was accidental, the last thing she wanted was to touch him in any way, but his low, sharp intake of breath pleased her just the same.

'Well, say thank you to the boy, Daisy!' Michael smiled.

'It's all right,' Dessie grinned, 'I know how she feels. She never shows it, but I know how our Daisy feels.'

Our Daisy, she thought furiously, *our* Daisy!

'Yes,' she smiled, looking away, 'I'm sure you do.'

The next day, without telling anyone, she set about finding her own work, taking herself to Fenwicks, the department store in

Northumberland Street, to ask if there were any vacancies. Inside she was terrified, but the thought of spending every day under Dessie's gaze, at risk of being touched by him, however 'innocently', spurred her on.

Her wardrobe consisted of very little, but she washed and ironed a black skirt and loaded a white blouse with so much Robin Starch that it felt like sandpaper against her skin. Her father and Kay were at work and Kathleen was asleep as she slipped out of the house and made her way to Northumberland Street, then walked purposefully into the huge store. Fenwicks was the biggest and best store in the city, a Newcastle institution, a place for window-shopping as far as people like Daisy were concerned. Once inside she felt like turning and running out again, then she thought of the alternative and approached the first assistant she saw.

'I'm looking for the person who takes people on,' she said.

The woman, dressed in an outfit almost exactly the same as the one Daisy wore, with the addition of a black cardigan and a string of pearls, looked her up and down. 'You mean you want a job?' she asked in a peculiar voice, Geordie trying very hard to sound like BBC diction on the radio. 'Here?' the woman said, as though it was the most ludicrous idea she had ever heard.

'Yes,' Daisy replied, heart thumping.

'I don't think there are any vacancies,' the woman replied, still examining her as though something decayed had been blown through the door.

Daisy resisted the impulse to turn and flee, but the woman's sniffy manner riled her. She stared back at her, taking in the precise tight waves of her hair, the heavily powdered face and narrow red streak of her mouth. Then she glanced at the ring-less third finger of her left hand and understood.

40

Daisy knew how males reacted to her, that lesson she had learned, but there was yet another shock she was coming to terms with: namely, the attitude of women, particularly women of a certain age. She had thought she would have the support of other females against the unwanted attention of men and at first she had been puzzled by what felt like hostility instead. As a child she had their protection, but physically she was now a woman, and an attractive woman at that, so now she was regarded as competition and, in the case of women like the one who was staring at her with disapproval, an almost malicious jealousy came into it.

Anger made her stand her ground.

'Well, if you'll direct me to someone who knows that for a fact,' she said firmly, 'I can ask *her*.'

Just then Daisy was conscious of another black-clad figure appearing on the edge of her vision, and in the mood she was now in she was preparing to turn and yell, '*And who do you think* you're *looking at?*'

'Can I help?' a voice asked calmly.

Daisy turned and saw a woman, younger than the old harridan she was sparring with, blue-eyed, she noticed, and dark-haired with neat features.

'I was looking for whoever takes people on,' Daisy replied. 'You know, the person who gives you a job.'

The woman smiled. 'Come with me, Miss . . . ?'

'Yes, it's Miss,' Daisy said stiffly.

'But Miss What?' the woman asked, trying not to smile, but Daisy felt it there all the same. 'You do have a name?'

'Oh, yes,' Daisy stumbled, feeling a complete fool. 'It's Sheridan. Daisy Sheridan.'

'Well, if you'd like to come with me, Miss Sheridan,' the woman smiled.

What for? Daisy thought, as she wordlessly followed the woman into a lift with double doors like expanding gates. Why bother? Even if there had been a vacancy she had started out facing up to the first nasty old spinster she had met who did have a job, and now she had disclosed her Irish roots. The thing was settled; this woman was obviously setting her up to knock her down. *So back to where you belong, Miss Sheridan, it's the rope-works for you and you should be grateful for even that.*

In the lift the woman held out a small, cool, delicate hand. 'I'm Mrs Johnstone.' She smiled, a tight, polite little smile.

Daisy shook hands, knowing her own was rough and, at that moment, distinctly sweaty, wondering just what further humiliation Mrs Johnstone had in mind for her before kicking her out. The lift stopped and the double gate routine, this time in reverse, was gone through.

'This way,' Mrs Johnstone said pleasantly, and like a lamb to the slaughter Daisy followed her into a small office. All fight had gone out of her now. She had never been in a place like this and despite her best intentions she felt intimidated; she hadn't even thought to keep an eye on what floor she was on, so how would she find her way out again with any dignity, particularly after Mrs Johnstone had delivered a flea directly into her ear? She noticed the graceful way the older woman moved, sitting behind the desk without bumping into anything or knocking anything down, something she had learned to admire and envy since finding herself with so much more to move around.

Mrs Johnstone gestured with one of her small, cool, delicate hands to a chair on the other side. Look at that, Daisy marvelled to herself. Now if I'd tried that I'd have cleared everything off the desk. Her heart sank even further as she sat down.

'Look,' she said, her voice rising with panic, 'I think I'd better go. You're just going to kick me out anyway for fighting with the old woman. I shouldn't have come here, but it was either that or the ropeworks, and I don't want to work in the ropeworks, but maybe that's where I should go anyhow.'

Mrs Johnstone stared at her, eyebrows raised and a smile on her lips. 'But I thought you were looking for a job here?' she asked calmly, putting her pretty hands on the desk in front of her.

'Well, I was, but . . .'

'That's where we'll start, then,' Mrs Johnstone said briskly. 'What do you want to do?'

'Not go to the ropeworks!' Daisy replied.

'Well, I think that shows ambition,' the woman said. 'Nothing wrong with that. And it takes a bit of confidence to come into a place like this. I appreciate that, Miss Sheridan.'

'Stupidity, more like,' Daisy said quietly.

'Confidence, Miss Sheridan,' Mrs Johnstone smiled firmly, then looked at her for a moment, but Daisy knew it was a different look from the one the old woman downstairs had given her.

'May I call you Daisy?' she asked.

Daisy nodded.

'Well, Daisy, if we took you on here, you'd have to start at the very bottom, doing whatever anyone else wanted you to do. You understand that?' She watched the expression on Daisy's face and laughed quietly. 'Yes, even Miss Manders downstairs,' she said, 'and I have to tell you that there's a great many just like her.'

Daisy smiled; her thoughts had been read. She nodded.

'What I can promise you is that if you don't have stand-up fights with her or the others like her, if you work hard and learn, you will get on here.'

'You mean you'll give me a job?' Daisy asked in amazement.

43

'I think you have a lot to learn, but, yes, if you abide by what I've said to you.'

'Why?' Daisy asked.

Mrs Johnstone chuckled silently, shaking slightly. 'Daisy, you are a very good-looking young woman. Customers like that. I think you're bright and I think you'll get on. Besides,' she said, looking directly at her, 'before I married my name was O'Neill and I grew up in Byker. I know what it is to be judged on things other than my ability, as I suspect you do. Everyone deserves a chance and I didn't get mine till I changed my name. I don't think that's right, do you?'

Daisy shook her head. 'You don't sound as though you come from Byker.'

'I can when I want to, pet,' Mrs Johnstone said in a strong Geordie accent, and they laughed. 'It's like playing a part, Daisy,' she said kindly. 'Here I'm the way you see and hear me; outside, in my own home and with my own family, that's different, a different me, in fact. Where do you live?'

'In Heaton, now,' Daisy replied, 'in Guildford Place.'

'My sister lives in Guildford Place! What a coincidence, and what a difference a mile up the road can make, can't it? Well, that's settled then.' Mrs Johnstone got up and glided gracefully out through the door as Daisy followed. She put Daisy in the lift, pressed the button for the ground floor and closed the two gates. 'I'll see you on Monday morning, Daisy,' she called. 'And don't worry, you'll be just fine.'

Daisy walked out of Fenwicks in a daze, marvelling at how good life could be when you least expected it, smiling as she passed the old woman she had first spoken to, and then smiling all the way home to Guildford Place. Once she was back home she changed out of her best clothes and set about catching up with her chores. She opened up the fire she'd banked up with dross before she had gone out and coaxed it into flame again. She finished the family washing, started the evening meal, and only then did Kathleen awake.

Michael came home first; he was on early shift these days. Then Kay arrived with Dessie, who seemed to spend more time in the Sheridan house than in his own. Daisy set out the evening meal and listened as the others went over the events of their day, saying nothing herself. When she had cleared away the dishes she deliberately left them on the draining board and closed the door before returning to the family. She knew that if she started washing them Dessie would offer to dry them. It earned him the praise of Kathleen and Michael, but Daisy knew he used his offer of help as a means of legitimately brushing against her as often as possible in the small space. Out of necessity she had learned to think ahead, to block every move before it happened.

Dessie looked up.

'Not washing the dishes, then, Daisy?' he asked, grinning at her.

'I don't feel like it,' she replied casually. 'I'll do them later.'

'Well, if you're fed-up washing, I'll do it and you can dry?' he offered.

He never gives up! she thought grimly.

'If you're that keen you can wash *and* dry,' she suggested calmly, and the others laughed. Dessie laughed, too, but he didn't take up her suggestion.

Didn't think you would! she said to herself, sitting on the single stool beside the fire because then he couldn't move beside her.

'I have some news for you that might change your mood,' he said, still grinning.

You're running away to sea? she thought hopefully.

45

'I've arranged for you to see one of the managers at the works.'

'Why?' she asked, staring into the fire.

'I've fixed you up with a job, of course,' he bragged. 'I don't think you'll have any bother.'

Kathleen and Michael made 'oooh' noises, as though Daisy had been presented with the greatest prize in the world.

She waited for silence. 'I've already got a job, thanks,' she said evenly, and the tone of the silence changed.

'What job?' her father asked.

'In Fenwicks. I start on Monday.'

'*Fenwicks?*' Michael asked, as though he had never heard the word before. 'You mean the one in Northumberland Street?'

'There is only one, Da,' she smiled.

'So when did this happen?' Michael asked.

'What does it matter when it happened?' Daisy shrugged. 'I've got a job there and I start on Monday.'

'A job doing what?' Dessie demanded.

'Anything they want me to do,' she said without looking at him.

'Well, that's a bit of a turn-up when you knew Dessie was putting in a word for you!' Michael accused.

'I didn't ask him to put in a word for me; I didn't say he could!'

'But it was understood,' Kathleen wheezed.

'Not by me it wasn't,' Daisy returned tartly. 'I'm not Kay, he doesn't rule *my* life!'

'Daisy!' Michael said. 'That's no way to talk! Dessie was doing you a favour.'

Daisy straightened up and looked directly at Dessie. 'Was he?' she said flatly. 'Well, I don't need his favours, I've got a job and that's that.'

★ ★ ★

Lying in her bed that night she heard the usual backdrop to night-time in the Sheridan household. Downstairs her mother breathed in her tortured way and upstairs Kay snored gently. Nothing disturbed Kay's sleep: she didn't seem to dream and wakened each morning in the same position she had gone to sleep in – a skill, if it was a skill, that Daisy had always envied.

She thought over how they had greeted her news. From Kay there was no response, but that was Kay, she had no opinions; and from her parents there had been something like disapproval. She lay in the darkness trying to analyse the feelings in the room when she had announced that she had found a job on her own.

The disapproval, resentment even, hadn't just been because kindly Dessie's good word had been thrown back in his face. It was more than that, it was because she was going to work in Fenwicks. Her parents saw her as getting above her station in life, she realised. The very people who complained about anti-Irish prejudice holding them back objected to her getting on. Why was that? she wondered. Because if one of them got on it proved that it was possible for all of them? It undermined their cherished victim status? Well, they could keep that; she had no intention of living her life as a victim, being grateful and resentful in equal measure for whatever crumbs those above threw down to her. For a start, she thought furiously, she didn't accept that those above had that power, and, even if they did, she wouldn't put up with it in future, in *her* future. And as for Ireland, the fabled Emerald Isle their hearts ached for generation after generation, well it was someone else's country as far as she was concerned and she longed to be free of it too.

In the future she now planned for herself, she decided, neither the place her family still referred to as 'home', nor Newcastle, would have any claim on her. Granny Niamh would have applauded her, she knew that, and Aunt Clare would have cheered her on, but no one else in her family had that kind of mind. She'd been aware of that for a long time, from when she had first started to question her father's stories; from the time, in fact, when she had begun to think for herself.

And Dessie? Well, Dessie understood perfectly well why she had done what she had done, and Dessie didn't like it. She knew that from the look in his eyes as she had met his gaze for that fleeting defiant second. It had taken him by surprise so he had no time to think up a reply, and that night he had left the Sheridan home early. She had shaken him off *and* he'd gone home early, so she had scored a double victory, and the thought warmed her.

But being young, Daisy didn't know that there were as many male reactions as there were males. She had misread Dessie that night. She thought she had beaten him at last, and she had no way of understanding the difference between battles and wars. In Daisy a different female had emerged from the union between Michael and Kathleen, as had happened in the family in the past, and lying in her bed in the Guildford Place house she was filled with optimism and ambition. There were no doubts, no threats to cloud her horizon, at least none that she was aware of, because she was young.

5

Fenwicks became Daisy's refuge in the years that followed. She lived for and through her job, and even if Mrs Johnstone was true to her words and made her work hard, it became work she loved.

On her first day, though, it was clear that the word had got round. She could tell that from the stares of a few of the old dears, no doubt tipped off by Miss Manders. She glanced at them as she made her way to the rickety lift that would take her to Joan Johnstone's office. Their lips were set in disapproving straight lines. She knew why they disliked her, of course. These women of a certain age didn't take kindly to competition that beat them hands down, and in their eyes, just by being young, attractive and from the wrong part of town, Daisy had beaten them. Maybe there was a trace of anti-Irish, anti-Catholic bias in there too. That was something you never knew about unless they spat in your face, but the Newcastle Irish had what they regarded as a sixth sense about such things, although Daisy wondered if it was also a kind of paranoia. Anyway, none of it had anything to do with her. She couldn't help her background nor her shape – if only she could! As her hand reached out to press the lift button, Miss Manders said behind her, 'You're expected down here to sweep the floor.'

'I was told to report to Mrs Johnstone,' Daisy said.

'Well, do that,' the older woman replied tersely, 'then you're expected back down here right away. Is that understood? You're only a junior, that's what juniors do.'

Daisy nodded. 'Miserable old cow!' she said to herself once the lift gates had clanged shut, but as she ascended she could feel her mood doing the same.

Mrs Johnstone was behind her desk, a tiny, bright presence set against dark woodwork and piles of paper. She indicated with a gracious hand movement that Daisy should sit down.

'Now, Daisy,' she said quietly, 'what I have in mind is to teach you the business. I want you to see yourself where I am now in a few years, or even beyond. How would you like to be working in one of the big Paris fashion houses?'

She giggled and Daisy giggled too.

'But first you have to work your way up, as I explained. Now there's one thing you'll learn about me, and that's that I hate paperwork.'

Daisy looked around. She'd never have guessed.

'I do it, of course, because I have to or it would overwhelm me.' She followed Daisy's gaze and laughed. 'You're thinking that it already has, aren't you?'

'No . . .'

Mrs Johnstone clapped her hands and laughed again. 'What I'd like you to do is help me keep it all in better order. I know it doesn't look as though it's in any order now, but it is, believe it or not.' She looked around, shaking her head. 'Now, that pile there, it needs to be properly filed, you know? It should be to some extent already, well, roughly, but if you could make sure it's by date, strictly by date, that would be a great help. Now,

I have a client to see to, so off you go, walk around the store first, familiarise yourself, and come back to my paperwork.'

They travelled down in the lift together and when they reached the ground floor went in different directions. Before Daisy had gone two steps she was stopped by Miss Manders. 'I want the stockroom floor sweeping,' she said shortly. 'There's a brush behind there.'

Daisy said nothing, but turned from the splendour of the shopfront towards the dark dinginess of the stockroom and started brushing. It was an impossible job; there was an endless supply of dust and fluff that seemed to elude every pass of the brush and land exactly where it had been before.

Miss Manders reappeared. 'You're not doing much of a job, are you?' she asked, before turning and disappearing again. Half an hour of useless brushing later, Miss Manders reappeared with seemingly no interest in whether the floor was dust and fluff free, and proffered a bottle of bleach, sniffily instructing Daisy to clean the staff toilet.

Daisy stood thinking for a moment. The only thing stopping her from telling Miss Manders precisely where to put her bottle of bleach and walking out was the thought of the alternative. '*Ropeworks, Daisy*,' she said to herself, '*ropeworks*', though she knew there was no telling how long that thought would hold her.

Just then she heard Mrs Johnstone's voice in the distance, then she burst in through the door. 'What are you doing here?' she demanded, though by the wretched look on Miss Manders' face as she followed, Mrs Johnstone already knew. 'Didn't I tell you to file the paperwork in my office?'

Daisy didn't reply, sensing that Mrs Johnstone's anger wasn't directed at her, and looked behind her to the older woman.

'Miss Manders,' Mrs Johnstone said tightly, 'can we please

have a word? Daisy, if you would be so good as to go up to my office and I'll see you there in due course.'

Daisy made her way through the sudden silence of the stockroom, past the even louder silence of the shop floor and the cold stares of all the Miss Manderses who watched her, and went through the lift procedure that seemed to take forever before it actually moved. She wasn't entirely sure what would happen, but she couldn't help feeling apprehensive. She wasn't to blame for what the old cow had made her do, but Mrs Johnstone had told her to look around the store and return to her office. She should have done that, she realised. Now she could be out on her ear and on her way to joining Dessie's harem after all. But if the old cow had complained to Mrs Johnstone that she had refused to do as she was told by her elders, if not betters, she could have been out on her ear anyhow.

When 'in due course' arrived, Mrs Johnstone came into the office and sat down.

'Well, that's that all sorted,' she said brightly.

Daisy looked at her blankly.

'Well, don't just sit there, girl, get on with my filing!' She suddenly laughed. 'On second thoughts, let's have a cuppa and biscuit, what do you say?'

'So I've still got a job?' Daisy asked, surprised.

'Well of course you have! Whatever made you think you hadn't?'

'The old, um, Miss Manders,' Daisy mumbled.

'Oh,' Mrs Johnstone said with a dismissive wave of her hand, 'that was all a misunderstanding. My fault really, I should've explained to the other ladies that you weren't to be treated as a normal junior. I have something different in mind for you: you are to be my assistant. I should've explained that to the ladies on the shop floor,' she repeated briskly, if unconvincingly. 'It was my mistake, but they understand now.'

Daisy lowered her head to hide a grin.

'I do hope you're not smirking, Daisy!' Mrs Johnstone said. 'Because I would expect better from you. It wouldn't be ladylike to gloat over the old, um, Miss Manders, you know!'

'No, no, it's not that,' Daisy said, laughing despite her best intentions. She looked up and as they met each other's eyes they both laughed out loud.

Mrs Johnstone sat back in her chair, rubbing her chest. 'She really is an old cow, isn't she?' she said breathlessly, now dabbing at her eyes. 'I'm sure you've met a lot like her, Daisy. I have, too. You won't get any more trouble like that, but I fear you'll always be regarded as my favourite and that won't help you make friends here. Does that bother you?'

Daisy shook her head. The fact was that it honestly didn't. She was a loner; she had always been a loner, partly because the life she had been given had made her one by separating her from girls of her own age, and partly because of her own nature – and that was before Mother Nature had aided and abetted the process by giving her a body and looks other women would have died for, and would have killed her for as well. All her life she had had to take on responsibilities beyond her years; maybe it was her destiny to always be older than her years, too.

She soon fell into a routine with Mrs Johnstone, who already had her own highly personal system of keeping track of pieces of paper that worked for her; but gradually Daisy brought an order to the office that even her boss fell into without noticing. She also made the tea, kept track of stock and learned how to use the telephone, an instrument of mystery to someone of Daisy's background, and, even more daunting, how to modulate her strong Geordie accent while doing so.

'You're not betraying your background, if that's what you're thinking!' Mrs Johnstone would tease her. 'You'll still have your own voice, but you'll have another as well that will make it easier to converse with people who don't have Geordie.'

'It's not that,' Daisy grimaced. 'What has my background ever done for me that I owe it any loyalty? It's just that I think I sound like such a fraud that the people on the other end will know and they'll laugh at me.'

'Daisy,' Joan said, staring at her with wide eyes and smiling, 'they're doing just the same as you! Everyone puts on an act of some kind for other people, doesn't matter who they are!'

Daisy worked in ladies' fashions, a man-free environment where she could relax, gradually being introduced to the well-heeled ladies of the area as they came in for fittings, seeing their fine clothes and the ones they left with, which were even finer. From Mrs Johnstone she learned that fashion wasn't just about wearing something nice, but it was affected by what was happening in the world at any given time. In Daisy's own lifetime the Flappers of the 1920s had caused a mini revolution when they threw away their Victorian corsets – torture garments reinforced with whalebone, tightly laced to give fashionably narrow waists of fifteen or eighteen inches.

'But I really like the dresses in these old pictures,' Daisy said, flicking through a magazine of the Victorian era. 'Don't you?'

'Heavens, no!' Mrs Johnstone screeched. 'I can't even look at them without thinking of women in torture! My mother wasn't rich, but as a young girl she had a waist of seventeen inches, can you imagine that?' She shook her head and tut-tutted. 'No woman was intended to be that shape, and the tightness of the corsets made them deformed. They couldn't breathe and couldn't move, and I've heard they were so tight that the marks of their ribs were imprinted on their lungs underneath, can you imagine that?

Then on top they wore layers of slips, vests, bodices, knickers, and stockings as well, and those heavy floor-length dresses with bustles.' She shook her head. 'It was all a trick, of course.'

'What do you mean?'

'Well, they were trussed up, weren't they? Which meant they couldn't move, so they had to stay at home, delicate flowers who had to be cared for and kept away from the world; but it kept them from taking their place in the world, didn't it? Because the world belonged then, as it still does, to men – only a little less now, thanks in part to the Flappers.'

'So what else changed then?'

'The First World War, Daisy, that's what changed,' Mrs Johnstone said grimly. 'The men were sent to the Front, God help them, and for the first time women were needed. They either freed more men to be killed by taking over their jobs or they worked in munitions factories, and they couldn't do that trussed up, so they were freed. Men's rules again,' she said thoughtfully. 'The only problem was that once they'd been allowed a few years of freedom they didn't take kindly to being shut up again. It was as if freeing their bodies had freed their minds as well. But do you know the strangest thing?' she laughed quietly. 'The Flappers of the 1920s did everything they could to look like boys.'

Joan got up from her desk and lifted a bound book of magazines from a shelf and handed it to Daisy. 'Look at those tubular shapes. Ladies of means went to men's tailors to have masculine clothes made. It even became an insult to compliment a woman on her nice figure, and they bound their breasts to be as flat as possible.'

'I can sympathise with that,' Daisy said glumly.

Mrs Johnstone laughed. 'Your shape is coming into its own, Daisy,' she chided her. 'You should be grateful for the 1930s, these days the fashion is for womanly women. But back then, well, I think in a strange way those ladies were trying to replace the poor boys lost in the war by almost becoming boys themselves.'

'Did you wear things like that?' Daisy asked.

'Heavens, no! I couldn't afford it, for one thing, but I was always a feminine kind of woman, if you know what I mean. The "Gay Thirties" suit me much better, though I still can't afford the wardrobes of our customers. Besides, who has time to be constantly changing into morning, sports, afternoon and evening wear? And they can't seem to be able to make up their minds where their hemlines should be.' She produced another book and opened it at a *Punch* cartoon. 'This always makes me laugh,' she said, pointing to two pictures of the same young woman, one in her afternoon suit six inches below the knee and pencil-slim, so that she could only manage to walk in 'the nine-inch hobble', in the second wearing a loose-skirted evening dress, enabling her to perform 'the metre stride'. 'These are the kind of ladies we come into contact with, Northern women who desperately want to keep up with London and Paris, women like us, I suppose, only we don't have their wealth!'

Daisy became as fascinated by the lives of such women as by their clothes, which she loved. The dresses sewn into sections, or on the bias, garments so well-cut that they didn't need fastenings, so craftily designed that making your own was beyond most females, even for someone as experienced with a needle as Daisy. She gradually became familiar with the names of designers like Chanel and Schiaparelli, and learned the tricks of film stars like Joan Crawford, who wore impossibly wide, padded shoulders, giving the illusion of the still-prized narrow waist without the agony of corsets. She couldn't have afforded the magazines that were part of her working tools and she and Mrs Johnstone spent breaks devouring each one, discussing and dissecting every detail.

'I love the dresses Ginger Rogers wears,' Daisy said, looking at the still photos of floaty, frilly dresses worn by the actress as she flew down to Rio to dance backwards and in heels with Fred Astaire.

'Is that what you'd like to do, Daisy?' Mrs Johnstone smiled. 'Dance with Fred Astaire?'

'Wouldn't it be wonderful?' Daisy replied, hunching her shoulders and clapping her hands together with feeling. She got up and laughingly improvised a tap dance, caught in the dream of being Ginger for a moment, a dream shared with thousands of other women.

'You couldn't wear her clothes, though,' Mrs Johnstone said quietly.

'Why not?' Daisy demanded, stopping suddenly mid-step.

'You're a different shape.'

Daisy looked down at her 'lumps'. 'There they go,' she muttered, 'ruining it for me again!'

'Daisy, Daisy, there's nothing wrong with your shape!' Mrs Johnstone said, shaking her head at the girl. 'Ginger's built for frills, you're built for good lines, for well-cut clothes. If ever a girl was designed for her time, it's you. I saw that the first time I set eyes on you, especially now that we have brassieres to guide and support the bust rather than flatten it.'

'I'd give anything to be like you and not need one,' Daisy said with feeling.

'Are you suggesting that I'm flat-chested?' Mrs Johnstone asked, faking outrage.

'No, no,' Daisy replied. 'But you're built like Ginger, you're built for frills; I just wish I was.'

'And I wish I had your curves. Never satisfied, are we?'

Joan Johnstone was impressed by the courage of the girl from Heaton via Byker, but she also had an eye for business. In recognising that Daisy was built to wear the fashions of the Thirties, even if she couldn't afford them, she knew that the girl would be perfect to model them for prospective buyers, once the rough edges were smoothed over, of course, and once she knew something of the business she was now in. From the very first day she had changed her lunchtime habit, and it became established that she and Daisy ate together in her office. 'I have hopes for you, Daisy,' she had told her. 'You'll get fed-up with filing and dealing with bits of paper, but you mustn't give up, you have to know everything, it's part of my plan.'

Daisy had nodded, though she didn't understand. For her the choice was simple, work with pieces of paper at Fenwicks or, if she was lucky, pieces of paper at the ropeworks with Dessie always on hand, leering at her. No choice at all, really.

Joan Johnstone was a smart woman, though. She was a good judge of when routine became drudgery, especially for a bright youngster like Daisy, so every now and again she would take her to the shop floor to watch some wealthy young woman buying a new wardrobe. Daisy was forbidden to speak, only to watch and learn, and what she learned was that the divide between her and the customers was much wider in some ways than she had thought, but in other ways much narrower. She would have to save for a very long time to buy one dress and she would think it was the world, while these women bought a whole collection complete with accessories, and they didn't just buy the best, they recognised it when they saw it. Sometimes Daisy was allowed to help them change and was always amazed by the finery they wore underneath, the embroidered silks, satins and gossamer laces that weren't seen as they moved grace-fully through their lives. She was impressed, too, by the way these wealthy women treated her. Not as an equal – that would have been too much to expect – but as a human being, when all her life till then she had lived in a world of Us and Them.

One day they had Mrs Armstrong in for a fitting, a lady in her forties who wasn't married but carried the title as a courtesy. She was a tall, slim woman, with dark, waved hair in the style of her young womanhood, and very pretty, with neat features and a sweet smile. Joan Johnstone had brought Daisy into the fitting room with Mrs Armstrong because she knew the woman had a kind disposition and wouldn't make Daisy nervous, even if she was very rich.

'They say there's to be another war, ladies, what do you think?' Mrs Armstrong asked, as Daisy did up the long row of tiny buttons on the back of her dress while Mrs Johnstone evened out the hem.

'It's too horrible to think about,' Mrs Johnstone said. 'You just can't believe they would do it again, can you?'

Mrs Armstrong sighed. 'I lost everything in the last show, you know,' she said sadly. 'Three brothers and my fiancé, all in the same regiment. At the Somme.' The words hung in the air. 'My parents didn't last more than a year afterwards, so that was me, all on my own. I had the family money, but nothing else. My lovely chap wanted to get married before he left, but my family wanted a huge society wedding for their only daughter and there wasn't time. The times I've gone over that in my mind and cursed myself for being a damned fool!'

Daisy stared at her, transfixed. 'And you never married?' she asked before she could stop herself.

'Daisy!' Mrs Johnstone said quietly.

'No, no, Joan,' Mrs Armstrong said, 'I really don't mind.' She turned towards Daisy, taking the girls hands in her own. 'You're a very attractive girl, Daisy,' she smiled, 'one day you'll be a very beautiful woman.'

Daisy shrugged with embarrassment.

'You *will*!' The two older women exchanged amused glances. 'I was, too, you know, though you'd hardly believe it now!'

'You *are*,' Daisy stammered, 'you really are beautiful. I think you're one of the most beautiful women I've ever seen!'

'Oh, that's kind,' the woman replied. 'But if you've lost the love of your life, Daisy, as I hope you never will, it doesn't matter how beautiful you are or how many men chase after you, you're not interested. I regret not marrying him every day of my life, I'd give anything, everything, for the chance to go back and change it. He was the only one and he still is, even all these years later.' She sighed. 'You see, everyone looks at the Great War and feels horrified at the millions of young lives that were sacrificed on the battlefields, but they don't understand that there were other lives lost here at home – the young women who never married their men. They weren't *actually* lost, of course, but they might as well have been, and if they never married, then they never had children. I often think of that, you know, what our children would have been like. But by the sounds of things if they had been born they would now be getting ready to fight the Germans all over again.'

'Do you really think it will come to that?' Mrs Johnstone asked quietly.

'I'm afraid it sounds very much like it.' Mrs Armstrong looked thoughtful, then she gave herself a shake that was transmitted through her hands to Daisy. 'Now look at us!' she said brightly, her eyes shining a little too much, 'standing here gloomily like MacBeth's witches!' She turned to Daisy again, still holding her by the hands. 'I was brought up to respect and obey my parents. I expect you were, too, Daisy, but they're not always right, that's all I'll say. Just don't you let the love of your life get away from you, Daisy, no matter what anyone else thinks or says. Joan here is living proof that marriage works: she found her man and held on to him!'

Daisy listened for the rest of the fitting session as Mrs Johnstone kept the conversation going in a polite voice with the strong Geordie inflections evened out, and thought how much she had to learn. Later, over sandwiches in the office, she talked about Mrs Armstrong.

'Money really isn't everything, is it?' she asked thoughtfully.

'No, it isn't, Daisy.'

'She sounded so sad, poor woman.'

'Well, she is,' Mrs Johnstone replied.

'But you'd think she'd have found someone, wouldn't you? I mean, she must've been a looker in her day, and she's so wealthy.'

'It doesn't always follow, Daisy.'

'And she's so nice, she'd have made a lovely mother.'

'Well, there are a whole bunch of lessons there for you,' Joan Johnstone said quietly. 'Just because she's got lots of money doesn't mean she should be horrible; just because she's beautiful doesn't mean she's able to forget – what did she call him? – the love of her life? And just because she's rich and beautiful doesn't mean she doesn't have her sadnesses or that she shouldn't be nice. Now stop it, you're getting morbid!'

'Do you think there is such a thing?' Daisy asked. 'As a love of your life, I mean. Does everyone have one?'

'Now how would I know that, Daisy? Maybe there is one for everybody, but not everybody meets theirs.' She looked at Daisy's serious face and suddenly laughed. 'You'll have us both in tears in a minute! Let's change the subject. I want you to model a dress for a couple of customers the day after tomorrow.'

Daisy choked and stared at her.

Mrs Johnstone chuckled. 'What's wrong with you?' she teased. 'Something go down the wrong way?'

'You mean put a dress on and walk up and down?' Daisy asked, horrified.

'You see, it's simple, isn't it?' Mrs Johnstone replied, calmly getting on with her lunch.

'But I can't!' Daisy spluttered.

'Why not?'

'I'll fall over, I'll trip, I'll . . . they'll just laugh at me.'

'No they won't, they won't even see you, they'll only see the dress.'

'But why me then?' Daisy persisted.

'Because you're the right shape to *let* them see the dress.'

Daisy glowered at her.

'Now what's that look for?' Mrs Johnstone demanded.

'I hate my shape. I didn't think it mattered here.'

'Of course it matters, you daft girl! And why would you hate your shape?'

'It's all lumps and bumps and men grab me or leer at me, that's why!' Daisy said bitterly. 'I wasn't always this shape, I used to be normal. My sister's two years older than me, she's nearly twenty, and she's still normal, they don't grab at her.'

'Oh Daisy,' Mrs Johnstone said, 'you are quite beautiful. Has no one ever told you that?'

'No. Women hate me and men just grab at me and rub themselves against me.'

'My dear God!' Mrs Johnstone whispered. She looked at Daisy's embarrassed face across the desk. 'Daisy, from now on you have to have a different outlook. You *are* beautiful, and that's a plus, not a minus. You have to rise above the creatures of the gutter who don't have the intelligence, education or natural graces to know how to behave.' She looked at her again. 'I want you to have your hair lightened,' she said.

'What?' Daisy demanded. 'Where I come from it's bad enough already, what do you think will happen if I become a Peroxide Blonde?'

'You will look like a million dollars, that's what will happen,' Mrs Johnstone said firmly. 'Daisy, you never intended staying in Heaton, did you?'

Daisy sat in silence. She had always wanted to 'get out', but it was a vague notion. She had no plan, in her mind it was a kind of 'someday' thing. 'No,' she said uncertainly, 'but '

'But nothing, my girl! You've seen the young ladies we get in here, do you think of them as "Peroxide Blondes"?'

'No, but . . .'

'There you go with that "but" again! Daisy, today we will practise walking without falling down or tripping, and tonight you will become a golden blonde, not a Peroxide Blonde.'

'But I can't, I have to go home and do the chores,' Daisy protested.

Mrs Johnstone looked puzzled. 'You have a mother, haven't you?'

'Yes, but she's an invalid,' Daisy replied.

There was a short silence as both women acknowledged to themselves that Daisy had never openly discussed her family circumstances before.

'How long has she been ill?' Joan Johnstone asked quietly.

'All the years since I was born,' Daisy replied in a small voice. 'One doctor told my father it was her heart, something from when she was a child, but my father says it's really her lungs.'

'And she's bedridden, Daisy? Totally?'

Daisy nodded.

'And you do everything?' Mrs Johnstone asked, suddenly remembering clues the girl had inadvertently dropped in the past and putting the pieces together. 'The shopping, washing, cooking, cleaning?'

Daisy nodded again.

'But you mentioned a sister at the ropeworks, she must help, surely?'

'No, no, Kay doesn't do chores,' Daisy said, shocked.

'Why?'

'Because one day she's going to be a big star, she has her music to practise and she can't have rough hands, and . . .' Daisy stopped, realising for the first time that it sounded strange.

'I don't understand . . .' replied Mrs Johnstone, who did think it was strange.

'My sister's Little Kay Sheridan,' Daisy explained, 'though she's not all that little now, of course.'

Mrs Johnstone thought for a moment. 'The little girl who used to sing in the clubs?'

Daisy nodded. 'She's still going to be star,' she said defiantly. 'My mother says it always happens with child stars, there's a slack spell while they grow up, then they become adult performers.'

'But for now she works in the ropeworks and you do all the housework?' Even as she said it Mrs Johnstone looked and sounded as though she thought it was all nonsense.

Daisy looked at her glumly. 'It's not how it sounds,' she protested, 'Kay still has a beautiful voice, she's still going to be a star. She'll sing for the world one day, not just the Irish clubs in Newcastle,' she continued, falling back on her mother's oft-repeated mantra. She looked up at Mrs Johnstone and they both laughed. 'That's what my mother says,' Daisy said quietly.

'Well I'll tell you what, Daisy, tonight the star will do the housework.'

Daisy opened her mouth to protest. Kay didn't know how to fill a kettle, the thing was unthinkable.

Mrs Johnstone held up her hand and turned her face to the side. 'No "buts", Daisy. I'll get a message to your sister at the ropeworks that you'll be late tonight, and the star can get her hands dirty for once.'

Daisy's stomach leaped. The thing wasn't just unthinkable, it was impossible, maybe even a sin to be confessed. Even if she had beginner's luck with the kettle, Kay opening up the banked fire and putting coal on? Making a meal – even if all the basic work had been done earlier so that she just had to heat it up? Kay washing dishes – even with good old dependable Dessie drying – seeing to Kathleen, washing her and emptying the bed pan she had taken to using since the distance to the bathroom had become too much for her? *Kay?*

Later that day she looked in the hairdresser's mirror and once again saw a complete stranger, this time a *very* blonde stranger.

'Now I look like, like . . .'

'A million dollars,' Mrs Johnstone beamed beside her, 'just as I said you would.'

'I was going to say that now I really do look like a street-walker,' Daisy said quietly.

Mrs Johnstone exchanged a look with the hairdresser. 'What can you do?' she asked, shaking her head with a smile. 'Can you tell her we haven't ruined her forever?'

The hairdresser held a mirror this way and that for Daisy's approval. 'We've just lifted the colour, Daisy,' she wheedled. 'It's not as if you had jet-black hair and we dyed it blonde.'

As she headed home that evening, having parted with Daisy in all her newly golden glory, Joan Johnstone, despite her earlier confidence, wondered if she had done the right thing. Daisy was eighteen years old, a woman in the eyes of many, but a child to her parents, she had no doubt, for all her bravado. Perhaps she should have asked them before pushing their daughter into dying her hair? They would have said no, of course, she knew this for a fact. The fact being that she had grown up with parents just like them, who ruled her every moment and tried to do the same with her thoughts, even to the extent of trying to arrange her marriage to a 'suitable' man, which meant someone Irish. Marrying 'out' was regarded almost as something to be ashamed of; they preferred to stay in their little communities, marrying only their 'own kind' and grumbling about how they were kept in ghettos. Like Daisy she had wanted more out of life than living up, or down, to someone else's label, having her future mapped out for her. She had told herself that when she had children of her own she would help them reach for the stars rather than accept what was considered to be their lot. It hadn't happened, though.

Out of spite and defiance she had married George Johnstone, a draughtsman at the Vickers-Armstrong engineering works, a man unconnected with the Irish Geordie community, and she had married badly. Not that George was a bad man or she a bad wife, and they still liked each other, even though they weren't suited. But the love of her life he wasn't, nor was she the love of his. They had a nice Victorian terraced house in Holly Avenue in the Jesmond area, to the north of the city, with enough bedrooms to house the children that would come in time. They'd had more than enough money and a bright future ahead. However, less than a year into their marriage, when they should have still been basking in that honeymoon glow, they'd run out of things to say to each other. It was as simple as that. It was a great disappointment to them both, but they had rubbed along quietly enough these fifteen years or so, both of them giving the other room in a partnership that existed in name only. They had an understanding, an unspoken but nonetheless still firm understanding, that neither would embarrass the other, that whatever arrangements they made would be discreet.

And George, decent man that he was, had abided by that, carrying on his liaisons with her tacit approval, and never letting her find out officially. Joan, for her part, would have done the same − if she had been interested in seeing other men, that was, which she wasn't. There was nothing like having sex with someone you'd once thought you loved but now knew you didn't for putting you off the whole notion. She'd thought about it over the years and knew that even if she ever found a man she did love − that elusive love of her life − she would've run off with him without a second thought, abandoning all security and propriety. However, she could never abandon George, he really didn't deserve that, so seeing other men was a risk she had decided not to take. To the outside world she and George looked like a well-set-up, happily married if child-less couple, for which she was always blamed, as women always were.

Joan was now a career woman and career women were disap-proved of. Her job in Fenwicks took the place of children. She knew that was what others said, and it was true, but only because there would be no children. It was a deep regret in her life, and sometimes she felt guilty that George would never have any either − she felt absolutely sure of that − but then she came to the conclusion that the arrangement must have suited them both or they would have found ways out. Divorce wasn't for people like them anyway, that was for Hollywood stars, and neither of them could have handled the stigma if they'd parted.

Joan especially did not want her family to ever have a whiff that she had made a mistake. She acknowledged that to herself, but it was not the one they would see of marrying, 'out'. She had made the mistake of not knowing the man she had married, and she was hardly alone there. It even happened to those who married 'in', not that her family would ever have admitted that.

The only one who'd turned up at their wedding had been Joan's younger sister, Myra, who now lived along the road from the Sheridans in Guildford Place, with her handsome, adoring Irish husband and their four children. So Joan had children near her life, if not in it. She had never hinted to Myra that her own marriage had been a mistake. If Myra had been taken hostage by the rest of the family they'd have got it out of her by some means or other and Joan didn't want to put her in that position.

So she had settled into the routine of attentive wife just as George had settled into his role, and they would sit quietly most evenings, sometimes reading, listening to the radio and playing Scrabble, before settling down for the night in their twin beds in the same bedroom, good pals but never lovers.

So why had she taken this young girl under her wing, Joan wondered. Was it for Daisy's sake or for her own? The daughter she would never have? Daisy reminded Joan of herself, of course, that need to stretch and grow, but where Joan had been quietly determined Daisy was more of a firebrand. There was potential there, she thought, for the girl to self-destruct, and that would be a shame. She was an exceptionally bright and pretty girl who would be a beautiful woman, but she wasn't handling it well, she was fighting it, and in some ways she was incredibly innocent.

The situation with the sister, for instance, Joan thought, shaking her head and laughing to herself. What a complete nonsense! Little Kay had been well-known in her day, but her day was long gone and she was just a girl working in a rope-works now. Yet Daisy thought it was perfectly acceptable that she should do all the work in the house, plus caring for an invalid mother, so that one day Little Kay would be transformed into Big Kay: Big Kay with soft hands! Well, if Joan had helped to put a spanner in those works with this day's events it would be all to the good, and the scene Daisy was sure to face at home would do her good, too, in the long run. It would help open her eyes if nothing else.

So there they were, Joan and Daisy, a childless mother helping a child who hadn't known what it was to have a mother, who had, in fact, become mother to her mother.

She would have done the same for her own daughter, had she had one, Joan Johnstone decided. She would have helped her own daughter to reach new heights, so she would go on helping Daisy, but she still didn't envy the girl walking alone into the lion's den in Guildford Place that night.

As Daisy walked home, deep in her own thoughts, she knew they would be waiting for her with their recriminations, the family she had left in the lurch just so that she could be trans-formed into this streetwalker. And they were, the entire family, meaning Dessie as well. As she walked in there was an audible 'Oh!' as her newly golden tresses registered, but her father's rage had been too pent-up and ready to go and at first he didn't notice. In fact his face was so red that Daisy felt she might be doing him a favour by finally giving him something to aim at. He opened his mouth to unleash his fury, then he stopped, his diatribe thrown off course by suddenly registering the hair, so that he opened and shut his mouth several times before he could utter a word.

'So!' he shouted, and standing in front of him Daisy almost laughed because it was so obviously not what he had intended to say.

'It's come to this, has it?' Michael demanded.

Daisy closed her eyes tightly and lowered her head, trying not to laugh, whether from fear or amusement or a mixture of both, she didn't know, though her father assumed it was from shame.

'Well may you hang your head, madam!' Michael shouted, marching about the room, picking up his tobacco pouch and putting it down again. 'So this is why you left your family to starve!' he yelled theatrically. 'So that you could be made to look even more like the brazen hussy you are!'

'Oh Da,' she said quietly, 'I'm sure Kay could be trusted to heat up a stew.'

'Kay has never had to do such a thing,' Michael threw back at her. 'She didn't even know how to turn the gas on!'

The newly gilded Daisy was finding it harder and harder with each passing moment not to laugh out loud, and the thought of Kay struggling to light the gas made her cover her face with her hands.

'Well may you hide your face in shame!' Michael shouted. 'What people must think of you, walking into a respectable home with that head of evil hair, as if it hasn't been bad enough these years with you and your woman's bits provoking decent men to carnal thoughts!'

Daisy took her hands away from her face and stared at him, horrified. All these years when she had been trying to disguise her shapely body and feeling afraid of what the next man she met might say or do, and her father had blamed *her* for it. She couldn't believe it; he saw it as *her* fault. This was the only man in her life she had counted on, the one she'd thought was on her side, who could be trusted to defend and protect her against the world, and all the time he was disgusted by her 'woman's bits'. *She* disgusted him, it was in his eyes and in his voice; she *disgusted* him! She felt tears prickling at the corners of her eyes and turned and ran to the bedroom she shared with Kay, but she couldn't hold in a deep sob as she went, provoking her father's triumphant remark,

'That's *her* sorted now!'

Up in the bedroom Daisy lay on her bed sobbing as Kay came in.

'Daisy, I didn't mind making the dinner, honestly I didn't,' she said in her childish voice. 'I told Da that; I said as soon as I worked out how to light the gas it was all right, and next time I'll know and I won't burn so much.'

Daisy looked up at her sister and suddenly laughed out loud, picturing the scene in her mind. 'Oh, Kay, was it all burned?'

'Not all of it,' Kay replied solemnly, watching Daisy laugh, 'a fair bit, but not all of it. Why are you laughing?'

'I don't really know,' Daisy said, her voice between a sigh and a sob.

'And your hair is lovely, Daisy.'

'Is it?'

'Yes, I'd love to have hair that colour, I hate this red stuff.'

'Well, it sent Da off the deep end,' Daisy replied.

'It wasn't just you,' Kay said innocently, 'it was me too.'

'Was he mad because you'd burned the stew?'

'I don't think it was that as much as me expecting.'

Daisy sat bolt upright, her eyes wide. 'What did you say, Kay?'

'I said Da wasn't happy that I was expecting.'

'Expecting? As in expecting a baby?' Daisy asked incredulously, and Kay nodded.

'How? I mean, Christ, Kay, a baby? You? Dessie and you? Why?'

Kay looked at Daisy with her usual blank expression. 'He just sort of did it, said we were getting married anyway.'

'And you didn't tell him to stop?' Daisy asked.

'Well, no, he would only have got annoyed with me and shouted,' Kay explained. 'Da says we'll have to get married as soon as possible, but as Dessie said, we were always going to get married anyway.'

'But Kay,' Daisy said sadly, taking her sister by the shoulders, 'do you want to get married?'

'Why not?' her sister responded dreamily.

'Do you even want to have this baby? There are women who can take care of it for you. There's Mrs Young down the road, you must've heard people talk about her.'

'Oh, that would be a sin,' Kay said calmly, 'and I already have this one to confess to Father Connolly. I don't think I could confess another, he'd be angry with me.'

'So what? Aren't *you* angry, Kay?'

Kay wrinkled her eyes, looking up into the corner of the room as though wisdom lay there. 'No, not really,' she replied gently. 'Babies are nice, aren't they?'

'But Kay, would you really want to marry Dessie if there was no baby?'

'Why not?' Kay asked again, already tired of the conversation.

'But how can you be a big singing star if you have a baby to take care of?'

'Oh, that's all right,' she replied brightly. 'Dessie says it doesn't matter, I can always sing in pubs and clubs here, that'll bring in a few bob; and Da says I can still sing in London and big places like that, and you can look after the baby for me. I mean, it would only be a very little baby and you're looking after the house anyway, and the little baby will be in the house, won't it? So that's all right.'

Daisy looked at her sister's smiling, innocent, *stupid* face and had to fight the urge to slap her, but would that bring forth any sign of intelligence, she wondered? She felt that her head might explode off her shoulders at any moment, taking her gold-plated locks with it.

It was all arranged. Kay would marry Dessie and still be a big star, and as well as everything else she was already doing, Daisy would look after her child, or children. In the eyes of her family she was Aunt Clare one generation on. What was there to say except that it was madness and she would refuse to do it. What could they do if she said that? Throw her out? How could she look after them all and care for her sister's family if they threw her out? she wondered.

Then, through her confused thoughts came Kay's next piece of news, delivered in her usual blank, expressionless tone. 'As soon as we're married Dessie and I will move in here, to our bedroom. Da says you can always sleep on the couch downstairs.'

As Daisy drifted off to sleep that night, for what was possibly one of the last times she would ever do so in her own bed, she thought over the day's events. All the way home she had been expecting to be denounced as a harlot by her family, and she couldn't even get that to herself. Kay had already stolen Daisy's thunder with her own news, so though she had indeed been denounced, it was with second-hand anger. Maybe that was why her father had accused her of deliberately provoking the male population, because he was already angry that Kay was pregnant, but still, he had said what he'd said and there was no way those words and thoughts could be taken back. She felt that they were seared across her forehead for the world to see, and even if they weren't she knew she would carry them for the rest of her life as a shadow over her memories of her father. To think that had been in his mind all this time. She closed her eyes tightly to squeeze away the tears: she *refused* to cry over the slur ever again, whether he could see her tears or not.

And Dessie would be moving into her home. He would actually become a physical member of the family. The thought made her feel sick. It seemed that for every step forward she took, someone, somewhere, had decided that she would always take two back. She thought of Mrs Armstrong who was, strictly speaking, Miss Armstrong, and went over the sad conversation in the fitting room earlier in the day. Everyone was talking about another war; the newspapers were full of it and people discussed it every day on buses, in shops and in the streets. Like her nice, rich customer they talked resentfully of how they had lost an entire generation of young men in the last one – and to the same foe – and now here they were, getting ready to do it all again twenty years later.

Daisy had felt so sad for Mrs Armstrong that she had almost cried, but now there seemed more pressing problems in her life than worldwide bloodshed.

6

The next day, before her debut as a model, there was little time for talking, which was a relief because she didn't want to talk about the previous night's events, even if she had known what to say. Her hair was soaked in diluted sugar water, combed to the side at the crown and clamped in fearsome wave-making clips, the sides and back in metal curlers. Joan Johnstone danced around the fringes of the beautifying team, making suggestions that were ignored. 'Not too heavy with the face powder . . . a little less rouge, perhaps? . . . Are lips *really* so magenta in Paris this year?'

Daisy watched in the mirror as her eyebrows were plucked almost as thinly as Marlene Dietrich dared, then drawn in again with a special pencil before false eyelashes were applied, with only the finest Elizabeth Arden cosmetics used. Then her new hair was released from the instruments of torture she had endured since early morning and brushed, combed and teased into the latest fashion of deep waves and shoulder-length curls. It was the first time she had looked in a mirror and not even recognised her *real* self in there somewhere. The reflection showed a stranger, one she liked, she realised.

Daisy then calmly went about the business of learning how

to walk well enough to show off the three chosen evening dresses to Mrs Johnstone's customers. They were all made of silk, not the new wonder material, Rayon, that everyone was talking about. Fenwicks' ladies had their standards.

She stepped into the first gown, a cotton cape around her shoulders to stop the make-up transferring to the high-necked silk creation with a row of tiny buttons from the bowed sash at the waist to the neck. It sported two collars, the peaks of the first hanging over the bodice, almost like a bolero, and on top of that a tiered collar of white lace. As a change to ordinary puff sleeves, where they fell from the shoulder was shirred like the fronts of babies' romper suits, so that the gathered red silk burst forth from the tight stitching to billow out luxuriously halfway to the elbow.

The next dress she would be wearing was pink and square-necked, the line straight across the throat decorated with flowers and embroidered panels at either side from the shoulders to the bust. It had simple puff sleeves, but the waist was highlighted again with a slim sash held in the middle by a smaller panel of the same embroidery on the bodice. The most attractive feature, though, was the fishtail detail of tiered silk from knee to ankle, which compelled any woman to walk with a deliberate sashay. The last dress was a deep peacock blue with a completely plain skirt, but above the bust it had three exaggerated wavy frills all the way across, so that they formed both bodice decoration and short sleeves.

Daisy felt, as Mrs Johnstone had predicted, like a million dollars. Like most women of the era she followed the fashions in magazines like *Women's Magazine* and *Eve Pictorial* and she was a practised needlewoman, using patterns from *Butterick's, Vogue, Weldon's* and *Mabs Fashions*, but she had never worn dresses of this quality and she was surprised not only by how comfortable they were but how confident she felt wearing them. The feeling of silk against her skin for the first time had taken her by surprise. She could never have imagined anything so cool, so light, so luxurious, and made the decision there and then that the little money left over from the wages she gave to the family would be saved for something silk.

She took a close look at the different features and worked out in her mind how she could copy them, the little bowed sashes that drew attention to a slim waist, the row of covered buttons that accentuated the bust in a stylish way rather than an overt way, emphasising a graceful neck; and as for the fish-tail, she would defy any woman not to kick out glamorously wearing that. That's what they did, clothes like that, they could make anyone glamorous, even a Heaton girl on a cold, wet day in Newcastle.

Daisy's first step on the catwalk had been tentative and she had to fight the urge to turn and run. They were looking at her, all those well-heeled, beautiful women who spoke so nicely; if she tripped up and fell her length they would laugh at her.

They'll laugh even more if you run away, she told herself, and, shrugging slightly, she put on her act. Slow steps, looking up, shoulders back, hearing Joan Johnstone's despairing voice in her head: 'No, it *doesn't* make your bust look bigger, Daisy, it makes *you* look taller! Heavens above!' Count the steps, all worked out in advance, pace it carefully to six and turn. Drop the hip, hand resting on it just so, and a smile to the audience, then back up the catwalk again and behind the curtain.

She had done it, she had walked six steps, turned, stopped, smiled and walked six steps back again without falling over or being laughed at!

'Well, what are you waiting for, girl?' Mrs Johnstone demanded, trying to sound businesslike while fussing round her. 'We've got to get you into the next dress and back out there, they won't wait forever, you know!' Then the pink dress was fastened up and she was performing her six steps, turn, drop hip, smile, six steps back routine over again, her head lost somewhere in the clouds. That was really how it felt, she realised, as though her head was somewhere else, somewhere high, lofty, floating along in another world.

She felt so disappointed when the third act of the performance was over that she wanted to beg the ladies to wait where they were, that she could easily find another ten, twenty dresses they would love to see. Then the down set in. It was over; she had felt all that power and now it was over. The beautiful dresses had gone and she stared in the mirror at all that was left, the face she had inhabited for the short time the session had taken – how long had it been? Fifteen, thirty minutes? – and saw there Daisy Sheridan trying to pretend she was what she wasn't. She began rubbing off the make-up that had been applied so carefully.

'Oh Daisy! You've scrubbed off your lovely make-up!' Mrs Johnstone said behind her.

'If I went home wearing that lot my father really would put a red light above the door,' Daisy grinned wryly.

'Well, I think your debut went well. I think we've found your talent, Daisy.'

Daisy nodded though she didn't agree; she felt deflated now that she was back to reality, face scrubbed, in her black skirt and white blouse.

Joan Johnstone looked at her. 'What's wrong?' she asked gently. 'You've just had a triumph but to look at you anyone would think it was a disaster.'

'Well, it was all pretend, wasn't it?' Daisy said. 'It wasn't really me: this is the real me.'

Joan Johnstone put her arms around the girl and hugged her. 'You still don't understand, do you?' she said. 'Daisy, how you felt wearing those lovely dresses, that *was* the real you, it's who you should be, who you will be. How did you feel out there?'

Daisy looked upwards. 'Like, like a million dollars, I suppose!' she said with a little laugh.

'So after that you intend feeling like tuppence in future?' Joan demanded, shaking her a little. 'Daisy, that should've given you a sense of who you can be, a sense of who you will be. You have to look forward now and tell yourself that one day you will wear clothes like that because you have a right to, because it will come naturally to you.'

Daisy laughed uncertainly. 'You really think that?'

'I know it, Daisy, I *know* it. Class isn't about where you're born or who your parents are, it's about who you make yourself . . . and you have all the ingredients.'

'You make me sound like a cake!' Daisy laughed, trying to stem the tears in her eyes.

'You must make your looks work for you, Daisy,' Joan smiled. 'The way you looked out there on that little catwalk, it was obvious how you felt. There's no reason why you shouldn't always feel like that.'

Daisy didn't reply.

'Everything go OK at home last night?' Joan asked lightly.

'Oh, as well as could be expected, I suppose,' Daisy said quietly. 'The big star couldn't turn the gas on and when she did she burned the stew, and before I got there she had announced that she was pregnant.'

Joan sat down beside Daisy and drew in a shocked breath. 'Little Kay Sheridan *pregnant*?' she asked in a hushed voice.

'Somehow I think we'll have to drop the "Little", if not now, certainly soon,' Daisy replied. 'Before I even got there it was all arranged that she'd marry her horrible boyfriend and they'd move in to our bedroom. I'm to sleep on the couch from now on, apparently. I don't think my father had much rage left to waste on me, but he had enough. He accused me of deliberately exciting every male in the world with what he called my "woman's bits", to which I'd added my harlot's hair.'

She looked up and found Joan with her hand covering her mouth, laughing as she imagined the scene. Despite her mood, Daisy smiled too. 'Do you think that's funny?' she asked in an aggrieved tone.

'Well, not funny exactly,' Joan giggled. 'I'm sure it was all awful, Daisy, it's just the picture it paints in the mind. I'm sorry, honestly.'

'Well,' Daisy said wryly, 'here's the punch-line. When the baby arrives, the big star will continue with her career, because it will only be a very little baby.'

'But they all take the same amount of looking after, big or small. Who's going to do that?'

Daisy kept looking at her, holding her gaze as the penny dropped. She nodded. 'That's right: me!'

'Oh, Daisy, you've got to be kidding!'

'It was all worked out before I got home,' Daisy said.

'You're not going to do it, are you? I mean, it's impossible!'

'No, I'm not going to do it, and I agree, it is impossible. The question is, what happens now? I walked past a new recruiting office for the WAAFs this morning, and for a mad moment I thought of walking in and signing up.'

'No, no, you can't do that, there has to be some other way out, surely?'

'Oh, I don't know,' Daisy said, grinning. 'It seemed just the thing, off into the wide blue yonder, leaving all your cares behind.'

'Yes, well,' Joan replied, 'I think we've all felt like that from time to time. Mind you, women were sent to work in the factories last time, so if it's war again, Daisy, you could still end up in the ropeworks!' she teased.

'Wouldn't that be just like it?' Daisy said, pulling a vexed expression. 'Avoid it now, only to be *sent* there because of some war,' and they both laughed.

'So what are you going to do?' Mrs Johnstone asked. 'About things at home, I mean.'

'Nothing for the moment,' Daisy sighed. 'All I can think of is waiting to see how things work out. Even if it isn't the solution, it'll buy me some time now.'

The joyful union of Dessie and Kay took place at St Theresa's in Heaton Road as quickly as possible a few weeks later. Kathleen, whose health seemed to have taken another dip, wasn't well enough to be at the church for the nuptials; but Michael was there, looking stern and embarrassed, sure that everyone in the community knew and disapproved – either of Kay or of Daisy, which one wasn't clear. The bride wore a white dress made for her by her sister, the bridesmaid, which had to be let out surprisingly early in her pregnancy, but then Kay was no genius and had no real idea of how far on she was.

Dessie's belongings had already been moved into Kay and Daisy's bedroom and all that was left for him to do was move himself in. On his wedding night he dallied longer in the sitting room than seemed necessary after his new wife had gone upstairs to bed and his father-in-law to work, sitting on the couch that was now Daisy's bed.

'So we're related now, Daisy,' he said, watching her as he blew a stream of cigarette smoke out of pursed lips.

Daisy kept her back to him, trying to find things to occupy her till he had gone, and didn't reply.

'I get the feeling you don't approve any more than Michael does.'

'I think Da feels the same as I do – that you shouldn't have got my sister pregnant,' Daisy said, damning herself for replying.

'We were always going to get married,' he replied casually, still lying back, still smoking and still watching her.

'Well we'll never know about that now, will we?' Daisy said tartly, her back still turned to him. 'She didn't exactly have much choice, did she?'

'She does what she's told, your sister,' he grinned, 'though she was happy enough with how it was done.'

She knew he was hinting at the child's conception, a picture she had been fighting to keep out of her mind since the news first broke. She tried to change the subject.

'Well, that's the musical career gone, isn't it? All the years we've each worked to help her, and it's been for nothing.'

'She can still sing in the clubs and pubs, it's not all been wasted,' he replied. 'She'll still be able to bring in a few bob.'

'Yes,' Daisy said calmly, 'you taught her to parrot that well enough, but that's not what it was for, you know that fine. Kay's better than that; singing in pubs isn't enough.'

'It's enough for me.'

'But is it enough for Kay?' Daisy spat at him, turning round.

'Oh, all that big-star talk, it was always hogwash,' he said wearily. 'The only people who believed that shite were you Sheridans and the Clancys, and everybody laughed at you as well. She's just a woman and women marry and have kids, that's what they all want, what they're all for.'

'Well, that's how it will be now, that's for sure,' Daisy whispered angrily. 'Now will you bugger off upstairs to your wife? I have work in the morning, I want to go to sleep.'

He got up slowly, grinning at her, collected his cigarettes and matches and stood watching her as she moved towards the couch, her arms full of blankets, for protection more than anything, a barrier between them. Then he caught her by the shoulders from behind and held her tightly, his body pressed against her, and she could feel his breath through her hair.

'That hair drives me wild, Daisy,' he whispered, 'but then you know that.' She tried to shrug him off but he held on. 'That's where we did it, y'know, on that couch,' he whispered against her ear. 'It was one night when I brought her home and everyone was in bed. Just think of that as you're lying there, Daisy. That's where we did it, can you see it now?'

She dug her elbow into his stomach much harder than the time she had accidentally hit him before, throwing him off so firmly that he staggered, but he was laughing as he regained his balance before moving towards the stairs.

'I'd have preferred it if she'd put up a bit of resistance like that, Daisy, I like a challenge,' he said, climbing the steps.

Daisy looked at the couch and cringed with disgust, wrapping her arms around her body. She had no idea if he was telling the truth or just trying to upset her, and, much as she didn't want him to succeed, she was tempted to sleep on the floor.

She sat in the darkness, fully clothed, for another hour, listening, afraid he might be there, watching her, but the only noise was the sound of Kathleen's laboured breathing. Michael had gone on his shift at the pit just like any other night, so she got up and crept into the bedroom to ask if her mother needed anything. To her horror she found Kathleen even more breathless than usual, and as she moved closer she saw tears running down her mother's shiny red cheeks.

Daisy didn't need to ask why. Kathleen Sheridan was crying

for the loss of her ambitions for her daughter with the beautiful voice, the loss of the future she had planned and dreamed of for herself and then for Kay. Her daughter would have put right what had happened to Kathleen Clancy's career, but now there was only a double tragedy that no one and nothing could put right. Daisy knew she couldn't put an arm round her; it only increased Kathleen's sensation of being unable to breathe. It was space her mother's body craved, so Daisy sat on the bed beside her, holding her hand till she fell asleep, then she went and put three blankets on the couch, pulled one on top of her and lay down to sleep herself.

7

In the months that followed, Daisy kept her distance from the rest of the family as much as possible. She saw to her mother's needs and still ran the house, but it was with a new detachment that she didn't understand herself.

Mrs Johnstone had given her a second-hand Singer sewing machine saying she had bought it out of vanity and knew she could never get the hang of it, so Daisy might as well be doing some good with it. Daisy had made polite refusals for form's sake, but she loved the machine. It was the most precious thing she owned, though it had to sit in the hallway because there was no room for it anywhere else in the house. Before Kay's marriage, Daisy had sat there by herself, sewing her versions of the clothes she saw and wore at work, fuming over her inability to create a skirt sewn on the bias and fuming even more when Joan laughed at her for trying anything so ambitious.

Sitting at her machine she had mastered French seaming, sewing a seam on the right side then turning it to the wrong side and sewing another that enclosed the first, so that no ragged edges showed. Quality was the key, that was what Joan always said. There were no shortcuts, the basics were important, and even material that wasn't silk – Daisy's favourite – could be made to perform well and look good if the basics were mastered. Daisy learned the importance of detail, too, sewing little frills of lace on her blouse collars while removing anything tacky that betrayed cheapness. 'When you come across anything of bad taste,' Joan would say severely, 'you must avert your eyes, Daisy, or it will mar your judgement forevermore!'

Daisy would laugh at her, but gradually she understood and her confidence in her eye grew stronger. She and her machine changed plain buttons for unusual ones, added matching colours to brighten up the ordinary, and attached white collars to everything, because, as Joan said, that Chanel woman was absolutely right, there was no face so perfect that it couldn't be improved by the reflected glow from something white underneath.

The little machine had become her best companion out of working hours, but when Dessie had moved in all that came to an end. If he wasn't going out to the pub he would stand behind her as she worked, making her so conscious of his presence that she could feel his eyes and his breath on her; and if he was out drinking he could still come back at any moment and then loom behind her. She knew he did it to make her feel uncomfortable; the other household doors were shut and might as well have been miles away. It was his way of establishing power over her, but she preferred to give in rather than join in with his games, so the sewing machine was abandoned and she went back to sewing everything by hand when the household chores were done – even when he wasn't there. She had thought of sleeping in one of the cold, damp, unused bedrooms upstairs, though they had no beds, but the thought of him being so close at night put her off. Once he'd joined Kay, Daisy was at a safer distance downstairs. Besides, what if he came in one night, blocking the doorway? She would be trapped.

So she decided to continue to sleep where her father had suggested, on the couch near to the black-leaded kitchen range. That at least would provide some heat, and there were too many doors leading off for Dessie to try anything.

Kay was no longer working at the ropeworks but lay about all day awaiting the birth of her child. When Daisy came home at night she would feel irritated that her sister seemed to be sitting in the exact position as when she had left in the morning; then she remembered that Kay had always slept that way too and knew there was no point wasting energy getting angry about it. What she had to do, she realised, was teach Kay to do the things 'Background Daisy' had been doing since birth, but with Kay's expanding girth it wasn't easy to make her into a housekeeper. There were things she couldn't do, like lifting Kathleen to change her sheets and her nightclothes, or carrying coal – though other pregnant women did so – but Daisy decided that she could learn to cook.

Somehow it wasn't a huge success, though, as Kay forgot the simplest tasks, like how to peel potatoes, from one day to the next, and had to be taught all over again. It was as if all her learning ability had been devoted to music, leaving nothing to absorb other skills, and somehow she was incapable of clearing the now useless music out to make way for them. Still, Daisy persevered. Kay had to learn these things, Daisy decided, she would need them: as though Daisy knew 'Background Daisy' might not always be there to do them for her. She didn't know where this notion came from or where it might lead, it was just a thought that was there in her head, and that for the time being she didn't take any further.

As Kay waited, Daisy spent the time encouraging her sister and caring for her mother, worrying as the months passed that Kathleen had shrunk into herself more than ever and wondering if anyone else had noticed. Years ago Michael had told her that her mother would not live to old age. The doctors had told him this long ago, and though Daisy knew this she had never really applied the knowledge to the everyday reality of Kathleen being there, trying to breathe. It was how things had always been, so Michael's words had taken on all the importance of his other tales, the ones about 'home'.

But back then Kathleen had something to live for – Kay's future career – and now that it had vanished, Daisy sensed a change in her, a deeper low than she had known before. She couldn't discuss it with Michael as once she would have, because these days she avoided her father as much as she did her brother-in-law. She felt bad about it, not guilty, more deeply sad, but her years as Daddy's Little Girl had disappeared when he had mentioned her 'woman's bits'. She didn't know how all fathers should be, having only had one, but deep down she felt no father should have spoken to a daughter in those terms, and, on the occasions when they passed each other in the house in Guildford Place, she pulled her clothes around her and crossed her arms to hide her body.

Being used to seeing life as a series of difficulties and problems, Daisy didn't know she was going through a more hurtful form of what all daughters do with their fathers, that often bitter parting of the ways when they change from adoring little girls to women. Michael wasn't the first or the last to be thrown by his daughter's developing sexual allure, all fathers are acutely conscious of it and confused by it. He had already been faced that night with the sexual development of one daughter when he inflicted hurt on Daisy with his remark. She knew how other men regarded her, but that she disgusted her father was too much for her to bear and from then on she withdrew from him.

As Daisy had suspected, Kay was further on than she knew, two months further on, and the child was born healthy and loud only four months after her marriage. It was delivered by Mrs Young, the woman down the road whom Daisy had mentioned to Kay, and who also specialised in abortions.

When Daisy went into the bedroom to view the new arrival, Kay was sitting up holding her daughter, and Daisy took one look and burst into tears. Everyone was crying, of course, all the disapproval of the shotgun wedding had disappeared with the arrival of the little girl. There was joy all around, but Daisy's tears were different. She was crying because she knew everything was finally over for Kay; poor, dim Kay who had the voice of an angel but would now be a brood mare instead. There was no doubt about it, her music, her fantastic and mesmerising talent, would wither and die. It had indeed all been for nothing, and she felt such pity for her sister as she held the little black-haired child that it was a physical pain.

She took the new baby downstairs and put her in Kathleen's arms, just as she herself had been taken to Granny Niamh.

'Look, Mum,' she whispered, 'another Kathleen.'

As Kathleen looked down at her granddaughter she smiled and the child cried briefly.

'Did you hear that?' Daisy asked. 'She even cries in tune! I think you've got another singer there!'

It was a desperate attempt to give her mother something more to live for, because the first one had faded to nothing and they both knew it. Kathleen nodded and wept quietly as she stared, bright-eyed, at the baby, but there was an air of doom, a bitter foreboding that Daisy could almost taste.

Everything in her family had changed so quickly, she thought, and it wasn't helped by the talk of war that was occupying the minds of everyone in the country, making for feelings of doubt and fear. It was the end of May 1939, and it seemed nothing could stop the strange little Austrian with the funny moustache as his Forces tramped over Europe. Certainly not another strange little man with a funny moustache waving a piece of paper in London, no matter how loudly the cheers of the listening crowd resounded. The people of Newcastle, as in other cities, were preparing for a war no one wanted or had really believed would happen.

'We've got an Anderson shelter going up in the back garden,' Joan Johnstone announced one day. She exchanged a disapproving look with Daisy. 'They say it will withstand everything but a direct hit, so that's comforting, isn't it?'

Daisy smiled. 'I suppose it depends on whether the Germans will be understanding and bomb from the sides,' she said.

'And that we don't drown from the flooding. Why does no one mention that? They're under ground-level, all the rain will get in.' Joan shook her head. 'And all my flowers have gone,' she continued. 'George has planted vegetables instead. They say all the public parks will be ploughed up and used for vegetables soon, too.'

'But do you really think it will happen?' Daisy asked.

'If it does we'll all be sitting in three feet of water – eating carrots, by the look of things!' Joan replied.

At the end of August, three months after the birth of baby Kathleen, a tearful Kay confessed to her sister that she was pregnant again. Mrs Young thought she was about two months gone.

That was what Daisy was for, sorting things out, making them all better.

'I don't want it,' Kay whimpered, 'I don't even want the one I had. It hurt, Daisy, it hurt really bad. I was all torn, you know, down there.'

'But Kay,' Daisy said, 'you knew it was too early, why didn't you stop him?'

'I don't know how to stop Dessie,' Kay wept. 'He says I'm his wife, he can do what he wants. You don't know what he's like,' she added fearfully.

'Don't I?' Daisy fumed. 'Seems to me I'm the only one who knew what Dessie was like from the first time I set eyes on him, but nobody would listen.'

That Thursday night Daisy waited till Dessie came home from a night of drinking. He spent more time out of the house than in these days, not that she minded, but she never slept till he was safely upstairs. She would lie on the couch in the darkness, her eyes closed, deliberately keeping her breathing slow and deep so that he would think she was asleep, but underneath the blankets she was fully dressed, ready to run if he touched her. Sometimes he stood beside her for ages, and though she controlled her breathing she felt her heart thumping loudly and was afraid he might hear it, too, and know she was still awake. The relief when he finally moved off and made his unsteady way upstairs was always so acute that she felt like crying, but this night she wanted to see him, this night the lights were on and she was fully awake and angry.

He was singing under his breath as he came in, then she heard him curse as he bumped into the abandoned sewing machine in the hall before he made his way through the sitting room.

'So you've made it back, have you?' she asked.

He looked at her as she stood by the couch, her arms folded. 'And what's it to you?' he challenged her. 'Have you a rolling pin handy to hit me with there?' He laughed at his joke.

She didn't answer him. 'Kay says she's expecting again.'

'I wouldn't be surprised,' he said, sitting down and taking off his shoes. 'Not with my bloody luck anyway.'

'*Your* luck? What about Kay's luck being stuck with a bastard like you? Sure, you know you shouldn't have touched her for six weeks after the baby, no decent man would have done what you've done.'

'She's my wife, I can do with her and to her what I want,' he replied calmly.

'Yes, she told me you'd said that. She'll have two babies only nine months apart, do you understand that?' Daisy said angrily.

'So have many women,' he grinned.

'Only the ones married to bastards like you!' she whispered fiercely.

'Ah, shut up!' Dessie said wearily, getting up and moving towards the stairs. 'Your trouble is that you need someone to slap you around to make you think less of yourself, Daisy Sheridan. You need to be taught less cheek and more respect.'

'Respect for the likes of you? Don't kid yourself, you're the one who needs slapping around a bit, and if I were a man I'd do it, believe me!'

That was when she made her mistake. Thinking the conversation was over because there was no point talking to him when he'd had a few, thinking that because he'd headed for the stairs he had actually climbed them, she turned her back to him and began making up her bed. Suddenly he grabbed her from behind again, but he didn't make the same mistake as last time by leaving his stomach exposed to her elbow. He caught her and threw her, face down, on the couch, then fell on top of her, knocking all the breath out of her lungs so that she suddenly realised that even if she had wanted to, even if there was someone in the house who could help her, she couldn't shout.

'You know your trouble, Daisy?' he whispered. 'Your trouble, Daisy, is that you're jealous of your stupid sister. You want what she has and plenty of it! Well, all you had to do was ask.'

He felt under her, grabbed her wrists tightly and almost whipped her round onto her back. Then he caught both wrists in one hand above her head and started ripping at her clothes with the other. She tried kicking him, but he knelt on her legs, then eased them apart with his knee. She would never have believed it was possible. How many times had she heard girls talking about men who forced themselves on females? How many times had she said to herself that the girl *must've* co-operated, or else he couldn't have done it, could he? They could've lashed out, couldn't they? Kicked him, scratched him, fought back by instinct? No man, she had always told herself, would dare think he could do such a thing to her.

Only she hadn't reckoned for the shock, the paralysing thought going through her mind that he wouldn't do this, not really, he couldn't. If she just kept quiet and didn't provoke him any further, he would stop.

Then there were other thoughts as she felt him between her legs, pulling at the red silk pants with the lace edges that she had saved up to buy. Her father was working, her mother was in her bedroom and upstairs her pregnant sister lay with the baby. Her mind was full of panic; she must get away from him without making any kind of noise that would attract attention, and as it was she was afraid someone could already have over-heard. If they came in and found her and Dessie entwined on the couch, they wouldn't believe she hadn't wanted this. That's what he would say, what he would have to say, so she had to keep as quiet as possible. If she did manage to shout out there would be chaos, the family reaction would be one of hysteria.

So go along with it, she told herself, and he'll think of that, too, and he'll stop. If he didn't she could always roll him off her before he got any further.

Only she couldn't. It was a position she had never been in before and she didn't know the physical rules, whereas he did, and his weight was too heavy, too overpowering, and he knew how to pin her down. She was gasping, taking in his stinking breath every time she inhaled, and she was trying to talk to him, trying to put together soothing words about his wife, his child. It was all a mistake; she wouldn't tell anybody, honest, Dessie. Right up to the last moment she thought he'd stop, till the sharp pain that made her call out, but Dessie was aware enough of what he was doing to silence her by roughly putting his mouth over hers.

That's when she gave up; when she realised that he *knew* what he was doing. This was no man in his cups making some vulgar, feeble attempt at a pass that he wouldn't remember in the morning. This was Dessie doing what he had always planned to do.

She stopped struggling. He was inside her, and there was no way to dislodge him anyway, so she lay under him, eyes tightly closed to disassociate herself from what was happening to her body, telling herself it wasn't happening, at least not to her, not to the real Daisy Sheridan. He had let go of her wrists and her arms hung limply by her sides as she thought herself out of her body till he had finished, not uttering a word, not looking at him.

Finally he pulled away from her.

'You've been wanting that for years,' he said, 'and don't bother denying it.' As he climbed the stairs he turned and said with quiet satisfaction, 'Two sisters on the same couch, not bad going for Dessie boy, eh? I'll say this for you, Daisy, you're a damned sight tighter than your sister. Since she had the brat she's too slack to be any use.' Then he was gone.

Daisy lay where he had left her for a long time, hiding in the darkness, wishing she could stay there forever. When her mind slowly began to function she started to feel panic overtaking her and lay down on the floor and covered herself with a blanket, leaving one ear uncovered for sounds of him returning. She had no sense of time, but slowly she began thinking more logically. The wetness between her legs, she'd have to attend to that. And there would be blood on the blanket, that would have to be got rid of, along with her lovely, ripped, stained underwear.

Move quietly, though, she thought, don't give Mam or Kay any reason to think something might be wrong, nor him any excuse to come back down. Ssh. A glass of water, cold water, she thought, running the kitchen tap at a low, quieter capacity for a long time, before holding the glass in her hands, then rolling the wet mist on the outside over her forehead. Every sound was magnified, making her fear that he might return, though common sense told her he would be asleep by now, thanks to the effects of the booze alone.

And what of the morning? How was she supposed to behave? Was there anyone she could tell? And if she did, what would that do to a family already in turmoil?

Her sister; she had to think of her sister and the baby, two babies soon. How could she tell Kay what her husband had done, and, come to that, how could she not tell her? She couldn't run to her mother – Kathleen couldn't help her in any way – but, worse, she couldn't run to her father either, because he would say it was all her fault, wouldn't he? He already had.

There was no real plan in her mind, just the mental crossing-off of a series of things she couldn't do that left only one that she could: she had to leave.

She crept carefully up to the bathroom and locked the door, closing her eyes as she slid the bolt home, silently praying that it wouldn't make a noise then lodging the back of a chair under the handle just in case. Slowly and quietly she washed herself. Once safely downstairs again, she changed her clothes for some drying on the pulley above the range, gathered a few more things together and put them in a small cardboard suitcase, stopping every few moments to listen, like an animal, for approaching danger. The blood-stained blanket and her red underwear were wrapped in newspaper and tied with string, then she sat waiting for time to pass and the first light of the new day to appear. She placed the pillows and the remaining blankets on the couch, so that if Kay came down very early in the dark she would think Daisy was still asleep there. It would buy her a little extra time, and when the mistake was discovered they'd all think she'd just left early for work.

She let herself out, the case in one hand, the newspaper parcel in the other, and walked down the street till she came to a bin where she placed the parcel. She was an hour early at the store, so she walked down the street to pass the time, her mind whirling, wondering what to do next, wondering if it had really happened. It was a pleasant Friday morning, the first day of September, and the world looked just as it always had. Surely everything would have seemed different if it had really happened?

The WAAF Recruiting Office was just opening up and she had to step onto the road to let the RAF people pass. Then she walked on a few steps, turned back, and walked in.

'I want to join up,' she said calmly.

The WAAF Recruitment Officer looked up at her. 'You do?' she asked cheerfully. 'Now this is how I like to start the day. Do come in and sit down, Miss . . . ?'

'Sheridan. Daisy Sheridan.'

'And you really want to join us?'

Daisy nodded. 'I walk past every day on my way to work,' she said. 'I work at Fenwicks, down the road there. I've been thinking about it for a while.' She was amazed at how calm and in control she seemed, how normal her voice sounded.

'And what do you do there?' the officer asked.

'Well, a bit of everything really. I know how to type, file things, chase-up orders, answer the phone, and I do a bit of modelling as well. For customers, like. I model the dresses they're interested in.'

'And you want to swap that for our uniform?' the woman asked her kindly.

'Well, I know in the last war women were sent to work in factories, and if this one lasts that's probably what will happen to me.'

'And you don't want that?'

Daisy shook her head.

'I don't blame you, I'm sure you'd be far better off with us.'

'I want to go today,' Daisy said firmly.

The woman looked up. 'Not sure that will be possible, Miss Sheridan,' she said. 'You see, the trains will be packed, the evacuation of all the children in Newcastle begins today.'

'I thought they'd gone on Tuesday?' Daisy replied.

'No, that was just a rehearsal just in case, but I don't think anyone's in any doubt that we'll be at war within days, so the children are being evacuated now.'

'Well, if I have to I'll stand all the way on the train. I'll sit beside the driver in the cab, I'll help him shovel coal,' she laughed, surprising herself even more by how relaxed and confident she sounded. Mrs Johnstone was right, everything came down to how well you could act a part. 'I've made my mind up, there's no reason to hang about. I'd rather be busy than hang about. See? I've even brought my case.'

'Well, can you come back here at noon?' the officer asked her. 'I'll see what I can do.'

8

When Joan Johnstone saw Daisy that morning she knew
something was wrong and took the girl straight to her office.
She took in the paleness of Daisy's face and the look in her
eyes, like a rabbit not only caught in the headlights, she
thought, but one that had had a real fright. Then she looked
at the battered case in her hand and knew it was something
bad.

'So what's happened?' she asked.

'I've joined the WAAFs,' Daisy said, sitting down. 'Honestly,'
she smiled, 'my case is packed, I just came in to tell you.'

Joan looked at her seriously. 'Daisy, I know you. Wasn't I the
one who taught you all you know? Well, don't try to fool me.
What's happened?'

Before her, Daisy crumpled onto the desk, her head on her
folded arms, sobbing.

'He . . . he forced himself on me,' she said, keeping her face
hidden.

Joan tried to put her arms round the girl, but couldn't because
of the way she was sitting on the chair and leaning forward
onto the desk. 'Who did, Daisy?' she said distractedly. 'Look at
me. Who forced himself on you? Daisy?'

Daisy looked up. 'My brother-in-law,' she said softly.

'Little Kay's husband?' Joan said in a shocked voice.

'Well, she's not going to be little for another while,' Daisy said, trying for humour but dissolving in tears once again.

'Daisy,' Joan said severely, 'you have to stop crying and tell me. Blow your nose and settle yourself.'

Daisy did as she was told and sat back in her chair. 'I've always liked this office, you know,' she said quietly. 'I've always thought of it as my refuge from what's out there.' She looked up at Joan and sighed an uncertain shudder. 'Kay told me yesterday that she was pregnant again so I waited for him when he came home from the pub and told him he shouldn't have touched her so early.'

'Oh, Daisy, that wasn't very clever. You should know better than to talk to a man when he's drunk.'

'I know, I know, I was just so angry. She's not bright, our Kay, she can't stand up for herself, and the birth wasn't easy, she was all torn down below, and he still –'

'And he *raped* you?' Joan said, aghast.

'Threw me onto the couch, trapped me there, I couldn't do a thing.' She pulled up her skirt to reveal the bruises on her shins where he had knelt on her legs before forcing them apart with his knees.

Joan Johnstone drew in her breath and stared, horrified.

'My thighs are the same,' Daisy said miserably, 'and my wrists.' She held out both arms, pulling back her sleeves to show vivid reddish-purple marks around each wrist. 'He held my wrists above my head,' she explained, then pulled the sleeves down before placing her hands below desk-level, as if ashamed of them. 'I never believed women who said they couldn't stop men,' she said quietly. 'I always thought they must've been able to do *something*, you know? But I couldn't, I really couldn't, and I kept thinking he'd stop, and wondering what would happen if I did manage to scream. The only one who could have come would have been my sister, and I couldn't do that to her, could I? And my mother would hear too if I made a noise, and she's so ill, I didn't want her to be upset.'

Joan nodded. 'And were you . . . I mean, had you . . . was it your first time?'

Daisy nodded and started crying again, her head down.

Joan Johnstone walked up and down the floor of the office. 'There must be something we can do, Daisy, we can't let him get away with it,' she said in a troubled voice. 'Does no one else know? Your father?'

Daisy laughed coldly. 'My father?' she said. 'He told me I went out of my way to provoke men. As far as he's concerned I'm no better than a street-walker. Anyway, he was on night shift at the pit. They don't know yet that I've gone, and, if my luck's in, when I go back to the WAAF office at noon they'll get me away from here before they find out.'

The two women sat silently for a moment. 'Can you do something for me, Mrs Johnstone?' Daisy asked. 'If I write a note to my mother, can you make sure she gets it? I thought maybe your sister could take it round.'

'Of course, Daisy, of course,' Joan said absently. 'I'll go along to the cashier and get your wages while you do that.'

But Joan had been making plans, too, and, before seeing the cashier, she decided to go to her bank. She left Daisy writing to Kathleen, telling her that she'd decided to join up on the spur of the moment, that she hoped they'd all forgive her but she'd only have been sent to work in a factory anyway.

Not that she would be forgiven, of course, Daisy knew that. To her father she would be Aunt Clare all over again, another woman who had abandoned her family, her ill mother and her sister who'd just had a child and would soon have another. How any female could abandon her own family was beyond Michael, and now he had two who had done it. Just up and left, not caring what misery they left behind, the shame of it, there was definitely a flaw in the female line. Daisy could almost hear him. She'd be no daughter of his, Michael would say, just as he'd pronounced Clare no sister of his, despite the fact that she'd brought up him and his brothers and seen him safely married. Daisy knew this even as she wrote her note, but she hoped her mother might understand, even if just a little bit.

When Joan came back, Daisy handed her the note, and in exchange Joan handed her an envelope containing her wages. Daisy looked inside and then back at Joan.

'I can't be due this much!' she said.

'I've put a little something in there for you, to help you on your way.'

Daisy counted out fifty pounds, a fortune. 'I can't take this!' she said.

'Daisy, George and I have more than enough, we don't have children and we have a nice house. You've been like a daughter to me, you must take this little bit of money as a kindness to me. Please don't embarrass me by throwing it back in my face.'

'No, I wouldn't . . . it's not that I'm not grateful, but you've already done so much for me.'

'Nonsense! You're a clever girl and you've applied yourself well here. You've done it all yourself, so let's hear no more of that.' Then she looked at Daisy and the two of them hugged. 'I'll miss you,' Joan said tearfully. 'You must keep in touch, write to me here at the store but mark your letters "Personal", now promise me?'

'Of course,' Daisy said.

★ ★ ★

When Daisy went back to the Recruiting Office there was good news. A new intake of WAAFs from various parts of the north were headed for Innsworth in Gloucester via Newcastle for initial training. Daisy was to meet up with them at the station and travel south. So it was goodbye to Newcastle and to her family, who wouldn't even know she had gone till she didn't arrive home that night. And then, hopefully, her note to her mother would be delivered. She thought suddenly of Kathleen's reaction and a wave of panic almost knocked her off balance. There was nothing she could do, though, no other way out, she realised. But she would make it up to her Mam some day, somehow, she decided.

At the station, all around were weeping mothers as their children were sent off on the mass evacuation of city children to the countryside, to keep them safe from the expected German bombs. As the mothers sobbed the children looked worried and confused, each carrying a little bag of possessions, their gas masks in boxes round their necks and labels with their names and addresses on pinned to their coats.

Joan Johnstone saw Daisy off, the platforms milling with children, the smoke from the engines filling the high glass ceiling and noise everywhere.

'I keep thinking there has to be another way,' Joan said, clutching Daisy's hand.

'There isn't,' Daisy said shortly. 'Don't worry, I'll manage.'

'But it's been so quick,' Joan said helplessly, and Daisy nodded.

'And what if you're . . . ?'

'I'll cross that bridge when I come to it, *if* I come to it,' Daisy said.

'But you'll keep in touch? You'll let me know? I feel I should be able to do more for you. I feel so useless!' Joan said angrily.

'You've done everything for me,' Daisy replied. 'Who else

would I have turned to if you hadn't been there?'

They both started crying, but it went unnoticed because everywhere around them there were crying people.

'You could come and live with me and George,' Joan said desperately. 'How about that?' What was the worst that could happen, she thought, that the girl would think there was something odd about her and George? There *was* something odd, and anyway, in these circumstances, what did it matter?

Daisy shook her head. 'How could that help?' she asked kindly. 'I have to go, there's nothing else to do. Besides,' she smiled, 'I've signed the papers.'

Joan looked at her, recognising a show when she saw it being put on, feeling proud of her girl and devastated at the same time. No one said life had to be fair, but this went beyond unfair. 'I've become so fond of you, Daisy,' she sniffed into her handkerchief.

'I know,' Daisy smiled back. 'You're so funny,' she said, 'you even blow your nose like a lady.'

Then they collapsed into each other's arms before Daisy forced herself apart and moved towards a carriage. Joan handed her little cardboard suitcase up to her, trying to think of something memorable to say before they parted, aware that time was running out before either of them was ready for it. They had come so far, further than many women related by blood. They meant much more to each other than fellow-workers and the pain they were both feeling at losing each other was hard for either of them to put into words. The parting was too sudden, too tragic for them to articulate feelings that ran even deeper than they had realised.

'I'll take your letter to your mother, and don't worry, I'll make sure she's all right,' Joan shouted as the train moved off. 'And remember what I told you — life's an act, just a series of parts. Don't take it seriously, just learn your lines and say them as though you mean them. As long as you know inside what's what, you'll be fine!'

That was the memory Daisy would always carry of Joan Johnstone, a small figure dressed in black, hopping up and down and cheerfully throwing kisses with wild abandon as the train gathered speed. All the while getting smaller until Daisy couldn't see her any more and so couldn't see Joan crying from pity and frustration. But she knew, because she was crying the same tears herself.

On the train Daisy found herself sitting between Violet from Darlington and Celia from Middlesbrough, two of the other northerners bound for life as WAAFs, but it was so packed and noisy that she was hardly able to exchange a word with them. It suited her, though. She was withdrawn, needing her own company, still in shock, she supposed. She hadn't understood shock before, she'd thought it was a bit like getting a fright, you just calmed down and got on with things fairly swiftly. But this was different, this was almost like being ill. The other two girls were already chatting on as though they had known each other all their lives, the kind of conversation that didn't need to be listened to. Daisy was glad to notice that all that was required was a nod of the head or a smile occasionally. She was trying not to go over it all in her mind; rape wasn't unheard of, after all, and girls did get over it, so why dwell on it?

'God, I'm hot!' Celia said beside her. 'I didn't know there were this many brats in the world.' She was a tiny, talkative blonde, Daisy noticed, her mind flitting back and forth, while Violet was a tall, hippy brunette.

But Daisy couldn't stop thinking about the implications of what had happened. Suppose she was pregnant: could she get pregnant first time round? She'd heard that you couldn't, and was slightly relieved by that, but there again, suppose that was wrong?

And had she wanted it, as Dessie had suggested, even subconsciously? She knew that wasn't so, the very thought of him had always revolted her, long before he took any notice of her. But what about those times when he had pushed against her, touched her or just stood there, staring at her in that way, that sickeningly raw, animal way. She had never told anyone, never drawn attention to what he was doing, how he was making her feel, because he could have, and would have, said she was imagining it. No one would've believed her anyway, they would have asked why she hadn't spoken up earlier if he'd been behaving like that, as indeed she was now asking herself. After all, any decent girl would. Besides, Dessie had always been there, a member of the family, an asset they were all grateful to have around, or nearly all. And that was another thing, she had made it clear that she didn't like him, so they'd have accepted his denials and would have said she was making it up.

Her father had always thought her dislike of Dessie was based on jealousy, though it wasn't, and now that she was grown up he'd shown that he believed she went out of her way to entice all the poor, innocent men around. He would've taken Dessie's side and she'd have been thrown out of the family whether she was needed or not.

So she had lost nothing. Nothing but her virginity that was.

Daisy shuddered. Then she thought about her mother and wondered who would look after her now; who would wash her, make sure she had clean bedclothes and was comfortable, remember to take her tea without her asking. She lowered her head and tried to stop the tears. Her poor Mam, who didn't deserve anything that had happened to her in her entire life and now she would think Daisy had deserted her.

Well, there was nothing for it. There was no going back so the family would have to manage. Kay was stuck in the house anyway, and she'd be stuck even more with two children to look after, so she'd just have to get to grips with the situation Daisy had lived with all her life. It wasn't ideal, she knew that, but there was nothing to be done.

That evening Joan Johnstone didn't go straight home to Holly Avenue. She went first to see her sister in Guildford Place, then she walked to the other end of the road, to the Sheridan house, and knocked on the door.

Dessie answered her knock. He wasn't hard to identify: Daisy had described him often and she knew there were no other young men in the house.

'Mr Doyle?' she asked politely.

'Who wants to know?' he asked back.

He stared at her in an arrogant way and she knew she would've marked him down as trouble even if she hadn't already known he was.

'My name's Mrs Johnstone, Mr Doyle,' she said. 'My family and the Clancys were good friends and when I said I'd be in the neighbourhood I was asked to pass on their good wishes to Mrs Sheridan. I have a message here for her,' Joan continued, a sweet smile on her face.

Dessie looked her up and down, and she saw him deciding from the way she dressed and spoke that she wasn't from these parts; in fact she represented the kind of people he both feared and felt inferior to: she was a toff. He looked at the letter in her hand.

'Who's it from?' he asked suspiciously, putting his hand out.

'Well, as I said, it's good wishes from old friends, but I think Mrs Sheridan should read them first, don't you?' she said, head to one side, still smiling. 'If you don't mind I'll give it to her myself.'

She made to walk past him a split second before he tried to stop her. 'It's all right, Mr Doyle, I know she doesn't keep well, I won't upset her,' she said brightly, and headed inside the house. In the hallway she saw the Singer sewing machine she had given Daisy. She'd told the girl she couldn't master the thing, it was just gathering dust in her house so better to give it to someone who would make use of it, but that hadn't been true. Knowing Daisy was a skilled needlewoman and liked to copy the clothes in Fenwicks she had wanted to give her a machine, but she knew Daisy would've refused a brand-new one, so she had bought a second-hand one and spun her a yarn so that she would accept it.

She paused for a second, imagining Daisy sitting there, happily sewing her creations, remembering the skirt on the bias that had been such a disaster and how annoyed Daisy had been, and she closed her eyes for a moment. The girl had so enjoyed making things on her machine, even the disasters. Such a little pleasure, and now the machine looked as forlorn as a head-stone. She gathered herself and looked up at Dessie.

'This way?' she asked perkily, heading for the likeliest room without pausing for a reply. Not that she had to use too much imagination, she could hear Kathleen's laboured breathing as she put her hand on the door handle.

Even though Daisy had told her of Kathleen's ill-health, Joan was shocked by her first glimpse and had to work hard to cover her reaction. She couldn't tell if Kathleen was awake or not at first, her eyes were hooded and her cheeks were a shiny bright red against discoloured, unhealthy-looking skin. Her whole body wheezed, and her arms were unnaturally swollen. Joan supposed her legs, hidden under the blankets, would be, too.

'Mrs Sheridan?' she asked quietly. 'I'm Mrs Johnstone.'

Kathleen didn't move, apart from an almost imperceptible nod of her head indicating that she knew the name. Then her eyes looked behind Joan, to where Dessie was still standing in the doorway, smoking despite Kathleen's breathing.

'It's all right, Mr Doyle,' Joan said, smiling her false smile. 'You won't mind if I shut the door, will you, Mrs Sheridan?'

Kathleen shook her head slightly, but said nothing. Talking took too much effort.

Joan shut the door and returned to the bed.

'Mrs Sheridan,' she said quietly, 'I'm Daisy's boss at Fenwicks, I assume you know that?'

Another slight nod.

'Please don't upset yourself, but I have a note from her and some news. Would you like me to read it?' She didn't wait for the nod this time, but carefully opened the envelope and read the contents of the letter, and found herself suddenly overcome, hearing Daisy's voice in her head. Not that Daisy had revealed anything of her real reason for going, just that the house was too crowded now and would be even more so when Kay's next child arrived, so she had decided to join the WAAFs before she was sent to a factory and she hoped her mother would forgive her. She made no mention of her father or of anyone else, which Joan found more significant than Daisy had intended.

Joan looked at Kathleen, prepared for some sort of reaction, but there was none.

'I can assure you that she's all right, Mrs Sheridan, I saw her off myself. She wanted to do this in a way that would cause you least upset and thought it would be better for you if you didn't know she was going. All those long goodbyes, you know the sort of thing.'

Still nothing, then Kathleen lifted a hand and pointed to the door.

'Do you want me to go?'

Kathleen closed her eyes then opened them again.

'Do you want me to get someone for you, is that it?'

Kathleen shook her head just once again and Joan looked at her helplessly, trying to decipher the limited communication.

'Him,' Kathleen croaked. 'It was him.'

Joan looked at her, wondering how much knowledge those few words covered, but she had no right to patronise this woman. 'Yes,' she said sadly, 'it was him.'

Kathleen pushed her head back against her pillows and closed her eyes, and Joan tried to comfort her.

'Mrs Sheridan,' she said helplessly, 'Daisy truly is all right. I've made sure she's all right, please don't be concerned.'

Kathleen didn't reply, but lay there trying to breathe. Joan put the note in her hand and moved towards the door.

'I couldn't,' Kathleen's voice came from the bed, a faint whisper. 'I couldn't help her.'

'You heard?' Joan said.

Kathleen nodded. 'And before,' she whispered. 'She always said he was bad . . . she was . . . right. I couldn't . . .'

'Of course you couldn't, don't blame yourself,' Joan said kindly, going back to the bedside. 'I always got the feeling from the little she said about the situation that he'd had his eye on her for a long time.'

Kathleen nodded more firmly this time.

'Let her down . . .' she wheezed, and was immediately lost in a paroxysm of moist coughing.

'I'm sure you didn't,' Joan said helplessly. 'What could you have done?'

Tears were coursing down Kathleen's cheeks, more from

concern about Daisy, Joan was convinced, than from the fit of coughing.

'Not even her own father,' Kathleen's voice rasped, then shook her head slightly, her eyes closed.

Joan Johnstone felt wracked with pity for the woman, imagining what it must have been like for her to know what Daisy's life had entailed. No one else had noticed, no one but Kathleen herself, so there had been nowhere for her daughter to turn for help. She thought of Kathleen lying in this room and listening, and then she pictured poor Daisy, thinking that if she didn't cry out Kathleen would be saved the knowledge of knowing what Dessie was doing to her. Only Daisy was an innocent, she wasn't to know that even if she didn't scream out, the accompanying sounds were unmistakable if you already had the knowledge.

'Can't tell Michael anything,' Kathleen cried. 'Still, should've done something. My own Daisy!'

'Mrs Sheridan, please don't distress yourself. Daisy would be beside herself if she knew you were upsetting yourself over this,' Joan said, laying one of her own delicate, ladylike hands on Kathleen's swollen one and noticing with some horror how pink her own was in comparison.

'Cool,' Kathleen whispered, and Joan immediately moved her hand to the woman's forehead. Kathleen nodded slightly with gratitude.

'Don't worry, Mrs Sheridan,' Joan said. 'I'm very fond of Daisy. I'll be keeping in close touch with her and I'll keep you up-to-date. I would imagine her father won't approve of what she's done, she'll be an outcast to him, so it will be our secret; yours, mine and Daisy's. We'll say our families were friends in the old days; I've already said as much to that beast at the door. All right?'

A slight smile turned up the edges of Kathleen's mouth as Joan left. 'Oh, by the way, Mrs Sheridan,' Joan said. 'My father really was a great fan of yours, he had quite a crush on Kathleen Clancy.' It was a lie, but what the hell. 'It was lovely to meet you and I'll be back the moment I have any news of Daisy. I promise you, you have nothing to worry about where she is concerned. Good night.'

Kathleen's hand lifted slightly in farewell, but her eyes were again half-closed. Dessie was waiting outside the bedroom door.

'Ah, Mr Doyle,' Joan said pleasantly, 'how nice of you to show me out,' and she nudged him in front of her and out the door. Then she turned quickly, grabbed him by the front of his shirt, yanked him down a foot to her eye-level and rammed him against the outside wall, leaving him so shocked that he didn't even protest.

'Listen to me, you evil, mucky bastard,' she said in thickest, purest Geordie, 'I know what you did to Daisy last night.'

He tried to shake her off, laughing, and she tightened her grip.

'Keep those arms by your sides or I'll scream blue murder,' she ordered. 'Who do you think they'll believe is being assaulted, you or me?'

Dessie thought for a moment then stopped moving.

'I was brought up in Byker, laddie,' she said menacingly, 'there's nothing I don't know about how to deal with scum like you, so don't try anything.'

'She asked for it,' he said, in a bravado attempt to sound casual. 'She's no angel, no matter what tale she told you. She was all for it.'

'She was a virgin, you bastard!' Joan said furiously, slapping his face with the other hand that was holding her handbag, so that the clasp cut him across the nose as a bonus. 'If she wanted to lose it there were real men out there for her to choose to lose it to. She'd never have picked you.'

He opened his mouth, wiping the blood from his nose, and she silenced him.

'Don't lie to me. I *know*,' she told him, 'and all I want you to be aware of is that in future when I come to see her mother I'll carry a knife in my bag. If you ever come near enough I'll cut your heart out and feed it to the nearest dog. Do you understand me?' She shook him violently. 'Do you understand?' she demanded again.

He didn't reply but she knew males like him. She'd grown up with them just as Daisy had, even if she no longer looked or sounded as though she had, and she knew he understood. She let go of him, patted her hat, straightened her coat, put her bag back in position over her arm, and went home without looking back.

She knew his type, could sense them a mile off. Brought up by an Irish mother who had convinced him the world was his oyster, no doubt, the kind who treated her sons like gods and her daughters like god-worshippers in training; she had never understood why Irish mothers did that. Then he had had the good fortune to find himself near to the Sheridans, to Kay in particular, a beautiful child by all accounts and with a talent that could make him money, see him leave his poor beginnings far behind. Only he had miscalculated and the sister he had treated like dirt had turned out to be the more beautiful woman, and she was smart with it; while apart from the voice Kay was dull and thick, and once she had grown up a bit and was no longer a cute little girl, nobody wanted her talent either. So there he was, trapped and bitter, but that didn't mean he had the right to take it out on Daisy, to try to drag her down to his level, the nasty, vicious brute.

She would make sure he learned a lesson before she was finished, she decided, stomping her way homewards. He'd regret meeting up with Joan Johnstone.

Daisy, of course, knew nothing of this. She was far away by the time her former boss attacked her brother-in-law, and further away in mind. She had been thinking constantly about that night, reliving the horror in slow-motion, trying to make sense of it, and had come to the conclusion that rape was really about power, not really about sex at all. Compelling a woman to have sex against her wishes, either by physical force or mental bullying was, to the male psyche, the ultimate declaration of dominance. In attacking Daisy, Dessie wasn't just taking his pleasure from a particularly attractive female, he was paying her back for all the open dislike and snubs over the years. And that included her attempts to better herself, because to his mind it implied that she regarded him and where they both came from as beneath her. Plus, that night she had told him what she thought of him for getting her sister pregnant again so soon after the birth of her first child. She had assumed the upper hand and told him off, so he had brought her down a peg or two with a simple, brutal act of aggression to teach her that she was only a female and that she meant nothing.

But it wasn't that simple. For Dessie the matter was over once he had demonstrated his power by teaching the sexy but uppity Daisy Sheridan a lesson, but he'd done more than that. He had changed Daisy's entire life forever.

9

The first thing Daisy, Violet, Celia and the others discovered when they finally arrived at RAF Innsworth in Gloucestershire after a sixteen-hour train journey was that they weren't expected, or only in the vaguest of ways. There they were, anxious to do their bit, but there were no means of doing anything. Even the food provision was minimal, and on the first morning they were handed a thick slice of bread, a lump of cheese, two pickled onions and a mug of tea.

The majority arrived wearing summer dresses and sandals, quite reasonably thinking they would be kitted out with uniforms: only there weren't any. As in most aspects of the war, Britain was ill-prepared and ill-equipped to deal with the WAAFs. Neither was there much idea of what to do with them, beyond the things women were considered to excel in, like cooking, washing dishes and sewing, all of which Daisy had decided she would have nothing to do with.

The WAAF director had further problems in that the Equipment Directorate had recently moved to Harrogate, complicating every normal difficulty tenfold. In desperation she sent her staff out to look for suitable clothing in the London stores, and meantime the influx of newcomers would have to train as best they could, wearing civilian clothing.

War was officially declared two days later, on 3rd September, but Daisy's intake had even more immediate considerations than that. At RAF Innsworth they were undergoing full medicals, parading naked but for a towel about their waists in front of the medics, who were really more on the look-out for lice or signs of pregnancy than ill-health. A WAAF officer told them encouragingly, 'Just give them a quick flash, girls, and it will all be over in no time!'

Before the Dessie incident, being near-naked in front of a group of men would have bothered Daisy greatly, but it seemed to her that as the worst had already happened this was of no real importance. She was relieved that they were allowed to wear towels round their waists, so that she could hide the bruising on her legs, and she took care to keep her arms behind her back as much as possible so that no one would question her black-and-blue wrists.

What could she have said? How could she have explained them away? Leg bruises could have happened in a fall, but the ones on her wrists were so obviously what they were, that someone had held her very brutally, and there were few circumstances where that could happen.

It was soon over. She had been too wrapped up in her own terrors to understand that there were too many girls to examine for the medics to indulge in close inspection, though they did make a point of sifting through the hair of each one for nits, which she did take exception to.

All around she heard cries of 'FFI!'

'What does that mean?' she whispered to Violet, who was behind her in the line.

'Free from infection,' she whispered back, introducing Daisy to her first piece of service slang.

Daisy shrugged, wondering why they just didn't say that. 'I suppose it's better than NFFI,' she said quietly, and Violet looked back quizzically. '*Not* free from infection,' Daisy said, and they giggled together.

Suddenly Daisy realised that she had never envisaged laughing again, that she had expected to remain as frozen as Dessie's attack had left her. But life hadn't stopped after all, it would go on, and she would move forward.

'What are you two laughing at?' Celia asked in front of them. 'Are you making fun of my fried eggs?' she demanded, covering her breasts with both hands.

'Are you kidding?' Violet snorted back. 'We can't even see 'em! We were wondering why you had your head on back-to-front, Celia, but that *is* your front, after all!'

Celia leaned around Daisy in a vain attempt to pinch any area of Violet's flesh.

'I'm spoiled for choice,' she whispered fiercely, 'I mean, there's so much of *you!* You'll never blow away in the wind, will you?' She stopped and looked at Daisy. 'And as for you, Daisy Sheridan,' she said mournfully, 'well, what can I say?'

Since their arrival the three girls had stuck together and were therefore placed in the same hut.

'Look at it!' Violet said, surveying it distastefully from outside. 'It's more like a chicken coop!'

Celia stared at the scene. 'I've got news for you,' she said, 'that's exactly what it is. I know chicken shit when I smell it.'

'Well, I have news for you, ladies,' Daisy laughed. 'It's now officially home.'

'These Newcastle broads!' Violet snorted.

'They can't help it,' Celia agreed, 'it's what they're used to.'

Once inside they were shocked again.

'These are *beds*?' Celia moaned, looking at her mattress,

consisting of three hard slabs – known as 'biscuits' – in a row. 'They're made of concrete, how are we supposed to sleep on that?' She picked up a pillow. 'And this,' she wailed. 'It's made of straw! I can't sleep on that!'

'Yes, you already said,' Violet commented wryly, 'but you can forget about sleeping anyway, there's no space between the beds to get into them. I reckon we're supposed to pole-vault in and out!'

There was a lot of crying in the hut that night, from girls who simply didn't know what had hit them but were only too aware that there was no escape, for even if they ran away, the girls were told, they would be dragged back. For Daisy, though, it was a time of starting again. This new life was tough, but what she'd had was tougher, and she found herself reverting to type with the others: Daisy the carer started caring for the other girls. All her life that was what she had done, taking on adult responsibilities long before she should have, long before she was truly able to, if the truth were told, but there had been no choice. She was older than her years, and naturally slid into the role of mother hen, even if she was in the company of girls of her own age for the first time. They were all together in the same awful circumstances and needed each other to get by. She was learning much about service life, but more than anything she was learning how strong women could be and how much easier they could make life when they stuck together. With Joan Johnstone she'd had the closest relationship of her life, but with the other WAAFs she began to appreciate how supportive female friendships could be. In those first days, weeks and months she heard different accents, found herself in close proximity with girls from different backgrounds, and yet it didn't matter. It was as if they had all reached the same conclusion at the same time: that they were in this thing together and had to get through it together.

As one they endured injections against every disease known at that time and lectures on subjects as varied as history, VD and military life. They were introduced to the delights of square-bashing in pouring rain and high winds, then sitting through lectures on 'toilet paper, use of', which came down to 'one piece per sitting, one sitting per day'. This was delivered by a male officer, naturally, followed by an hour and a half of classical music played on a gramophone as they sat soaked through, water dripping off them into pools on the floor, all of them cold, shivering and sneezing. Fifteen minutes of wearing their gas masks came next, having first rubbed anti-dim solution into the glass of the eye-pieces to prevent them steaming up as they breathed, and they learned how to adjust the respirators within five seconds of hearing the rattle that sounded for a gas alert.

'I don't know why, maybe it was just the silliness of the day, but suddenly it struck us all as funny,' Daisy wrote to her mother, via Joan Johnstone. 'There were 250 girls there, and every time we breathed there was a sort of snort. We looked and sounded like a roomful of black pigs, and Violet, Celia and I started to laugh, which didn't please our officer a lot.'

There were lessons on marching, saluting and, more importantly, who to salute to, and all of it seemed like a waste of time. But those weeks gave them the basics, as far as the discipline of military life was concerned, and when they looked back on it very few of the girls objected as much as they had while it was happening.

After the Declaration of War everyone had expected the Germans to come visiting immediately, and all eyes were trained on the skies for the predicted hail of bombs, but what they got instead was the 'Phoney War' that ran from September 1939 till April 1940. When nothing happened the entire country relaxed.

'*You remember all those children on the train with you that day?*' Joan wrote to Daisy a few weeks after she'd left. '*Well they're all home again.*' This was a pattern repeated all over the country when the Germans didn't arrive, not on foot, nor by tank or plane. All that happened during the 'Phoney War' was that both sides had the opportunity to send planes over each other's territory to gather reconnaissance photos and to size each other up.

At least it gave the WAAFs breathing space to gather together their uniforms in a bits-and-pieces, haphazard way.

As autumn passed in a blur of personal indignities and basic training, Daisy and the other Innsworth girls were sent on to a training camp, West Drayton, on the outskirts of London. They would become a select little band who were able to talk of their early days there as 'the nightmare winter at West Drayton'.

As if the harshness of that winter wasn't bad enough, when the London Blitz began they spent most nights quaking in fear in trenches that were inches deep in freezing water. After a few weeks, blue-belted RAF raincoats and berets arrived, complete with metal RAF badges and navy armbands with WAAF in red. Some girls even managed to take delivery of grey lisle stockings and a small quantity of black lace-up shoes, though they didn't always fit. It would take till February 1940 to lay hands, by various means, on enough shoes for them – except for size eight and a half, for some reason. Skirts, it was discovered, wouldn't be available till December, so slacks were issued temporarily. Then fleecy linings for the raincoats arrived, then gloves and cardigans, and it was discovered that for 7/6 of their own money, Moss Bros. of London would supply soft crowned caps with black patent peaks, making those who bought them the centre of attention at their bases.

And it wasn't just a bad winter, with ice forming and staying put for months at a time. It also started unusually early, but pleas for more clothing only produced a promise of airmen's greatcoats – for next winter. In December the camps were hit with flu and German Measles epidemics – 'Hun Measles' as they insisted on calling them – prompting Lord Nuffield to present the WAAFs with a Christmas gift of eighty-two wirelesses to amuse them as they recovered.

Still, most of the girls mucked in and coped as best they could, and Daisy wrote to Joan Johnstone that Christmas: *'Freezing cold, no hot water or heating, cold food and flimsy clothing, but great people.'* She was also able to write, with great relief, that there had been 'no after-effects' of her leaving home, which was code for not being pregnant. Added to that joy was her knowledge of the arrangement that Joan would visit Kathleen every Friday with her letters, which meant that Daisy could now write with her mother in mind. Even if Kathleen couldn't reply, the fact that she wanted to hear how she was doing was proof of what Joan had already told Daisy, that her mother hadn't turned against her for her 'desertion'.

Joan didn't tell her, though, that Kathleen had lain in her room that night, listening to the unmistakable sound of Dessie raping her daughter. She knew that would be too much for the girl to cope with.

From April 1940 things did improve. Uniforms arrived, even if they were built to last rather than complement the female figure. Widespread building of accommodation slightly more advanced than chicken coops was underway everywhere, and station establishments were being settled. Married women were admitted for the first time, and it became more accepted that the WAAFs were not just there to cook, clean and 'serve' the men of the RAF, but to substitute for them, thereby freeing them for combat, the one area women were never allowed to enter.

Even in uniform Daisy drew unwelcome male attention. The curves were all too obviously all in the right places under the WAAF uniform, it was almost as though the unflattering uniform had been designed specifically to showcase them. The other WAAFs said that Daisy in uniform proved that there was no justice, and she knew it was true that it also appeared to have been designed to make them look frumpy. Why else give attractive young women a heavy, long, grey serge skirt and a tunic that didn't even fit where it touched? And a shirt and tie was designed to be worn by men: flat-chested men. On women it rolled into bunches, making them look misshapen. And let's not to go near the hat, Daisy thought. Add to that thick tights and sensible shoes, and how could anyone find that lot alluring? No, it had to be a deliberate attempt by 'them' to disguise normal female attributes so that the RAF men were not distracted from war work. That's what the girls thought.

There was another problem for the girls too: people in and out of the RAF thought the WAAFs were only there to provide the men with sex. That's why the uniform-as-disguise theory hadn't a chance of working, because Daisy knew, and the girls would find out, that men would crawl over broken glass to get close to anything female, especially in wartime, when the thought of the Grim Reaper looking over every shoulder somehow upped the libido.

Daisy understood how the girls felt about their uniforms, and their complaints were valid. Just because there was a war on was no reason why they should be made to dress like men with inconvenient body shapes. Somehow the uniform didn't have that effect on Daisy, though. The masculine constraints seemed magically to emphasise her shape; plus, of course, she had an understanding of the business of clothing the female form, and having been an accomplished needlewoman since childhood she had made a few, well, adjustments.

As a fourteen-year-old working in Fenwicks she had learned about well-heeled, stylish women and what made them walk with that uppity air. They dressed beautifully from the inside out, and even if no one knew what kind of knickers they wore, *they* knew, and it made them feel confident. Daisy took it to heart. She'd had no intention of staying in Newcastle and regarded her days in Fenwicks as training for the life she would one day lead. The very best silk underwear, that had been her first purchase as soon as she had saved up enough, and one day soon she would no longer settle for anything on the basis of what was functional and hard-wearing, she promised herself, and the quality of what she wore outside would one day catch up with what was underneath. One day soon.

The war had arrived to release her sooner than she had planned, but the principle remained the same: Daisy would never settle for second best, even if she had to put up with it temporarily. There was no wearing of the regulation underwear either, where she was concerned. No 'blackout' or 'twilight' long-legged knickers touched her contours, and she had dispensed with the uniform bras and vests at first glance without even trying them on. She would make her own silk fancies out of parachute silk if nothing else was available, she decided, but elastic was in short supply. It made her laugh to think of all those women being prepared to do anything for a length of elastic to hold their knickers up, when that same 'anything' often involved their knickers coming down.

So Daisy became the unofficial WAAF seamstress, adjusting ill-fitting uniforms in secret, as long as no word leaked out, because the last thing Daisy wanted was to be shunted into tailoring for the duration. She wanted excitement, she wanted adventures, she wanted a different life than she had ever known before, because as far as she was concerned, that old life had gone forever.

Now she was one of the girls, though, and she was gradually emerging as the leader. They worked under the same conditions as men, went through the same tests, and were reclassified and remustered in exactly the same way, although there would always be those who refused to accept the very idea of women actually doing real work in the Air Force.

In due course Joan reported that Kay had given birth to her second child, a boy named Patrick. What else? Daisy thought wryly. Joan also wrote that her mother loved hearing of Daisy's exploits and was much as she had been, her father too. Daisy knew what that meant: there was no way to any relationship with Michael. Dessie had volunteered for the army, either keen to do his bit or desperate to escape life at Guildford Place, but at least he was gone, and Kay was safe from another immediate pregnancy.

Every now and then Joan would send Daisy the kind of feminine underwear she loved, saying it was pre-war stock and just lying around the store, though Daisy knew better. As it enabled her to avoid the terrible RAF long-legged knickers on offer, she was doubly grateful.

'*Everyone with a garden has an Anderson shelter,*' Joan wrote to her. '*George has planted a garden of vegetables over ours, and we've all got gas masks because they say the Germans will attack us with poison gas. George is on a decontamination squad, they run around doing exercises with buckets and garden hoses. I suppose they know what they're doing. And everywhere you look women are standing about with skeins of wool across their outstretched arms, rolling them into balls for Heaton Social Services to knit things for servicemen. They've taken all the garden railings down to melt them down for armaments, apparently, and we're having to salvage everything. Paper, aluminium and scrap iron are valuable, so they say. The parks are being ploughed up to plant vegetable crops and lots of people have pigs. In many back gardens, Pig Clubs are springing up. It's all so strange, Daisy, you just wonder if life will ever be the same again.'*

Of course, everyone wondered that, and many, like Daisy, hoped it wouldn't be. After the initial enthusiasm of those first girls who had joined the WAAFs, the hardships proved too many for some, and around a quarter had left by May 1940. But nothing could be done about deserters, as the Judge Advocate General had ruled that WAAFs couldn't be charged.

The reaction of those who stayed was one of annoyance; they saw it as a sign that they couldn't be up to much if they weren't to be treated the same as deserting airmen. It seemed to strengthen the attitude they had been working hard to dispel, that their real function was to be 'officers' home comforts', but on the other hand it acted as a kind of natural selection process, ensuring that the WAAF ranks contained only the best and strongest.

Daisy had made some firm friends, all of them from different backgrounds, yet this no longer mattered. They were in this together and that was that. Just like the boys who had volunteered, most of the girls had joined for their own reasons – to get away from home, parents and boring lives.

Gradually, the attitudes towards WAAFs changed. Maybe Dunkirk had something to do with it. When the evacuation got underway in late May 1940, the WAAFs sat around Lord Nuffield's radios in absolute silence, listening intently as the BBC newscaster's chilling tones described the rescue of 220,000

Allied troops from the advancing German army, plucked to safety by every ship and small boat able to travel across the Channel. British ships picked up more soldiers from Cherbourg, St Malo, Brest and St Nazaire, and by the beginning of June 558,000 men had been saved to fight another day. In three weeks the Germans had taken one million POWs, losing only 60,000 of their own men, but the threat of invasion was over. Britain alone remained unconquered.

Even so, everyone knew that all RAF stations would now be under attack, every aerodrome and aircraft would be a target, as well the eyes of the RAF, the Operations Rooms and Radar stations, staffed mainly by WAAFs, would be in the firing line.

Daisy wrote home to Joan and Kathleen about the aftermath of Dunkirk. *'They've taught us to handle handguns and rifles and we have to watch out for German paratroopers. We go around checking doors and windows every night in our nighties and fluffy slippers, a .45 pistol hanging out of our dressing-gown pockets, then we turn and look at each other and break down in fits of giggles. We're always getting told off and we do know it's serious, but it does look so funny, and if we ever come on a German paratrooper I think there's more chance of us laughing him to death than shooting him.'*

And that was one of the big questions for the RAF, how women would react under fire, but they quickly got over their self-conscious feelings. As station after station came under attack, Fighter Command signalled, *'The C in C has heard with pride and satisfaction of the manner in which WAAFs at Dover, Rye, Pevensey, Ventnor and Dunkirk conducted themselves under fire today. They have abundantly justified his confidence in them.'*

Daisy and the others exchanged glances as this commendation was read out by an officer in their hut, as they stood to attention at the bottom of their beds. When the officer left, the girls lay down.

'Did he think we'd all run home to Mummy saying the naughty Germans had thrown big bad bombs at us?' Daisy asked indignantly.

'Exactly,' Celia replied. 'Women with families in civvy street are being bombed every day and coping with it, so why wouldn't we? Damned cheek!'

As things had settled down the girls knew that part of the assessment process to be allocated jobs, meant they would have to go through Intelligence Tests, and for the first time Daisy regretted her lack of schooling. There would be fractions and decimals and percentages to be worked out, the girls who had already gone through testing reported back, all 'as easy as pie' they said. Only Daisy hadn't learned any of that, she had been looking after her mother and running the Sheridan household.

Daisy confided this to her friend Edith, a small, serious girl. Edith had been head girl at her school and about to apply for a university place she didn't want when she saw the prospect of escape through the WAAFs. So, in the evenings, as they huddled round the coal-burning stove in the hut, Edith taught Daisy how to conquer the black arts of fractions, decimals and even long division, while Daisy introduced Edith to the intricacies of darning – a skill, she was coming to understand, that did not sit well with those of an academic mindset.

Daisy went over a mental list of her strengths as the IQ Test loomed. Her handwriting, she knew, was good. It had often been commented on at Fenwicks. And she could spell and do sums – all of that was part of practical learning from her years as a child housewife. But the more complicated stuff had terrified her, till she realised it was all based on logic and was therefore just as easy as the others said.

When the time came to sit her twenty-minute test in spelling, arithmetic and general knowledge, she passed with ease – and a little bit of play-acting as someone who possessed supreme confidence. The two officers asked about her schooling and she conned her way through by simply replying that the Sacred Heart was considered to be the leading Catholic school in Newcastle, without actually saying she had never set foot in the place. It wasn't really a lie, it was more not answering the question they had asked and hoping that in the circumstances no one would have the time to check up.

The fact was that Daisy was bright, and it showed, so no one thought of looking more closely at her replies. More than anything else she wanted a posting that wasn't based on housework. She didn't want to cook, clean, be a seamstress or be stuck caring for the sick, the very things she had experience of, so she kept quiet about them and stressed her office skills. She could type – she didn't say she had taught herself – she knew about filing and handled phone conversations with real as opposed to pretend confidence; and her voice, with the Geordie accent toned down, was clear and precise. She came across as calm and efficient, so they made her an administrator, a rather grand name for a clerk, and asked her where she'd prefer to be posted, and having been clued up by Dotty, another friend, she said London.

Thanks to Dotty's advice most of the girls asked for London, where there were perks, like free or reduced-price theatre tickets, clubs and places to stay when on leave, and the possibilities for fun loomed larger than they did in the sticks. After a time, of course, those allocating the girls to their postings got wise to the London requests and simply ignored them, so that girls asking for London would find themselves consigned to a remote Scottish island with no right of appeal.

Back in the hut the three original friends were re-united to find out their respective fates.

'What've you got? What've you got?' Celia demanded excitedly.

'Administrator,' Daisy said.

'Where?'

'Here.'

'Oh,' Celia said sadly.

'What about you?'

'Pigeons,' Celia replied.

'*Pigeons?*' Violet and Daisy screeched in unison.

'Who the hell gets pigeons?' Violet asked.

'I do!' Celia replied, hurt. 'It's what I wanted, I just didn't say because I knew how you two would react.'

'Well, put it another way,' Violet said wryly, 'why the hell would anyone – even you – want pigeons?'

'My father's been a pigeon-fancier all his life,' Celia said defensively. 'There's nothing I don't know about pigeons.'

'But what do pigeons do in a war?' Daisy asked.

'All sorts of things,' Celia replied. 'Shows how much you know! They go up in kites and if the crew are shot down or have to ditch, the pigeons fly back with their position so that the boys can be rescued.'

Daisy and Celia laughed out loud, staring at her.

'You're serious, aren't you?' Violet demanded. 'Look at her, the least pigeon-chested female I've ever seen and she's a sister to pigeons!'

'So what've you got, then, Miss Lardy Buttocks?'

'I,' said Violet, rolling her eyes and sticking her tongue in her cheek as she nodded her head cockily, 'am to train as a mechanic.'

'Where?'

'RAF Langar,' Violet replied.

'Me too!' Celia shouted. 'We'll still be together!'

Then they looked at Daisy. 'So,' Violet said quietly, 'this is the parting of the ways, then, my fellow flower. It's just me and the pigeon lady from now on.'

'What do you want?' Daisy demanded. 'A couple of verses of "We'll Meet Again"? I'll survive without you two, you know!'

'I know you will,' Violet said. 'The question is, though, how am I to survive with just the pigeon lady in future?'

And the three girls hugged each other, as others were doing in WAAF huts all over the country. Partings were part and parcel of war.

By this time Dotty Bentley had already found a place among Daisy and her friends. Though she had arrived at West Drayton in the same batch, until the night of the NAAFI incident she had just been a face, noticeably of different means to most of them, but they were all girls together now.

There in front of them Dotty had been engaged in a conversation with an RAF officer who had approached her, though there was an impression from their greetings that they had met before. Then she had left with him, a beaming smile on her face.

'Bit brazen, wasn't it?' Celia asked. 'I mean, everybody saw, didn't they?'

Daisy shrugged. 'It's none of our business, is it?'

'Well, it is,' said Violet, 'in a way. If she trots off to tango with the first officer she meets, it reflects on us all, doesn't it?'

'Don't see why,' Daisy countered. 'Anyway, it looked as though they knew each other.'

Violet and Celia were shuffling about uneasily in their chairs, not entirely convinced. The thing still didn't look right. Suddenly they heard raised voices outside and ran to the door. There stood Dotty, and sprawled at her feet was the officer.

'What happened?' a voice asked.

'Nothing,' said Dotty sweetly. 'You just slipped, didn't you, *Sir*? Let me help you up.'

It was clear by the way she said '*Sir*' and by the way he pulled away from her as she proffered a hand, that something *had* happened.

'Must be the new shoes, you forgot to roughen up the soles,' Dotty continued. 'We've all done it.'

As the officer departed with his friends among the crowd he was rubbing his face, and Daisy said suspiciously, 'He was sitting down, but he was rubbing his jaw. Just where did he land when he, er, slipped?'

'Ssh!' Dotty hissed, turning and heading back to the hut, the others at her heels. 'What are you? Military police?' Then, when they reached a patch of darkness, she almost bent double. 'My hand!' she shrieked, hopping about. 'I think I've broken every bone in my hand!'

The others watched her, bemused. 'So what really happened then?' Daisy asked.

'You won't tell anyone?'

'Oh, get on with it!' Violet said impatiently. 'It's obvious you clocked him one, he looked a dicey character to me anyway.'

Dotty was still hopping around, holding her right hand by the wrist and waving it about. 'I knew him before, he went to school with my brother. Had the bloody cheek to ask for his 'officer's perks', his 'home comforts'. I said I didn't know what he meant, though I did, of course, I was just giving him the chance to be joking. Then he said everyone knew WAAF duties were to keep the men of the RAF happy, that it was the only reason to let women into the RAF.'

'Bloody cheek!' Violet shouted.

'You think he's the only one who thinks that?' Celia said. 'I had one erk say to me that he'd never go out with a WAAF because everyone knew we were no more than prostitutes.'

'What did you say?' Dotty asked.

'I said his problem was that he was bitter at being turned down by some sensible WAAF and he couldn't get it even if he did pay for it.'

'Good for you,' Dotty smiled painfully, 'but I didn't expect it from someone I actually knew.'

'So why did you go outside with him?' Celia asked.

'He was an officer!' Dotty said, shocked. 'I couldn't whack an officer in full view of everyone, could I? Whose word would they have taken, his or mine? I'd have been on a charge and chucked back to civvy street.'

'And you just whacked him one under cover of darkness, then?' Daisy laughed.

'Landed a damned good right hook, if I do say so myself. Floored the erk!'

'Only he's not an erk, is he?' Violet said. 'He's an officer. And where did you learn to deliver right hooks anyway?'

'From my older brother, of course. He boxed at school. If he tries to make trouble I'll just have to tell Freddy. He's a pilot,' Dotty replied proudly.

'And we'll all have to swear blind that we saw him slip and Dotty trying to help him up then, won't we?' Daisy said. 'Those leather soles can catch anyone out.'

'Oh, I say,' Dotty cried, 'would you girls do that for me?'

'Course we would!' Celia laughed. 'We're all in this together. Right, girls?'

'Right!' they shouted in unison, then they fell about laughing and stumbled back to the hut.

★   ★   ★

Dotty stood about five feet four, attractive with a lovely figure that was much the same shape as Daisy's but less pronouncedly so, a pretty brunette with bright, brown eyes. When Celia and Violet moved out, Dotty moved to the bed on Daisy's right, joining Daisy's already-existing alliance with Edith, though it would be Daisy who would hold their friendship together.

Edith was from Norwich, the daughter of a doctor who had worked his way up to become one of the best-known consultants of his time. What he had really wanted was a son to carry on his name and his work, but Edith was an only child and so she carried his hopes by default. 'He says it all the time,' Edith said dolefully. '"I've worked hard to get where I am today." What does he want – a medal?' Edith's father wanted Edith to take his ambitions further, which meant going to university, but Edith had side-stepped his plan by nipping into the WAAFs instead.

'He sees that as the height of respectability,' Edith mused. '"My doctor daughter",' and she shook her head.

'So what do you want to do, when this is over, I mean?' Daisy asked her.

'To not be a doctor,' Edith replied wearily. 'What about you?'

'I haven't the slightest idea,' Daisy replied. 'I'm like you, I just wanted to get away from where I was. What about you, Dotty?'

In the dark they heard Dotty sigh. 'I think the only thing I can say is "Snap",' she said.

Dotty, they had always known, came from a rich family. Because her uniform was specially tailored in the finer air-force material used for officers' uniforms, she had never had any need of Daisy's skills with needle and thread. This was disapproved of, though tolerated by the WAAF hierarchy, none of whom seemed to notice that all the girls had their uniforms tailored to a degree, thanks to Daisy.

To the others it was a curiosity that anyone would spend money buying a uniform, as even specially tailored it was far from the height of fashion, but Dotty herself was regarded with affection, partly because of her ever-cheerful disposition, and partly because of her father's generosity. Pa Bentley despatched the family Rolls carrying the family butler to the railway station at West Drayton every fortnight, with strict instructions that the hamper he carried should be left there for Dotty to uplift. Dotty didn't want the Rolls to come to the base gate where it would be seen by the others, or the guards would pass the word around. However, Dotty's ploy had no chance of working because the guards said instead that a Rolls had dropped the hamper off at the station.

The hamper contained cake, sweets, bacon, hams, butter, and eggs which were subsequently boiled in an illegal kettle, as well as tinned delights that Dotty happily shared with the rest of the hut. When asked what her father did for a living, Dotty became slightly flustered and explained, apologetically, that he had inherited a farm from his father. Hence the abundance of treats in the fortnightly hamper.

Some of the others in the hut came from farms, too, and had their suspicions: which they kept to themselves, they were all sharing in the bounty, after all. What Daisy quickly became aware of, though, was that Dotty knew the places to go in London, where her name opened doors. If there was a party, Dotty and her friends were welcomed with open arms, and they never had to rely on the YWCA for accommodation either.

The first 'wizzo do' the three girls went to was at the Savoy Hotel – to mark the posting abroad of some titled youth, Dotty said, though Daisy and Edith quickly learned that no excuse was actually necessary. The three girls arrived in their WAAF uniforms to be met with unbearable shrieks of delight by Dotty's non-service friends, and much over-the-top hugging and kissing – the normal mode of welcome, it seemed.

'Bit, um, well,' Daisy whispered to Edith, 'much?'

'I was thinking insane, actually,' Edith said, as another wave of emotion engulfed Dotty.

'Yes,' smiled Daisy, 'that too.'

'But darling,' a male voice yelled from the crowd around Dotty, 'your uniform is absolutely divine!'

'Almost makes one want to join up!' a female screamed in reply.

Edith and Daisy exchanged looks.

'You must meet my friends,' Dotty said. 'This is Daisy, and this is Edith. Girls, this is Rupert.'

'My God, darling,' the same male voice said in a hushed tone, as the owner looked Daisy up and down. 'This one's uniform's even more divine!'

'It's not the uniform, silly,' Dotty squealed, 'it's Daisy! She fills it out better than the rest of us!'

'I'll say!'

'You've already said,' Daisy added calmly.

'But it bears repeating, my dear!'

'And it's been repeated.'

'Feisty one, this,' he said to Dotty. 'How delicious!'

'Too rich for your palate, that's for sure,' Daisy remarked.

Dotty screeched loudly at her side. 'You'll get nowhere with Daisy, Rupie, she'll eat you alive!'

'And my God, wouldn't it be worth it?' he grinned.

Creep, Daisy said to herself. Erk would have been too much; Daisy didn't do RAF slang and swore she never would.

They then discovered that it wasn't just the welcomes that came at ear-shattering levels; it was the only kind of communication anyone in the suite seemed to understand. Daisy and

Edith had expected a gramophone, but what they found was a jazz band in dinner suits, as were most of the male guests, though some wore uniforms bearing higher insignia than the girls normally consorted with. The females all wore amazing evening gowns that Daisy identified as coming from the best designers, and more jewels than she had ever seen in her life. There was a great deal of wild dancing that grew wilder with the limitless alcohol on offer. They watched one gorgeous girl being gleefully thrown about like a rag doll.

'That's an actual dance, is it?' Edith asked.

'Damned if I know,' Daisy replied, 'but if it is it must be the jitterbug, that's exactly what she looks like.'

The girl stopped mid-jitter to push a handful of pearls into Daisy's hand, saying, 'Be a dear and hang on to them for me, darling, damn things have almost had my eye out a dozen times,' before jumping back into action.

Daisy looked at the string of pearls. 'I think they're real,' she said to Edith.

'How can you tell?'

'Oh, there must be ways, don't you bite them or something? Shall I try?' She raised the necklace to her mouth, laughing.

'Why don't you just slip them into your pocket, then you, me and the pearls can slip out of the door?' Edith giggled back.

'Don't think we could. Don't know how she can walk wearing them never mind throw herself about like that, they're enormous!'

Just then two men approached them, bearing a huge bottle of champagne and two extra glasses, announcing themselves, and hoping for a favourable reaction by doing so, as diplomats from the American Embassy.

Daisy felt a wave of panic rising up. She didn't want any man to approach her, couldn't bear the thought of him leaning towards her, leering at her, and the idea he might touch her made her feel so instantaneously sick that she swallowed quickly. So she bristled just enough to put them on notice that they were not automatically welcome, in her company at least; but Edith, who wasn't used to familiar behaviour from men, American men in particular, showed fear rather than reserve by stiffening up completely.

Oh God, Daisy thought, she's turned into a rabbit. She watched one of them taking advantage by sitting beside Edith and slipping his arm around her shoulders, while 'Daisy's' kept a respectful distance as he poured champagne for both girls. Daisy gave a serene nod of the head and took a sip. It was like fizzy cider, she decided, another illusion gone, though her expression didn't change.

'So, tell me, sweetness,' the American said, 'what's your story?'

'I don't think I have one,' Daisy replied coolly.

'What's your name?' he laughed. 'Mine is Walt.'

'Well, Walt,' Daisy smiled back, 'my name is Daisy.'

'Well, don't tell me then,' he winked back at her, 'you little minx!'

Daisy tried to exchange a wry glance with Edith, but Edith remained stiffly transfixed, staring straight ahead.

'So what are you?' Walt persisted.

'A WAAF,' Daisy said.

'But are you a Lady or an Honourable somebody?'

'I'm an honourable lady, if that makes things any clearer.'

Walt guffawed loudly and slapped his sides, the bottle still in one hand.

'You'll hurt yourself doing that,' Daisy said, looking around the room disinterestedly, then turning to look him in the eye as he moved closer and tried to slip an arm around her shoulder. 'And I'll hurt you if you do *that*,' she said icily.

'What's the matter?' he asked in a thick voice. He waved the hand with the bottle in the air, indicating the room, wine spilling out in a wide arc. 'Look, honey, everybody's doing it.'

And they were. A group of four were perched precariously on the piano, to the anxiety of the pianist, swaying madly as they sang out of tune, drowning out all but the beat of the music. Of the others, those not dancing wildly or conversing loudly were lying about on top of each other, while those carousing, dancing and conversing continued as though they hadn't noticed.

'Yes,' Daisy replied, 'but perhaps I'm just choosy, or maybe not drunk enough.'

'We can soon fix that,' Walt chuckled, lifting the bottle to pour her more wine, but Daisy had already placed her hand across the rim of her glass. 'Make that just choosy then, Walt,' she smiled sweetly.

Afterwards she thought about how she had handled herself and took stock. She hadn't planned any of it, she had simply taken a deep breath and launched herself into an act, becoming an ice-maiden with a glib turn of phrase. Joan Johnstone had been right: life was all a question of choosing your part and performing it with confidence – even if you were quaking inside. She had wanted to keep Walt at a distance and it had worked. She had got away with it without doing a Dotty, so there was no reason why it shouldn't work just as well in future. She had discovered a means of taking back control.

Not that all Dotty's soirees were like that. Some were held in private apartments in Knightsbridge or Pimlico, but there was always some degree of bodies lying on top of each other, it had to be said, and always some male or other trying his luck. It was an attitude that had spread worldwide, though. By all accounts the outbreak of war had prompted a steep decline in morality both inside and outside the services, and across the social barriers, too, for that matter. As Daisy's male-deflecting act developed, it was becoming the one everyone accepted, and she was increasingly regarded as a bit of a character. Mae West they called her, and soon everyone knew that it would take a pretty special male to get past her guard.

Not that it stopped them trying, of course. It was in the nature of the beast, but the last thing they wanted was to be humiliated in front of their friends, so the first rebuff, however humorous, usually sufficed.

After her disappointment at her first sip of champagne, Daisy decided alcohol wasn't for her. As a child she had seen how much damage it could do, and at the London parties she saw how it lowered the resistance and inhibitions, and she wanted to keep both. One thing the Dessie escapade had taught her was to always be alert; to learn how to spot situations before they got out of hand. She realised that everyone else was too intent on how much fun they were having to notice how little she was drinking, so she accepted a glass of whatever was on offer and kept it by her side, unconsumed, for the duration. When top-ups were offered she would indicate her full glass. It worked, because everyone was more interested in themselves.

After champagne there were other disappointments to come. Caviare was disgusting, she discovered, though Dotty assured her it was an acquired taste and she should persevere, which she didn't. Truffles, on the other hand, were quite nice, really, which was more than could be said about anchovies; while smoked salmon and scrambled eggs was pretty amazing, considering the salmon hadn't even been cooked first.

Soon, though, these forays consisted of just Dotty and Daisy, Edith having decided none of it was for her. Edith was a serious-minded girl who saw little value in small-talk and so had never perfected the art. She was acutely aware that this was a handicap, even if she had no wish to change it. She just wasn't made for parties, certainly not on Dotty's level.

Daisy, on the other hand, had some experience of the landed gentry in her years at Fenwicks and was better equipped to deal with almost any company, so she adapted effortlessly, though with her own rules. At the beginning of her healing time, when she had needed calmness and quiet, Daisy had been closer to Edith, who was capable of sitting for hours in silence reading a book. But now she was recovering and re-grouping mentally, putting what had happened to her behind a closed door in her mind and trying to find a way of going forward.

Edith remustered as a Radio Telephone Officer and moved to Langar along with Violet and Celia, so it was natural that Daisy and Dotty became closer. At first Daisy had seemed, on the surface, like just another girl away from home, a bit anxious but trying her best to learn as much as she could; but underneath the turmoil of her escape from Newcastle had raged. She had struggled to make sense of the rape and come to terms with why she had let it happen to her, as though it had been her fault. She'd become full of a guilt and anger that had nowhere to go. As she made those first steps forward it seemed that every attempt to put her old life behind her was caught up in her dreams as she slept, jumbled up with details of her new life, twisted and mixed up together, reminding her of what she wanted to forget.

Being in the company of females helped, even if they were all in view of males every day. The men had so many girls to choose from that she could hide in the pack, to a certain extent anyway: there was safety in numbers. However, men still noticed her in this new life, her outward appearance hadn't changed for the worse, and the airmen pointed her out to each other.

Crossing her arms and determinedly not walking in the way her hips tended to guide her didn't disguise anything, and gradually she was coming to terms with the attention. It was boring going around all the time thinking of ways not to look the way she looked, there were more pressing matters to dwell on, so she was trying to devise a plan of survival.

Slowly Daisy was taking control of the situation, finding within herself the ability to rise above the whistles and the winks, and to deal with them whenever and wherever they came at her, and her closer friendship with Dotty had helped her with the next steps along that path.

10

In July 1940, Joan Johnstone's latest letter to Daisy carried various bits of news. First of all, her father had been taken off night shift at the pit.

'He isn't happy about it, I can tell you,' Joan wrote, adding gleefully, 'he says it's because he's Irish! I don't think he'll ever accept that he isn't the only one being messed about by the war. At least he's there at nights now to look after your mother, whose health isn't good, I have to be honest, Daisy. She loved the picture of you and your friends in uniform, made her eyes sparkle for a bit. And Spiller's old factory has been bombed, it's just standing there like a skeleton, though everyone says the High Level Bridge was the real target, not that the Spiller's people will find much comfort in that. The next bit of news is in two parts, good and bad. Kay's husband has gone abroad with his regiment, so it's good riddance to bad rubbish there, but the bad news is that he got leave before he went and Kay is now expecting baby number three. Yes, I know, my dear, it's terrible, but there's nothing you can do about it, you have worries enough with what you're doing. In fact I wasn't sure whether I should tell you, but I thought you'd want to know, so forgive me if I've upset you.

'By the way, I've found a whole box of those cotton nightdresses that your mother likes, it was under all sorts of rubbish in the stockroom. I wish I could embroider flowers and things on them like you did, but you know I'm all thumbs when it comes to needlework. But at least she'll have the ones she likes, even if they are quite plain. And please don't think of sending me a penny for them now, I've told her I've put them on account for when you come home. I'll take them to her this evening and report back in my next letter.'

Reading the letter, Daisy smiled, remembering Joan trying to find a way of giving the nightdresses to Kathleen without making her feel like a charity case.

By late 1940, partly because of Dunkirk and partly the news of the bombings throughout the country, Daisy's attitude to being a WAAF had changed. She wasn't alone, though. It wasn't just about escaping the home situation any longer, like most of the girls who had joined up; she wanted to do something, to be part of the war by working in an operational unit. So, early in 1941, along with Dotty, she asked to remuster as an R/T Operator – a Radio Telephone Operator. There was an excitement about being where planes flew out on missions and, hopefully, came back, Edith had written from Langar, a feeling of being involved in a way that would make a difference.

Daisy was successful, and was put on a course that had been compressed into six weeks, something that would cause friction throughout the war from regulars whose training had taken years. Dotty, to her bemusement, was to be a medical orderly.

In Guildford Place, Joan Johnstone was making her way home after visiting Kathleen. She was thinking how strange it was that her life had become so entwined with the Sheridan family. If she had taken the lift down to the shop floor ten minutes later all that time ago she would probably never have known Daisy existed. Miss Manders would already have sent the girl on her way with her usual dismissive tone. What kind of powers governed such things, she wondered? And who was to know that she and Daisy would develop such a deep bond, one that had encompassed Kathleen too? Joan had never had the opportunity to care for her own mother, the family breach had never been healed, but at least she could do something for Kathleen.

That was what Joan was thinking that Friday evening, on how much of their lives they now shared, and all from being on the shop floor when she had been. Then she gave herself a shake. Never mind the past, if she didn't get a move on the blackout would descend and she might have no future.

At West Drayton the following Thursday, as Daisy and her fellow WAAFs waited for news of their postings, there was a call for Daisy to report to the Senior WAAF, Gwen Thomas. Thinking she was about to be reprimanded again for wearing silk stockings, the absolute cardinal sin as far as WAAFs were concerned, she dashed from the Admin Block back to the hut, dug out the old lisle horrors and put them on before making her way to the unit office.

Gwen Thomas was in a situation she had never handled before, though it was becoming common enough. On the previous Friday evening, there had been a German raid on Newcastle. Byker and Heaton had been hit, especially Guildford Place, and the Sheridan home had been destroyed. There were no survivors, so she would have to tell Daisy that her entire family had been wiped out.

Thinking how she would break this news, the officer decided it would serve no purpose to beat about the bush. Not only would that be pointless, but it would also be wrong. Besides, any girl called to the office would already be geared up for bad news, she mused, so it was better to say it straight out and to be prepared to go over it two or three times after that as the girl took it in. As she waited for Daisy to appear she was practising in her mind what words to use. The girl's whole family, my God, what a thing to have to come to terms with, and it was worse that she was so far away. Still, there was no way of not telling her, or of holding out any hope. Daisy had to have the truth, that much she knew.

There was a knock at the door and Daisy entered and saluted.

'Sit down, Daisy,' the officer told her, and as Daisy did so she could see by the expression in the girl's eyes that she had no idea of why she was really there.

'Daisy, I have something to tell you and I'm afraid it's bad news.'

Daisy was horrified; surely they weren't going to take her new job away from her because she'd been reported for wearing silk stockings again? All the way to the office she had been practising her speech, too, but for her defence, unaware that Officer Thomas had been doing something similar.

'If it's about my stockings, I swear I won't —'

'Daisy, it's not about that, it's much more serious, I'm afraid. I'm sorry, but last Friday there was a raid on Newcastle and your home was hit. I'm sorry,' the officer repeated, playing for time rather than saying what she had to say. Then she paused for a moment and cursed herself mentally. The girl, the poor girl, had to be told. 'I'm afraid everyone is accounted for, your mother, father, your sister and her children, and there are no survivors. It's a blessing that your sister's husband wasn't in the house, as he's currently abroad on active service,' she said quietly.

Daisy stared at her as though she was speaking in a foreign language. She hadn't anticipated this — how could she when she knew for a fact that it always happened to someone else?

'It's taken this time to be sure they've got everyone, and, of course, they had to be buried quickly, you understand . . . Then they couldn't find you and neighbours said you were in the Forces.' Gwen talked on, giving Daisy time. 'They pointed the way to your last employer and that's how you were traced here. There were letters in the office of a Mrs Joan Johnstone, I believe,' she said, looking at the papers on her desk for confirmation.

Daisy nodded, staring into space. There was a curiously detached feeling in her head, as though she was floating on the ceiling, right there in the corner, and watching and listening to what was going on. As though she were eavesdropping on a conversation that didn't concern her.

'As it turned out, Mrs Johnstone's body was found near your home too,' the officer continued, more to fill the silence than supply details, and because she couldn't think of anything else to do. 'Apparently she has a sister who lives in the same street, so presumably that was why she was in the area. The sister's home was untouched, so if she'd reached it she would've been safe. Just one of those things, I suppose, a few minutes in either direction makes the difference.'

Daisy nodded again and tried to speak, but her throat was dry. The officer handed her a glass of water and she took a sip. 'When did it happen?' she asked.

'Friday evening, after nine p.m.'

Daisy didn't reply, but she knew Joan hadn't been visiting her sister. On Friday evenings after work she went to see Kathleen with Daisy's latest letter. What had she written about? Oh, yes, the girls having a bath, a little tale to amuse Kathleen. She smiled, remembering how all the girls had laughed when they'd heard the story first-hand from a new arrival, and she'd made a mental note to include it in her next − now her last − letter home. Somehow it became of crucial importance to remember the exact story at that moment. How had it gone again?

In the WAAF in question's previous posting she had been one of four girls billeted in a former boys' school, where they had been told there were plenty of baths.

'We set off in search of this luxury,' the girl had explained, 'and found a dozen baths lined around three sides of this enormous room. Myrtle, Sheila, Ethel and I kind of laughed, a bit embarrassed, then we thought, "What the hell? There's a war on, y'know, this is no time for modesty!" We stripped off and found there was nowhere to hang our clothes, so we put them in the middle of the room and ran these beautiful deep, warm baths, absolute heaven. We were lying there singing and telling jokes till we couldn't stay in any longer, then we pulled the plugs and got out. And that,' she sighed, 'was when we realised the baths didn't have individual plumbing, and we watched aghast as the water ran to a central drain in the middle of the room.'

The other girls were by now giggling.

'That's right,' she said wryly, sipping her tea thoughtfully, 'to where we had left our clothes.'

That was what Joan had read to Kathleen last Friday as the German bombers were on their way. She must have left for home just before the blackout, then the explosion had struck. All of them gone, her entire family, even Joan who had done so much for her.

Daisy cast her mind back, picturing Joan jumping up and down on the station platform on that day a lifetime ago, in tears but blowing wild kisses and waving frantically. It was hard to take in, impossible really, the words playing in her mind over and over: 'All of them gone.' The only survivor, by 'a blessing', was Dessie, so there was no justice in the world after all, just as she'd always suspected. She shook her head slightly and the officer got up and called for tea to be brought in.

'Daisy, I'm so sorry,' she said helplessly. 'I wish there was something I could do. You'll get compassionate leave, of course, I'll arrange that, we'll talk about it over tea.'

Daisy hadn't said anything, but her mind had been busy. If they were all dead and buried and the house had been flattened, what was there to return for or to? A cup of tea was placed in her hands and she sipped it slowly, tasting only the extra sugar that everyone said was good for shock. Why was sugar good for shock? she thought. She must remember to ask someone one of these days.

'Does anyone else know about this?' she asked eventually.

'The CO,' Gwen replied.

'Well, could we please keep it between us?' she asked in a small voice. 'I'd rather no one else knew.'

'But Daisy, you'll get support from the other girls, you know that.'

'Yes, I know, but I'd find it easier to deal with on my own; the last thing I need is a lot of sympathy.' She looked at the officer. 'I'm not explaining this very well, but it's just that I feel that it could have me on my knees if everyone crowded round to comfort me. The best thing I can think of doing is carrying on as normal.' In her mind she chided herself. 'On my knees' indeed, so much for not using RAF slang. She took another sip of her tea.

'But Daisy,' Gwen Thomas said quietly, 'they'll know when you go on leave . . .'

Daisy shook her head. 'What's the point of leave?' she asked. 'They're gone, there's no one to see, and the house is gone, too. Why would I go all the way up there to look at . . . well, nothing?'

Gwen nodded. 'But you must have other family?' she suggested.

'Oh, cousins, I suppose.'

'And you don't think it might make all of this easier if you were to spend some time with them?'

Daisy shook her head. 'Haven't seen them in years,' she murmured. 'I could pass them in the street and not recognise them. They live in another world, there are people here I'm closer to.'

'I understand what you're saying,' said the officer, 'but perhaps it would help you to accept it if you saw it?'

'No, I don't have any trouble accepting it,' Daisy replied quietly. 'It's happening all over, not just to me. There's nothing to go back to Newcastle for, ever again. I'm still on duty –'

'No, no, we'll get someone to cover for you.'

'Then they would know something was wrong,' Daisy said logically. 'The best thing for me is to get on with my work.'

'Do you think you're up to it?' the officer asked kindly.

'Yes, I'll be fine, honestly, I wouldn't say that if it wasn't true. If I can just sit for a minute or two to get my mind straight? And you don't have to talk to me,' she said, 'I'm really OK.'

The two women sat in silence, the only sounds the clinking of their cups and saucers, accompanied by little gulps as they swallowed their tea. After ten minutes Daisy replaced her cup on the desk, stood up, smoothed a hand over her skirt and took a deep breath.

'Thank you for being so kind,' she smiled tightly.

'Daisy, you're sure?'

Daisy's head dipped in a firm little nod.

'If you change your mind . . .'

'I won't,' Daisy said, 'but thanks.'

She saluted and left, and as she closed the office door behind her there was an echo as another closed in her mind. Then she went back to the hut where Dotty was waiting for news.

'Another ticking off?' she asked, arching her eyebrows.

Daisy nodded. 'The risks we take to wear silk stockings,' she said, bending to remove the detested lisle ones. 'Still, it was only a slap across the wrist, it could've been much worse.'

The next day, news of their postings arrived. Daisy and Dotty would report to RAF Langar, nine miles south-east of Nottingham, where Edith had already joined Violet and Celia. Life would be different now that her entire family and Joan had gone, but she had her friends, all of whom she had met since leaving Newcastle and her old life behind. It would be an entirely fresh start where she could become whoever she wanted to be, because now there was no one alive who knew the old Daisy Sheridan. No one, that was, apart from the 'blessedly' alive Dessie, but Daisy closed another door on that thought.

11

A Utility – a van – took Daisy and Dotty on the long journey from London to Langar. The base was set among fields just showing their springtime foliage, though the houses near the airfield, like the Langar buildings, were painted in green and brown camouflage colours. This was a different world from West Drayton, where they had been aware of airmen but didn't really mix with them much. This was an operational station, so as the van took them into the airfield they tried hard to behave like seasoned service personnel who weren't impressed by the sight of aircrew and planes, even though they were.

At the WAAFery they got out, collected their belongings and calmly booked in, before heading to the dining room for a meal of cheese-on-toast, bread, butter, jam and tea, a marked difference from their breakfast of 'dry rations'. From there they made their way to the bedding store to collect blankets and sheets, then to their hut, where they found they were sharing a room.

Daisy immediately thought of Gwen Thomas and smiled. Her former officer at West Drayton must have arranged that Daisy would be with her friend, and she had also been as good as her word. Nothing had slipped out before they left the camp

about the raid on Newcastle. Now Daisy had a fresh start with
a new job in a new place, with different people as well as old
friends. She and Dotty were both tired from their journey, so
before tracking down Violet and Celia they made up their beds
and slipped between the rough sheets, the background noises
lulling them to sleep.

Footsteps on the highly polished lino; someone drawing the
dark blue blackout curtains; two girls talking as they polished
shoes and uniform buttons; more sitting on a bed laughing at
something; another writing a letter and someone singing in
the distance. As Daisy drifted off into that first stage of slumber
where nothing makes sense, in her head she converted the
tune the girl was singing to 'I'll Take You Home Again
Kathleen', and turned her face into her straw-filled pillow.
Sometime later she wakened with a start to a deafening noise
and a girl looked at her and laughed. 'It's only the planes,' the
girl said. 'Ops tonight. We always cheer the boys as they take
off, but you stay where you are tonight.' Later Daisy dreamed
of thunder as the planes returned from their missions. There
were so many sections to inform of their arrival in the days
that followed, but luckily Violet and Celia found them first
and were there to help, having descended with screams and
hugs as soon as they heard of their arrival. Edith, they told
them, was on leave. There was the Pay Accounts, the Gas
Section, the Orderly Room, and everywhere they went they
had to collect the correct number of signatures from the officers or NCOs in charge. Finally they parted and made their
ways to the guardroom, where Dotty was sent off to the
Medical Unit, while Daisy was taken to the Orderly Room
and handed a pile of train timetables to study, as they thought
she was a Railway Transport Officer. When she pointed out
that she was, in fact, a Radio Telephone Operator, she was

looked at with complete confusion. She realised that not only did no one there know what that meant, but they hadn't been expecting her either, regardless of what she did. 'Sounds kind of Signalish,' a voice said. 'Send for a Signals Officer.'

When the Signals Officer arrived he pointed Daisy in the direction of the Watch Room, a square, two-storey box-like building in front of the aircraft hangars. After climbing the concrete stairs she approached the Squadron Leader in charge, saluted and explained who she was and why she was there. He was a good-looking, dark-haired man, in his early forties, she thought, watching him walk up and down, look at her, say 'Hum' rather a lot, look at her again and walk up and down once more. His face was contorted with concentration and he was biting on the knuckle of his first finger. Suddenly he stopped, threw his arms into the air and beamed at her.

'I know what!' he said with deep happiness. 'How would you like a few days' leave?'

'Sir?' Daisy replied.

'I'm sure you could do with it,' he continued. 'Get out in the sun, take long walks, that sort of thing, eh?'

Daisy didn't know what to say, so she continued to look at him.

'Yes, yes, that's the thing,' he said cheerfully, returning to his seat. 'You take a few days off. The thing is, I haven't the slightest idea who you are, why you've been sent to me or what to do with you. It'll all be clear when you get back. Have a good time, then!'

Daisy stood in silence for a few seconds, gradually taking in, by the fact that he had closed the conversation and turned away from her, that she had been dismissed. So she made her way down the stairs again and went back to the guardroom.

There she found Dotty.

'I've been told no one knows anything about me,' Dotty said in an offended voice.

'Snap,' Daisy replied.

'I've been told to go on leave till it's sorted out.'

'Me too. I've to get some sun and go on a long walk, apparently,' Daisy smiled.

'It's a bit rum, don't you think?' Dotty asked, still offended.

'So you're going to turn down a spot of leave, are you?'

'Not likely!' Dotty grinned. 'Where are you going? Home?'

'No,' Daisy said casually. 'My family's away.'

'Why not come home with me to Rose Cottage then, that's our farm in Gloucestershire?' Dotty asked. 'There's loads to do and Mar and Par love having people to stay.'

'You sure there's room?'

'Positive! I'll ask to use the telephone and get Par to send the car to the railway station. We'll get a lift to the station, surely?'

'Why not get your father to send the car to the camp, then we wouldn't have to find a lift to the station?' Daisy asked.

'No,' Dotty replied. 'We'll get a lift OK.'

The farm wasn't quite what Daisy had expected, and Dotty's father was not pottering about in the byre, hay sticking out of his ears as he fed the cows; but there again, the chauffeured Rolls that arrived to pick them up wasn't a tractor either, so she already suspected something. She looked at the huge country house in front of her, ivy growing rampantly all over it and threatening to cover the many windows on the front.

Daisy laughed.

'What is it?' Dotty asked fearfully.

'Rose Cottage?' Daisy asked.

'Oh, that's just Par's sense of humour,' Dotty replied, flustered.

'It used to be called Bentley Manor, but Par thought that was terribly pompous, so he changed it to something terribly silly. I mean, there's not a rose in sight, is there? Ivy Cottage, now that –'

'Dotty, the point is that it doesn't look much like any kind of cottage; doesn't look much like a farmhouse either for that matter,' Daisy commented.

'Oh, don't be a clot, Daisy,' Dotty replied curtly – to cover her embarrassment, Daisy thought. 'This is where we live, and it's not my fault. I just happened to be born here, I had no say in the matter.'

'I'm not saying anything against it,' Daisy said, dragging her kitbag out of the Rolls only to be relieved of it by someone in a black suit. 'I'm just saying, that's all. You said it was a farm; you've always said it was a farm.'

'Well, there is a farm attached,' Dotty replied defensively, 'so technically it wasn't a lie.'

'And I asked you if you were sure there would be room for me,' Daisy said, shaking her head. 'I feel such a fool!'

'Well, I don't know why, it's just a house really.'

Just then a tall, rangy man in his late forties bounced out of the front door, threw his arms around Dotty and swung her round in a great bear hug as she screeched with excitement.

'Dorothea, how wonderful to see you again!' he yelled.

'Now, Horace Alfred,' Dotty yelled back, hugging him and laughing, 'two can play at that game!'

She freed herself from the embrace and introduced him. 'Daisy, this is Horace Alfred –'

'All right, all right,' he laughed, cupping her face in his hands and kissing the tip of her nose gently. 'Pax, pax!'

'This is my father, Daisy. He prefers to be known as Farmer Jim, but we call him Par. Par, this is my friend Daisy.'

'So this is Daisy?' he said in a hushed voice, looking her up and down. 'I've heard a great deal about you. You've been to a variety of very naughty parties with my daughter, I understand. Our London friends speak very highly of you, and now I can see why.' He lifted her right hand and kissed it. If you relied entirely on looks and disregarded the affection in his expression and in his eyes, then he was probably the ugliest man Daisy had ever seen, a large face with huge features, huge teeth especially, a great hawk nose and a shock of wiry, prematurely silver-grey hair that seemed to grow in all directions at once, as did the eyebrows above his twinkling blue eyes.

'Oh, stop it, you dreadful old rake!' Dotty chided, leading the way indoors. 'Daisy, treat him with contempt. He's a married man and you know what they're like!'

'Just because I'm married doesn't mean I can't admire a beautiful young woman,' Par protested, placing Daisy's arm through his own.

'But it doesn't mean the beautiful young woman should take any notice of you,' a voice said amiably but loudly from inside the house. 'Leave the girl alone, you old goat.'

'Mar!' Dotty shouted, and threw herself around her mother. 'Daisy, this is my Mar!'

'You don't have to call me that if you don't want to, my dear,' said the woman. 'My name is Emilia.' She looked at Daisy with kindly dark eyes just like Dotty's. 'The old goat was right, though, you are indeed a beautiful young woman. How d'you do.' She retrieved Daisy's hand from Par's and shook it with such gusto that Daisy wondered if she would survive the welcome, yet Mar was a small woman, an older version of Dotty in build, and, recalling her friend's famous right hook, she mused that the Bentley women must all be stronger than they looked. Beyond that, Mar was in her early forties, though that seemed ancient to Daisy's generation. She had a strikingly pretty pink complexion, her curly hair just showing early strands of greying in places, swept up haphazardly and kept in some sort of order with a variety of pins, as though every time a tress escaped another pin was brought into play in an attempt to keep it in order.

It must take her hours to remove them all every night, Daisy mused, watching the family's open affection for each other with a kind of awe. It was open and *noisy*. Where she came from, people not only stood back but held back from expressing real emotions, and she was suddenly struck by the thought that she couldn't remember ever being held or kissed by anyone in her family. And now she never would, of course. She felt a wave of, well, of panic rather than grief and put her head down.

'Now we've embarrassed the girl, look what you've done, Par!' Mar reproved her husband. 'Come in and have a cup of tea, Daisy, we're delighted to have you here; and just ignore that randy old goat.'

Par followed them, smiling happily and talking excitedly. 'We'll be quite a party this weekend,' he boomed. 'Your brother's bringing a couple of his chums this evening.'

'Freddy's coming?' Dotty asked, swinging round as she took off her cap. 'Oh, wizzo, I haven't seen him in months!'

'Wizzo', Daisy thought. Why? It was one of the things she resented, this strange way of talking in the RAF. Everything was 'FFI', a 'bad show' or a 'shaky do' and, of course, most of all there was the dreaded 'wizzo', and she had always sworn none of it would ever pass her lips. Apart from 'on my knees', of course, but she was allowed one lapse under difficult circumstances . . .

The inside of the house was like nothing she had ever seen before, except in the movies, and as she looked at the sweeping staircase she pictured herself dancing down the steps with Fred Astaire, suddenly shaking her head again to banish the memory that thought provoked. It was that kind of house, or mansion – it seemed to have been built to put on grand events, to be a backdrop to the grand noise of Dotty, Mar and Par that echoed and ricocheted off every surface.

Daisy was shown to a room next door to Dotty's about the size of the hut at Langar, with its own bathroom and dressing room, all in co-ordinated shades of pink. It had the softest bed she had ever known. Lying down to test it, the silence of the countryside hit her like a cosy, warm blow, and she fell instantly and deeply asleep.

She woke when the light was fading and the room was growing dark, to find that someone had placed a blanket over her. There was a tap at the door and Dotty came in.

'I didn't want to wake you earlier, you looked so peaceful, but you've just got time for a bath before dinner.'

'Fine,' Daisy smiled, though she would far rather have slept on.

'And we dress for dinner, I'm afraid,' Dotty continued self-consciously. 'It's a bore, I know, but Par thinks it cheers everyone up, though being a man he doesn't appreciate the work that goes into dressing up for us. I'd far rather wear my PJs, bet you would too.'

'But I don't have anything to wear,' Daisy murmured, thinking this might be her way out of dinner. An evening of sleep in this glorious bed appealed far more.

'That's all right, you can borrow one of mine.' Dotty produced a black silk dress with a bolero of black lace. 'What size shoe do you take?' She peered at Daisy's feet. 'Size five?'

Daisy nodded.

'Thought so,' Dotty said triumphantly, holding out a pair of black satin high-heels with an ankle strap and a diamanté buckle. 'I'm next door, give me a knock when you're ready.'

Once again, when Daisy got into the bath she didn't want to get out again. All that warm, soapy water and it belonged to her alone, with no one hammering on the door and shouting to her to get out. But she did the decent thing as far as guests were concerned, and bathed, towelled herself off and got ready. She then knocked on Dotty's door as instructed.

'Oh my God!' Dotty cried theatrically, looking at her, her hand flying to her mouth.

'What?' Daisy asked, horrified. 'What? Tell me, what have I done wrong?'

'Wrong?' Dotty cried. 'Wrong? Look at you!'

'What?'

'I wouldn't have believed it! We're about the same size, but you're, well, you're distributed differently. It never looked like that on me! I mean, it's not fair! It looks just like it did on the model when I first saw it. I thought they'd tricked me, but it looks like that on *you*! Daisy, you look absolutely fabulous! I won't get a look-in if I stand beside you. You must promise me,' she said in a mock-serious tone, 'that you will sit, stand and dance at the opposite end of the room from me all night. Is that understood?'

'You had me terrified there!' Daisy protested. 'I thought I was wearing it back-to-front or inside-out!'

'Oh, that's an idea,' Dotty said. 'Would you? Just for me, please? Especially back-to-front, then your unfair advantages won't show.'

'Stop it!'

'And here I am in this baby-pink rag with awful puff sleeves. I look like Shirley Temple beside you!'

'Will you shut up?' Daisy begged. 'You look gorgeous and you know it!'

'Seriously, Daisy, you have the most wonderful shape. Where did you get it? Can I buy it?' she giggled. She linked her arm through Daisy's and propelled her down the winding staircase, stopping at the bottom. 'Now pause for a moment so that everyone turns round to see who's come in,' Dotty whispered. 'Take a deep breath and right foot forward, making sure you don't make eye-contact with anyone. You're above any of the erks here.'

The two young women walked forward arrogantly, superior expressions on their faces, then ruined the effect by laughing loudly and throwing their arms around each other.

'Doesn't Daisy look wonderful, Mar?' Dotty demanded of her mother. 'I won't bother asking you, Par, your eyes are on stalks as it is.'

'My word!' Par kept saying over and over. 'My word, what a pair of stunners!'

'And I don't think he's including me there, Daisy,' Dotty said archly, her eyes dancing with laughter.

The butler came in with a tray of drinks and bowed as the ladies took a glass of champagne each, or fizzy cider as far as Daisy was concerned. Then there was a noise like a football crowd coming nearer and nearer, before a bunch of young men in dinner suits burst into the room. Dotty leaned across to her. 'This will be the erks,' she whispered.

'Freddy!' Dotty screamed, throwing herself into the air like a ballerina in the direction of one of the young men, who caught her in his arms and spun round with her, hugging and kissing her with shouts of 'Dotty! Little Dotty! How marvellous you're here!'

Seeing Daisy's bemused expression, Mar leaned forward. 'My son Freddy,' she whispered. 'Noisy pair of perishers, ain't they?'

Daisy smiled in reply.

'I'm afraid we're all like that,' she said apologetically. 'I suppose you've noticed that? I'm not sure if it comes from living in a big house where we can shout a lot, or if we'd be like it wherever we were.'

'I'd guess the latter,' Daisy said, laughing, as they watched the performance.

'And your family, Daisy, they're not, um, loud?'

'No, nothing like this. Raised voices always meant trouble in my family.'

'Meant?' Mar asked gently.

'Well, they went abroad at the start of the war,' Daisy said easily, thinking to herself, Where the hell did that come from?

'I wanted to do the same,' Mar sighed. 'Where are your people? Canada?'

'No, America,' Daisy replied evenly. 'My father has a sister in New York.'

'And you didn't want to go with them?'

Daisy shook her head firmly.

'Wanted to do your bit?' Mar smiled. 'Good for you, Daisy, our young people have done us proud, though the last generation of young people did, too. Dotty and Freddy would've stayed, too, if we'd gone, but with Par getting this job, well, that was the end of that.'

Daisy looked bemused.

'Didn't Dotty tell you? Her father's in the government, very junior of course, very, very hush-hush, too. I don't know what he does, won't even tell me, but I do know that in the bowels of Whitehall there is a lavatory kept exclusively for Winston, and it has a big white door marked "WC". You've no idea how much amusement Par gets out of that, and when no one's looking he sneaks in and has a pee. Watch this. Par! Par!' she shouted across the vast room. 'I was just telling Daisy here about WC's WC.'

Par immediately laughed so hard he had to lean on the wall to stop falling over.

'You see?' Mar said to Daisy. 'Now be honest; is this a man you'd trust with anything *really* important?'

'I see what you mean,' Daisy smiled.

'To be perfectly honest,' said Mar, 'I wouldn't be in the least surprised if that was all he actually did. He's never in any of the pictures in *The Times*, and I never hear his name mentioned, so for all I know his contribution is to go to London frequently to spend a penny in WC's WC. One day they'll catch him midstream and he really will be in the papers, unmasked as a fraud and unbuttoned into the bargain!'

It struck Daisy afterwards that Mar was a kind woman, that their little conversation had been to take her away from the frantic screaming and hugging, to save her embarrassment. Maybe Mar had seen through her outward show of confidence and knew she felt exposed in this foreign land.

When the noise had died down a bit Dotty came over to where her mother was talking to Daisy, grabbed her friend's hand and dragged her to the group of young men. To Daisy, whose experience of groups of young men was of being leered at, shouted at and made to feel dirty, they didn't look so much like a group as a herd, and she was conscious of fighting against hunching her shoulders, and straining back, even as her feet moved forward. When she looked up she deliberately didn't make eye contact with anyone, that always made her feel like running and hiding, but looked coolly at no one in particular.

'This is my brother, Freddy,' Dotty said with obvious pride. 'He's a pilot.'

Freddy held her hand in both of his and when she looked at him she saw he had the same bright, dark eyes and brown hair as his sister. A very good-looking boy, she thought, even if he did have Par's nose. The rest of the young men stood watching her, waiting to be introduced, one or two with the kind of looks in their eyes she was used to, others slightly shy. However, one man stayed at the back, looking away from her except for a few swift glances that she felt rather than saw. As she shook hands with the others she felt him there, like an electric presence, and when she finally had to shake hands with him there was the strangest sensation. Suddenly her mind was full of a host of confusing feelings and she was struggling to separate them. It wasn't that she had known him before, she didn't believe in that kind of romantic nonsense. It wasn't even that there was an instant attraction: she didn't know what that meant. It was more a feeling of peace than of falling madly in love at first sight. Not that she believed in love, let alone love at first sight, she had no use for either one, but in the moments when their hands met she felt a peace. It was the only word she could ever come up with to describe it, yet there was an excitement as well; and just how did she reconcile those opposing emotions when she didn't understand them? Added to the confusion was a kind of desperation to be gone, a feeling of wanting to escape, and she had to concentrate on her breathing to stop herself turning and running.

With barely a glance at the man – what was his name? – she accepted Freddy's invitation to sit beside him at the dinner table, and managed to put up with the usual boyish banter – 'Trust you, Skipper!' 'Hey, we didn't vote on that!' 'Pulling rank again, Frederick!' – the kind of remarks that normally had her employing a glance that would freeze them to the marrow. All she could think of was keeping away from the last chap, whatever his name was, then she realised that she didn't know what he looked like either. Nothing of his features had registered, so how would she know him if he approached her later? You'll know all right, she said to herself, feeling her eyes being drawn to the end of the long table and glancing up quickly to see him there, glancing at her then away again.

She decided to keep her eyes down so that she could only see those on either side of her, not that it was difficult to limit her gaze with the amazing food and amounts of it on offer. There was pork, beef, chicken, duck, and that was all she recognised, with various vegetables and a confusing array of knives, forks, spoons and glasses on the table. She remembered Joan Johnstone telling her that dinner-table etiquette was simple, you just started at the outside and worked your way in. So that's what she did. 'Act the part,' she heard Joan's voice in her head. 'That's all it is, Daisy, acting.' And Daisy found herself thinking 'Wait till I tell Joan about this!'

Suddenly she stopped, spoon halfway to her mouth, remembering that Joan was no longer there, but gone. Completely and forever. She hadn't reached the personal grief stage yet; she was grappling with the nothingness where her family and Joan should be, trying not to dwell on the thought of them all just being dead, because if she did so she had to force down an accompanying wave of panic that she would never – *never* – see them again.

'Is the soup too hot, Daisy, dear?' Mar said at her side.

'Just a little,' she smiled, putting her spoon down again, bemused and confused by the tumble of emotions all happening inside her at once. There was the horror of losing everyone who mattered to her, and yet whoever this new chap was, he had brought a kind of electricity to the air that she had never experienced before.

After the lavish dinner there was lots of good-natured chat and teasing, with Daisy making sure she kept a safe distance from the young man. She found she could keep track of him just by feeling that he was nearby, and then she would move away. She had the curious illusion that everyone else was standing still and the entire room was in black and white, with only him and her moving and in colour. He eventually caught up with her, as somehow she had always known he would.

'I have the feeling that you're avoiding me,' he said shyly.

'Now why would I do that?' she asked evenly, registering his deep tan, blue eyes and fairish hair.

'I'm sure I don't know,' he said, laughing gently.

Australian accent? she thought.

'Maybe you just don't like me,' he suggested, looking at her.

'Well, why would you think that? I don't even know you, Mr . . . ?'

'Frank Moran,' he replied. 'Royal Australian Air Force.'

Moran? she thought. Isn't that *Irish?* You'd think I'd have registered *that* first time round.

'Oh,' she said, in a disinterested voice.

He laughed. 'You're thinking "Another Fly Boy on the make", aren't you?'

'I wasn't, strangely enough,' she said quietly, casually looking around the room as though for someone, anyone else, a technique she had perfected to deflect unwanted male attention. 'And I really wouldn't advise it if you are. The big, brave flying-ace thing has no effect on me.'

'Ouch!' he said. Then, 'What do you do?'

'I'm an RTO at RAF Langar,' she said, trying not to sound as pleased with herself as she felt.

'So you'll be in the tower, talking to pilots?' he asked.

'That's the general idea.'

'Maybe we'll have a proper conversation one day,' he said. 'I fly a Spitfire.'

'I doubt it, then,' Daisy smiled tightly back at him. 'We're a Bomber Command Station.'

'You could still find yourself talking to a Spit pilot,' he grinned.

'I'll make a point of looking forward to that,' she replied in a deliberately weary voice.

He looked at her seriously. 'Would you rather I just left you alone?' he asked.

'To be perfectly honest, I would,' Daisy said calmly. 'No offence, but I spend my working life surrounded by Fly Boys, I really am immune to every line you can think of.'

'Maybe I wasn't trying to spin you line; maybe I just thought you'd be pleasant to talk to.'

Daisy looked him straight in the eye. 'Yes,' she said coldly, 'that sounds *very* likely. But don't worry, everyone makes mistakes.'

Then she turned her head away as though still looking for that anyone else in the room rather than him, so she didn't see him move off; but she felt it and was relieved that he had gone. Despite her outer coolness she felt confused, disturbed even, which scared her in a way; the days were long gone when she could be thrown off-balance. There was a feeling deep inside her that she had to keep this man away from her, a conviction that this thing had to be nipped in the bud.

And what was this thing, exactly? Attraction? Yes, she conceded, pretending to sip the fizzy cider, it was attraction, like metal to a magnet, there was no way of denying it, but it made her want to flee, not hang around for more of him. Even so, she couldn't help smiling to herself at the impression she had given him of the work she did, when the only time she had been in the tower at Langar the Squadron Leader hadn't known who or what she was and had told her to go away for a few days and he'd try to find out.

★   ★   ★

After the dinner party had ended Dotty followed Daisy into her room, and Daisy's heart fell. She wanted to go to sleep in that beautiful, soft, warm bed in that silent, comfortable room, but she knew that Dotty was the kind of person who had to wind down before she could sleep, and as she was responsible for providing Daisy with all this luxury, she couldn't bring herself to throw Dotty out. The night's events were discussed, each young man's character, action and conversation dissected, with Daisy supplying the occasional response when required, a skill she was perfecting.

'You and that Spitfire chap didn't seem to hit it off very well,' Dotty said.

'Who?'

'Frank Moran.'

'Which one was he?' Daisy asked.

'The one you were talking to last. I've been just dying to meet him. Freddy's been talking about him forever, he's terribly well-known you know.'

'Is he?'

'Cripes, yes! Didn't he tell you?'

'Tell me what?' That was another skill she was picking up: not completely answering the question asked.

'About the Battle of Britain, of course.'

'No,' Daisy said honestly, 'he never mentioned that, as far as I can recall. I wasn't really listening to him, to be honest.'

'Well, he flew a Spit in the Battle of Britain, and Freddy says that out of one thousand men over four hundred were killed, but Frank was in it all the way through. He had a tremendous kill-rate, so Freddy says.'

Daisy felt crushed and ashamed of the way she had spoken to him, and she was glad she was hearing this in darkness – darkness had long been her friend – so that Dotty wouldn't see her blushing. 'Mm,' she said sleepily.

'Oh, Daisy, you're almost asleep, I'm being so selfish! See you in the morning.' Dotty jumped off Daisy's bed. 'Night!' she called.

'Mm,' Daisy repeated, then she lay in the lovely darkness and thought, Dear God, to have spoken to a Battle of Britain ace like that! Fair enough that she'd wanted rid of him, but the man deserved some respect, a little dignity at least.

Then there was Mar. The only outright lie she'd told her was about her family being in New York, but what was she to say? That they had been wiped out by a bomb a week ago and the bits that had been recovered were buried days ago, and there she was, attending a posh dinner-party in a mansion and chatting as though she hadn't a care in the world?

At least she had worn black, she thought wryly. Should she have told the truth? What good would that have done anyone, her dead family included? But still, now that she'd told the lie, there was no way out. She would have to maintain it forevermore, though it wouldn't cause any problems that she could see. She was coping with it in her own way, she told herself, as was her right, but somewhere in her heart there was a doubt that she couldn't locate because she didn't want to.

Next morning both girls had a lie-in before a breakfast consisting of eggs – boiled, fried, poached and scrambled – bacon, tomatoes, fried bread, kidneys, mushrooms, sausages, porridge with cream, kippers, and something called kedgeree that Daisy had never come across before. Once again the amount and array of food shocked her, and Dotty watched her with a look of misery on her face. They were alone; Par and Mar were out with Freddy and his friends.

'Daisy, I feel really rotten about this,' Dotty said.

'About what?'

'All this food. You see, the farm produces most of it, not the fish, of course, a friend of Par's sends that down from Scotland. Par says what good would it do if we did without it, there isn't so much that it would make the slightest dent if we gave it all away. And we do keep the estate workers fed with it, it's not as if we hoard it all to ourselves.'

'Dotty, relax,' Daisy smiled, tucking into her eggs. 'I'm not complaining, I'd fight a duel with my own grandmother for this egg.'

'But you won't tell the others, will you, at Langar, I mean? Please? I'd hate them to find out and treat me like a toff. That's why I asked for the car to come to the station rather than the base, it'll drop us there on the way back, too. People can be strange when they see the Rolls, and I don't want them to hate me because of all this.' She looked around at her luxurious home and grimaced, and Daisy laughed at her.

'Your secret is safe with me,' she replied. 'Who knows, I might need you to cover up for me one of these days.' She looked at Dotty's serious expression and laughed. 'Anyway, I'm your partner in crime now, I've eaten the forbidden food.'

The next two days were spent walking, cycling and talking in the clear, quiet air. It was a million miles away from the life Daisy now led, and much more than a million away from Newcastle. You could hear birds singing and, in the distance, the sound of cows and ewes calling to their young. If Daisy could get away from Dotty she could stand alone, watching the lambs leaping around together as though they had springs on their feet, and for some reason the grass seemed greener and lusher than she had ever noticed before. Along a country lane she found a pond with ducks and returned later with bread to feed them, feeling guilty, knowing that food was in short supply everywhere, then thinking that Rose Cottage existed in another world, a world of plenty, even for ducks. Sometimes she wandered alone, but mostly she went with the other young people who were there.

Daisy tried to think of ways to make amends with the Australian but decided she couldn't actually apologise, that would leave her in a vulnerable position, open to his advances. He didn't make any, though, merely exchanging the fewest words possible when their paths crossed, much to her relief.

He watched her, though; she could feel that, and wondered why the sensation should be different. She had been watched by males before, after all. It was different, that was all she could say, it just was, and she couldn't work out why. But the rest of it, the calm, quiet countryside, she could get used to that, she decided. If she survived the war, and many wouldn't . . .

She lowered her head – many hadn't – then she looked up again, over the green fields. If she survived, she wanted to live in the country. This was where the new Daisy belonged.

As they were leaving after three days of peace, quiet and comfort, Mar drew her aside.

'Daisy, I want you to know that you can come here any time you want, whenever you have leave you don't want to spend in London, though I know you'll be in great demand there for parties and fun. Doesn't matter if Dotty is here or not, if you need to be quiet, just let me know and I'll send the car for you.'

Daisy was overwhelmed and hugged Mar.

'And may I ask you a favour?'

'Of course,' Daisy said, 'anything.'

'It's about Dotty,' Mar said quietly. 'She's a bubbly little thing, always has been, much more than the rest of us, and that's saying something. I have no idea why they should think she could handle being a medical orderly, and I'm afraid she might not be able to, that's the thing. I have this fear that she won't admit it. She's always been overshadowed a bit by Freddy, he's the kind of chap who excels at everything he tries, while Dotty has to work at it, so if she's struggling she won't say because she'll think she's a failure, do you see?'

Daisy nodded; she did see. She stood there half-listening, thinking back on the days when everything her family had to give went to Kay. All that time she'd thought she was the only one it had ever happened to; it had never occurred to her that there were other people in the same boat.

'The thing is, Daisy, you're a level-headed girl, mature for your years, and I'd like to think you'd keep an eye on her, and if you think it's all going wrong, that you might let me know.'

'Of course, of course,' Daisy said brightly. 'Don't worry about it, Mar, I'll watch out for her. But she's tougher than you think. I've never seen a female throw a right hook like Dotty!'

'Oh, she'll have learned that from Freddy,' Mar laughed, then looked at Daisy, 'but what . . . ?'

'She floored an officer at West Drayton,' Daisy chuckled, 'an old school friend of Freddy's. Apparently he'd suggested that she should provide him with the home comforts WAAFs are expected to provide officers with.'

'And Dotty let the blighter have it?'

'Well,' Daisy laughed, 'depends what you mean by "it", but she certainly let him have a right hook to the jaw!'

Mar was overcome with mirth and slapped Daisy's shoulder so hard that she was put off-balance for a moment. 'Had much the same effect on him as that slap had on me, in fact!' Daisy giggled.

Mar threw her arms around Daisy and hugged her. 'Oh, I

wish there was some means of letting her know I've heard that,' she laughed, 'but I don't suppose there is, is there?'

'*No!*' Daisy chided her. 'There *isn't*, Mar!'

The two girls left in the Rolls, the usual hamper from home on the front seat beside the chauffeur, as the band of young men took off in the opposite direction for London in sports cars – the upper-class RAF pilot's only possible land-borne transport. Dotty was chattering away good-naturedly, as Dotty always did, while Daisy thought about her conversation with Mar. She didn't understand why people thought of her as mature and sensible. It was all an act, inside she had no idea what she was doing or thinking most of the time, yet she was always put in the position of carer, as though that was her natural role. It wasn't, though, that was the thing, it really wasn't, so why did they think it was? Was it something she was doing that gave them that impression?

Just then there was a rapid tooting of a car horn and one of the sports cars that had headed for London drew alongside the stately Rolls with a great screeching of brakes, forcing the car to stop. Dotty rolled the window down and Frank Moran's head appeared.

'I was just wondering,' he said, looking from one to the other, 'if you girls would write to me?'

Daisy and Dotty exchanged glances.

'You see, my next posting is to Orkney and Shetland, wherever that is. I gather it's pretty remote.'

'I'll say!' Dotty giggled.

'And I thought if you felt like it you might take pity on a lonely Fly Boy far away from home and drop him the odd letter. He'd be very grateful.'

'Of course, that would be wizzo!'

Daisy closed her eyes. Wizzo indeed, she thought, and when

she opened them again Dotty was holding on to Frank's hand for dear life, but he was looking at Daisy. She hadn't said a word in response and that was how she wanted to leave it. Let him correspond with Dotty, who was already totally besotted with him before she had even met him. Let Dotty reply, and she knew Dotty would, and that would be an end to it.

'It was good meeting you,' he said, still looking at Daisy, 'even if I did bore you to death.'

'You didn't bore me, Frank!' Dotty squealed 'Whatever gave you that idea?'

Then Frank went back to his little car and the Rolls moved off. Dotty turned round and waved out of the back window. 'He's still there, waving,' she said in a hushed, excited voice. 'I think I have a chance with him, who'd have thought it? Look, Daisy!' and she continued to wave, but Daisy stared straight ahead.

12

The Rolls dropped them off at the station again and they found a lorry going back to Langar, stowed their gear in the back and climbed in beside the driver. On the way to the base they chatted as much as the engine noise allowed, but Daisy's mind wasn't really on it, and she had to fight to keep the conversation going. She was thinking of him – the Aussie – not thinking of him exactly, but he was there in her mind and she couldn't get rid of the image. When they were within sight of the camp they saw an aircraft lying at a strange angle in a field. The driver followed their gaze.

'Happened last night,' he said. 'A Wimpy.' Wellington bombers were nicknamed Wimpys because of their rotund shape, which had reminded some wit of Popeye the Sailorman's well-fed, hamburger-eating friend, J. Wellington Wimpy. 'It was shot up pretty badly and couldn't make it back.'

'Are the crew safe?' Dotty asked, looking at the charred remains of the aircraft as they passed.

The driver shook his head. 'They were alive when she crashed, but then she exploded. Nobody could get near her for the flames, the boys all died. The firemen and medics were pretty upset, they could hear them screaming but couldn't do anything.' He shrugged and glanced at them. 'That's how it is sometimes,' he said. 'You know how it is.'

The two young women, fresh from a leave spent in luxury, eating good food and sleeping in comfortable beds, didn't know how it was, as it happened, and sat in subdued silence for the rest of the journey, painfully aware that they soon would. They made their way to the WAAFery to sign in and were immediately set upon by the WAAF CO. The front entrance, she told them coldly, was reserved for officers and senior NCOs; common or garden WAAFs must use the back door. She was prepared, she informed them grandly, to overlook their transgression this time, as they were new to the base, but she could have put them on a charge, and would if she caught them using the front door again. They headed for the dining room, suddenly aware they had wandered back into the real world.

'After what we've just seen and what the driver told us, you have to wonder where her head is, don't you?' Dotty said testily. 'What a bitch!'

'Well, at least we know one thing,' said Daisy with feeling. 'Avoid WAAF officers here at all times.'

Then they went their separate ways, Dotty to the medical unit and Daisy to the tower, the Watch Room where she had met the Squadron Leader a few days earlier. It was just beginning to get dark, so the room was gearing up for another night of operations and the atmosphere was anxious and taut.

'Ah,' the Squadron Leader smiled brightly at her, 'you're back! Good leave? Jolly-D, that's the ticket, ticketty-boo.'

'You left out "wizzo",' Daisy thought wryly.

'Now this is Reg, he'll explain procedure to you and act as your instructor.'

Daisy shook hands with Reg, an airman of about thirty, fair hair becoming sparse, grey eyes, nice, shy smile. Married with a couple of kids, she imagined, the kind of man born to be a husband and father.

'I'll explain our shift patterns now, Daisy,' Reg said quietly, indicating a seat to his right. 'Best get the nasty stuff out of the way first, I always think.'

Daisy looked at his station and saw a snap of his wife and children, a boy and a girl.

'My family,' he said proudly.

'Lovely,' she replied, sitting down.

'Yes, they are, rather,' he smiled, then pulled himself back to business. 'You'll have a four-hour watch, a break, then an eight-hour watch, and if there are enough operators to cover, you can have a day off between each twelve-hour day and the next. If not, every third day after an eight-hour day, week in, week out.'

'Week in, week out,' she grinned.

'Apart from leave, of course,' he laughed.

'I bet you say that to all the girls.'

'I do, actually, now you come to mention it!' he chuckled, smoothing down what was left of his hair.

'Incoming calls from aircraft have to be answered in the officially set-out manner. We have a local-range microphone and a long-range one. You give the strength of the signal back to the plane, so that the aircrew know how good their contact is. – "Strength Two" is very faint, "Strength Nine" – a niner – is the loudest, and all conversations have to be logged. On the wall there is a special loudspeaker tuned to Bomber Command's 'Darky' frequency, that's for aircraft in trouble who can't make it back to their own home base and have to find somewhere to land quickly. We don't get many, but if we do it takes priority and has to be answered immediately. The first thing you say is "This is Langar" – so that the crew know where they are.'

'You make it all sound so routine,' she said uncertainly.

'Well, it's not, Daisy,' he replied seriously, 'it's never that. You'll find that this job takes its toll on you. Don't expect it to be easy.'

'Cripes!'

'Oh, I don't mean to put the frighteners on you,' he said pleasantly, 'I just think it's best to be prepared.'

She nodded. Looking out of the tower she could see the planes already queued up on the runway waiting for clearance to take off, an amazing, overwhelming sight. The great lumbering machines patiently moved up the line as the one in front took to the sky.

'This board,' Reg explained, 'lists each plane's identification and its estimated times of takeoff and return. The names of the crews are there too.' He didn't dwell on that and there was silence. 'We preserve radio silence before takeoff,' he said, watching the planes on the runway. 'They're bound for Germany tonight. Have you been on an operational station before?'

Daisy shook her head.

He pointed to a lorry by the tarmac. 'That's delivering pigeons,' he said. 'If a plane ditches, a message of its last-known position can be sent by pigeon – if there's time and if any of the birds have survived.' He paused. 'And, of course, if any of the crew have.'

'One of my friends works with the pigeons,' she said, wondering if Celia was one of the dark little figures scurrying about down there. 'She thinks it's the most important job in the RAF.'

'Well, she'd have to, we all have to, don't we?' he replied quietly. He pointed to another lorry with a red cross on the side. 'That's the medical orderlies on Drome Duty. They're handing out boxes of tablets to the crews to keep them awake on the return journey.'

Was Dotty part of that side of the operation? Daisy wondered. Funny to think of all the different things the girls were doing, it made you feel part of it all.

'They stay in position until takeoff is completed.' He turned to look at her. 'You never know,' he said, 'could be a situation where every second counts. They go back to Station Sick Quarters, then back here again when the planes are expected, to count them all in and take the injured to the SSQ.' He pointed out the WAAFs lining the runway. 'Every spare WAAF stands on the airstrip to cheer the boys as they leave. Not that they can hear them over the engines, but the boys say it means a lot to them.'

The lumbering planes, heavy with bombs, taxied and then stopped for a second before revving up and gathering speed for takeoff.

'And you'll always see the odd one standing by herself,' Reg smiled, pointing again. She'll be watching her special boy take off. Sometimes they'll have a scarf, a hankie or some other keepsake in their hands, and he'll have something of hers, a silk stocking, a letter, anything that might bring him safely back home.' He shrugged. 'It's just a superstition, as old as the ages, though they all think they've invented it. If you've left something behind then you have to return to reclaim it, right?'

'And if your special girl has given you a keepsake, you have to live to bring it back to her,' Daisy nodded, and to her shock the thought that popped into her mind then was of Dotty carrying something of Frank's as a talisman, and the next thought was that for some stupid, inexplicable reason she felt hurt by that. She was still trying to banish the thought from her mind when Reg took a break. There was a tap on her shoulder and a hand appeared.

'Edith Turner,' a solemn voice announced. 'Shake hands.'

'Yes,' Daisy said, leaping up to hug her, 'I thought the face looked familiar! Have we met before?'

'Didn't I see you at a party in London once with two Yanks?' Edith joked.

'I only had one, a strange, frightened rabbit of a girl had his chum, as I recall!' Daisy laughed. 'So, how was your leave?'

'Oh, I dunno, Daisy,' Edith said, sitting in Reg's seat. 'It's all so strange. You spend all your time on duty thinking of the wonderful things you'll do when you see your family, you know?'

Daisy nodded wordlessly.

'Then when you get there, well, you're bored, somehow. It's lovely to see them, of course, but after you've said hello you're counting the days till you can get away again. I feel bad about it, but there we are. My father told me off for saying damn, and I felt like walking out. Of my own home, mark you, where I've grown up and all that. I almost called him an erk!'

'You?' Daisy laughed. 'I don't believe it!'

'Yes, I know,' Edith grinned wryly. 'But I did think it could stand me in good stead later, when he's trying to browbeat me again into becoming a doctor! Anyway, this job's a piece of cake once you get used to it, so don't worry about it. If you feel tired it's OK to wrap yourself in a blanket and have a doze,' she suggested. 'There won't be anything much to do till the boys are on the return leg. This is your first night-duty, it takes a while to get used to it.'

Daisy knew she had a lot to learn and was glad Edith had got here before her. It was always better to learn from a real friend.

'When the mission's finished, the first aircraft over the coast on the return journey will call in,' Edith explained. 'As it nears home it will come into local frequency and we'll land it under instructions from the Control Officer. Priority is always given to planes with wounded on board, and the fire and ambulance crews will be waiting for them as they land.'

'Does that happen often?' Daisy asked. 'Injured coming in, I mean.'

'Pretty often,' Edith said quietly. 'As soon as they land the uninjured crew are taken to be debriefed by intelligence officers, though you wonder how much info they can pass on, given the state of them. Doesn't matter how many "stay awake" tablets they've swallowed, they're usually too mentally and physically done-in to pass on anything meaningful, but them's the rules.'

'So what do we do when all the planes are safely back?' Daisy asked.

'Well, they don't all come safely back,' Edith replied. 'We know which ones are still missing from the board there with their details, so we sit up all night, listening for any Mayday calls. Sometimes we get a call from another base to say one of our crews has emergency-landed there, but when all hope has gone we'll be ordered to wipe the names of the lost from the board and stand down for the night. That's the hardest part,' she said quietly, 'wiping the names from the board. It's like erasing them; actually condemning them not to return. I don't think you ever get used to that part, so if you find it upsetting, don't worry, we all do, just don't let it show.'

Whatever Daisy had thought her job might entail, however exciting she'd imagined it could be, that first session of instruction brought home to her how daunting it *would* be, and the impact was all the more intense for the calm, ordinary manner of those already doing it. Although she would have expected that from Edith in any situation, bar being told off by her father for swearing. There was no overdramatising up in the tower, it was a crucial job. The lives of men who had already been shot at from the ground and from the air would depend on these people doing their jobs properly, and so the details had to be clear, calm and logical. Still, sitting in there that first night, trying to watch, learn and listen, she wondered if the world of passing forms around, typing and filing had been so bad after all.

Added to Daisy's work in the tower was the ever-present threat of an air raid, as the Germans tried to destroy as many planes as they could. There were terrible tales about these raids. Those not engaged in landing planes were supposed to head for slit trenches if the base came under attack, and, shortly before Daisy had arrived at Langar, some NAAFI workers and a sergeant pilot had done just that, but there had been a direct hit where they were sheltering and all were killed.

Thankfully, Daisy had been in the job for a month before she experienced her first raid. The planes were returning from a mission and were being landed when the warning Red came through. Immediately the airfield lights were doused, leaving weary bomber crews to circle aloft in the darkness.

'It's a lone German aircraft dropping a stick of bombs,' said the Squadron Leader calmly; but sitting in the tower, listening as each explosion came nearer, Daisy wondered what reassurance this could possibly be. She was convinced she was about to die, they all were, but there was no hysteria. They all just waited for the next bomb, which was so close that the tower shook. That's it, Daisy thought, the next one will hit us. And all the while their own aircraft, some running out of fuel, were asking what the hell was going on, and Reg was answering them in a cool voice as Daisy logged each exchange.

'I don't want to die,' said an annoyed female voice nearby. 'I've only just learned Morse Code, and anyway, my parents would be really upset if I croaked,' and the others laughed nervously.

'What?' the Squadron Leader demanded. 'Since when have you known Morse Code?'

'I told you, Sir, I've just learned!' the voice responded in the dark.

'Well don't just sit there, you clot, send out an SOS and maybe someone will come and rescue us!' said another voice.

Suddenly the noise stopped. The lone German had departed, and the airfield sprang back into life. The Control Officer very quickly inspected the airfield, declared it damaged but fit for landing, and the Langar planes were rapidly and safely brought down. Afterwards, mixed in with the relief, shaking and chattering teeth, there was also a feeling of euphoria. They all sat together, making jokes and laughing, blankets around them as they sipped hot, sweet tea and reflected that it had been frightening, but exciting, too. If she had to be bombed, Daisy decided, she'd prefer to be on duty in the tower. There would be no slit trenches for her.

And though it looked to everyone else that Daisy got used to it, she never really did; but she did learn to cope, because there was no alternative. There were so many sad sights, and they didn't seem any less sad because they happened often, such as 'the girls' as the other WAAFs called them. At the end of every mission, with the planes that had made it safely home standing still and silent, the anxious girls could be seen, still waiting. As dawn broke, bathing the field in first pink then golden light, their heads would turn upwards, this way and that, as they gazed into the morning sky with worried faces and red-rimmed eyes, listening intently for the sound of engines, willing a special plane to suddenly appear on the horizon.

When they finally gave up and returned to their huts the others would try to help. Maybe the plane had landed somewhere else, or it had ditched and the boys were all safe, just waiting to be picked up. Perhaps, at the very worst, they had been taken to POW camps and they'd hear confirmation any day . . . but in their hearts they knew the loss-rate was high and the chances the boys had survived were slim.

When she stood down after a night on Ops, Daisy would watch the girls and swear it would never happen to her. They must be mad to fall for aircrew who had a less-than-even chance of surviving till tomorrow. But as she left the tower with all hope effectively gone, she couldn't pass them. She would stop and hug them, standing wordlessly in the dim light, the dawn chorus bursting into life all around, intruding on the early morning silence.

There was nothing to say; all she could do was let them cry. How could you help feeling for them? They inhabited a world of their own, all these youngsters united by war, living their strange existences on a piece of ground set in the middle of civilian territory yet apart from civilians, every soul on or off duty held together by their common responsibilities to the boys who flew off into mortal danger, night after night, not knowing if they'd ever be seen again.

Dotty and Daisy settled into their room in the hut, seeing less of each other because of their different duties, but getting to know Edith and the other girls all over again. Violet was a trainee mechanic and already planning her wedding to a Rhodesian gunner, inevitably named Cecil after Rhodesia's founder.

'So how did that happen?' Daisy demanded. 'To Violet of all people, and so quickly, too.'

'Probably because you weren't here, Daisy!' Celia laughed. 'You should've been here to make sure no Fly Boys got near us!'

'Us?' Daisy raised an eyebrow. '*Us*, Celia?'

Celia looked sheepish. 'Well, who else is there to go out with, Daisy?' she protested.

'Does no one listen to a word I say?' Daisy asked. 'They are not to be trusted, you must not be fooled by them.'

'But a drink isn't actually banned, is it, Daisy?' Celia laughed at her. 'I mean, as long as we don't actually fall for them.'

'Like Violet hasn't fallen for her Fly Boy?' Daisy laughed back, shaking her head. 'I can see I've arrived here just in time!'

Then there was Molly, the girl who was singing as Daisy fell asleep on her first night at Langar and who, she was to discover, sang all the time. Molly drove a lorry and loved every minute of it. She was engaged to a bomb-aimer in a Pathfinder Unit in 8 Group. His job was to drop incendiaries to mark out a path to the targets for the heavy bombers coming behind. Every day she would drive her lorry down to the Admin Block, wheels screaming, to see if her transfer to 8 Group had come through, so that she could be near her Dave. They wrote to each other every day, though there were times when days would pass without a letter and Molly would worry, then four would arrive all at once and Molly would sing again.

While she waited for Dave, his letters and her posting, Molly sang, and though it was sure to get on someone's nerves, Daisy understood it was Molly's way of coping. Everyone had their own way, she did, too, taking long, solitary walks into the countryside around the camp, sitting under a tree and letting her mind and her eyes relax, watching the waving greenery of the crops. She would go over in her mind all that had happened in her life, trying to make as much sense of it as she could, then filing it away and closing the door on it. If only she could find a way of closing the door on all thoughts of Frank Moran, but he was there, stubbornly there, intruding to absolutely no avail.

One fine day she might open the door and give all the other thoughts and memories a proper going over, but not now, there was no point just now, she was busy and, as everyone said, there was a war on, you know. She was still reinventing herself to fit her present situation, sifting through Daisy Sheridan from Guildford Place and deciding what to keep, bend or discard.

By the end of 1941 Daisy was the superb RTO whose family were in New York with Aunt Clare for the duration, which explained her lack of conversation about them. Mail across the Atlantic was far from reliable, with U-Boats waiting to have a go at any passing ship, so it was little wonder that she got very few letters. One sadness was that someone had noticed serious Edith's cleverness and she was sent to Special Ops at Bletchley Park, about fifty miles north of London, otherwise known as Station X, which everyone knew was involved in intelligence and secrets, but no one ever asked more.

'I actually want to go,' she confided in Daisy. 'I'm afraid you'll confine me to quarters for this, Daisy, and I deserve it, but I've been seeing an Australian.'

'Oh dear God!' Daisy said. 'Not another damned Fly Boy?'

'My father would tick you off for that sort of language, you know,' Edith smiled. 'He's a Lanc navigator,' Edith went on, 'a really nice chap.'

'Aren't they all?' Daisy sighed wearily.

'Thing is, I've found it really hard to be in the tower when he's on a mission, wondering if he's for the chop and trying *not* to wonder in case that makes it come true.'

Daisy was about to say she hadn't noticed Edith having a hard time, but then Edith wouldn't have shown it – not even-tempered, sensible Edith.

'I think I'll find it easier being somewhere else, not watching his kite taking off and waiting for it to return.'

'So you'll still be seeing him?' Daisy asked. 'Even though you'll be away from the base? It's serious, Edith?'

Edith nodded.

'Well, all right,' Daisy said grudgingly. 'But let him know I'll be watching him, that's all, and if he as much as glances at another female he *will* be for the chop! If the Germans don't get him, I will!'

And so Edith left for calmer waters, but that was always happening. Friends came and went, and, if you were lucky, kept in touch and might even come back again.

These days Dotty had quietened down and didn't attend so many parties, which pleased Daisy, who mainly spent her leaves, with or without Dotty, but mostly without, with Mar and Par in Rose Cottage. At Langar she became known to live it up in the Big Smoke and wouldn't stoop to entertain any of the boys at the base; she was well out of their league. She never corrected the impression, it gave her new persona strength. There she was, a non-smoking, celibate teetotaller who was known as the definitive Good-time Gal, a tribute to her acting abilities, backed up, of course, by the outer packaging.

'Off to some orgy at the Dorchester?' the girls would giggle as she left the base.

'Why not?' she'd smile back, 'but if I remember correctly it's the Savoy again,' never once saying that she was bound for Rose Cottage. Dotty was sworn to secrecy, but Dotty wasn't the chatterbox she had once been. She too had changed character and her bubbly nature had been harnessed in a way no one expected when she had been made an orderly. It suited her, it brought out abilities no one, least of all Dotty herself, had ever suspected she might have, and she had made her mind up that she wanted to train as a nurse.

'You sit with them, Daisy,' she would explain, 'and they can be terribly injured. The smell of their burned flesh clings to you and you can smell it all along the corridors, but it's just a smell, after all, you have to get over it. All they want is someone to hold their hands and tell them they'll make it, even if they know it's a lie. They tell you about their mothers or girlfriends or wives and ask you to write to them saying it's not so bad, really, even when it is. We get them off to better-equipped hospitals if it's possible, but there are times when you know they won't last that long, so you just sit there and keep them company, even if they're unconscious.

Did you know that hearing is the very last thing to go? They can hear you even if they're spark out and about to die, so I tell them what happened in the NAAFI the other night, which pilots were getting engaged, drunk, or in a fight, all the usual stuff. At least then they can go calmly and peacefully, without any fear or panic because they don't know they're going. Do you see what I mean? I mean, if it ever happens to Frank, I'd hope someone would do the same for him.'

Daisy didn't reply. Something had struck her to the core about Dotty's words, confirmation if ever she wanted it that there was something between Dotty and Frank, and she couldn't understand why she was so struck by it. She had wanted that, hadn't she? His attention elsewhere? And nowhere better than on good, kind, adoring Dotty, so why did she feel tears spring to her eyes and have to bite her lip to distract herself? Why?

It wasn't as if he was betraying her in some way, was it? If anything he probably didn't deserve Dotty. When Fly Boys were lost it was Dotty who always wrote to their families, telling them what a fine young man Ted, Tom or Tim had been, how everyone liked them, and she kept up the correspondence as long as they wanted it. They were hungry to hear of the last months they hadn't shared with their boys, so she asked Daisy to help her with the letters, and Daisy agreed, too overcome by the change in her friend to refuse.

Dotty had found her niche in a place where everyone doubted that she could cope, her mother included, and if her patients did survive, as often as not they would be sent off to Rose Cottage to convalesce, which gave Mar something to do while Par was peeing in Winston's private lavatory.

Meanwhile, the Frank situation was worrying Daisy in other ways. He wrote to both of them and she saw how Dotty looked forward to his letters. She would lie on her bed and read them out, completely unaware that Daisy had one hidden under her pillow that she didn't mention, far less read out.

There was a difference in the letters, though. To Dotty he wrote about his work, about the islands closer to Scandinavia than Britain where he had been posted and how he missed having fun in London. But he told Daisy all about his home in Australia and what he wanted to do after the war and about his feelings. He had been so excited at the prospect of getting away from home, just like all the others, and he swore they would never drag him back again.

'My home's in the Darling Downs, a black-soil plain and a very productive agricultural region. The family farm is in Dalby, a farming community in Queensland, it grows grain and grazing crops in summer and winter. The topsoils store a lot of rain, so you can grow a good crop of wheat in three or four weeks, but when it does rain, even pretty lightly, you can't drive around the farm for two or three days. It isn't as hot as other places, in fact people come to the Darling Downs from all around in summer to keep cool.

'In winter we get fine, sunny days, though the nights and mornings can be frosty. Then dry, cold NW winds come in August and the landscape can look a bit brown and desolate, but it warms up in September, though you still have to watch out for a late frost that could destroy the wheat crops when they're in flower. In October the crops are close to harvesting and the soil's warm enough to plant summer crops. Usually the days are warm and the nights are mild, even in November. When it does rain in summer it comes in storms, they come from the west and bring wind and hail, blowing the crops over and knocking the heads. The storms are very localised, though, you can get fifty millimetres and the guy up the road will only get ten.

'I miss it so much that it hurts – it was all that kept me going through the Battle of Britain, the thought of going back home again. Though I didn't think of it when I was in the air, only when I was waiting to go up again. I came over with one of my mates, Gerry, and we always tried to look out for each other. We went up once south of Manston to intercept a raid of 109s, and we saw a seaplane below. The Germans were very good at that, they flew seaplanes all along the English Coast to rescue their boys, and we had very little in that line. I decided to go after the seaplane and Gerry went after the 109s, but he found himself on a collision course with one and it fired as fast as he did, then crashed into him underneath. I could see that his engine had seized up and as he passed me his cockpit was full of smoke and he was having trouble opening it. I don't know how much you know about Spits, Daisy, but the hoods are made to fit one plane. If it has to get a replacement at some time the hood doesn't always fit, and that was what happened to Gerry.

'There he was, trapped, and the burning fuel coming back at him and filling the cockpit as he tried to glide it down. I saw him hitting some open ground, where anti-invasion posts had been put in to stop enemy gliders landing, and I thought that was the last I'd see of him. He came back that evening, though. He'd found a little jemmy thing and smashed the hood with that, then somehow he got out and watched the plane burning and his fuel exploding. He was sitting there on the ground, his hair and eyebrows singed and his knees pretty badly hammered, and this woman came out of a nearby house and calmly asked if he'd like a cup of tea! And Gerry said, "Struth, haven't you got anything stronger, lady?"

'We were pretty short of pilots so he went back up the next day, but I think he would've done anyway, to get over the fear quickly. Taught us all a lesson, though. You'd see us every spare minute we had, opening and shutting hoods, opening and shutting, over and over, to make sure it would give if needed.

'I had this sergeant pilot who used to give us tips. They were looked down on, the sergeant pilots, the RAF officers wouldn't let them be commissioned, you know, treated them like scum pretty often, wouldn't even share their cosy billets with them. Most of them lived in tents along the airstrips, so when the Germans came calling they got the chop, even though pilot numbers were getting fewer by the sortie – that crazy class thing went on. This sergeant pilot gave us better training than the RAF did, told us never to fly straight and level for more than thirty seconds when the enemy was likely to be about, even when you're attacking, keep an eye on what's happening around you, and never watch your kill, your flamer, going down, because that means you've taken your eye off the real ball. And you should never identify with the men in the enemy planes. You're in a tin box, he used to say, trying to knock other tin boxes out of the sky. Sometimes you'd see this little human being on the end of a parachute and you'd realise it was someone's son, you know? But then it would descend and you were still up there and one of those little human beings might do the same thing to you, so you couldn't hang around to see if he was OK.

'Then once we came across a single Heinkel and we went after it, hitting the fuselage and setting it on fire, so we stopped the attack and tried to escort it back to land. I was flying on its port side, where the fire was, and I could see the crew clearly. I almost wanted to jump across and help them. It was strange, we spent all our time trying to blow them out of the sky and they did the same with us, and now I just wanted this lot to survive. We were within a few miles of the coast when a Hurricane from another squadron came in behind us, didn't even think of us being all around, and poured a long burst of fire into the Heinkel. It blew up in our faces and ditched into the sea. There were no survivors, and I had this urge to turn and open fire on the Hurricane. I just felt such a sense of loss.

'There are times when I can't make any sense of the war, Daisy. I can't wait for it to be over and to get back home. I want to raise a family, with a wife first, but you know that already, there's only one candidate. I can't wait to see my mother and father again. There are times when the hunger to see them is so strong it almost hurts. But it must be like that for you, too, bet you can't wait to see yours again.'

Daisy lowered her head for a few seconds. She had to find a way of getting out of this situation, she decided. She wasn't getting drawn into the dream, so she replied to his letters by telling him about *her* work, while Dotty, she knew, told him of the life she had planned for when it was all over.

So there they were, in a bizarre *ménage à trois*, with one of them completely unaware they were three. Daisy wrestled with it every time she received a letter, but decided she couldn't tell Dotty. The girl was in love, and even if only with the idea of him, it didn't matter, so she kept quiet. Besides, there was no danger of anything developing between Frank and herself, so she wasn't deceiving Dotty, she reasoned. At the same time she worried in case Dotty might find out and feel betrayed anyway, though there was nothing to feel betrayed about, except that she had never told her Frank wrote to her, too, and now it was too late to tell her.

Daisy felt there had been too much loss in her life. Not that she was the only one to claim that, but she needed time to readjust to what her life had become, and she didn't yet know what that was. She was alone in the world, there was no family to welcome her back, all sins forgiven and forgotten when all this was over, a thought that sometimes caused her moments of panic.

Somewhere, in the back of her mind, she realised, she must have held on to the hope that one day she would be accepted back into the family fold, though she couldn't see how with Dessie still around. Now that would never happen and she would have to find her way through life on her own.

Sometimes she would waken in the night hearing her mother's tortured breathing, a sound that had terrified her all her life as she waited for the next and the next breath, and now that there was no hope of ever hearing it again, she wept. At the same time, much as that prospect frightened her, there was a feeling that she didn't want anyone else to be close to her ever again. They hurt you and then they died – being alone was preferable. She didn't want marriage and children, never had, which probably made her unusual compared to other girls of her age. Look at Violet and Molly, aching to be with their boys – for Daisy those feelings had merged with the fear of closeness. When she thought about closeness she saw Dessie's face again, mouth gaping and dribbling as he sweated on top of her, inside her, eyes unseeing, intent only on using her, making her dirty, amid the smell of stale cigarettes and booze. If that was closeness she had no use for it, no one would ever get that near to her again.

So there was nothing there in her future, and no one of her own. What could she do, where could she go? Shut the door, Daisy. Shut the door and put on your act. Let the future wait, for now there was still a war on.

13

At the end of the year one problem was solved: Dotty was transferred to non-operational Station Sick Quarters, where there
were both British and Polish patients. She had already moved
away from Daisy before that, of course, when she became so
absorbed in her new life and work, and it was time for Daisy
to move on too – from Dotty at least. When she'd been recovering from Dessie's assault she had needed Edith's silence; and
then she'd wanted Dotty's cheerful noise to hide behind when
her family had been wiped out. But Daisy had come out the
other end and needed different company from both the old and
the new Dotty. Not that she'd lost her affection for Dotty, and
no one ever made any goodbye speeches. They would still stay
friends and in touch, but from a distance that she felt ready for.

Daisy wondered what this said about her, but she suspected
that people must grow out of other people all the time, and in
wartime you had to get used to partings anyway, it was the way
of life in the services. It was a time of replenishing the spirit and
rebuilding the parts that had been damaged, and she would walk
alone through the different seasons, thinking sometimes, at others
trying not to. In summer there were apples and plums on the
trees and the smell of the fruit made your mouth water, followed

by the rustier yellow of the autumn sun complementing the oranges and reds of the trees, the hedgerows full of elderberries, brambles and rose-hips. Almost imperceptibly winter arrived, bringing crystal-clear air one moment and snow blizzards the next, so that you couldn't see more than a few inches in front of you and the freezing wind blew through you. Everyone went to work to clear the runways, no one would have thought of refusing, especially when some besotted Fly Boy had smuggled a pair of sheepskin boots to the object of his desire.

Daisy loved the snow: now that she could see it in the country she knew that's where it was meant to be. It was wasted on cities, where it was all-too-soon trampled into a cold, wet brown sludge. The only problem was that when they set off to steal coal from another hut to keep the stove burning – which they all did – their footsteps left clear trails to the guilty. But springtime would be just around the corner, or so they told each other as they shivered in their beds every night, usually to yells of 'The next one to say that dies!' It would be fresh and green and there would be flowers for the first time in many months. There would be snowdrops.

'They're quite beautiful when you see them up close, you know.'

'Last warning, no more or you die!'

'And crocuses – or should it be croci?'

'Right, that's it! I'm coming to get you!'

'And the world will be bright again!'

Then they would all join in a wry chorus of 'There'll be blue-birds over the white cliffs of Dover', followed by raucous laughter.

And even though they made a joke of it, it still made you believe the world could be clean and free again, one day, one day soon.

★　★　★

By the time American Forces were arriving in 1942, having joined the war rather belatedly again, Daisy was established in her little world, the only one she had, up in the Langar tower. She found the work suited her and she did it supremely well. It had been reported by her colleagues that she was completely calm in the worst circumstances and she had a voice that carried well on the radio. More than this, she seemed capable of taking the stress – though no one called it that in those days – of talking to aircrew in desperate trouble, boys who were about to die and would have Daisy's voice as the last sound they would hear. Knowing this as she talked to them, she never cracked and stayed on the line till the end, chatting to them in non-military language when she thought it was appropriate, a great sin in the eyes of the hierarchy.

She was good with the girls, too, looking after them in the early days of their service careers, the first time away from home for most, and making sure they were protected from predatory aircrew, even if she had already conceded general defeat on that one.

By spring 1942 she had got to grips with service life and grown in confidence, and she also had the respect of the aircrews for the way she handled her job. They all tried to bed her, of course, that's how they were: when tomorrow might never come, young men's fancies turned to fornication and, crudely, in Daisy's case, to a rolling sweepstake that grew to a fortune for the first one to manage it. Daisy knew this and dealt with it by treating them with her Mae West attitude, friendly but distant contempt, when they were on the ground. When they were flying it was different, then she did everything she could to coax them safely home, and when they didn't make it she would write to their families, telling them what heroes their boys were.

The constant quest of the airmen for sex had nothing to do

with love, nothing really to do with sex, if the truth were told. It was a reinforcement of life at a time when it was cheap. It reassured them that *they* were still alive, when they saw their comrades blown to bits on a daily basis. They were young, they were performing inhuman acts in a brutal war; they, too, needed to find coping mechanisms, and flower-pressing wasn't on their agenda.

Some wanted to marry so desperately that they would propose to every female in the universe – that was *their* salvation, to know there would be someone to come home to. If both parties survived, many of these marriages proved to be enduringly happy, but just as many fell apart because husband and wife hadn't known each other when the ring was slipped on, or didn't know each other once the war had changed them – and those six years changed everyone. Still, even the hasty unions gave hope to many at a time when they needed it, so who could blame them?

Others, the vast majority, took the opposite view. They saw death beckoning and tried to pack as much living into each day as they could, or so the myth said. It was a myth because they mainly indulged in sex and booze, and there had always been more to life than both, so it could be argued that they packed each day with sex and booze as a means of coping with the nights, when they would fly over hostile territories with guns blazing at them, and drop their bombs on terrified people below. They risked death, saw it and brought it to strangers, so sex made them feel their lives were still going on. They were vital, and the booze dulled the horror of their vital lives. And the boys of the RAF weren't alone in over-indulging, whatever that meant at the time. It was happening in every service, and post-war alcoholism would become a common problem, another marriage breaker.

As it was, heartbreak was always around. Daisy saw it so many times that she could spot it in advance, feeling truly older than her years. A remuster would take place and the empty bunks would be filled by young girls who hadn't heard the aircrews' lines before, whereas Daisy soon knew every one by heart. Once, in the NAAFI, she heard yet another 'I could be dead tomorrow' speech being given to a young WAAF and she wandered over and stood behind the pilot as he delivered his heartfelt entreaty.

'He's never felt like this before,' Daisy said wearily, buffing her nails on her shirt then examining them intently. 'And you're not just another notch on his joystick. You didn't think you were, did you?'

The pilot turned round, grimacing, and Daisy smiled sweetly.

'And what's more, he'll still respect you in the morning,' Daisy continued. 'Now let me see, have I left anything out? Ah yes, and he hasn't got a wife. How's that?'

As the pilot slunk off to the cheerful catcalls of his crew-mates, he turned to Daisy and said with a grin, 'Do you *never* go on leave, Daisy?'

'When are you next in the air, sunshine?' she snarled back at him. 'I'll arrange it for then, OK?' knowing that the last thing any of them wanted was for Daisy not to be in the tower when they were flying a mission.

'Don't you think it's enough that we're fighting one war already?' he asked, laughing. 'Then we come back to base and have to fight another one, with *you!*'

'And that one, sunshine,' Daisy said lazily, 'is the one you will never win.'

In the hut, a day had passed for Molly without a letter from her Dave, then another and another. The girls reassured her as they always did. He was a Pathfinder, they worked flat out, she knew that, he'd be too exhausted to write, or there had been a hitch as usual. Any day now four or five letters would arrive together. How many times had that happened?

Only this time was different, and instead of those four or five letters from Dave there was one from his commanding officer with the news everyone dreaded. The instinct of the others was to throw their arms around Molly, to comfort and protect her, but she didn't want anyone to touch her if Dave couldn't.

Daisy understood that. She had felt the same when her family had been killed, and she advised the others to let Molly handle it in her own way, until she saw the girl grow paler and more withdrawn and reported it to their officer. Molly was taken to the sick bay and sedated, and when the girls visited her they found her distant and reluctant to even acknowledge their presence, far less talk to them. Within a few weeks she was taken to a civilian hospital and they never saw her again, nor heard what had become of her. She just disappeared from their lives as completely as her Dave had disappeared from hers. Every now and then, during the domestic nights imposed by the WAAF hierarchy when the girls had to sit around the stove together, mending and being 'domestic', inevitably there would be a lull in the conversation and someone would say wistfully, 'Isn't it quiet without Molly's singing?'

'I used to throw things at her to make her stop,' another voice would reply. 'I wonder where she is now and how she is?'

Then, just as they were settling down after that tragedy, Violet's wedding plans came to a sudden halt only days before the big event, when it was discovered that her handsome, tanned Rhodesian Fly Boy was already married. He had been transferred to another unit where a former Langar girl working in Pay had discovered that some of his pay was being sent home to his wife in Bulawayo. Naturally, she passed this information on. WAAFs always protected WAAFs, after all.

'Just as well you found out before you married him,' Celia comforted Violet. 'I mean, if you'd found out after you'd already, you know . . . done it . . . well . . .'

Only poor Violet had, and under her mechanic's overalls she was hiding a healthy four-month pregnancy, so before she could think she was bundled off the base, out of the service and home to Darlington and a doubtful welcome from her parents.

'What have I told you?' Daisy demanded of the hut. 'Keep away from Fly Boys, do not listen to Fly Boys, got it? They'll leave you one way or another. If they don't die they'll put you in the club and scarper, usually back to their wives.'

The girls all nodded sadly. 'He told Violet he might be dead tomorrow,' Celia said wistfully. 'Can you imagine Violet falling for that one?'

'If I could get my hands on him he would die today!' Daisy replied angrily.

'What I can't understand is that he went along with all the wedding plans,' Celia said bemusedly. 'Can you imagine? I mean, he would actually have shown up and gone through with it, knowing all the time that he already had a wife. Can you imagine it?' she asked again.

'I can, I can,' Daisy said with feeling.

'And he said, why wait, they were going to get married, weren't they? She fell for that one, too, smartarse Violet of all people,' Celia continued.

'There we have it, girls,' Daisy stated, walking up and down the hut. 'He managed to come up with the most obvious lines of persuasion and poor old Violet fell for them. Now, what must we do?'

'Keep away from Fly Boys!' the girls chorused, giggling.

'And if they give you the old lines?'

'Tell Daisy!'

'And what will Daisy do?'

'Throttle the swines!'

A couple of nights later, not long after the bombers had taken off and so no one in the tower was expecting them back yet, a 'Darky' call came in from a plane from another base that was in trouble, the first Daisy had ever heard.

'Hello Darky, hello Darky,' said a voice. 'A for Apple calling. I have to land.'

'Hello A for Apple, this is Langar,' Daisy replied. 'Permission to land.'

The airfield lights were switched on and the crash crews and medics informed.

'Hello Langar, I have one engine out,' the voice said anxiously.

'It's a Wimpy,' the Control Officer said, watching through binoculars.

'I've lost him, Sir,' Daisy said, and called again. 'Hello, A for Apple, Langar here.'

'Hello Langar . . .'

Daisy tried twice more and there was no reply, though the plane could be seen in the distance. There was a final despairing 'I can't . . .' as the plane passed low over the runway, then there was loud creaking, followed by crashing, then an explosion from the far end, when flames lit up the sky with the orange glow everyone dreaded seeing. Still, the emergency teams were right there and the Control Officer had followed them. They'd get them out, they'd be OK.

Everyone waited, trying to make out what was happening through the darkness and the smoke, then the Control Officer came back, looked at Daisy and shook his head. Five boys dead, five silly, boozing, fornicating, brave, wonderful Fly Boys just snuffed out before her with that frantic voice still ringing in her ears.

The others all crowded round in silence, shaken and shocked, but the first of their own Fly Boys would be coming back home from the night's mission in a matter of hours, they had to get a grip.

'Tea?' a voice said, and they all nodded. There was nothing like tea – indeed, in those circumstances it was all they had.

It had an effect, though, living that life, being efficient and businesslike at all times, though Daisy had a few lapses from military language from time to time. Daisy and Celia went to a film in Nottingham one night, something forgettably senti-mental, when without warning someone in the audience was sniffing, followed by Celia, and finally Daisy. One by one they left the cinema and met up outside, both of them crying over nothing and trying to laugh then subsiding into more tears. A group of aircrew saw their chance and offered hankies. There was nothing quite like happening upon not just one but two WAAF damsels in distress.

'Get lost, erks!' Daisy snarled, and the girls laughed then cried again. Eventually, when they were completely exhausted, they stood looking at each other and blowing their noses.

'What the hell was that all about?' Celia demanded.

'Oh, I suppose it's just been a hard spell, what with Molly and Violet and then the boys in the Wimpy,' Daisy sniffed.

Celia started crying again. 'I thought it was just that rotten film!' she wailed.

'Oh, no,' Daisy said, 'it had to be something more than that. We're WAAFs, we never fall for nonsense.'

'Poor Violet did,' Celia muttered, and they started crying all over again.

14

The crew of Lancaster Bomber ED498 EM–O arrived at Langar in late 1942, and Bruiser entered Daisy's life, though she did everything she could to keep him out. His name was Graeme Shaw, a Canadian flight-engineer on one of the Lancs, but everyone called him Bruiser because of his habit of bringing irritating disputes to an end with a punch. Not that he was violent, so everyone said, but having taken on board that life was short, terribly short these days, he didn't mess around making his point verbally if he thought there was no chance of his point being considered. Instead, without any malice or fury, Bruiser let go with a very good left-hook. It was the equivalent and had all the emotion of 'check-mate', as far as Bruiser was concerned.

Bruiser's Lanc was the talk of Langar because it had 'Lady Groundhog' and a red maple leaf painted on the side. The maple leaf everyone could understand, with the pilot, Calli MacDonald, being Canadian too, but there was much discussion about Lady Groundhog's origins.

'It's probably a sarcastic description of a female,' Daisy opined. All she and everyone else on the base knew was that Bruiser loved her, and not in the lecherous way she was used to with

Fly Boys but in the manner of a large abandoned adoring puppy she couldn't shake off.

Passing him in the NAAFI one night, the other girls giggled as he gazed adoringly at her. Daisy remarked sourly, 'Canadians everywhere', which prompted Bruiser to loudly and joyously proclaim that Daisy was looking at him. Daisy tried to keep a straight face, she was now a Langar fixture, she had a position to keep up, but his puppy-dog eyes generally followed her in such a good-natured way that she couldn't help smiling about him – not *at* him, that would have been fatal, but just when she thought about him.

When Bruiser had first arrived at the base he had approached Daisy as she sat on her own in the NAAFI, reading a fashion magazine she had read ten times before. He'd been put up to it, it was something of an initiation ceremony imposed on newcomers by the sweepstake organisers.

'Can I get you something, Ma'am?' he asked.

Without looking up, Daisy replied loudly and dismissively, 'Go away, you idiot,' and continued reading.

'Yes, Ma'am, thank you, Ma'am,' Bruiser said, bowing, then went back to his seat where the others were slapping each other and falling off their chairs laughing.

'What did she say, Bruiser?' one asked sweetly.

'She said she loved me and begged me to go to her hut tonight,' he replied, smiling stupidly at her.

A great raucous cheer went up.

'But I said I'd rather save myself for our wedding night.'

Daisy looked up as she turned a page of her magazine, briefly making eye contact with him, and she couldn't help smiling very slightly; and even though she tried to turn it into a grimace, he smiled just as slightly back at her. It was the start of Bruiser's many and frequent approaches, all of which she firmly rebuffed, but he was so pleasant, so unthreatening, she could never bring herself to really squash him.

He went everywhere with his skipper, young MacDonald, which wasn't unusual – crews were closer than most families. The younger pilot was not tall but strongly compact with a steadiness, a stillness about him that drew your attention. Handsome, too, with dark, crinkly hair and very direct brown eyes, whereas Bruiser was tall, thin and fair, with that incredibly silly grin whenever he looked at Daisy. The two of them – pilot and engineer – were always pushing each other and laughing. Bruiser's talisman was a green scarf that he wore at all times, and he once approached Daisy and asked her if she would mind bestowing a kiss on it to ensure his safe return from that night's mission.

'Fine,' she said calmly, 'as long as I can bestow a fist in your mouth in return, sunshine.'

'It would be an honour, Ma'am,' Bruiser replied, 'to be touched by you in any way.'

Daisy shook her head and walked away, hearing his voice in the background telling the others, 'She's thinking about touching me, she said so, she actually wants to touch me!' and his friends yelling at him derisively.

There was just something about Bruiser that stopped her going for the jugular, but she didn't know what, and it made her pay more attention to his kite, much as it annoyed her. When she was on duty in the tower she always checked where Lady Groundhog was and when it had landed safely, all the time reminding herself that this must be some kind of slippery slope. Attachment of any kind was a distraction she didn't need.

Frank. There he was again, she thought savagely. Bruiser made her smile and Frank made her angry. Why was that? Celia had recently announced her engagement and, as ever in wartime, the marriage plans had been hurried along, though being Celia everyone had to know every tiny detail. To Daisy's mild surprise her friend was lost in the romance of it all, as though by marrying Bobby the world would once again be full of roses. Daisy didn't even think the world pre-war was like that, so she was troubled by Celia's expectations. True, Bobby wasn't quite a Fly Boy, he was an aircraft mechanic, so that was something, but you had to wonder about these rush-jobs that always took place in the first mad flush of love. How many times had she seen the more sensible ones cooling down in due course, so who was to say how many of these marriages wouldn't do the same? In normal life only shotgun weddings took place faster than child-free ones did, but after living like this for years it was hard to decide what normal was.

Maybe life as Daisy had known it pre-war had gone for good. She was absolutely sure that Celia's wasn't a shotgun wedding, but her friend's romantic view was full of fantasy, and every time she talked to Daisy about it the whole thing seemed to have become a tad more unrealistic than the time before.

Eileen Reilly arrived at the base with the latest consignment of WAAF recruits in spring of 1943. Daisy had been on duty in the tower the night before, or she would have taken them in hand immediately, but she met up with them when she stopped off for a bite to eat before going back to the hut for some sleep.

Celia had returned from her short honeymoon the day before, and Daisy knew that when she went back to the hut Celia would be waiting to tell all, so she had taken refuge in the NAAFI to put the dreaded moment off for as long as possible. All she wanted to do was sleep, but if she went back to the hut she knew Celia would still be there, waiting to go on duty, so she sat sipping tea she didn't want, wondering in a resentful way why she was always the one the girls came to, why they didn't take their thoughts, fears and hopes to someone else. Why was she regarded as some kind of authority anyway?

'Are you Daisy?' a girl asked beside her, smiling.

'And you are?' Daisy said, looking at her over the rim of her cup.

'Eileen Reilly,' the girl said, holding out a hand. 'I thought I'd better introduce myself, I've been given the other bed in your room.'

'Oh, yes,' Daisy replied. 'Eileen Reilly?' she said thoughtfully. 'But you sound Scottish. Not exactly a Scottish name, is it?'

'As Scottish as Daisy Sheridan is English!' Eileen replied with a grin. She was a pretty girl, petite, Daisy thought they called it, with reddish-fair hair and bright blue eyes, and she seemed to be taking the horrors of early service life in her stride, even if she didn't like them. Daisy approved of that; she had no time for the ones who sat down and wept for their mothers, even though she became all of their mothers while they were WAAFs together. If she didn't look after them, who would? So she and Eileen obviously shared the get-on-with-it attitude, and the Irish thing, of course, though by the sound of it as they glee-fully compared notes in the canteen that first morning, the bias was worse in Glasgow than in Newcastle.

'When they meet someone new,' Eileen explained cheer-fully, 'they ask "What school did you go to?" This is to sort out Catholics from Protestants. With a name like mine, though, they didn't have to ask, they just saved time and snubbed me straight off.'

'It's that bad?' Daisy asked.

Eileen nodded. 'I'm the second generation born in Glasgow, but as far as they're concerned I'm still Irish.'

'Same in Newcastle!' Daisy said. 'I'm the third generation,

but it doesn't matter a damn. Doesn't matter to the Irish either, come to that, they still see themselves as natives of the ould country.'

'And do you have Orange Walks?'

'Yes,' Daisy laughed, 'not that we take much notice, because that's what they want. My father says when he was young everyone used a bucket during the few days before a march instead of the toilet, and they welcomed the Lodge with the contents.'

'Same in Glasgow!' Eileen replied delightedly. 'Yet they always march through Catholic areas.'

'That's what always puzzled me, too,' Daisy giggled. 'They knew what was waiting for them, yet they kept coming back year after year.'

'Are there certain jobs the Irish can't get in Newcastle?' Eileen asked, making a face at the plate of food in front of her. 'Do you ever get used to this stuff?' she added.

'Well, you do or die, as they say,' Daisy replied.

'Like in the shipyards on the Clyde,' Eileen continued, 'Catholics aren't allowed to work there. Not long ago they weren't allowed to be tradesmen of any kind. I don't think it's changed much, to be honest, it's just gone underground. Employers don't turn people down and *say* it's because they're Catholics any longer, but my father remembers job adverts in the twenties carrying notices that no Catholics should apply, and that meant anyone with an Irish name.'

'I don't think it was as blatant where I come from, but put it this way,' Daisy said with dark humour, 'on Tyneside, Catholics know better than to look for jobs in the shipyards.'

'They know their place!' Eileen chuckled.

'That's about the size of it,' Daisy said cheerfully.

They sipped at their teas.

'One of the pilots over there offered to take me up for a spin,' Eileen said, 'but I was warned by another WAAF to check with you first.'

Daisy scowled. 'Which one?' she demanded, and the girl pointed out the culprit. Daisy nodded. 'OK,' she said, 'I'll deal with him later. Never understood the desire to fly, but lots of girls seem to want to do it.'

'Do they?' Eileen asked, sitting down.

'Yes, and the Fly Boys know it, too. They take them up unofficially hoping for action of the other kind in return. One girl went up in a fighter a while back, it crashed and she and the pilot were killed. Didn't seem so exciting after that somehow.'

'Good heavens.'

'Maybe,' Daisy replied, 'but very definitely hard earth.'

Just then the crew of Lady Groundhog arrived and sat down not far from them, Bruiser smiling stupidly at Daisy and regarding her with soft adoration.

'Are they friends of yours?' Eileen asked.

Daisy, who had seen them arrive, didn't look round. 'That's a nice boy,' she said wearily, 'a couple of other guys, and the one that's smiling soppily is an idiot.'

'He seems to be quite sweet on you,' Eileen said.

'I told you, he's an idiot,' Daisy replied. 'He's harmless, really, he's called Bruiser because he hits people.'

'And he's harmless?'

'Totally. He's not violent or anything, he just gets fed-up when people won't give in to the obvious, so he belts them one as a kind of full stop. But don't look at them, that's what they want. If you look at them it encourages them and they'll talk to you, and if they talk to you you'll have to waste time slapping them around to get rid of them.'

Eileen put her head down and laughed.

'Well at least you're laughing,' Daisy said, looking at Eileen's fellow recruits. 'Look at that miserable bunch of perishers.'

'They've had a rough night. The recruiting office kind of led them up the garden path and they all want to go home. You should've heard the sobbing in the hut last night.'

'Heard it before,' Daisy sighed. 'Were they promised nice sitting rooms with plush furnishings, by any chance?'

'Exactly!' Eileen said. 'And we're all still looking for it. I have this feeling it doesn't exist.'

'I've got a feeling you're right on top of this!' Daisy smiled. 'Look, I've got to get some sleep. See you later?'

Daisy got up and walked past the table where the nice boy Calli, Bruiser and the others were sitting, sashaying her hips slightly more than necessary for Bruiser's benefit and giving him the very slightest irritated glance. Then she walked out, knowing without looking that Bruiser was blowing her a kiss and still smiling stupidly behind her back as usual.

'I wish to God you'd give up on her,' Calli said, shaking his head.

'Calli, my man,' Bruiser said contentedly, 'you have no idea about women. She loves me.'

'Oh yeah?' Calli MacDonald asked. 'And just how do you work that one out?'

'Her hips.'

All the others laughed and threw playful punches at him.

'Her *hips?*' said the rear gunner, who really was called Charlie.

'I tell you, Charlie, her hips wiggle every time they see me.'

'Her hips see you?' Charlie asked.

'And they wiggle,' Bruiser nodded.

'You're a sad creature, Bruiser,' Calli laughed at him, 'and you bring Canada into disrepute by virtue of being such an idiot.' He slapped Bruiser on the head with a teaspoon.

Bruiser smiled his stupid smile. 'I know, I know, Skip,' he said. 'But this is love, you wait and see.'

'She does nothing but give you the elbow!'

'Ah,' said Bruiser cunningly, 'that's just what it looks like to guys like you lot, but I can tell – I can tell. Every remark she makes to me might sound like a putdown, but her tone of voice is a give-away.'

'That she'll crush you like a bug!' Calli teased.

'No, no, fair dos,' said Taffy, 'I can see something of what Bruiser says he sees.'

'There you go!' Bruiser shouted happily. 'The mad Welshman here can see it!'

'Only,' Taffy said seriously, lining up Bruiser's usual claim, 'I think it's me her hips see when they wiggle.'

Bruiser took his cap off and beat Taffy over the head with it.

Much to her relief, Daisy managed to avoid discussing Celia and Bobby's first night as man and wife on a one-to-one basis for a couple of days. But the other girls crowded round her on domestic night, desperate to hear every detail in an era when virgin marriages were in the majority, even though there was a war on. Celia described the dress, the flowers, the church, the reception, the small sponge cake hidden under a highly decorated cardboard cover before the girls got down to the nitty-gritty.

'What was it like?' a voice asked as they sat round the stove. 'I mean, when you did it for the first time, what was it like?'

'Oh, it was fine,' the bride replied, head bent over her darning.

'Yes, but, what did he, you know, *do*?'

There was a pause as Celia struggled to untangle a very difficult knot and Daisy glanced up at her and saw tears brimming.

'Oh, come on!' she said to the others. 'That's private. How'd you feel if you were asked to describe every detail?'

Mother Hen had spoken and the others giggled and changed the subject. Later, though, Celia sought Daisy out and threw herself into her arms. They all brought their problems to Daisy, and the fact was that, however reluctantly, Daisy was always there.

'It was awful!' she sobbed. 'I hated it, Daisy, and I wanted to like it for Bobby's sake. It hurt and it was just awful. Every time he came near me after that I froze, and he wasn't very pleased. I don't know if he's even talking to me now. He's been posted away and I'm glad I won't have to see him for a while. I feel such a failure.'

'There, there,' Daisy soothed her. 'It was your first time, I'm sure it'll get better.'

'But it was *horrible*, Daisy, I never want to do it again,' Celia sobbed. 'Was it horrible for you the first time?'

'Ssh,' Daisy said quietly, 'don't get in such a state, it'll all work out.'

Sitting in the tower that night, the boys having flown off and with little to do till they were on the way home, Daisy thought about Celia. They all assumed Daisy was a veteran, a sexual acrobat who regularly took part in those fabled London orgies, so Daisy knew it all. And she couldn't blame them; it was an image she had created all by herself.

'Was it horrible for you the first time?' Celia had asked. If only Celia had known, she thought. If only the leader and protector that Daisy had become to her girls could reassure confused, disappointed Celia by telling her about her first time. But she couldn't. She relived it in her dreams often enough and wakened terrified and feeling sick, but she could never tell anyone. More times than she cared to think about she had heard airmen, full of bravado, make crude remarks about her as she passed. She had a body made for sex and that's what she used it for, it was common knowledge, that's what they said, as though because she had swapped bodies with a sex bomb one night years ago, the sex bomb's experiences had come as part of the package. She had reinvented herself as Langar's Mae West, quick, witty and choosy, and she *never* chose Fly Boys like them.

Long ago she had decided to walk away if the remarks were not intended for her ears, pretending not to hear them if they were far enough away. But if they were being really loud as well as offensive, and for her benefit, she would walk up to the big mouths, the crudest creeps, lean close with her breasts almost touching them and say, 'Fancy your chances, sunshine? Take my word for it, you're not man enough, you wouldn't have a clue what to do with them.'

The creep, now having to deal face-to-face with Daisy, or as near as, would always gulp and look sheepish as she called his bluff, then she'd walk away slowly and calmly with a bored expression on her face, to the cheers of the others.

It was like water off a duck's back to Mae West, but inside Daisy she was still Background Daisy Sheridan from Heaton via Byker, who cringed as she lay in her bed in the darkness – her old friend – and released her real feelings. To men like that she was no more than an object but she would never let them know how they made her feel. Never.

As the first call came in from a homeward-bound Lanc, she was recalling Celia's anguish.

'I never want to do it ever again,' the girl had said.

'Amen to that,' Daisy thought. 'Amen to that, Celia.' Then she went back to work.

15

It was some weeks before Daisy and Eileen caught up properly with each other again, and by that time Eileen had been put through her truncated Radio Telephone Operator's training and was about to join Daisy in the tower. Celia had just returned from a leave with her husband that Daisy had assured her would make everything right, but it had ended in tears and, naturally, it was Daisy she sought out.

'How did it go?' Daisy began brightly.

'It was terrible, Daisy,' Celia replied, her face a blank.

'I just froze again. I tried not to, but I didn't want him to touch me, and he got angry and shouted at me, then he made me.'

'He "made" you?' Daisy asked. 'What do you mean?'

'He said I was his wife and he had rights, and he just made me do it,' Celia said flatly.

'Did you try to stop him?' Daisy asked, her mind a mass of emotions.

'I said I didn't want to and Bobby said he didn't care whether I wanted to or not, I'd have to, and if I didn't buck my ideas up there were plenty of other females who'd be happy to do it with him. He said there was something wrong with me;

other women don't mind, why should I?' She sat silently on Daisy's bed then looked up at her. 'I think I hate him, Daisy,' she said flatly.

'Oh, it's just how you're feeling,' Daisy said, trying to sound encouraging and worldly wise. 'Remember how excited you were about the wedding? You didn't hate Bobby then, did you?'

'Well, he didn't behave like that then. I watched him the other night, you know, afterwards, and he couldn't look me in the eye, and I thought "You bloody coward!"'

'Celia, remember that Bobby's being worked off his feet, he's probably not behaving as he normally would, none of us are.'

Celia nodded. 'I know that, I've been making every excuse for him, but none of them work. I hate him. He forced me, he knew I didn't want to, Daisy, he's supposed to love me and he forced me. I've tried to pretend that it doesn't matter, but it does, and now I just feel so angry and stupid for letting him. What kind of man does that to his own wife?'

To any woman, Daisy thought, but didn't know what to say. In defending Celia's husband she was putting up defences Dessie could have used, and there was no defence.

'Look, Celia, you're not likely to be seeing him for a while, are you? So take this time and think it through, wait till you've calmed down and you'll probably find that it'll work out. You've got off to a bad start, and no wonder, you're not having a chance to have a normal married life, are you? When all this is over you'll forget it ever happened.'

Daisy didn't add 'like I did', because she hadn't.

She sighed, thinking of Celia's husband. Odds on Bobby was just a boy, every bit as inexperienced as Celia was, who had no more than a general idea of what to do; a boy who belonged to the 'have someone waiting' way of thinking. He would have left home too early, though in years he was old enough for war, but he wanted to be looked after as he had been at home, with regular sex thrown in.

Once, down in the pub, Daisy had overheard two airmen talking. The younger one was about to marry and the older one, who obviously regarded himself as the re-incarnation of Rudolph Valentino, was giving him advice for his wedding night. 'Just keep jabbing away and it'll be all right,' he said, in a leering way, and Daisy had turned round and thrown her drink in his face. She could imagine Celia's Bobby confiding in one of his colleagues that all was not as he had expected of marriage, probably after he'd had a few, and he would have been advised to put his foot down, show her who was master, demand his rights. Daisy could almost hear it. And the boy had done it, of course, and look where it had landed him and Celia.

It was just like Fly Boys to think they knew it all when they didn't, and then to pass on what they didn't know to impressionable boys like Bobby. There was nothing Daisy could do about that, she was on Celia's side here, so she took her on a night out in nearby Nottingham to cheer her up, and invited Eileen to join them.

They had signed themselves out and were sitting at a little café they had found that sold pancakes and syrup, but only to Forces personnel.

'Tell Eileen about the pigeons,' Daisy ordered, to get Celia thinking and talking about something other than Bobby and their marital problems. 'Something big's just happened in the world of pigeons, Eileen, you've got to hear this.'

Eileen looked at Celia, her eyes shining. She had heard about the pigeons but she didn't really believe it.

'I'm a pigeon handler,' Celia stated.

'Oh, get on with it!' Daisy said, dabbing some syrup on Celia's nose with her spoon.

'So what does that mean?' Eileen encouraged her.

'Well, we're part of Signals,' Celia said self-consciously. 'We breed pigeons and train them, then when they're ready we put a metal tag on each bird's leg, with the date, the basket number and the aircraft's number. There's a container on the leg with a white SOS strip and one showing the station, then they're put aboard the planes before takeoff on Ops.'

Eileen was chuckling, sure this was a joke, and Daisy kicked her under the table and threw her a warning look.

'But why?' Eileen asked.

'Well, if the plane goes down, one of the aircrew writes down their last position on the SOS strip with an indelible pencil. Then the pigeon flies home and we know where to pick the crew up. That's the theory — it doesn't always work.'

Daisy threw her arms up in the air. 'Will you get to the point?' she demanded. 'Tell her about Winkie before I thump you!'

'Winkie?' Eileen asked, looking from one to the other.

'Yes, Winkie,' Daisy said impatiently, 'she's a damned pigeon! *Tell* her!'

'Oh, I see, yes,' Celia smiled. 'Well, Winkie is a blue chequered hen —'

'Does it matter?' Daisy asked, rolling her eyes. 'I mean, would it make any difference if she was polka-dotted?'

'— and she was on a Beaufort in the North Sea last winter when it was brought down. The crew got into the raft and they didn't see Winkie had got herself free, so they were just sitting there waiting to die of cold or to be picked up by the enemy. But Winkie flew over a hundred miles covered in oil, and her code number was relayed to the Ops Room of her home station, and even though there wasn't a message, the number gave an idea of where the crew could be, and

217

they were picked up. Winkie got a medal.'

'Good old Winkie,' Eileen said diplomatically, wondering if pigeons could get medals and, if they could, where they were pinned.

'Wait, there's more,' Daisy said.

'What?' Eileen giggled. 'A pigeon with a medal, and there's *more?*'

'And you won't get to hear it if you don't stop being sarcastic,' Daisy reproved her. 'Will you tell her the rest, Celia, or do I have to get the electric wires out?'

'You only want me to tell her so that you can both laugh again,' Celia protested.

'And what's wrong with that? Don't you think we could do with a laugh?'

Celia sighed. 'Daisy thinks this is really funny for some reason, but the crew the pigeon helped save had a big celebration dinner for her and, as Winkie was the guest of honour, she was placed in her cage at the top table.'

At that Daisy dissolved in laughter and had to search through the make-up in her gas-mask container for a hankie to wipe her eyes, as Celia looked on disapprovingly. Then Eileen joined in, though she wasn't sure if she was laughing at Winkie's celebration dinner or Daisy's giggling.

'Oh, stop being so po-faced,' Daisy said to Celia. 'If you weren't so close to your pigeons you'd laugh too.'

'I just don't see what's so funny,' Celia said primly, shrugging her shoulders, 'though I can see by the two of you that I'm in a minority of one!'

'It's the picture of old Winkie sitting inside her cage at the top table being honoured, and she's just a pigeon, she doesn't have the slightest idea what's going on!' Daisy cried, dabbing at her eyes again.

'Well, you don't know that,' Celia said defensively. 'Pigeons are very clever, you know.'

But by then neither Daisy nor Eileen could hear her above their own laughter.

'We're not finished yet!' Daisy screeched.

'Oh, surely we *must* be!' Eileen giggled.

Daisy shook her head helplessly. 'Tell her about the hawk project!'

This time Celia giggled too. 'Well, our lot discovered that the Germans were using pigeons, too,' she said.

'They would, wouldn't they?' Eileen responded.

'And so our lot came up with this idea to train hawks to kill the German pigeons, only –'

'How could the hawks tell the difference?' Eileen interrupted, wide-eyed. 'Between our pigeons and German pigeons, I mean?'

'I was just coming to that,' Celia protested, reaching for a hankie of her own. 'That was the fatal flaw, you see, they couldn't!'

When the three girls got back to the hut later that night, Daisy's good mood changed. Normally she collected her mail up at Admin, but, presumably as she hadn't done so for a while, some kind person had picked up a letter and put it on her bed. She knew by the handwriting that it was from her Australian pen pal in Orkney.

When the correspondence had first started she had made her replies as boring as his own letters to Dotty, then she tried leaving her responses later and later, in the hope that he'd stop writing all together. Foreign servicemen often asked WAAFs to write to them, and even to write to their mothers to let them know how their boys were, so Frank Moran wasn't unusual, except that usually in the normal way of things contact slowly but surely died out after a while, as both parties found their time eaten up with work and other pursuits.

Not Frank, though. Frank stuck to it. He was in Shetland now, at a place called Sumburgh, which was as different from his beloved Dalby as anyone could imagine. With the Germans now in Norway they were just 180 miles from the northernmost part of the British Isles, so these tiny islands had been flooded with army, navy and RAF personnel; they now outnumbered the natives. There were few trees to be seen and little greenery, and even with so many service people about it was cold, lonely and remote.

'*The people are wonderful, though,*' Frank wrote. '*God knows, we've disrupted their way of life more than we do anywhere else, but they can't do enough for us. Every door is open to us. We're like family, and though they're on rations they're always baking for us. One Shetland sailor came home on leave and found his home full of other sailors – his family were on first-name terms with them. He said it felt like he was the stranger; it was like being back aboard ship. We have dances in the town hall and concerts in the RAF gym. Service personnel come from all over in lorries. Gracie Fields has been here a couple of times, though I've never heard her – I'm told I might not be missing a lot!*'

And then it was back to Dalby. '*I don't know if I've told you, but we have about 3000 acres all told, mostly open tree-land and grass with a paddock of maybe 100 acres for growing crops. Our main income is from wool, so we grow some oats for feeding the sheep in winter and some lucerne to give them good summer forage. A lot of the work is fencing to keep the blighters in, making sure they're healthy and checking the water supply – water's really important. We have an underground bore a hundred feet down and a windmill to keep the sheep trough supplied and a horse and a couple of dogs for mustering.*

'*Every couple of months we bring the sheep in for crutching (you don't want to know!), drenching, branding, lamb-tailing and paddock* rotation – if they stay on the same pasture they get worms. Six weeks off shearing we drench them to get rid of the lice. Lice are bad news: the sheep rub themselves against trees and fences to get rid of the itch and that affects their wool, and you have to keep an eye on blowfly that strike at the crotch and shoulder in the hot, wet weather. You have to shear the patches where the blowfly has laid and put on some oil to kill the maggots. And there's always burrs and poisonous weeds like prickly pear to look out for. I used to hate it, couldn't wait to get away from it and swore I'd never be back, but now I get sentimental thinking of blowflies! The house has a diesel-powered generator for electricity, a kerosene-fired fridge and a wood-burning stove for cooking. I'm going to build a new house when I get back, though, make it of cypress pine on two-foot stumps of hardwood like ironbark or spotted gum, they don't rot in the ground like cypress. Galvanised iron for the roof, and I'll have a phone in and a wireless, everybody will have them after the war.

You can have anything you want, Daisy, furnish it how you like. You'll be a long way from your family, but they can visit. You've never told me about your family. Have you got brothers and sisters?'

It was all getting too much, too involved. Even though she didn't respond in kind he was getting under her skin to the extent that she found herself picturing Dalby, wondering what his mother and father looked like. And there was Dotty to consider, Dotty who thought she would be the one to find that out after the war, if he survived that was.

And that was another thing. If he didn't survive she didn't want to know. She would hear from Dotty afterwards, but that would be one step removed, she didn't want to be the one who heard first.

She would have to tell him plainly not to write again, Daisy decided. She would use Dotty's undying love for him as an excuse, though the real reason was that she didn't want him or anyone else to fix themselves to her. So she wrote to him for the last time, telling him that she was far too busy to write, that she had nothing to write about other than work, that Dotty would be upset if she knew he was writing to her and she didn't want Dotty to feel something had been going on behind her back all along, even if nothing had been, couldn't and wouldn't. Anyway, they didn't know each other apart from that one brief meeting when they didn't get on, so maybe he should stop now, and, for her part, there would be no more letters.

There was nothing but the truth in what she said, but she still left it a couple of days before posting it, aware of some deep feeling of not wanting to hurt him and puzzled by it. When she had posted it, she felt bad in some indefinable way.

Still, that was that. It was over. She wouldn't think of him again. Until another letter arrived that didn't refer to the one, the very last one, Daisy had written to him. She didn't reply, and when yet another arrived she got Eileen to write on it 'Transferred' and posted it back to him.

'Aren't you going to open it?' Eileen asked.

'No.'

'But why not?'

'Because he's the kind of guy you don't want to let near you,' Daisy said, looking at the envelope with distaste.

'You mean he's a Fly Boy?' Eileen sniggered.

'Exactly. I'm trying to keep you lot away from them, and here's this guy I can't shake off. I think I may have to kill him to get rid of him if this doesn't work.'

And so they posted Frank's letter back to him, unopened, on the way out of the base.

In June it was Edith's birthday, and though she'd been posted to Station X, she wanted to celebrate with her old friends and see her Australian, of course, at Langar.

As many WAAFs as were off-duty made their way to a favourite pub. First of all they had a good gossip with Edith, who'd just had a letter from her cousin, who was working with barrage balloons in Birmingham.

The Balloon Operators were a hardy lot, often billeted in isolated areas, hands raw from splicing metal cables, winching balloons up and down, releasing the cables that were attached to 120 lb concrete blocks, and throwing around 40 lb sandbags. The idea of using balloons was to force the German planes to fly above them to avoid their wings being sliced off by the wires, and once they were higher they were easier prey for British artillery and fighter planes. Unlike the girls on settled bases, Balloon Operators didn't have prepared food provided, so each day's meals depended on whoever was on cook duty actually being able to cook.

The most frightening part of their duties, though, was standing sentry against intruders, two girls keeping vigil while the rest of the crew slept. Men on sentry duty had rifles for protection, but some higher authority had decided that WAAFs should have whistles and truncheons. Edith's cousin was based in Birmingham and the week before two men had attacked and assaulted the two sentries. Luckily the noise had wakened the others, and, when they rushed to help, one of the men had attacked Edith's cousin, choking her till she passed out. The police had arrived shortly afterwards and arrested the men, but the girls had been badly shaken and felt very vulnerable.

'They've asked for rifles,' Edith said, 'but so far nothing.'

'But they've got to give them rifles!' Daisy cried.

'I know, seems like common sense, doesn't it?' Edith replied, shrugging.

Just then the conversation was interrupted by a great commotion involving Lady Groundhog's nice skipper, the Canadian boy, Calli. He was drinking cider, under the impression that it was non-alcoholic, an impression his caring co-pilot, Bruiser, had given him. Calli had seen Eileen laughing at him and had first challenged her then asked her to marry him before passing out. As his crew tried to get him onto his feet with all the WAAFs cheering, Daisy found Bruiser looking up her skirt.

'Avert your eyes, sunshine,' she snarled. 'What's up there isn't for the likes of you.'

Then the crew slow-marched out of the pub, carrying the unconscious Calli aloft and humming the Death March, and all the others joined in. Someone grabbed flowers from a vase and placed them on his chest.

'How can you let him get in that state when you know he doesn't drink?' Daisy asked Bruiser, who almost dropped his skipper in order to converse with her for the first time.

'He'll be fine,' he replied, giving her his soppiest grin.

'He's on Ops tomorrow, though, doesn't that worry you, you idiot?'

Bruiser grinned as though she was addressing him with words of warm endearment. 'But that's when he'll be fine,' he said fondly, now looking down her blouse. 'As soon as he gets a whiff of oxygen it'll clear his hangover. It's the best cure there is.'

Daisy sighed deeply. 'Avert your eyes again, or you'll need more than oxygen as a cure.'

'How can I help it?' he asked. 'I love you, you love me, you're mine, and that gives me rights over where my eyes go.'

Daisy shook her head in exasperation and wandered off.

Daisy next saw Calli the following day, when he sat down at her table in the NAAFI and asked where he could find Eileen.

Daisy looked at him as though he were an insect. A nice boy she might have thought him, but a Fly Boy he still was.

'You can forget it, she didn't take your silly proposal seriously,' she replied, looking away from him as an indication of dismissal.

'Why not?' he asked.

'Why not what?'

'Why didn't she take my proposal seriously?'

Daisy gave him one of her severest looks, but he didn't flinch. 'Look, sunshine,' she said, 'Eileen's an innocent, a good girl. A *really* good girl, if you get my drift, and there's a childhood sweetheart to consider, bastard that he is.'

'Oh, he doesn't matter now,' Calli replied amiably. 'And why is he a bastard?'

'Because all childhood sweethearts are,' Daisy snarled. 'They get their hooks into some nice girl and hang around so that no one else can get near her – while he's bedding everyone else's girl – then they marry her and destroy her.'

'And this childhood . . . ex-childhood sweetheart of Eileen's, he's like that?'

'They all are,' Daisy said quietly. 'I'll bet you're a childhood sweetheart yourself.'

'No,' Calli chuckled back at her.

'What? A good-looking boy like you and you don't have some poor little deluded female waiting for you back in Canada?' Daisy sneered.

'No,' Calli replied again, looking directly into her eyes. 'For me there's just Eileen.'

Daisy looked at him for a moment, then she laughed. 'Look, Fly Boy,' she said firmly, 'I'll get her, but understand this – if you mess her about I'll remove your balls with a fork. Is that clear?'

Calli lifted a fork from the table and handed it to her. 'If I mess her about, I'll help you,' he grinned.

So Daisy fetched Eileen for him, against her instincts, it had to be said, and within minutes he and Eileen had disappeared to change into civvy clothes and had departed from the base in a borrowed sports car.

Daisy had been thoroughly dazed. It was so unlike Eileen, and after all Daisy's warnings, too. They tended to listen to her, at first at any rate, so it was hard to take in that Eileen had just upped and gone off with a Fly Boy like that. She felt she should protect Eileen; she had recognised her as someone like herself, that's why they had become such good and close friends, the closest friend Daisy had ever had.

She had been closer to Edith than Celia and Violet, and closer still to Dotty, but Eileen was a good degree closer than any of them had been. How long was it? Two short months, but life-changing seeds had been sown, and not just in one life, but in many.

Daisy had her mind on other things, that was the point. It was just one of those times, so much to think about. Frank Moran was still writing to her and she was still ignoring him and having his letters sent back unopened. Edith had written to say her cousin and the two sentries who had been attacked had recovered well, but when the two men had been brought before the court, the judge, on hearing they were merchant seamen on Russian Convoy Duty, had admonished them and set them free without penalty. They were important, that was the message every WAAF took from that, far more important than some females playing with balloons, anyway. The WAAFs had asked for rifles to protect themselves like male sentries, the *Daily Mirror* even took up their case, but nothing happened. The girls were left with whistles and truncheons between them and rape and murder.

Then, Daisy had another letter, this time from Dotty, something that was happening less and less. Daisy dreaded opening

Dotty's letters in case they contained a hurt accusation over the unwanted contact Frank still insisted on making with Daisy, but although this letter was painful, it wasn't about the handsome Australian.

'Daisy, darling, I have a favour to ask, and I'd like it passed to as many of the girls as possible. I know you're terribly busy, but can you possibly spare the time to help? I know you're such a good person and I'm imposing on our friendship, but I'm hoping you'll agree.

'We have a Corporal here at Princess Mary's RAF Hospital, a male nurse who's come up with a brilliant idea. As you know, being burned is the greatest fear of all aircrew, apart from dying, of course, because the pain is excruciating. Even if the patient lives, the disfigurement all too often makes normal life impossible. As burned hands heal they also contract into claws, and so more painful surgery is needed to release the fingers.

'The answer is a strong but pliable frame to support the healing tissue without letting it contract, but there's been no such thing, until our Corporal had his brainwave – WAAF cotton suspender belts! You know those two bones in the front panel? Well how many of us really need them? We just take them out and throw them away.

'So I got to thinking and gave our Corporal a bundle I got from the girls down here, and he experimented, placing one bone at the wrist, and others inside each finger, fastened loosely at the top and then tied to the bone at the wrist. The result was that the fingers couldn't curl up as they healed, because they weren't strong enough to push against the suspender-belt bones. Then, as they became stronger and stayed straighter, pushing against them helped exercise the muscles too.

'What I was thinking was that if we could get all the girls to help, we could get a box in every base to drop the bones into and then they could be sent here so that more frames can be made to treat burned airmen. Do you think you all could be bothered? I keep thinking of Frank. Spit pilots are more at risk from burns than others because they

sit behind the fuel tank, so if they're hit and go down the burning
fuel comes into the cockpit, and sometimes there's a problem with the
hood. I don't know if you know that.'

Yes, thought Daisy, I think I've heard that somewhere before . . .

That evening, another of the dreaded domestic nights, Daisy read out the letter – missing out the last part – and produced a box.

'Right, everyone, if you've left your bones in, off with the suspender belts and out with the scissors!' she ordered, and the girls removed the garments, giggling, and set to work.

'I'm sure I saw a little pile of them somewhere,' said a voice.

'Remember where and get them,' Daisy said.

'How does she know we don't need them?' demanded a well-built WAAF.

Daisy looked at her sternly. 'Well, even if you *do* need them,' she replied sweetly, 'the lads need them more.'

'Fair enough,' replied the WAAF with a shrug.

In a short time the letter was read out in every hut on the base and other letters were sent to other bases, though no one realised at the time that the anonymous Corporal had made a breakthrough in the treatment of burned hands, or that they were contributing to it, even if one or two waistlines would bulge slightly for the cause.

But Dotty had also told Daisy another story, one that did the heart less good. At her base, which was non-operational, word had come through that a badly damaged Lanc was coming in to make an emergency landing. The place was full of Americans and B-17 Flying Fortresses – their version of the British Lancs – and when the word spread the American aircrews rushed to the tarmac to have their first look at the real thing. Two of the

Lanc's four engines had gone, the turret and the tail – the areas that housed the mid-upper and tail gunners – were no longer there, and the fuselage was riddled with bullets. As it came to a halt everyone was relieved that there was no fire, so the fire crew weren't needed.

Then the pilot stepped out and said, 'My navigator's injured, both gunners are dead,' and an American doctor and orderlies removed the navigator and rushed him to hospital in the waiting ambulance. Other medical orderlies moved in to remove the bodies of the two gunners, coming out with the mid-upper gunner first, then making their way to the tail to recover the other body. Tail End Charlie no longer existed in any recognisable form, though; he was simply splattered on the inner surfaces nearest the tail. The orderlies came out of the plane and sat on the ground being sick. They had never seen such horror and were too shocked to act professionally. The pilot climbed into a Jeep to be driven away.

'Is it *always* like this?' an American voice had asked.

The pilot looked at him wearily. 'It sometimes is,' he'd said.

Dotty said the Americans had been as boisterous as everyone expected them to be up till then, giving out handfuls of candy to everyone, making a noise, sure that now they were in this little war it would soon be cleared up, they'd have a little fun and get back home again in no time. But after the Lanc landed they changed, they seemed to understand for the first time what the boys had been up against during the years of the war America had missed.

One August night at Langar, Eileen wasn't on duty in the tower. A new lot of WAAFs had arrived, giving them more than they needed, so there were more rest days and leave. One of the new lot, Pearl, was with Daisy in the tower. Pearl was a small, dark-haired, very pretty girl who had a way of turning her head at an angle when she looked at you, and Daisy had immediately identified her as being a magnet for Fly Boys. It was raining lightly, but takeoff was just takeoff, nothing to mark this one as different from any other.

Lady Groundhog had been shot up shortly before, the mid-upper gunner and Tail End Charlie had been badly injured and the two replacement boys had barely had time to shake hands. When they'd come back from the first incident Daisy and Eileen had been on duty and had watched the ambulances take the injured gunners off, then Calli, Bruiser and the others lay on the tarmac, wrestling with each other and capering about like children in their relief that they'd made it home.

Tonight didn't seem different, but it was. Daisy couldn't explain it, but she'd bumped into the Lady Groundhog crew in the NAAFI earlier and Calli had seemed subdued. Daisy had grown quite fond of him. He was a decent boy, she thought, though she hadn't given him any more of a chance than the others at first. He was treating Eileen well, too, no messing about.

Once, Calli had stared at Daisy from a distance with such concentration that she had turned round as though he had called her name, and she found she couldn't look away. Usually it was Bruiser who caught her attention. Bruiser would and frequently did do anything to make her look at him, and finding herself staring at Calli had quite unnerved her, though she hadn't known why. She was sure she had read his lips saying 'Poor Daisy'.

'Do you see that Fly Boy of yours?' Daisy had demanded of Eileen. 'He called me "poor Daisy". What the hell does he mean by that, cheeky bugger!'

'I'm sure he didn't,' Eileen had laughed, 'he wouldn't have dared!'

'He'd better not,' Daisy scowled. 'I don't mind him calling me an old hag, but I won't have him calling me "poor". You tell the blighter that.'

She'd never forgotten it, though. It irritated her because she couldn't really be sure what he had said, if he'd said anything, and she couldn't ask him either because it would have sounded silly, even to Daisy. Still, she liked him, and that night in the NAAFI, as he sat with his crew, he looked particularly anxious, though going up with two gunners he didn't know would do that to any pilot.

'What's wrong with you, Fly Boy?' she asked. 'Eileen finally come to her senses and given you the elbow?'

'No, your luck's right out there, Daisy,' he replied. 'But keep hoping, you never know.'

'Then what's up with your ugly mug?'

'Oh, nothing. Just thinking, you know.'

'I'm thinking, too,' Bruiser said, smiling at her. 'Ask me what I'm thinking about.'

'You have no capacity for thought,' Daisy retorted, dismissing him with a look and returning to Calli.

Bruiser jumped up and offered her his chair with exaggerated gallantry. She glanced at him and sat down without thanking him.

'You're not worried, are you?' she asked Calli.

'No more than usual,' he grinned. 'I've always thought about my family back home, but now there's Eileen to think about as well, that's all.' He looked up at her. 'It's just me letting myself be spooked, new gunners and all that. Just me being spooked.'

Daisy didn't know why, but on the spur of the moment she kissed him on the cheek. 'See you later,' she smiled, drawling in her best Mae West tradition, 'I'll be waiting for your call.'

As she turned to leave, Bruiser shot to his feet, yelling, 'She's mine, you Canuck bastard, she's mine! You should never trust these farm boys!' and started wrestling with Calli. Then the others joined in, apart from the two new gunners, who weren't quite part of the family yet.

'Daisy, Daisy!' Bruiser yelled after her. 'Daisy, I'm more spooked than this Canuck bastard, I need a kiss!' and she waved a regal hand in his direction and smiled without turning round. 'I'll be coming to collect when I get back!' he shouted, and the boys all laughed, but she felt Calli's heart wasn't in it and for some reason it made her feel cold.

He had such a decent expression in his eyes, she remembered. He was the real thing, no longer the nice boy from Canada, but *the lovely boy*, she thought, now that she had got to know him a little better through Eileen.

Lady Groundhog was bound for Italy, a long mission, and as the plane went off all the girls cheered, waving frantically, wishing the boys a safe journey and an even safer one home again.

But Lady Groundhog didn't come back.

Daisy sat in the tower all night with Pearl and a few of the others, long after all the planes had been accounted for, long after they had been stood down, waiting for something more than silence. They were chatting in that nervous way, trying to sound so natural and unconcerned that they sounded unnatural and concerned, then they heard steps on the concrete. Daisy opened the tower door, ready to curse Lady Groundhog's crew for keeping them from their beds, but there was no one there.

'Did you hear that?' she asked one of the girls.

'Yes, it was flying boots, but I didn't see a plane coming back.'

'Doesn't matter,' Pearl grinned, 'just so long as they're back.'

They looked out of the door and across the tarmac but there was no one there.

'Stop messing about, you bloody idiots!' Daisy said, trying to cover her relief. 'Some of us have beds to go to, you know!'

Still there was no one there, and the girls sat down again, confused and a little shivery, to wait for Lady Groundhog to return or make contact.

Soon after that they received a message ordering them again to stand down. The last aircraft was now confirmed lost. The message was timed exactly to when they had heard the foot steps.

'I was sure I heard flying boots,' someone said. 'You can't mistake them, can you?'

'No,' Daisy smiled tightly. 'I thought I heard them, too. Maybe someone put something in our tea tonight.' And suddenly it hit her that she would never again see Bruiser's silly grin and she fought down a sob. She was a WAAF, more than that, she was Daisy Sheridan, and Daisy Sheridan was always in control. Besides, she had something to do now and she would need all her self-discipline and her wits about her.

16

Daisy walked back to the hut with Pearl to face Eileen, unsure of how she should break this news, unsure even of how it would affect Eileen, but knowing it had to be done. After her officer at West Drayton had broken the news of her own family being wiped out, Daisy had thought about it and realised that she'd done it quickly, no holding back in a kindly attempt to break it gradually, so she decided she would do the same with Eileen.

It was six in the morning when they reached the hut, and before they went in Daisy and Pearl arranged that, as Eileen's closest friend, Daisy should do it alone. Pearl had been very quiet, understandably so, and Daisy was afraid she might break down in front of Eileen, and that couldn't be allowed to happen.

Eileen was standing by the window, her back to the door, as Daisy came in.

'Are you all right?' Daisy asked. 'Why are you up at this hour?'

'Just couldn't sleep,' Eileen said, smiling. 'What about you? You look exhausted.'

'It's been a bad night,' Daisy said wearily. 'You know the kind.'

'How bad, Daisy?' Eileen asked, her arms folded, watching her.

'The worst, Eileen,' Daisy replied, and fought to go on. 'Lady Groundhog has been confirmed lost. She was seen crashing, she was on fire and there were no parachutes seen.'

Eileen closed her eyes and rocked slightly on her feet.

'Eileen?'

The girl put a hand up and said quietly, 'It's OK, really, it's OK. Don't panic.' She stood for a moment then sat on her bed. 'The poor boys,' she said. 'My God, isn't it awful?'

'It is,' Daisy said, aware that it was inadequate. 'Can I get you something?'

'No, no thanks, Daisy, I think I'd like to lie down.'

There wasn't another word said for hours. Daisy stayed awake because she couldn't sleep and in all that time she didn't hear a sound from Eileen.

They both had a day or so off, a normal day off between two twelve-hour shifts for Daisy, and the final day of a three-day leave for Eileen. Daisy would spend the day with her friend, she decided, make sure she was really OK. The trouble was that she didn't know how close Calli and Eileen were. They had only known each other for two months and even then didn't manage to see each other that much because of their duties. And how close could two people get in that short time?

It was wartime, Daisy knew how fast things could progress in such times, but still, Eileen had liked the boy – who wouldn't? – but she hadn't said anything that gave Daisy an inkling of how Eileen really felt. Calli had made that remark earlier in the NAAFI about now having Eileen to think about, but what did that actually mean?

Daisy must have drifted off without noticing it, a deep, deep sleep that kept her under without a single dream, and when she woke up she was alone, she thought. Then she became aware of a group of WAAF hierarchy standing at the door looking at her.

'What is it?' she demanded angrily.

'Just making sure,' one of them said.

'Making sure of what?'

'That you really were asleep after night duty as it says on the notice on the door. There's a parade today, some girls will use any ploy to escape them, as you well know.'

'And that would be so bad?' Daisy shouted, jumping out of her bed. 'The whole world would come to an end if I got myself off some stupid parade, would it? We'd lose the war because I'd had a kip instead?'

'Consider yourself on a charge for insubordination, Sheridan.'

'Consider yourself a bloody clown!' Daisy shouted back, returning to bed. 'And what's more,' she yelled, taking the in-for-a-penny line, 'only poke your head back in here while I'm trying to kip if you're happy to lose it! Stick that on your charge-sheet, and now get out and shut the bloody door after you!'

Daisy didn't know why she had reacted as she had. The Squadron Leader blamed overwork and lack of sleep after a particularly busy and distressing spell, and he might have been right. They decided to let her off with a warning, something of a first, so either she was invaluable or everyone knew she had been in the right and the hierarchy didn't want to inflame the situation by punishing Daisy.

Not that she cared. She had reached that stage beyond and regarded the whole nonsense as no more than irritating. Her focus was on Eileen, who seemed to be coping amazingly well with Calli's loss, and there was something in the back of her mind that wondered if her friend was putting on an act.

After putting in a word for her a week later, the Squadron Leader ordered Daisy to use some of the leave she had built up and go off somewhere. She would have refused, but the weather was bad and flying was put off for a couple of weeks.

'And even if the weather was clear, you know perfectly well there won't be any flying,' the Squadron Leader teased her, 'the boys would refuse to go up unless you were at least on the premises.'

Eileen had already gone on weekend leave to London to meet up with Alex, her childhood sweetheart, before he joined his ship, but she was back in the hut when Daisy returned from being rapped across the knuckles.

'What did you get?' Eileen asked, looking up.

'Told to be a good girl in future,' Daisy smiled sweetly.

'They'll be lucky!'

'Told to take some time off, too.'

'One of your famous London orgies would do you the world of good,' Eileen grinned, 'they always put some colour in your cheeks.'

'You're sure you'll be all right?' Daisy asked Eileen, but she was already reaching for her bag.

Eileen was writing a letter. 'I'm fine, stop worrying, mother hen!'

'Who are you writing to?'

'Alex,' Eileen smiled in reply.

Daisy grimaced. 'The bastard childhood sweetheart?'

Eileen nodded.

'Typical of him to join the navy!' Daisy snorted. As far as she was concerned even the senior service was vastly inferior to the RAF. 'Never mind,' she continued sweetly, 'at least that gives us the possibility that he might drown.'

'Daisy!'

'Well,' Daisy muttered, 'bloody childhood sweethearts, they shouldn't be allowed.'

'Get on your way,' Eileen grinned at her. 'Leave this place, it's making you bitter and nasty!'

'Oh, no,' Daisy said seriously, 'I was like that when I joined up!'

Rose Cottage was just what Daisy needed; peace, sleep, comfort plus coddling and gossip from Mar, though it was hard to switch off at first. Mar still had no idea what Par did in London, but he was much busier these days, she said. Things had livened up since Dunkirk and he wasn't about as much, and when he was, he was very tired.

'Don't bother dressing for dinner, darling,' Mar told Daisy, 'that's Par's thing, not mine. Besides, we have a few of Dotty's waifs and strays at the moment and I think it would be a damned cheek to ask them to go to the trouble after what they've been through.'

'How is Dotty? I haven't seen her in ages,' Daisy said. 'We write every now and again, but she's busy, she really loves her work.'

'Yes, I know!' Mar yelled. 'Isn't that quite something? Who'd have thought it? She was here a few weeks ago, when that Australian Spitfire Johnny came down. Remember? One of the chaps Freddy brought with him the first time you were here?'

'Freddy!' Daisy said, neatly dodging the question. 'How is he?'

'He's in North Africa now,' Mar said. 'Been promoted, something big, no idea what. Keeps promising to send me bananas.

I was thinking about that the other day, in fact. Can you remember absolutely pining for bananas before the war, Daisy? I can't. Now I think about them a lot — lack of, if you see what I mean. Par says I'm not missing bananas at all, they're just phallic symbols and I'm missing a bit of the other with him being away so much.'

Daisy burst out laughing.

'I said he was wrong, of course, that I was thinking of very *large* bananas, and all I remember seeing when he was here more often were very *small* ones.' With that she threw her head back and shrieked, the noise filling the huge sitting room. 'He's been wandering about saying things like "Walls have ears", and "Down every plughole is an enemy lughole". I said to him, "Par, I do hate it when you've been drinking and you pretend to be witty." Didn't do a blind bit of good, of course, he just said "Careless lips sink ships".'

Tea was brought in just then, and sponge cake with jam and cream bulging out all round, and they sat in companionable silence for a while, then Mar leaned forward, looking around as though the walls really did have ears.

'Between you and me, Daisy,' she said, eyes narrowed to slits, 'I can't quite see our Dotty with this Australian chap, can you?'

'I have no idea,' Daisy said quietly. 'I remember him, but not all that well, we only exchanged a couple of words, but I do know they've been writing to each other since then.'

'Nice chap,' Mar said, shaking her head, 'and Dotty is clearly besotted, but I can't see that he is.'

'Well, I wouldn't worry about it, they obviously planned to be here at the same time, didn't they? There must be something there.'

'And you, Daisy? No one stolen your heart?'

'Not me,' Daisy replied. 'If you knew the heartache I've been dealing with up at Langar. No, not for me, I'll wait till after the war and just hope life will settle down first.'

'Good for you!' Mar leaned forward and gave Daisy's thigh a gentle slap. 'You're a sensible sort, Daisy, you've got the right idea. Have some fun and don't get caught too young!'

Upstairs in her luxurious bedroom, Daisy wallowed in the soft, comfortable bed and thought of Dotty and Frank Moran being at Rose Cottage together. Like Mar she had thought the affair was one-sided, but maybe she'd been wrong. Maybe Frank had finally realised that he'd be far better off with Dotty after all. As Daisy fell asleep she was trying to work out why she felt good and not so good about that.

Daisy had been at Rose Cottage for a week and was beginning to feel she should go back to Langar. It was always the same, that's what the other girls said when they went home. You yearned for it, but after you'd been back a couple of days you just wanted to leave again. Their war work had changed them; they had less in common with their relatives and friends at home, though they felt guilty about it.

Mar threw a spanner in the works, though, by producing a tall, thin American who had been sent by Dotty to recuperate.

'Just wondering, Daisy,' Mar said quietly, 'if you'd do me a very great favour. I wouldn't ask this of anyone else, but you and I know each other, don't we, Daisy?'

'Mar, what is it?' Daisy asked.

'Well, you know that lovely quiet chap, the one who survived being shot down in his Flying Castle?'

'Fortress,' Daisy said. 'Flying Fortress, Mar.'

'Really? Well you know these things, I suppose. Been here a month now, name of Hal. I think he needs some younger company and a bit of fun. Still a bit shaky, mind you, but would

240

you take him to London for a few days, show him the sights, take him to a few parties perhaps? You can use the flat, Par's never there, he's always doing whatever it is he's doing, probably sleeps at the Windmill, I shouldn't wonder.'

What Daisy wanted to do was go 'home' to Langar. Apart from anything else she was anxious about Eileen, though she certainly seemed to be coping well, but Daisy knew there was no way of refusing Mar anything, especially after all Mar had done for her.

So Daisy took Hal to London, holding his hand because it was trembling, taking small steps and pretending to believe he was as strong as he pretended. He'd been the only survivor when his B-17 had been brought down, and, though he was badly hurt, he still felt guilty that he had survived and the others hadn't. 'One of the guys had only been married two weeks,' he told her. 'Another one had this beautiful kid, barely two years old.'

Hal was, as Mar had said, still pretty shaky and prone to crying at odd moments, and Daisy found it incredibly difficult to see this tall, good-looking and obviously once strong man in tears. Only he wasn't a man, he was just like the others, a boy away from home and in danger. He wasn't anywhere near recovered, he had no real strength, and when she took him to parties at the usual haunts he had had enough in a very short time, and she had to take him back to the flat and sit by his bed talking to him until he fell asleep.

It reminded her of Dotty's descriptions of sitting by the beds of dying men, and Daisy understood her friend better for the time she spent with Hal. He was from Boston, his forbears were from Scotland, he told her, and she felt herself suddenly thinking of Calli, the Scot who was Canadian, Eileen's lovely boy. Still, she listened, knowing that Hal would talk himself out, hearing the words grow fainter and his breathing deeper, before going to her own bed and weeping for everything, for everyone.

They were due back at Rose Cottage the next day, Friday, so she took Hal to a farewell party at the Dorchester, watching him for signs of weariness or distress, which she could tell by the tremor in his hands and the way his eyes darted back and forth so quickly that they couldn't possibly be seeing anything. They left before the blackout to make their way back to the flat, her arm firmly linked through Hal's, almost holding him up, when she heard her name being called and looked round to find Frank Moran with a very attractive blonde.

For a moment she couldn't speak, only stared stupidly, then she tried to cover it by making it look like one of her dismissive expressions. It didn't work, though, she couldn't compose her features quickly enough, though she didn't know if anyone else had noticed. If *he* had noticed, that's what she meant, she realised.

'What are you doing in London?' Frank asked, examining Hal.

'Seeing the sights,' she replied as haughtily as she could, looking at the woman who was hanging on to Frank's arm, 'much the same as you are.'

'This is a friend,' he said in an irritated voice.

'Ditto,' Daisy said. 'Hello, friend, this is Hal, he's from Boston.'

'So where are you staying?'

'At Mar and Par's flat,' she said, and he nodded; he knew where it was and had obviously been there. Who with? she wondered, then wondered why she had wondered. 'But we're going up to Rose Cottage tomorrow,' she said, to forestall any invitation being extended or asked for. He nodded again and they stood looking uncomfortably at one another. Daisy was glad the other woman was there, her presence stopped anything more meaningful being said by either of them, but at the same time she was annoyed, which made her feel as if the situation was slightly slipping out of control.

'Well, we must get back to the flat before the blackout,' she said. 'Give my love to Dotty when you next see her.'

Frank looked distracted. 'Dotty?' he said. 'Why would I be seeing Dotty?'

'Why wouldn't you?' she asked. 'You were at Rose Cottage with her, weren't you?'

Frank's woman was looking bored. 'Look, how long does this old pals act go on for?' she complained.

'It's finished as far as I'm concerned,' Daisy smiled sweetly.

'I wasn't with Dotty!' Frank said, his face flushing.

'What? Oh, you still on about that?' Daisy asked distantly.

'I thought, well, I heard she was going to be there, but I'd hoped she wouldn't be alone.'

'Well, she wasn't, was she?' Daisy said. 'You were there too. Anyway, what does it matter?'

'It just does, that's all!'

'Look, if you two are just going to stand here and argue . . .' the woman said.

'We're not,' Daisy replied shortly. 'Good night, and if you can't be good, be careful!' It was the kind of trite remark she hated, but he deserved it, she thought, though she didn't really know why.

Daisy took Hal back to the flat and sat beside him till he slept, then she crept to her bed again and lay down, but she couldn't sleep. Instead she went over every word, every look, every slight silence that had passed between her and Frank Moran. Her nerves felt jangled. All those nights in the tower dealing with really crucial stuff and she had never felt like this.

Yes, jangled, that was the only word, and why? He was only a man, after all, and she didn't want him, had pushed him away more times than he should have needed to get the message.

Daisy lay on the bed trying to make herself calm down and stop going over the shock meeting. Sleep would come, she told herself, if she composed herself.

Then there was a loud knocking at the door. Daisy looked at the clock: it was after eleven. Maybe the wardens had noticed a chink of light. She checked the curtains just in case on the way to the door, but they seemed all right. She was always careful about things like that. Then before she could open the door she heard Frank's voice demanding to be let in. She opened it slightly and he strode past her.

'What the hell are you doing here?' she whispered fiercely.

'I want to know why you returned my letters,' he said, striding up and down angrily, and she realised he must have departed with the blonde and then worked himself into a temper.

'I told you not to write, that's why,' Daisy said very calmly; she wasn't going to allow him to dictate the tone of the conversation. 'Now would you please leave, I don't want you to waken Hal.'

'What was wrong in my writing to you?' he demanded.

'I've already explained that. What was wrong,' she said slowly and precisely, 'was that I didn't want you to write to me. Am I speaking to myself here? And keep your voice down, I told you, Hal's asleep.'

'I don't give a buggery damn if Hal's asleep!' he said loudly.

'Well I do!' Daisy replied. 'Now why don't you go? No one invited you in.'

'I want to know why you keep running around with Yanks!' he said, trying to lower his voice.

Daisy was surprised. She had never been out with a Yank

up till now, and this was a duty rather than a tryst. 'Why shouldn't I go out with Yanks?' she demanded quietly. 'And more to the point, what business is it of yours?'

'It demeans you,' Frank answered. 'It gives you a helluva reputation, or should I say it adds to it?'

'Say whatever you want, I don't care,' Daisy said casually, Mae taking over. 'But I don't see why Yanks give me a helluva reputation. Isn't it the same with Australians, then?'

'The point is,' he said, almost clenching his teeth, 'the point is –'

She looked at him, arms folded, and raised a quizzical eyebrow.

'– that you only seem to like these flash guys who're only out for a bit of fun.'

Daisy shrugged and smiled. 'Right so far,' she said.

'And I'm not offering a bit of fun, I'm offering something more than that, and you're not interested.'

'Well, we're agreed on that, so why are you worked up? And while we're on that subject, who are you offering what to? Dotty, or the blonde who was hanging on to you earlier on?'

'She was nothing!'

'Oh, nice,' Daisy said sarcastically. 'That says so much for you.'

'Well, I won't be sleeping with her if that's what you mean!'

'Blown you out, has she?'

Frank closed his eyes for a second and she could see the muscles of his jaws working. 'Whereas,' he said, opening his eyes, 'you are sleeping with that Yank.'

'And I repeat, this is your business in what way?'

He stared at her in silence, his eyes a mixture of anger and hurt. 'I should've known what you were like,' he said angrily. 'The other boys told me. Word travels, but I wouldn't believe them, I said there was something pure and good about you.'

'Next time you'll know better,' Daisy told him icily, 'next time you'll believe your friends, who obviously know better than anyone else, and next time you might even have the guts to call a whore a whore. Now, if there isn't anything else, I should get back to the bedroom before Hal wakes and realises I'm not there. Good night.'

As Frank's footsteps retreated down the stairs Daisy moved to the window, opened the curtains a tiny chink and tried to watch him, but in the blackout she could only see a vaguely moving shape. Well, that was the end of him, she thought, and then she did something that she would regret for the rest of her life, that she would feel such shame over that she would never be able to think of it without her cheeks flaming. What possessed her she would never be able to fully understand.

Creeping into the bedroom where Hal was sleeping, she pulled back the covers and slid in beside him. Then, holding her breath, she placed her hand on his stomach and slowly slid it downwards.

Suddenly her wrist was caught in a vice-like grip. 'I can't, Daisy,' Hal said quietly.

She was overcome with embarrassment. 'I'm sorry, Hal . . . please . . . I don't know . . . forgive me,' and she tried to get out of the bed.

'No, it's OK,' he said dully. 'I mean, I *can't*, physically, I mean. I'm sorry, Daisy . . .'

She felt even worse. After everything he had been through, to have put him in the position of having to admit that, to have made the boy say it to a female. What kind of person was she? She ran to the bathroom in the darkness, locked the door and was violently sick, then sat on the floor and wished she were dead.

If the roles had been reversed and she had been a man,

what would she have done about Hal's refusal? she wondered. When it came down to it, was she any better than Dessie or Celia's Bobby? How could she have done that, or tried to do that, to a poor, defenceless boy, and could she have gone through with it?

Hal knocked on the bathroom door and she came out, head down with weariness and defeat. He put his arms around her. 'It was that guy, wasn't it?' he said.

'Yes, it was that guy,' she admitted. 'I'm sorry, Hal, it didn't concern you, I shouldn't −'

'Ssh, I understand. You were mad at him, is all.'

'Yes, I suppose I was.' Her clumsy attempt to seduce poor Hal was a reaction to Frank's contempt, that was clear, but why inflict it on the first vulnerable human being she came across?

The next morning, thankfully, Hal didn't mention Frank's nocturnal visit, nor hers, and neither did Daisy. They travelled to Rose Cottage, where she collected her things before climbing into the Rolls for the journey back to Langar. There were hugs from Mar and the usual hamper, of course, and all the time Hal stood in the background till the car door had closed, then he went to her window. The boy reached in and took her hand, his thumb making little circles between her thumb and first finger, and finally he whispered to her, 'And when I can, Daisy, I'll come looking for you. OK?'

He had such a gentle smile that she felt on the point of tears. 'OK,' she said, squeezing his hand but not making eye contact.

As the Rolls pulled away she reflected on all they had been told about the Yanks, that they were crude, had no manners, and were full of bluster and noise. Yet Hal had been so gracious, so kind, when she had been the one to overstep the mark. She hadn't felt the least attraction to him, that's what made it all so vulgar. Whatever the reason she had made the tacky approach, it had nothing to do with him, she had only been using him. God, but she was feeling so mixed up she didn't know if she was standing or sitting. How could she let any man, least of all a Fly Boy, do this to her?

17

Once Daisy had arrived back at her hut in Langar she was met by a worried-looking Eileen. It must have hit her, she thought. As soon as Eileen had been left alone in their room, the reality of Calli's death had hit her, and instinctively Daisy reached out to hug her.

'It's Celia,' Eileen said, catching Daisy's arms before they could go round her.

'What do you mean?' she asked.

'Daisy, sit down,' Eileen said, still holding her arms and forcing her to sit on her bed. 'Daisy, Celia's dead.'

People talked about everything spinning; now Daisy knew it was true. 'Was there a raid?'

Eileen shook her head. 'They've told her relatives her appendix burst, but it wasn't that.'

Daisy stared at Eileen.

'After you'd been gone a week she came to me in a state. She was looking for you, really, not me, thought I'd know where you were. She was sure she was pregnant and wanted you to help her get rid of it.'

'But why? She was married!' Daisy gasped.

'She said that it had been a mistake and the last thing she

wanted was to be stuck with his child after how it had been conceived. She said you'd understand and that you were sure to know someone who'd help her. I told her I only knew you were in London, and that you'd be back very soon, and she nodded and left. I thought she would wait, but apparently she didn't.'

'What happened?' Daisy asked, all sorts of horrific pictures forming in her mind.

'I don't know who she went to,' Eileen said quietly, 'and whoever gave her the name isn't likely to talk now. Next day she went into Nottingham, as far as I know, that's where she said she was going anyway. When she came back she was quiet, but she had been for a few days. It was the next morning she was found. She didn't get up and everyone assumed she'd slept in, which of course she never did, and when they went to wake her she was unconscious. The bed was covered in blood, it was pretty awful. They took her to a civilian hospital, but it was no good.'

They sat together for a long time, Daisy on the edge of her bed, Eileen kneeling on the floor, holding Daisy's hand.

'I can't believe it,' Daisy said miserably. 'All she had to do was wait a few days and I could've arranged for someone to see her in London. She wasn't the first and she won't be the last, why didn't she wait?'

Eileen shrugged. 'All I can think of is that she really wanted it gone, that she couldn't bear the thought of it being inside her any longer.'

'But to think of her in such a state!' Daisy whispered. 'I never knew she was feeling so bad, I thought they'd just got off to a bad start.'

'Who knows what anyone else is really thinking, Daisy?' Eileen said sadly. 'It wasn't your fault, it was no one's fault. It just happened.'

'But she came to me so often, all I did was say it would all be better one day soon. What sort of a friend was I? I shouldn't have gone, I should've taken her more seriously.'

Daisy had woven such a convincing fiction, aided by the constant movements of service life, that no one would have been able to contact her. Dotty, the only one who could have tracked her down, had been posted at least twice since leaving Langar, and the girls now in the hut, Eileen included, knew nothing of her friendship with Dotty anyhow. Daisy's tracks had been superbly covered.

Celia's new young husband, Bobby, suddenly sprang into her mind. 'What about her husband?' she asked.

'He thinks it was her appendix, too. The other girls said she had been a bit off-colour for a few days, so that helped. One of the others said that was the usual story, that the girl had a burst appendix, but Celia was married, as you say, so why did they cover up that she had been expecting?'

'Oh, to save the boy, I suppose. Didn't want him to feel it was anything to do with him and leave him feeling guilty about it,' Daisy said wearily. 'It's a man's world, Eileen, no matter which way you turn.'

They sat in stunned, sad silence for a moment.

'And there's the other thing, not wanting to raise suspicions,' Daisy said.

Eileen looked at her quizzically.

'Well, if she wasn't pregnant then she couldn't possibly have died as the result of a botched abortion, could she? And it was her appendix, so she wasn't pregnant, was she? How is the boy anyway?'

Eileen shrugged. 'Pretty much as you'd expect,' she said.

It had all gone, Daisy thought, all her supposed ability to cope. Somehow she had lost any control over what was going on around her, and yet the more she thought about it, the less she understood how it had happened. Daisy had everything worked out, that's what everyone said, and what she herself had thought, yet in the past couple of months it had all gone wrong and now there was a hint of panic in her mind. For some reason her carefully constructed cover was collapsing and she didn't know how or why.

She'd felt something slip when Lady Groundhog hadn't come back. There had been real grief where there should have been simple sorrow for lost boys from her squadron. They had got through the outer shell she had created and she should have been aware of that at the time. She missed them as people, not just as 'some of our boys', and found it hard to picture Bruiser without her eyes filling up. Dear, silly, affectionate Bruiser, who punched people yet didn't have an unkind bone in his body. Once that crack in her armour had appeared others ran off it in different directions, so many that she was finding it almost impossible to hold the facade together.

Two weeks at Rose Cottage should have done the trick, but then Mar, who hadn't known how much Daisy needed the rest, had suggested the disastrous trip to London, culminating in the scene with Frank and her dreadful attempted seduction of poor, sick Hal. And all the while Celia had been in Langar and in a panic that would cost her her life.

Why hadn't she taken more notice of Celia's problems instead of just comforting her? 'There, there,' she'd said, when bright red flares should have been going off in her mind – had she been paying attention, that was, and she hadn't. She had let so many people down. Now Celia was another one to be mentioned in sad tones around the stove on domestic nights, another casualty of the war.

For weeks afterwards Daisy had dreams of trying to hold a

cracked jug together as the water came out in drops before inevitably exploding in a great flood that she chased after. The jug dream took its place with the others, of Dessie coming to find her, of the sound of her mother's breathing.

No one had breakdowns in those days. It wasn't the done thing, and even Molly, who had been removed from Langar in total secrecy and silence, was regarded as weak, somehow. You coped any way you could without bending, far less buckling; whatever it took, the stiff upper lip had to be maintained. In a bid to cope, Daisy had become this other Daisy, the one who knew everything, who supported everyone, who could withstand whatever life threw at her, her own life as well as everyone else's, and if she wasn't that Daisy, then who was she?

The war had dictated that coping was all that mattered and, like millions of other people, Daisy was doing that and had been doing it throughout her life. In her early twenties that was more than enough to break anyone's resolve, and she was just a girl herself when all was said and done, a girl with no one of her own to turn to.

As if to underline Daisy's failures, Eileen confided that she, too, was pregnant and was about to marry the dreaded childhood sweetheart, though the child wasn't his, it was Calli's.

'You won't think I'm a good girl now,' she confided in Daisy.

'You want to keep Calli's baby and so you have to marry somebody,' Daisy said simply. 'Why not? He thinks it was him anyway, doesn't he?'

'Yes,' Eileen wept.

The childhood sweetheart had been drinking to give himself courage on their night in London and Eileen had put him to bed. When he woke up the next morning he thought they must have slept together, so he was doing the decent thing in marrying Eileen before he went abroad on active service, as he had wanted to anyway, even before finding out she was pregnant.

'It's not fair, though, is it?' Eileen asked sadly.

'Nothing's fair, Eileen,' Daisy said, hugging her. 'Losing Calli wasn't fair, neither was losing Bruiser; the war isn't fair and neither is life. You just do what you have to do.'

Well, that was that loose end safely tied up, but she should have seen, and once would have, that the relationship between Eileen and Calli had been deep and sincere. So she had let Eileen down, too, left her to deal with her grief because she hadn't realised it was there.

They went through the motions, going to London for the marriage, with Daisy as the bridesmaid, and she was almost happy to discover how much she disliked the bridegroom. She had never reckoned much for childhood sweethearts and, as far as she could see, this one was typical of the breed, though Eileen insisted that he was a nice chap. Still, at least he would serve the purpose of giving Calli's child a father, though not the father he or she should have had.

It was a quick service in a Registry Office with the bridal party in uniform, as so many were these days, then back to a local pub for a 'celebration'. Every now and again she and Eileen would make eye contact, both thinking of Calli, and Bruiser too, who would have been best man, and they had to look away to stop breaking down.

Daisy imagined Bruiser's silly delight at being a real couple with her, and at a wedding of all occasions, and felt deeply sad. As it was, the best man had been unable to take his eyes off her breasts all day. At one point she wondered if he would have rather shaken hands with them than her, then realised she was being silly – of course he would.

As they sat in the pub being desperately bright and happy, Daisy quietly picked out a beer bottle in case she should need it. Finally, under cover of being drunk, the best man made the fatal mistake of trying to stick his hand down the front of her blouse, and in one gloriously graceful movement Daisy lifted the bottle and broke it over his nose, broke his nose, too.

At least it made Eileen laugh, genuinely laugh, for the first time that day. The groom thought Eileen's sadness was because he had to leave immediately and there would be no wedding night to make the earth move, so Daisy also got a wry smile out of the proceedings.

Then, the happy event over, the groom and his blood-stained best man made their way back to their ship and the bride and bridesmaid went back to Langar.

Three months later Eileen 'discovered' she was pregnant and left the service for home, to become a lady-in-waiting, both for the child and the return of her husband, the 'father' of her child. Daisy missed her desperately.

And there was the Frank situation, or lack of it. It had finally been brought to an end. He no longer wrote to her, which was what she had wanted, and yet she was bereft, suddenly feeling his loss on top of all the others. She recalled a conversation she had had many, many years ago it now seemed, with Joan Johnstone and Mrs Armstrong in Fenwicks. 'Don't let the love of your life get away from you,' Mrs Armstrong had told her, 'no matter what anyone else thinks or says.' And now, when it was too late, she wondered if that was what she had done.

Long walks in the countryside as autumn turned to early winter were Daisy's only solace. She tried to think of the past months as a wound that was healing and setting into a scar. All she had to do was calm herself and move on as she had done before, but there were times when a voice in her head would ask, 'Move on where?'

Still, there she was, all these terrible things had happened; things she would once have spotted and nipped in the bud; things, further more, that she had caused to happen. Now all she could do was try to recover and not dwell on the past, because dwelling on the past might well cause the floodgates to open completely and she would drown. Close those doors, Daisy, close the doors. Don't think about it; get on with life. Things could have been worse, there were successes. Look at Eileen.

18

One of the good things about friends moving on during wartime was that there were new ones always being recruited to fill the gaps. In Daisy's case, Pearl was one of her new friends. And you didn't always lose the old ones. Edith was frequently at Langar because of her Australian.

'You always call him my "Aussie",' Edith laughed. 'Can't you use his name? I mean, surely he's proved himself a non-bastard by now, Daisy. No secret wife and children, no other notches on his joystick?'

'*Other* notches?' Daisy said, faking shock.

'Forget I said that!' Edith said quietly. 'It was a slip of the tongue.'

'A slip of something, I'll grant you,' Daisy said, looking at Pearl beside them. 'And since when does clever, serious Edith make slips of the tongue anyway? The security of the realm depends on you and you make slips of the tongue?'

'Oh, shut up!' Edith said, embarrassed. 'Anyway, his name's Doug, I want you to call him that, OK?'

'Seems, Pearl,' Daisy said archly, 'that we are being presented with a true romance here.'

Edith pushed her and they all laughed. 'He'll be here tonight,' she said, 'and I want you to be nice to him. You remember nice, Daisy, it's when you bare your teeth without biting!'

They were on their way to an ENSA concert, one of the entertainments put on for service personnel, though things didn't always work out for the artistes who thought they were doing their bit for the war effort by performing for those actually involved in it.

It was here that 'Edith's Aussie' truly became Doug. He earned his stripes as far as Daisy was concerned, though she already half-approved of him because Edith had asked her to. He was a solid little man, dark eyes and fair hair and quiet, it seemed, until during the variety show a conjurer by the name of the Great Walendo asked for a volunteer from the audience and Doug got up and joined him on stage. When he was asked to pick a card he chose the wrong one, only to produce the right one from his pocket. The conjuror looked confused. Next was the hidden bottle trick, or it was hidden until Doug stepped forward and uncovered a whole collection of different bottles all hidden under each other, until the hapless conjurer's table was covered in them.

The audience roared with laughter and Doug gazed back in complete innocence, as though completely unaware of what he was doing. The Great Walendo decided to go for broke and brought on one of the leggy dancers from the show, a real trick, knowing that the attention of the males in the audience would be on her as he sawed her in half.

'Which half would you like to take back to base with you tonight, gentlemen?' he asked, thereby unwittingly losing the female section of his audience.

'Oh, get on with it, sunshine!' Daisy called out wearily. 'There's a war on, you know, or there was when we came in here!'

'Is that the one you took back last night?' the conjuror asked, addressing the males once again.

'Heard it all before,' Pearl shouted at him, adding for good measure, 'you *erk!*'

Now that the audience was taunting him the conjuror decided to get on with the act, and with a great flourish he pulled the trick cabinet apart to reveal two distinct halves of the lady in question. Doug didn't need a flourish, he just pulled a compartment door and revealed her real legs, still attached to her body.

The audience were now engaged in a contest. It was their boy or the Great Walendo, and their boy was willing, though he appeared to be unaware of being in the competition. In desperation the magician brought on a cabinet, enticed another leggy lady of the company to enter it, went through a diverting performance of locking the door, then unlocked it and revealed an empty cabinet. Doug stood applauding. Then another beauty was 'disappeared', and another, till the Great Walendo was visibly growing in confidence and stature. That's when Doug struck again. As the Great Walendo was taking extravagant bows at the front of the stage, Doug walked to the magic cabinet and pulled a curtain at the back, uncovering another door, from where the leggy lovelies had escaped behind stage. The Great Walendo departed to catcalls and opinions that he had misspelt his name – 'The Great Wally, mate, that's who you are!' – sweating profusely and glaring at the straight-faced Doug.

The show comic, Tony Hancock, was rushed on stage to save the night and quell the audience. He pulled it off by appearing before them wearing a tutu and army boots, but it had been a close-run thing.

Afterwards the girls wanted to know how Doug had managed to upstage the Great Walendo so effectively.

'I did a bit of conjuring back home,' he said quietly, 'and he was so sloppy I couldn't let him get away with it. I hate sloppiness. If we were as sloppy as that in our jobs we'd never get through a mission. As far as I'm concerned that applies to his war effort, too.'

From that moment Edith's Aussie was Doug.

Six months after Eileen's departure as a respectably married mother-to-be, word had come through that she had given birth to a daughter. More than anything Daisy wanted to see the two of them, but that would have to wait till after the war.

Meanwhile there was Rose Cottage. Freddy, Dotty's pilot brother, was there, insisting she come down to London with him for a party. By now this was a rare occurrence for Daisy. She was very choosy these days, much preferring to stay at Rose Cottage.

'Who'll be there?' she asked calmly.

'It's to welcome a crowd of Americans,' Freddy explained, 'so the usual crowd plus the Yanks.'

'Will Dotty and Frank be there?'

'No,' he replied sadly. 'Little sis is too busy attending to the sick these days, can't drag her away from the hospital, and poor old Frank is stuck in some God-awful wilderness off the map to the north.'

'Oh, that's a shame,' Daisy lied. 'It would've been good to see them both.'

Question answered, she was safe, so she agreed to go, with nothing more than the vague prospect of a little diverting fun in mind. There she was approached by an American Major – she was sure he had said his name, but she hadn't taken much notice. Why bother when she wouldn't see him again?

'Well,' the little man drawled, 'I'm glad I stayed single, this is the gal I've been looking for all my life!'

Her heart sank. She wasn't fooled for a minute, there was undoubtedly a Mrs Major stateside, as they liked to call America. Daisy had rarely seen a more married man. He was around forty, short and dumpy with a dark moustache and a swarthy complexion, of Italian extraction, at a guess. He probably imagined he looked like Clark Gable, though he'd have to stand on a box for a start, even before you got down to comparing the features, and he did not fare well there either. At best, a very bargain-basement Clark Gable, she thought. He looked the kind of man who was used to his shirts being freshly ironed and laid out for him every morning by Mrs Major, and more fool her for marrying him in the first place.

Still, presumably Mrs Major had been an innocent girl once herself and hadn't known what she was getting into. She was probably sitting at home now, maybe with a couple of swarthy kids who didn't look like Clark Gable either, being loyal and true, worrying about him and praying that he would come home safely at the end of the war. It was something she had noticed before, the tendency among the biggest prats to marry decent little women who doted on them and, more importantly, trusted them, so maybe she was right. More fool Mrs Major, she should've known better.

It was part of a universal male arrogance that made men think they knew women, and there was no reason why Yanks overseas with the Forces shouldn't believe it, too. Men were men, after all. All females want to get married, that's what they thought, and with some reason. Most unmarried females were regarded – and regarded themselves – as failures if they hadn't been graciously picked off the shelf and their lives legitimised by marriage by the time they were in their twenties.

But not all, Daisy thought, definitely not all, as she tuned out of the Major's pitch. He was saying something about dinner sometime and she smiled distantly.

'I work in the Langar tower and I don't get leave that often,' she replied, employing her tried and tested looking-for-someone gaze about the room.

'I can always get transport,' he suggested, 'and come up there.'

Her mind was only vaguely on him. She was thinking about that other Yank absolute: that the plucky little Brit variety of female, or dame – she cringed at that; no one ever called her 'dame', well, not twice, anyway – having endured years of drab existence before America entered the war, and who would doubtless have to endure years more when it had finished, wanted desperately to marry Americans and have access to the great American dream. It had become a joke with the WAAFs once she'd knocked them into shape. They'd return from a weekend leave in the fleshpots of London and announce, 'Guess what, girls? I'm off stateside next week, Beauregarde is having a mansion built for me beside his oilfields in Brooklyn.' The others would immediately chip in with news of their engagements to a host of similar oilmen and cattle ranchers from deepest Manhattan. 'Ah, but,' the first one would ask, 'do you have one of each variety? I think this one's my fourth this week!' Every American male knew this fervent desire of the plucky little Brit female to be whisked off stateside was carved in stone, so that's what they offered to get what they wanted, and the Major was no exception.

'Oh,' she said, still not concentrating on his conversation, plus she had found that 'Oh' worked pretty well in these situations for a while.

'In fact I can take you anywhere you want to go, little lady,' he boasted.

Suddenly a plan formed in her mind. Anywhere? Did he say anywhere? 'I'm sure you're just saying that,' she said in a flirty voice.

'No, no, I mean it, name your destination,' he said, delighted by her change in tone.

'Well . . . no, it's too much to ask,' she smiled, gazing at him over the rim of her glass.

'Say it,' he said excitedly, 'just say it and it's yours!'

'Well, it is far away,' she said, 'and please say if you can't do it, I won't think any less of you,' meaning, of course, that she would. 'I have this friend in Glasgow that I'm just dying to see, a girlfriend.'

He gulped.

'Oh, I'm so sorry,' Daisy said sadly, 'I've asked too much, please forgive me. Obviously that's way too far.'

'No,' he almost yelled, 'no, I can do that. No problem, just tell when you want to go and I'll arrange that!'

God, they were so easy!

Eileen's departure had left a huge gap in Daisy's life. It had taken her by surprise even though it was the way of their world these days, these years; after all, people were always coming and going for one reason or another. Eileen, she decided, was special. The affection and friendship between them would have been as strong even without the war, so it was natural that she should miss her, and she had turned her mind to her friend's new life.

It hadn't been as simple as love, marriage and family for Eileen, but to the outside world and, more importantly, to Eileen's childhood sweetheart, it looked that way. The plan had worked. If Daisy was honest she hadn't expected to see Eileen again, not really. A new leaf is a new leaf after all, who wants last season's mouldy ones turning up to spoil the greenery? But the Major's 'offer' changed her mind. On her next weekend she would pay a flying visit to Eileen and the baby in Glasgow, if he could pull it off, that was.

Much to Daisy's surprise, the Major came through, for which she was grateful, even if she hadn't yet worked out how she would make him pay for his generosity, rather than the other way round. The only usual way of getting around in wartime was on a slow-moving, cramped train, usually full of predatory servicemen, and it had been part of her reassessment of herself that Daisy Sheridan did not travel steerage. The little Major had promised transport and transport he had provided, and she felt a pang of, not sympathy exactly, more pity for the Major when she laid eyes on the staff car he turned up in at the base the following week.

This was no front-line vehicle, no basic London run-around either; the poor besotted and deluded Yank had obviously called in a few favours to lay hands on a more luxurious model than his rank allowed him, purloined rather than provided, she imagined. The back seat was roomy with comfortable leather upholstery and armrests, and the windows had dinky little curtains held back with a strap that made them look almost homely, despite being a boring shade of brown, colour being one of the many things that the world had to give up for the duration. It also had a radio that seemed unable to play anything other than the Glenn Miller Orchestra. Not that she minded for the first couple of hours, but she had grown up in a house full of music, and if she didn't hear dear old Glenn's 'Chattanooga Choo-Choo' ever again she wouldn't protest over-much.

Situated in front, on the board separating the passengers from the driver, was a flap that folded down to provide a serving table for a small bar, complete with booze, glasses, cocktail shaker, cherries and olives. If there was one thing Daisy had learned it was that wartime rationing applied to only the poorest sections of the population. There was always plenty of food, drink and luxuries in the circles she now mixed in, especially now that the Americans had arrived. On the outside of the passenger doors was the usual large star, and miniature stars-and-stripes flags flew on the bodywork above the two front wheels, so that everyone seeing the car pass by would be in no doubt that an American of some note sat inside.

America liked to advertise itself. It was a proud nation, or arrogant, Daisy thought with a silent grin, depending on your opinion of the Yanks being 'overpaid, over-sexed and over here'. On hearing this well-known put-down, some wit, usually someone who had joined up on the outbreak of war, would yell out, 'And over-late, just like the last time!', a judgement on the American habit of entering world wars somewhat later than the rest of the world. They had been embarrassed into entering the 1915–18 show in 1917, only because their President could no longer ignore the rising number of American ships being sunk by the Germans, and WW2 in 1941, when Japan launched its infamous attack on Pearl Harbor. Few Americans were spared teasing when they did arrive on the battlefield. Now that they were finally here the word was that the war was all but over. There were rumours of some big push coming up, but by May 1944 how many times had the world heard that kind of rumour? Until it did or didn't happen there was no point in thinking about it, let alone believing anything would bring the end of the war any closer.

If there was one thing Daisy had learned in her twenty-odd years it was that being cynical saved you a lot of grief. And she would shortly be in the place that had caused her most of it. Newcastle. It couldn't be avoided, it was the price she would have to pay to see Eileen and the baby.

They would be going via Newcastle, the Yank being sure she would want to see her home town, apparently. She didn't, as it happened, but why argue, so she steeled herself to see Newcastle again for the first time in years, gazing out on the depressingly dull landscape. Her home town, whatever that meant, and she had sworn she would never be back here, yet here she was, though she had no intention of stopping.

One thing was sure, she thought, the city slipping past her eyes as the car sped on, she wouldn't be back here again, never, not even if Eileen had quads! There was nothing to come back for and, furthermore, her home city had been full of that same nothing for her for as long as she could remember, with one or two exceptions, now all gone. Looking at familiar scenes she felt no emotion, just a deep gratitude that she had no connection to the place any longer, though there was an illogical anxiety to be gone, as though a huge hand might reach into the car and snatch her out, as a voice said in a thick Geordie accent, 'Got you, Daisy Sheridan! Thought you'd escaped forever, did you?'

The stuff of nightmares, she thought with a shiver, and it had been a recurring nightmare, that hand and that voice. The war had thrown up more horrors than she could ever have imagined and she had coped, but the 'Newcastle Hand' dream was something else. It told her Newcastle was where she belonged and was waiting to reclaim her when the war ended.

Not that it wanted her, it hadn't ever wanted her kind, the Irish were no more welcome nearly a hundred years after their arrival than they had been on their first day there. No, it didn't want her, but it owned her and at least there she wouldn't be allowed to be any better than she should be, the Geordies would see to that. Newcastle would take her back to punish her for Bernard's folly in coming to the area.

Not if Daisy could help it, though. In these last few years she had learned that it was possible to be noticed for what you could do, for your worth, not for the sound of your surname. And for how you presented yourself, she thought with a grin. A little acting ability went a long way.

They stopped at Coldstream, a little place in the Borders, where they lunched on the contents of a particularly fine hamper the Major had provided, full of succulent items that the people outside the car hadn't seen for a long time, if ever. Then it was on to Glasgow, a dark city showing the results and atmosphere of years of war.

When they arrived at Eileen's home she noticed that her friend had altered in some indefinable way. Motherhood, she supposed. After the hugs and tears she gazed at the beautiful, ugly little bundle Eileen held in her arms, a dark-haired little girl called Anne, after Calli and Eileen's mothers, and Martha, after both their grandmothers, two coincidences that doubtless had convinced them that they belonged together forever. The little girl had a vertical line of annoyance between her eyes that so reminded Daisy, and Eileen, too, no doubt, of her father, who had died without knowing she had been conceived.

'She's beautiful,' Daisy cooed, 'she's really beautiful!'

'I know,' Eileen laughed.

'And the image of –'

'Her father, yes,' Eileen said sadly.

'And you're well? Everything's, you know, all right?'

Eileen nodded. 'Everyone up here sees her like Alex,' she said. 'They had the same colouring, if you remember. Dark hair and eyes, that's all they see.'

'Well that's OK then, isn't it?'

267

'Yes,' Eileen replied, but it didn't sound convincing.

'So what's wrong?'

'Oh, I don't know. The plan has worked out, Daisy, but at the end of the day Calli's still gone, isn't he?' She laughed uncertainly. 'Just being ungrateful, I suppose. At least I have Annie, don't I? And what about you? The Yank, is he the one?'

'Oh please!' Daisy said dismissively. 'You know better than that! He was fool enough to try to impress me with claims that he could provide me with transport anywhere I wanted to go, so I called his bluff, that's all.'

'He'll be hoping for something in return, though!' Eileen chuckled.

'No harm in hoping, is there?' Daisy laughed. 'People do it all the time!' And they laughed together almost like the old days of nine short months ago.

'So there's still no one special?' Eileen asked.

'No,' Daisy replied brightly. 'I'm surprised you even ask!' Her mind tried to suppress an image of Frank Moran.

'And how are the others?' Eileen asked.

'Well, I think Edith and Doug are fine.'

'Doug?'

'Yes, I decided to graciously allow him a name other than "Edith's Aussie" after she asked me to, and besides, he's really all right.'

'For a Fly Boy,' Eileen teased.

'Exactly!' Then Daisy told the tale of Doug versus the Great Walendo to justify her change of heart about him. 'Besides, he doesn't consort, if you get my meaning. He and Edith may well win.'

'Well, then, that's good. And Dotty?'

'Up to her ears in sick Fly Boys, from the little I hear from her. Not at all the gadabout she once was.'

'It comes to us all, Daisy, we all have to grow up,' Eileen said. 'Except you, of course, you were born grown up!'

I wish, Daisy thought, laughing back, I wish.

All too soon the visit had to end so that Daisy could be back in Nottingham for her shift the next day. The two young women clung to each other and wept.

'Will you keep in touch?' Eileen asked.

'Of course, of course. And you'll send pictures of Annie for the girls to go gooey-eyed over?'

'Yes.'

'Eileen?'

'Yes?'

'Will we ever see each other again?'

'Of course we will!'

'Honestly?'

'Get on with you, you silly cow!'

The visit to Eileen had been a brief one. It had felt as though there had barely been time to say 'Hello' before the car was turned round and the return journey started. Daisy doubted if the driver had time to step out from behind the steering wheel, and now Glasgow had been left behind as they headed once more in the direction of Nottingham. On the journey south they would pass through Newcastle again. Oh joy, Daisy thought.

The anticipation that had made the journey up from Nottingham seem short had disappeared. Now she was pensive, a bit down, though she was having difficulty fully understanding why. The American Major beside her was totally oblivious, prattling on as usual. On the way up he had regaled her with the merits of the various bridges crossing the River Tyne, almost lapsing into poetry when he talked about the big iron one, as though he thought that just because she had once lived there he was praising her by association.

There was probably a compliment in there, she thought, if she felt like looking deep enough, which she didn't. Still, there was little to be gained from being unpleasant. Nottingham and Glasgow were both a long way off and she didn't feel like walking to either, especially if he pushed her out of the car in Newcastle. A fate worse than death, she thought glumly. So she sat there smiling as required, while thinking that the only good thing about the bridges, even the iron one, was that they took you out of Newcastle, north or south, it didn't really matter, just as long as they took you away.

On the return journey the driver had noticed the changed mood in the rear seat and was glancing back more often. He could have been watching the traffic very carefully, of course, except that he was making eye contact with her in the rear-view mirror, so either he was concerned about her or he was just giving her the eye. Probably the latter, she thought with a sigh. He was a man, after all, and few of the breed didn't chance their luck where Daisy Sheridan was concerned.

Sitting in the back of the staff car as it sped through Newcastle, Daisy was thinking of her life, past and present, and wondering what the future held. She looked at her reflection in the car window. If she had seen a woman like herself when she'd been growing up, she would have said, 'She's a film star.' The Adelaide or the Empire cinema screens were the only places women like her existed where she came from. She shook her head wryly, remembering the child she had been: Background Daisy. She had no idea how the transformation had come about, but somewhere inside the woman of the world who stared back at her from the window, she knew that 'the real Daisy Sheridan' was still alive and waiting, even if she wasn't quite sure what she was waiting for. Not that it mattered; she suspected life had been arranged so that there would always be something else to wait for, but maybe everyone felt like that, especially in wartime.

The war had been a godsend to young people like her. It had given them freedom, even if that freedom meant death. You never really thought about the death part, not at the time, just the freedom, until death touched you at any rate, and it had touched Daisy in many ways these last few years. She was hardly alone in that, though. There was no going back, certainly no going back home, not least because Newcastle had never been home.

Daisy could feel a sense of danger lurking if she let her mind wander down that road, so she sighed again and tried to turn her thoughts to something else. She had always had trouble switching her mind off. 'Too bright', that was what her father always said, though not bright enough to see *that* one coming, she thought, hankie at her eyes again. That was the trouble with long journeys, especially in boring company. They gave you time to think, and Daisy didn't want to think, at least not now. There would be plenty of time for that when she got back to the base.

RAF Langar was her domain, where real life existed. Now Eileen and their friendship existed in another time and she suspected that time was over.

Oh, God! There it was again, that prickly feeling behind her nose. She closed her eyes and swallowed hard, trying to think herself away from the moment, trying desperately to come up with a different thought. She opened her eyes again and stared determinedly out of the car window on her right, as the American Major's southern voice drawled on – about the bridges again! Dear God! Into her left ear the words went, as irritating as a buzzing insect she couldn't risk swatting, at least not yet, in case it stung her. Why did they always think they should, or even could, provide diverting conversation? she wondered, nodding at various intervals in his monologue as though she gave a damn.

Having finally managed to get up to Glasgow to see Eileen, she now realised she had been as unprepared for what she found as she had been for Eileen leaving Langar. An old friend and her new-born daughter, that was what she'd expected to see and that was what she had seen, but her own reaction had thrown her. And now here she sat, weeping quietly in this talkative Yank's staff car, or some other Yank's staff car, more likely, wishing he'd shut up.

It was over, completely over. As they parted it felt like they had just seen each other for the last time, which made the whole sad, sorry affair that much more touching. Daisy knew, knew without a shadow of a doubt, that they wouldn't keep in touch, far less meet again. The first time she had seen that beautiful, ugly little bundle Eileen held in her arms would be the last time, too, she realised, though she suspected she would always wonder about her and never be able to get her or Eileen out of her mind for the rest of her life.

The whole world was bleak, of course, had been for years, but Daisy had never felt so trapped in it as she did now. She felt alone and friendless now that Eileen – and Annie – would fade from her life. She pictured Eileen waving her off, Calli's precious child in her arms. There was something strangely touching about true love, and something infuriatingly stupid as well, almost as infuriating as the way her eyes kept filling up.

Why was this happening when everyone knew Daisy Sheridan didn't do tears? Tears were for the defeated, the ones who couldn't think themselves out of a paper bag. Tears were an admission that there was nowhere to turn, and, as a matter of principle, Daisy always had somewhere to turn. Daisy thought round corners, in advance, tactically. That's who she was: people, especially her girls on the base, depended on it. And yet, and yet. There had been something totally disarming about the sight of Eileen and the tiny, unsuspecting little soul that had caught her off-guard, another female brought into the world fighting from her first breath, before that, in fact. Why was it that females had to battle for everything?

It was always the innocents who came a cropper, Daisy mused. How many times had she said that to yet another intake of fresh-faced young girls into the ranks of the WAAFs? 'Look after yourself,' she would say, 'because no one else will,' even though she was doing just that. 'Don't take *any* chances,' she told them sternly. 'Don't have anything to do with Fly Boys. They're men, they're only after one thing, and they want it today because there might not be a tomorrow, for them especially. And they'll use that line every time, so don't fall for the "I may be dead tomorrow" routine. What you have to remember is that that's not your fault, it's Hitler's, and I don't see any Fly Boys demanding their oats from that bastard. Don't give in, because when they've had what they want they'll leave you in one way or another. They'll go on to the next innocent or they'll die, and you'll be left to pick up the pieces. Keep away from them at all costs, and if they give you any trouble, come to me and I'll sort them out.'

And she'd been right, too. Eileen was the latest living proof of that. She should add that to her next speech: 'Look at my friend Eileen, my ex-friend Eileen.'

She dabbed at her eyes again and the American Major smiled at her. 'Never mind, honey,' he said kindly. 'One day that will be you.'

Daisy returned his smile, but inside her head she said, 'Don't bet on it, sunshine!'

And it wouldn't be, it would never be her. Never. She glanced at the Major from the corner of her eye. They all thought they knew women, but they didn't, and the male chattering on beside her was no exception. All he had was the wherewithal to provide himself with a few luxuries, and he regarded Daisy as one of them, though she saw it differently. These days she knew how to deal with these situations.

For instance, with the Yank, she allowed him only what she chose to allow him. There was no chance of gaining Daisy Sheridan's favours with a couple of packs of stockings and a Hershey Bar. Daisy Sheridan was never short of stockings and she didn't like their Hershey Bars. There was nothing special about their Hershey Bars, yet the Yanks handed them out as if bestowing the purest gold.

She closed her eyes again to indicate that she would welcome silence from Major – what the hell was his name anyway? she wondered, and smiled to herself. She hadn't bothered to learn it, not that it mattered. She knew from the moment she'd met him that he would ask her to marry him. It was how all the Yanks operated, and she was tempted to accept with gushing enthusiasm, just to see the look on his face as he backed away in panic, but she would be civil to him until they reached Nottingham. He'd taken her to Glasgow and back after all.

Eileen and her baby popped into her mind again and she pictured Calli's handsome young face. 'Eileen's lovely boy,' she murmured.

Beside her, the Major – she must try to remember his name, she thought, or maybe not, seeing as she had already decided he wouldn't be around long enough to justify her taking the trouble – said, 'Boy? I thought you said it was a girl, Daisy?'

'Yes,' she replied quietly. 'Must be lack of sleep, it is a girl.'

He *had* been a lovely boy, Calli, she thought, slipping back into the company of her own thoughts. He had been one of the few males who hadn't tried it on with her and had looked her in the eye, so he was a hero to Daisy for that alone, even if she'd given him a hard time. She had given Bruiser a hard time, too, but he hadn't seemed to care, refused to even recognise it because he was so sure she would eventually fall for his charms.

She wished now that she could have done things differently. Calli MacDonald was different. Just when she had given up hope of ever meeting a male who wasn't like all the others, along came Eileen's lovely boy, with his dark brown eyes and matching dark brown curly hair. He'd certainly been a looker, but there'd been something more about him, too.

Daisy grinned, remembering. Decency, that was what he'd had. No wonder she had trouble putting it into words, it was a long, long time since she had seen it.

True love, she thought, true bloody love. Everyone seemed to be searching for it, but who needed it? Because Eileen had loved Calli she hadn't wanted to get rid of his child. Now she was condemned to the dreaded childhood sweetheart. Still, as Daisy had said at the time, with any luck the bastard wouldn't come back, then Eileen would be free, to an extent at any rate. She would survive the war with Calli's child but no Calli, though no bloody childhood sweetheart either.

In the back of the American staff car the Major was gearing up to strike. Daisy sighed and looked out the window. It was always so unoriginal, that was what insulted her, apart from the fact that they tried at all, of course. There was no wit, no finesse, either they weren't capable of it or didn't think she would understand it. She had never been able to work out which.

'I was thinking, Daisy,' he said in a smarmy voice, his attempt at seduction.

Without looking at him she imagined him twirling his moustaches like a villain from a silent film, if he'd had moustaches, that was, instead of a little bar of stubble under his nose.

'I was thinking,' he repeated, close up to her left ear, making her think of Dessie, 'that we could stop somewhere instead of going all the way back tonight.'

Out of the corner of her eye she saw the driver look in his rear-view mirror and grin at her.

'No,' she said lazily, 'I don't think so.'

'But you're not on duty till tomorrow night,' the Major persisted. He was clearly the kind who believed girls said 'No' when they meant 'Yes'. 'Surely you'd be fresher if we stopped somewhere.'

'No, I wouldn't,' Daisy replied. She turned to bestow a severe stare on him. 'What you have in mind isn't a night of rest and relaxation, is it? But I'm sure you're a real beast between the sheets, so I'd only end up exhausted.'

He looked bemused, not sure whether to deny he was a beast between the sheets or to say he intended being a gentleman and would leave her to sleep alone.

'Besides,' she said, before he could think his way out of that one, 'I'm emotionally distraught. Didn't you see me crying? What kind of man would force himself on a lady in distress?'

'I . . . uh . . .'

'Is *that* the American Dream you all talk about?' Daisy continued, her voice rising with every syllable. 'Are *all* American men like you?'

'Well . . . I just thought . . .'

'Oh, I see now what you thought!' she accused. 'Do her the tiny favour of supplying transport for two old friends to see each other after they'd been through a hard time together, and one's sure to join you in the sack, that's what you thought!'

'No, no . . .'

'You should've mentioned it back in Glasgow, maybe the new mom would have been so grateful she'd have obliged! Would that satisfy you, having your way with a mom with a baby at her breast? A mom desperately worried about her husband in danger on the high seas?'

He couldn't think of anything to say, so she delivered the *coup de grâce*. 'I'll tell you what,' she said tearfully, 'just stop the car here and I'll walk all the way back to Langar. I thought you were a decent man, a friend who was prepared to do a favour for another friend without asking for payment of any kind, and now I find out that . . .' Here she subsided into sobs. Well, it had to come somewhere and this was as good a place as any. If he accepted her offer she wasn't too far away from Langar, and she'd find a lift easily, everyone stopped for service-women.

'Now, Daisy,' the little man said, almost sincerely, 'you have misunderstood. I was thinking of you, only of you. I was thinking of how upset you've been –'

Clever! she thought.

'– and that what you needed was a good night's sleep before going back on duty. Not for one minute was I thinking of taking advantage of the situation, and you can take my word on that as an officer and a gentleman.'

'Well, I'll get a good night's sleep in my own bed at Langar,' she explained quietly and primly. 'Then I'll have the whole of tomorrow off to relax before I go on duty in the evening. We still have plenty of time to make it back before the blackout.'

'Yes, yes indeed,' the Major said firmly. 'My thoughts exactly. Driver, carry on!'

Which is more than you will, she thought. With me at any rate.

The rest of the journey passed in silence and when they reached Langar the car pulled up at the gates. The driver came round to open the door for her to get out.

'You're good, Ma'am,' he winked at her.

'Sunshine,' she said, fixing him with a look, 'I'm the best, I'm the best there is.'

'At what?' he asked, laughing quietly.

'Now *that* you'll never find out,' she smiled demurely, 'but you're free to fantasise.'

'Yes, Ma'am!' he said, chuckling as he saluted and turned to climb back in the driving seat, then he spun round to face her again. 'I was wondering,' he grinned. 'Just what *would* it take? I mean, what's the price?'

'More than you'll ever be able to afford, sunshine,' she said casually without looking back as she walked away, 'even if you live to have millions in the bank.'

As she walked to the WAAFery to sign in, taking care to enter by the back door, she knew the guards had noted not only her return but the staff car that had brought her back, and they would spread the word around. Another chapter in Daisy's reputation. It would do her no harm. Now she would go back to the hut and bring the others up-to-date with how Eileen was faring, or at least the sanitised version of it: happy and healthy wife and mother and beautiful baby girl.

God, but it was all so difficult at times, and when she thought back to how it had all started it made her feel like crying for real. She looked out at the planes on the airstrip, remembering that when the first Lancs arrived there had been so much excitement. And they were beautiful planes. WAAFs in operational bases knew about planes, and Lancs were so different from the Manchesters that went before them, and with so little alteration, too. The crews had had to learn about them, what they could and couldn't do, so they'd been flying round the clock doing 'circuits and bumps', as the exercises were called, with cross-countries, air-firing, fighter affiliation and all the other necessary ops. One farm worker had been bringing his herd in for milking when he found three of the new aircraft bearing down on him at low level, and he had thrown himself flat on the muddy, cowpat-strewn ground and covered his eyes, unaware whether they were friend or foe. Funny how quickly you got used to such a strange world.

'So how was Eileen?' Pearl asked as Daisy was unpacking.

'Oh, you know, tired.'

'But the baby? Is she pretty? Who does she look like?'

Daisy stopped and drew in a breath. 'Like her father,' she said quietly, 'very like her father.' Which was no more than the truth.

'Will we get pictures?'

'Yes,' Daisy said. 'She'll be sending some when she's feeling more like herself.'

'I expect she's still worrying about her husband,' Pearl mused, head to one side. 'Can't be easy having a brand-new baby and not knowing if the father will ever see her.'

Yes, Daisy thought, something like that. 'Well, there are a lot of women in the same boat, aren't there?' she smiled brightly. 'Can't be easy for any of them. So, anything been happening here?'

'Well, everyone's hinting that something big is about to happen, no idea what. It could all be rumours, though there does seem to be a lot of moving about,' Pearl sighed.

'There always is.'

'Yes, but more than normal, more units and squadrons moving south rather than here and there. It's probably nothing, they'll move back to where they came from and we'll still be hearing rumours.'

Daisy sat on her bed. 'I sometimes wonder if it will ever end,' she said wearily. 'Here we are, the end of May 1944 and we're still fighting a war that, in September 1939, we thought would be over in no time.'

'Yes, I know what you mean,' Pearl replied. 'I often wonder if we'd been told then how long it would go on, would we have been able to take it?'

'It never seems to end,' Daisy nodded. 'We hear things are going badly, going well, but I can see us spending our lives like this, making friends who just disappear, talking to boys in the air, avoiding officers in case we get ticked off for wearing nylons.'

'Trying to find a decent supply of nylons!' Pearl giggled.

Daisy reached into her bag, brought out a pile of nylons and threw them to her. 'Courtesy of a Yank,' she said, 'and don't ask what I did to get them.'

'Oooh, it must have been good whatever it was, or should I say bad? He has been generous beyond all expectations!'

'Oh, and here's something else he gave me,' Daisy muttered, 'another supply of bloody Hershey Bars!'

Not long afterwards they learned that the rumours of 'something big' were true this time. Operation Overlord, the D–Day Landings in Normandy, would be launched on 6th June 1944. It would be the true beginning of the end of the Germans, though the allied casualties would be terrible.

It would be the usual botch–up. Each landing craft carried fifty-six fully equipped and armed troops onto the beaches, but the weather wasn't what they had been expecting and the sea had a bad swell, so a great many died by drowning, dragged down by their packs before they could fire or take a shot. The design of the special tanks was faulty, taking many more to their deaths under the sea, and leaving the troops who got ashore unsupported.

Those who made it onto the beaches fought strong German gunfire that mowed down serried ranks of young men, not counting those who died after stepping on the heavily mined sand. From St-Vaast-la Hougue to Villers-sur-Mer on the beautiful French coastline, Canadian, British and American troops fought their way ashore on the beaches named Utah, Omaha, Gold, Juno and Sword. Names that would remain in the psyches of a generation of Americans in particular, because of the high number of casualties they suffered, especially at 'Bloody Omaha', where they had to climb high cliffs as the Germans shot down on them, turning the sand red with their blood. There may have been early British resentment about the Yanks being 'over here', but when they got 'over there' they earned admiration for their bravery, at the heavy cost of so many young lives. And among those supporting the troop landings was the only all-Australian Spitfire Squadron in the UK, who had earlier been sent to the south coast in preparation for the 'something big' that was D-Day.

Not that Daisy knew anything of this. They were all too busy with their own responsibilities to take much notice of what was happening elsewhere, and she had placed Frank Moran behind one of those doors in her mind marked 'Not to be thought about'.

The news came in a letter from Mar. That young Australian chap, the one Dotty had been keen on, had survived all the way through till the end of August and then been shot down. He was badly burned and had been taken back to a hospital in southern England, apparently, not expected to live. *'And to*

*think he survived the Battle of Britain, too. There's just no justice, my
dear Daisy, is there? Are we likely to be seeing you soon?'*

The words hit her like a brick between the eyes. She felt
dizzy and sick and wanted to get up and run, but her legs
wouldn't move. So what do you do when your bluff's been
called, Daisy Sheridan, not just knocked about a bit in a Mayfair
flat, but actually called? He was going to die. Dead, like Calli
and Bruiser, that kind of dead, the forever kind. Do you sit
here trying to work out your options? Well, there aren't any.
Dead, that's what he'd be. Try to push *that* door in your mind
shut now that it was pushing against the famous Daisy Sheridan
determination. Why? What do you have to gain?

Get up, Daisy, move. Dead. OK, first breathe deeply and calm
yourself, panic never achieves anything. Now put on the mask,
the calm one that people can't see through. D-Day is over,
you've got more leave to take, that's all you're doing, taking leave
that's due to you, no one needs to know anything. Mar would
help, but you can't tell Mar, what with Dotty being besotted
with Frank. Not to worry, any one of the boys will give you a
lift to London, they'd pay to do it and there was always someone
going there. The hospital is no problem, it's only some place
outside London, there's bound to be someone else who's going
that way, lifts are easy to come by. It'll be easy. But what about
Dotty? Well, nothing Daisy could do about that. If he was going
to be dead for her he'd be just as dead for Dotty, but she had
to see him, and sort things out with Dotty later.

She told the nurses at the hospital she was his fiancée, but
when they led her to his bed she didn't recognise him. What
she could see of him was covered in black skin, but, as he had
written to her, Spitfire pilots got the worst burns because they
sat behind their fuel tanks, surrounded by them, too. He was
full of shrapnel as well, and deeply unconscious.

'You're sure this is Frank?' she asked a nurse, and the nurse nodded. There were no points of reference. His skin, where it wasn't burned black, was red and oozing, and his hair had gone. She pictured him in her mind, the tanned, fair-haired, blue-eyed war hero, and couldn't see anything of him in the body in the bed. The smell was indeed awful. It smelled disconcertingly of roast meat, but she remembered what Dotty had said – a smell was just a smell, so what? And what was it Dotty said about hearing? That it was the last thing to go, that even when someone was dying they could hear. So talk to him.

It wasn't easy. She was still far from sure it was Frank, and even if it was, what could she say, especially now?

'Frank, it's me, Daisy. Bet you didn't think you'd see *me* again. If I remember rightly, the last time we talked you were angry, you called me a whore.' She laughed quietly. 'I just want you to know, I'm not. All those stories you've heard about me? Well, they're not true, I just let people think they are to, well, to keep them away from me. I did go to all those parties in London, but I didn't participate, if you see what I mean. But I was seen there, so that was good enough. I've only, you know, *done it* once, and I didn't do it, he did.

'It was my brother-in-law, he raped me, and next day I left home and joined up. There. I've never told anyone that, apart from Mrs Johnstone, and she's dead now.' She paused, near to tears. 'I don't know why I'm telling you this, there's no point, is there? I suppose I wanted you to know because I did everything I could to discourage you and maybe you thought it was something about you, but it was something about me. I wasn't ready to let anyone close to me, Frank, but if I had been, it would have been you.

'And the Yank at the flat? Well, he was an American pilot who'd been shot down. He was very sick. Mar asked me to take him to London to see the sights. There was nothing going on, we didn't sleep together, he was too ill, apart from anything else. All I did was look after him like a child. I was angry with you, that's all.'

It was all coming out in a rush, but there wasn't the slightest movement or alteration in his breathing.

'Besides, Dotty was absolutely stuck on you and Dotty is a good friend and a good person, I didn't want to do anything that would hurt her. I'm really surprised she's not here.'

Still no reaction, and Daisy lowered her head and wept.

For a week Daisy sat there beside Frank every day, reading newspapers to him, reading books, telling him stories about her childhood, about Bernard the 'Seaham Scab', Granny Niamh and how she had been named by the old woman, and her mother's wonderful voice that had been passed on to her sister, Kay. She even went to the local library and looked up the Darling Downs so that she could talk to him about his home. Then, with her leave up, she had to head back to Langar and decided to stop off at Rose Cottage, just for a couple of hours.

'Where have you been?' Mar screeched. 'You look like hell!'

'London,' Daisy replied.

'Well, you've obviously been partying hard by the look of you. Good for you, Daisy! And have you heard about that daughter of mine?'

Daisy shook her head. That was really why she was there, to find out why Dotty wasn't with Frank.

'Her lot were sent to France to bring the injured back, and she married one of the doctors before she went!' Mar giggled delightedly. 'Have you ever heard the likes of it? I don't even know the bounder's name, all she said in her telegram was *"Married a doctor, will introduce you when we get back."* What do you make of that?' She threw her head back and filled the room with laughter.

Well, that was Daisy's question answered, not that it made much difference. Frank might have been free, but he was no better, he could still die. Mar was disappointed that she couldn't stay and sent her back to Langar in the Rolls, thus preserving her reputation at the base, as did the fact that she had to be wakened when she got there. That Daisy, they'd say.

The next weekend she hitched down to the hospital again and spent three days reading to Frank, but there was still no movement and no improvement either, the nurses told her. As she was leaving a doctor stopped her and took her to a side room. He looked as though he hadn't slept in a month, and he probably hadn't.

'Look, love,' he said wearily, 'this chap you've been sitting with.'

'Frank, yes,' she replied.

'Well, I have to tell you, he's not going to make it.'

She stifled a cry and he put a hand on her shoulder. She shrugged it off; old habits died hard.

'The thing is,' he said kindly, 'he's pretty badly burned on the outside, as you can see, but what you can't see is how badly he's burned inside. He was breathing in the scorching fumes as the plane went down, you see, and then there are the shrapnel injuries.'

She looked up at him. 'So?' she said defiantly.

'Look, I'll do a deal with you. If he's still here in a fortnight, I'll call you. You can't go on doing whatever it is you do and hitching down here to sit beside him. You'll exhaust yourself. Where are you based?'

'Langar,' she said. 'I'm an RTO.'

He looked confused.

'A Radio Telephone Operator. I work in the tower, landing planes on their way back from missions,' she explained.

'Well, that's pretty important work, and pretty exhausting, too, I should think. You'll need your wits about you. Look, I'll leave a message with the Admin people there if this chap improves, but I've seen it so many times over the last few years, and there's no way he'll make it. I'm sorry. You would be prosecuted for keeping an animal alive in these circumstances. Sorry,' he said again quickly, 'bad taste. I do apologise.'

She nodded. 'It's probably true, though,' she said sadly.

The next two weeks passed slowly without any word, though she went to Admin every day to check there were no messages for her. Then another three days passed and she couldn't stand it any longer, so she risked being charged by waiting till her officer went off to lunch then nipping in to use her phone. She got through to the hospital, then through to the ward he had been on.

'It's RAF Langar here,' she said confidently. 'We're trying to trace a wounded Spitfire pilot, an Australian called Frank Moran.'

'I'm sorry,' said the nurse, 'we have no one here of that name.'

'You're sure?'

'Absolutely.'

Frank hadn't made it. Frank was dead.

Two days later a letter arrived from Frank. It had been written before his last mission and been delayed by events, as mail usually was. Daisy had been in the habit of returning his letters unopened for some time now, but this one came as a shock, his final letter, so she tore open the envelope and unfolded the pages.

'Dear Daisy, I haven't written for a while, but I have a mad feeling that I might not get another chance. Things are pretty hectic at the

moment. *I just wanted you to know I have never stopped caring about you, despite making an ass of myself the last time we met. We didn't get to meet often, but I knew from that first time, and I think you did too, there's something there, Daisy, though I can't explain it. When this is over, if I make it, I want you to come back to Dalby with me, and I won't give up. I think about you going home with me a lot, but then you know that, and I think about my family and everyone I took for granted while I was there. Had a letter from my Uncle Kevin the other day, my father's brother, he's always been there in the background, part of my life, but I don't think I ever took much notice of him before. Just the usual family stuff, but the thought of him bothering to write to me really choked me up, he has his own sons fighting in faraway places yet he took the time. He's the local ice man, delivers chunks of ice to houses for their ice chests, goes around in a cart with a canvas cover with a thing like scissors, only with clamps, that open wide enough to stretch across the big blocks of ice. People buy either a full or a half block and Uncle Kevin hits a line in the middle with the back of his scissors and splits the block perfectly. You won't know about ice chests, they're rectangular with legs that keep them off the floor, and there's a lid on top that you lift to put the ice on a shelf. Below there's a cabinet for food and a tray underneath catches the melted water. You don't have anything like that here, your weather isn't hot enough. Our ice chest at home is made of wood and Uncle Kevin brings us ice every second day for a few pennies. All the local children follow him around to get handfuls of the leftover ice chips. When I was a nipper it was my job to empty the water from the tray underneath our ice chest, but I always forgot, so we had the cleanest floor for miles around. Anyway, you'll meet him yourself soon enough and have your own ice chest too, if I get through this.'*

She folded the letter, put it back in its envelope and sat for a moment on her bed. So that was that. She closed her eyes to stop the tears and ripped the letter to shreds. Just as well you heeded your own advice about not getting involved with Fly Boys then, Daisy, she thought, even if no one else had. Think of the state you'd be in if you hadn't kept him at arm's length. So, good for you. Frank's dead. *C'est la guerre*, Daisy, *c'est la* rotten bloody *guerre*.

19

News that the end of the war was nigh had been heard so often that no one really believed it, but suddenly it was true. After D-Day the Allies fought on and by December 1944 France and Belgium had been liberated. With the end in sight, the 'Big Three', America, Britain and Russia, met at Yalta on the Crimea in February 1945 to carve up post-war Europe. Russia would carry off the trophies of Poland, Hungary, Romania and the Baltics; Greece, Yugoslavia and Austria would be shared between all three; and France, Luxembourg, Holland, Denmark and Norway would fall within the influence of America and Britain, without the people of any of those countries being given a say. Germany would be occupied by the 'Big Three', plus France, and the city of Berlin would be split into four districts, under the control and administration of the four countries.

Meanwhile the fighting went on and hundreds of thousands more were still to die.

On 24th April 1945, the last major German unit surrendered 200,000 men, though German soldiers were resisting elsewhere. Western POWs were, in the main, set free and made for Allied lines, but rather than let concentration-camp prisoners go free, the sick and starving were marched in front of the hard-driving Allied armies. Thousands more died as a result of the enforced marches and others were killed by their captors in an attempt to get rid of the evidence. Advancing Russian and American Forces liberated camps and found, to their horror, bodies piled high for urgent disposal as the killings were accelerated. General Eisenhower, touring Ohrdruf Camp, ordered local German citizens to be forced to see what had been going on, allegedly without being noticed, in their own backyard. The Russians, who had suffered a great deal in the war, were so feared by the Germans that many took their lives rather than fall into their hands, but even so, in another demonstration of male power, 100,000 German women were raped by the Red Army after the fall of Berlin, and Eastern Germany was sacked of anything of value.

On 26th April, German units in Holland and Denmark surrendered, and four days later Hitler married his mistress then they both took cyanide. Hitler, for good measure, also shot himself, and as Goebbels arranged for the bodies of the bridal couple to be burned, his wife killed their children and prepared their own suicides.

Meanwhile, all over Europe the Germans were laying down arms, and on 7th May 1945 Germany officially signed the instrument of surrender. The war was over. VE Day, Victory in Europe Day, was declared on 8th May 1945. On many RAF stations bonfires were lit to celebrate, and there was singing and dancing all night. At RAF Oakley, the New Zealand Squadron emerged in full Maori dress, descended on the WAAF billets and carried them out of their beds, while chanting, singing and banging dustbin lids. In other places WAAFs 'relocated' potatoes from cookhouses and roasted them over open fires, marvelling at a sight they hadn't seen in six years – fully lit windows all around. Others did mile-long congas around their bases and beyond, got drunk and headed for the streets of London, against orders, to swell the numbers celebrating there.

Dances and parties were held in bases all over the country, but the feelings of joy weren't universal. To many the gaiety was forced. Some felt there was little to celebrate, among them Daisy, who grieved for those who weren't there. She thought of Eileen in Glasgow with Calli's daughter and knew how she would be feeling, of her own family and Joan, of Calli, Bruiser and all the other boys who had died for this moment, including the ones who died with her voice in their ears and whose voices she would carry for the rest of her life. There would be little celebration in so many families, she thought, just renewed sorrow for sons, husbands, fathers and brothers.

And for Frank, of course. In a place called Dalby in the Darling Downs area of Queensland, the Moran family would be thinking of Frank, and they would never know she was sharing their grief. What was it Mrs Armstrong had said all those years ago? 'Don't let the love of your life get away from you, Daisy, no matter what anyone else thinks or says.' But Daisy had, she now realised, and she couldn't quite get her head round the concept of celebration.

Not that the world was entirely free. The Japanese and Burma still had to be dealt with, and while that battle was still raging, Operation Exodus got underway. The Lancs, Flying Fortresses, Ansons, Dakotas and every other plane of the RAF and USAAF were no longer delivering bombs to Europe but delivering human beings from it, bringing liberated POWs home after years of incarceration, one base dealing with 5400 arrivals in one day. Twelve boilers kept going throughout the daylight hours provided hot water for endless cups of tea and for washing, and inside hangar areas were set aside for the returning prisoners to sit quietly, read newspapers and listen to music while the ever-necessary forms were completed. No one could be accepted as safely home, it seemed, unless a piece of paper said so, and WAAF typists worked till their hands ached and cramped to get the bewildered men home as fast as they could.

When the men were fed the girls couldn't help noticing them quietly stealing an extra bit of food and hiding it in their pockets, unable to believe that it would be free from now on, unable to believe that *they* were free. Most of all they wanted to talk to someone, to anyone, and the WAAFs listened patiently, with no one complaining about long hours or watching the clock. How could they, when their main preoccupation during the war had been getting enough leave and nylons and avoiding parades? They had done more than that, of course, but they were only human and found being faced with the results of inhumanity a humbling, almost overpowering experience.

Most of the POWs had been reasonably treated, but not all, and the sight of some of the men would live with the WAAFs till the end of their days. They were like walking skeletons, their bones showing clearly through what was left of their grey skin, and their poor bodies, unwashed for years, created a smell few could forget, even years later. They were deloused, washed, given a medical and then taken by bus to secret locations to be given clothes and allowed to rest before being reunited with their relatives. Then, inevitably, there were so many little personal tragedies for men who had suffered more than enough. Those who returned clutching 'Dear John' letters at least knew what they would find, unlike others who only discovered when they arrived home that wives and sweethearts had gone off with someone else.

After the atom bomb had been dropped on Japan, the final surrender of the Japanese was signed on 2nd September 1945, VJ-Day, Victory in Japan, and the war was finally and completely over. For WAAFs on operational bases, like Daisy, everything seemed to stop. There were no more planes flying missions, and before they knew it, RAF and WAAF demobilisation was taking place. By the end of December 125,000 men had been demobbed and 45,000 women, and the process went on into 1946, on a first-in, first-out basis.

Married WAAFs were demobbed first, then the others waited for their turn to be bussed to Birmingham and turned into civilians again, leaving them with mixed feelings. Since operational flying had ended the military mind had reasserted itself with the urgent need for parades, route marches, PE sessions and the absolute necessity to have every item of kit as polished as possible and laid out for inspection whenever those above felt like seeing them.

It wasn't what the girls had joined up to do, it wasn't what they excelled at, so on the whole they were keen to go back to civvy street. Many had married during the war years and were eager to start normal married life and raise children. It was a fresh start, but adjusting wasn't always easy. Throughout the war they had taken on huge responsibilities and performed them well for years, and now they were expected to go back into the home to become housewives and mothers.

The returning men would, naturally, want to take up employment again, it was only right, so the women who had trained as mechanics, engineers and had driven trucks and ambulances found that though they still had their skills they were no longer able to use them. They were once again 'only' women.

When the time came for Daisy and Pearl to go to Birmingham to be demobbed they felt as bemused at the prospect as the others. They were taken to a large hall with tables around the walls that they had to work their way around, clockwise, being given fifty-six clothing coupons at one, a fourteen-day ration card at the next, then fourteen-days' pay plus credits and gratuity, which for Daisy amounted to £42 – she was rich! Plus there were two further postal drafts for fourteen days each, leave passes and £12 10s for the purchase of a civilian outfit, though they were allowed to keep the uniform they stood in. Little did they know at the time that a female adviser at the Treasury had argued long and hard against giving them such an outrageous amount, saying that a very good civilian outfit could be had for £8 15s.

They also went through medicals, and Sadie, one of the girls from Daisy's hut, was in line in front of her. The examining doctor was Polish, a small man who spoke heavily accented English. 'Show me your tiths,' he instructed, whereupon Sadie undid her bra and obliged without a moment's hesitation.

'No, no! Tiths! Tiths!' screeched the little doctor, pointing distractedly at his teeth as the other girls giggled.

'Now see what you've done, Sadie,' Pearl joked. 'You've caused a titter to run around the room!'

'The oldies are the best, Pearl,' Daisy commented.

'Anyway, what's he so annoyed about? He's the only man I've come across in years who *didn't* want to see them,' Sadie shrugged, doing up her bra again.

'I know some who would've paid,' Daisy laughed.

'I know some who did!' Pearl giggled.

'But never enough,' Sadie muttered, 'never bloody enough!'

Next they were given unemployment and health-insurance cards, their Service and Release Book, and informed that they could purchase 320 cigarettes and seven ounces of chocolate at the nearby NAAFI.

At the end of the bewildering process an officer waited to shake hands with each ex-WAAF and say 'Thank you for coming,' and that was that. Free at last, and, in Daisy's case, with no home to return to. All around her were girls like her who had lost their youth for their country, some crying, some just dazed, all of them bemused and swearing to keep in touch forevermore. Some would, of course, their friendships based on so many shared experiences that, like a great many returning servicemen, left them slightly adrift from their families.

Daisy had already been invited to stay at Rose Cottage for as long as she wanted, her people being 'abroad', and that was where she headed, clutching in her hand an invitation to a post-war cocktail party at the home of Lord Nuffield, the wonderful benefactor who had supplied sanitary towels, radios, sun lamps, wedding dresses and bicycles to the services throughout the war.

Presumably each station had put forward names for the grand event, Daisy thought, though she wasn't really sure why she had been chosen. As the queen of the Langar tower? The gorgeous, sexy creature all men lusted after? No matter, she had no intention of going.

'But you must!' Mar wailed when she told her.

'Absolutely!' Par agreed. 'Nuffield's a wonderful fellow, you know, far more interesting than any of us hereditary shower! If you don't go, I swear I'll throw on a blonde wig and falsies and go in your place!'

'But I haven't anything to wear,' Daisy said half-heartedly. What she really wanted to do was nothing. Her plan was just to drift along, taking walks in the countryside and hoping that a time would come when she could do so without listening for sick planes. What a luxury it would be to look at the sky just for the sake of it.

'Let's look in Dotty's wardrobe,' Mar said, taking her by the arm. 'As far as I recall you're much the same size, only you manage to inhabit it better.'

'You can't just go through her things!' Daisy protested.

'Oh, do be quiet!' Mar boomed in reply.

Dotty's wardrobe was far more extensive than Daisy expected, even though she had seen a few gowns when they'd dressed for dinner at Rose Cottage. They had lived it up together at parties throughout London in their time, too, but always in uniform, and the gowns hanging up were almost a statement of the social life of an upper-class gel in the pre-war era.

Mar saw her looking at them.

'You're thinking that Dotty is a terribly profligate creature,' she said, eyes narrowed.

'No I'm not,' Daisy protested, 'I'm thinking what a beautiful collection she has, and how she'd feel about me delving into it and picking out what I want. I know how I'd feel, Mar!'

'Oh, stuff and nonsense! Anyway, it wasn't Dotty's choice to have all this, it was mine. I was from the generation who survived the first war, you see, the generation that was scarred by it. So many young men just disappeared. I was determined that my daughter would have a jolly time while she was young, then the blighters did it again.'

She pulled out one or two evening dresses and laid them on the bed. The black one Daisy had worn the first time she stayed at Rose Cottage was inspected.

'No,' Mar said. 'Quite beautiful on, as I recall, but I think we want something brighter for this occasion. What about this one?'

Daisy turned and as she looked at the dress her heart gave an enormous thump in her chest. It was sky blue and covered with sparkling sequins, as though someone had thrown a handful of diamonds in the air and sewn them where they fell. For a moment a little girl stood before her, long russet hair tied with a bow the same colour as the dress, expressions of emotion she didn't understand on her beautiful, innocent face, her sky-blue eyes full of sadness as she sang 'I'll Take You Home Again, Kathleen'. The child was so real that she felt that she could reach out and touch her, and the sound of her voice was as hauntingly angelic as she remembered.

She sat on the bed, the colour drained from her face, tears brimming over her cheeks.

'My dear girl!' Mar said, dropping the dress and rushing to put her arms round her. 'Whatever is it?'

'Someone I used to know wore a dress of that colour,' Daisy said, smiling and trying to lighten the moment. 'I couldn't do it justice.'

Mar, a lady to her fingertips, simply turned back to the wardrobe and came out with an exquisite dress of pale pink silk cut on the bias, the kind of dress Daisy remembered from her days at Fenwicks.

'This,' Mar said quietly, 'is your colour, and it's terribly sophisticated. I think Dotty was trying to impress me. It's not her, you know what she's like, or used to be, Dotty by name and Dotty by nature. Now, try it on and I'll be back in a tick. I have an idea.'

Daisy loved silk and dresses cut on the bias and remembered Joan laughing at her when she had tried to create her own version on the little sewing machine in Guildford Place. As she examined herself in the long mirror she found it hard to believe it was really her. For six years now she had been in uniform and had hardly worn anything else, and yet the woman she saw looked so completely different she could've been another species. The cut of the material suited her figure, the subtle plainness emphasised her curves, and she couldn't resist walking up and down in the exaggerated way she had been taught for the benefit of Fenwicks customers.

'That's the thing!' Mar barked from the doorway. 'Flaunt it, girl, flaunt it!' and Daisy giggled. 'Now sit down while I fasten this.'

'What is it?'

'You'll see!' Mar said, placing a necklace around her neck, a series of diamond-studded open hearts, each one with a pink diamond drop in the centre. 'There are earrings to match,' Mar said.

Daisy was speechless.

'It was made for my grandmother's twenty-first,' Mar said. 'Been passed down the family. I wore it on my wedding day, thought Dotty might on hers, but there we are. It's yours for the night, Daisy. You *shall* go to the ball!'

Lord Nuffield lived in Huntercombe, in a large house nestling in the Chilterns, and it was something of a surprise. It had been extended from the original design, presumably in expectation of the children he and his wife never had, but though the furniture, carpets and tapestries were of fine quality, the Nuffields lived in a very 1930s style, with few precious antiques around them. Into this setting came the guests that night, the WAAFs, ever ready for a good time, seeking each other out without too much trouble and becoming a group, even if they didn't know each other. They were immediately identified and paired up with specially chosen escorts, something that didn't entirely please the girls. They had been ordered about and regulated for years – now that they were free they wanted to please themselves.

'Peter Bradley,' said a voice behind her, 'and you must be Daisy.'

Daisy turned to look at him. About fifty, she guessed, a good four inches taller than her, fairish hair, receding, but otherwise

298

well-preserved, must have been quite something in his day. Nice smile, distinguished-looking, but with a certain look in his eyes as well, an amused expression.

'Yes,' she said, gracefully taking his proffered arm without touching him too much, another technique she had perfected over the years to keep a distance between her and anyone who wanted actual contact. He simply grabbed her hand and tightened it through his arm, pulling them closer, then he held on to the hand. She pulled slightly to get more control.

'I'm not letting go!' he announced cheerfully, looking at her with that expression in his eyes. He was annoying her, but she didn't feel threatened in any way, she realised. This man must be a very good father, but she wasn't looking for one. She felt vaguely disappointed that he wasn't younger or handsomer, or something, watching the others walk off on the arms of those who had that something. Still, it was only for a few hours. She could be civil, as long as he behaved.

'I'm one of Lord Nuffield's directors,' he smiled. He seemed very sure of himself, but then if he wasn't by his age, she supposed, he never would be.

She nodded slightly in reply, wondering if he expected her to say, 'How clever of you', or 'Oooh!'

'Can I get you a drink?' he asked.

'Soda water, please,' she replied.

'That *all*?' he almost shouted, looking aghast. 'There's plenty to choose from, you know.'

'That's what I like,' she shrugged. 'And do you always make sure everyone in the room is looking at you?'

He threw his head back and laughed. 'You want a bit of decorum, do you?'

'No, but I think you do,' she said icily, and was rewarded with another great guffaw as he went off to get her drink.

299

'Trust me to land the nutcase,' she thought, wondering how long she would have to stay here.

'You'd be a very cheap date,' he smiled when he came back with her soda water.

'I don't think you'll ever have to worry about that,' Daisy countered; she had decided on arm's-length cool to freeze him out. If she could put him off the night might not be wasted after all. Judging by the glances of the younger men around them she wouldn't have any trouble finding a replacement.

He was laughing at her as she thought this. 'I know what you're thinking!' he yelled, and there it was again, that attention-pulling laughter. 'So where do you come from?' he asked.

'Originally from Newcastle,' she said, 'but that was a long time ago.'

'You don't *sound* Newcastle,' he grinned.

'I still think it, and if I spoke it you wouldn't have any idea what I was saying,' she said, 'so I don't.'

'Except to yourself?' he asked. 'And your family, I suppose.'

She didn't say anything.

'You don't make conversation easy, do you?'

'Well, we didn't exactly choose each other,' Daisy murmured, sipping her drink and looking around in time-honoured fashion. 'I mean, you're just doing your duty, aren't you?'

'Well, actually, that's not entirely true,' he smiled. 'I had been tipped off, then I had a look and said, "That one's definitely for me," and pulled rank.'

'Oh God, another awful chat-up line,' Daisy groaned. She wasn't sure if he was laughing at her or with her, but either way she wished he would stop.

'I suppose you've heard a great many?' he said, looking her up and down.

'Look,' Daisy said quietly, 'don't try that one either, I don't succumb to flattery. And for your information, the dress and the diamonds are borrowed. If they're not back by midnight I'll be standing here in my WAAF uniform.'

'Clothes and jewellery are just the outside trappings,' he said. 'I'm judging what's underneath.'

'If you're being filthy you may well get this drink over your head,' she sighed. 'I've heard more crude chat-ups than you have; I can see them coming.'

'My, but you're touchy,' he chuckled. 'I was talking about the person, actually, not the body, though now you've drawn my attention to it –'

'I did not draw your attention to it!' she said firmly. 'And what are you, psychic or something? How do you know about "the person"?'

'Our first row!' he said delightedly, spinning on his heels with delight.

Daisy glared at him. 'I don't think this is exactly a meeting of minds. Why don't we split up and perhaps we'll meet people we can get on with? That way the evening won't be totally wasted.'

'On the contrary,' he said brightly, 'I'm loving it so far, and no one else will dare come near you. I told you, I pulled rank.'

Then he guided her to the middle of the floor and danced with her.

'I'm not dancing,' she said pointedly.

'Yes you are,' he grinned. 'Look – you're doing it now.'

'I'm not, you're pulling me about!'

'You sound so childish!' he laughed, whirling her round. 'Now be a good girl and dance properly or you'll fall down in your borrowed dress and everyone will laugh at you, me included. And if you *are* a good girl and behave yourself, I'll let you dance one dance with a young buck later.'

'I'll dance with whoever I want to dance with!' she said angrily.

'Yes,' he smiled, 'but only if I let you.'

The whole evening he stuck by her, a cheerful, good-natured if annoying presence. He brought her food, carried drinks to her and talked even when she refused to reply.

'You haven't asked about *me*,' he said.

'There's a message there,' she replied, raising her eyebrows.

'Peter Bradley –' he started.

'Yes, you said.'

'Oh, good! You remembered! Aged fifty-one, widowed, two daughters, nineteen and seventeen – you'll meet them later – on the board of directors of Morris Motors and various other bits and pieces –'

'– and you bother girls young enough to be your daughter. There's a name for men like you.'

'You *are* fun, Daisy!'

'Or are you one of those guys who likes boys better and surrounds himself with the most gorgeous females to put people off the track?' she said, in an attempt to insult him.

He looked thoughtful. 'No,' he said eventually, and grinned.

'Took your time answering, though, didn't you?'

'Well, you strike me as the kind of young woman who needs an honest answer, Daisy, so I considered it carefully before I answered,' he said seriously.

'Is there *anything* I can do to dislodge you?' she demanded.

'Don't think so,' he said, shaking his head almost mournfully. 'I'm afraid you're stuck with me.' He looked at her amiably while she glared back at him. 'What's the fastest marriage proposal you've ever had, Daisy?' he asked, smiling down happily at her.

'Oh, *please!*'

'I mean it!'

'Yes, that's the trouble, you probably do.' She looked at him. He thought he was in full control, so she decided to sort him out. 'Just for the record,' she said, 'the fastest proposal I ever had was from a pilot of a Lanc.'

'Oh, those boys proposed to everyone,' Peter said dismissively, reaching for her glass.

'He was about twenty and his plane was shot to hell, all the crew dead and he knew he wouldn't make it either. I was on duty in the tower, you see, he was on my earphones, and he asked me if I'd marry him if he made it home and survived.'

'And what did you say?' he asked.

'I said I would.'

'And did you?'

'No,' she said calmly. 'The line went dead and he was never seen again.'

There was silence for a moment, then, 'That was a rotten story,' he said quietly.

'You asked the question.'

'And you play dirty.'

'You asked for that, too.'

'Maybe you're not a very nice girl.'

'I think that's a wise judgement.'

'Poisonous, even.'

'You said it.'

'I think it's my duty to marry you, to keep you from poisoning some nice boy, though.' He beamed down at her. 'Good try, Daisy!' he said happily. 'We're going to have such fun together!'

It was one of the worst evenings of her life, and yet he reminded her of someone.

When she reached Rose Cottage the next day a bouquet of red roses was waiting for her, and so was Mar, full of excitement.

'Who are they from? Who are they from?' she demanded, dancing up and down.

'You know very well who they're from, you silly old mare!' Par shouted from the sitting room. 'You read the bloody card!'

Daisy knew who they were from, too. She didn't need to read the card, and put the roses straight in the bin.

'Daisy!' Mar whispered very loudly. 'Red roses!'

'From an idiot,' Daisy said wearily.

'Peter's not an idiot!'

'Oh, you know him?'

'Well of course we do, we move in the same circles, my dear, God help us. He's a little odd, I'll admit —'

'Odd!'

'Kind of strange at times, granted.'

'Mar, listen to me, the man's an *idiot*!' Daisy laughed, throwing her arms round Mar and looking into her eyes.

'But Daisy, you don't know enough about him.'

'I know all I ever want to know, believe me!' Daisy said, heading for her room.

'He and his wife had such a happy marriage,' Mar persisted at her heels, 'and the girls are so lovely — did you meet them?'

'No, he threatened to introduce them, but I made sure he didn't.'

'She died in the Blitz, you know, his wife. She was staying at their London flat, terribly sad. I said to Par. "He'll never live without her," and for a while you could see the sadness in his eyes, but he's pulled himself together wonderfully. Lovely man, Daisy, strange, but lovely.' Mar's voice sounded almost reproachful. 'I know there's an age gap, but you're mature beyond your years and I'm sure your people will love him when they come back.'

Daisy spun round to face her. 'You set this up, didn't you?' she accused Mar.

'Daisy! As if I would!'

'You set the whole thing up!'

From the sitting room she heard Par laughing. 'Found out, you silly old mare. I told you she was too smart not to guess!'

'Shut up, you old goat!' Mar yelled back. 'Daisy, it wasn't like –'

'The invitation, everything, you set it up! I couldn't understand why I'd been invited, but you arranged it so that I would meet that, that *idiot*! Mar, how could you?'

'Well, you are two of my favourite people, you and Peter,' Mar said sheepishly, 'and as I say, you've always been older than your years and he's always been younger than his, so I just thought, well, who knows? And if you can't interfere in the lives of your friends, well, I mean, darling, what's the point of having them?'

'He's not younger than his years, Mar, the man is an idiot! How many times do I have to say it? He ruined the entire night for me, pulling me about the dance floor, laughing so loudly that he had everybody staring at us. And I couldn't get away from him, he was like a leech!'

Mar was chuckling fondly. 'That certainly sounds like Peter,' she said. 'I'm so glad you two hit it off!'

'Mar!' Daisy said in exasperation, then she turned and made her way upstairs. Her reaction had been too strong because Mar had mentioned her people and their supposed return any day now, and she had had to divert attention. There had been so many opportunities to explain about 'her people', and that had been another one, but once again she let it pass. She kept saying to herself that she didn't know why she did this, but deep down she did. She didn't want to open that door and think about them. There was too much stored up there, her entire life until she had joined up and reinvented herself. If she looked behind that door, who knew where it could lead? Lying to Mar, even by omission, made her feel guilty, but she was only resting for a while at Rose Cottage. Soon she would decide what to do with her life and move on and Mar need never know.

What to do with her life, now there was a question, and she had no answer. The more she thought about it the less sense it all made. One thing she did know, though: she had no intention of being found a nice, safe man, and certainly not a nice, safe *old* man. Nor an idiot.

20

The next day Daisy returned to Rose Cottage after a day spent wandering round the farm on the estate and going for one of her lone walks down the lanes. It was springtime, a time of renewal, when the buds were on the trees and birds were building nests. All around her was the wonderful feeling of growth. She had lain down under a tree and fallen asleep in the grass, something she was doing a lot these days, now that she was finally free of night shifts and living too closely with other people. Space suddenly meant so much to her, and silence, except that it made her sleepy.

There was a sports car in the driveway when she arrived back, probably some former Fly Boy trying to make sense of civilian life, she thought, aware that she wasn't looking her best. Her hair was tousled, her cheeks red and her eyes still heavy with sleep – and there *he* was, in the sitting room, Peter Bradley, with his back to her, thankfully.

She saw him out of the corner of her eye and instantly decided not to turn her head and officially see him. Instead she moved very quietly along the passageway to the kitchen and went up the back stairs to her room. Then she lay on her bed and thought how intolerable the whole thing was, this man, this *old* man, chasing after her. The thing was sick and he had no right. Mar had at least encouraged him, probably even invited him, and she had no right, either.

No, that was going a bit far, it was Mar's house after all, she had every right to invite into it whoever she wanted, even weird eccentrics and oddities, but that didn't mean Daisy had to get involved with them. She didn't want this, didn't want romance or closeness or love, the very thought of involvement made her feel queasy.

There had to be a way out. No one had seen her coming in, so if she could get out again they wouldn't know she had come back. She kept the light out and in the early nightfall packed a few things in a bag, wrote a note for Mar saying she'd popped off to meet up with one of the girls and would be back in a couple of days. Then she crept downstairs, listening for voices and footsteps, looking around furtively every few moments.

'Going somewhere nice?' a voice said pleasantly from behind her. 'Oh, I'm sorry, did I make you jump? I was in my room, changing for dinner.'

She felt like a child caught sneaking out without permission, but tried for all the calmness and coolness in her repertoire. 'I was going off to spend a couple of days with a friend,' she said.

'Oh, I see,' Peter smiled, walking downstairs with her. 'Female, I hope?'

'That has nothing whatsoever to do with you,' she replied primly.

'Well, it has, really, Daisy, as well you know,' he teased. 'I won't stand for lovers, I'm not one of these moral liberals.'

He walked in front of her to the bottom of the stairs then turned to face her. Standing on the second step her eyes were level with his.

'I would think it very cruel if you were to hurt me like

that, Daisy,' he said solemnly, then he turned and went into the sitting room, leaving her standing there, perplexed.

There was the mass sound of various voices from the sitting room, then Mar came bounding out and found her where Peter had left her. 'You're not going *now*?' she demanded. 'I mean, Daisy, my darling, you can meet your friend tomorrow. Surely you can have dinner with us?'

'Mar,' Daisy said, putting her arms loosely around Mar's neck and looking into her eyes, 'stop this, please. I can't take it, honestly, I can't. When I'm under pressure I run, I can't help it, and I don't want him or anyone. I have my reasons, Mar.'

'Daisy, my darling girl,' Mar said, reaching up and smoothing Daisy's hair from her face. 'It's only dinner, it isn't white slavery.'

And so Daisy stayed. She had gone back upstairs, bathed, changed into one of Dotty's gowns and joined Mar, Par, a selection of friends and neighbours, and Peter, of course. She kept her eyes away from him at all times, as she had once done with someone else at this very table, but she could feel his on her and had to fight the urge to get up from the table and run. Then her eyes filled as she thought of that first time she had been to Rose Cottage and had avoided Frank Moran all evening.

She was acting true to form, she mused, whenever there was anything she felt as a threat, she killed it with rudeness and took to her heels. It was, as she had told Mar, what she did. The slightest hint of closeness overwhelmed her, so she ran, just as she had kept running until Frank was nearly dead, and then she had lost him.

She had no idea if Dotty had been right about hearing being the last thing to go, or if Frank had heard her as he lay dying, but during those last days and nights she'd told him how much she regretted running and wished she could turn the clock back. It was too late, but maybe that was why she had told him. If he had lived she probably wouldn't have said a word, she would have chosen safety and silence. At twenty-five years old she still couldn't face any kind of closeness, not closeness with men at any rate, and so she was alone and that was how she would stay.

Sitting at the table that night she looked up and met Peter's eyes. He seemed a nice enough man, if slightly odd, and she felt an attraction to him, but there was nothing she could do, she decided. She could only be as she was.

The next morning she slept late and had breakfast in her room, hoping that by the time she finally appeared he would have left; but a note arrived on her tray with the eggs and bacon asking her to join him downstairs when she felt up to it.

It might well be a good idea, she thought. If she could talk to him seriously she might be able to make him see that his attentions were unwanted and could lead nowhere, that she honestly could never be interested in him. As she came downstairs, her speech arranged and rehearsed ready to be delivered in the sitting room, he shouted, 'There you are! Come on!' and walked outside to an MG two-seater.

'I didn't know that was yours,' she said, looking at it.

'Of course it is,' he smiled. 'I'm a company man, a Morris Motors company man, what else would I drive? Get in, I'll take you to meet your friend.'

'You know perfectly well there was – is – no friend, Peter. I was trying to escape.'

'Get in anyway,' he said, suddenly serious. 'We need to talk.'

Sitting in the MG with the hood down there was little chance of hearing each other, so she used the time to rehearse her speech again. He pulled up under a tree in a lane and turned to her.

'Daisy, we have to get this sorted out,' he said.

She shook her head and laughed.

'What is it?' he asked.

'We met three days ago and here you are, turning serious and sorting things out. What is there to sort out?'

'I am deadly serious about you,' he said. 'I fell in love with you the minute I set eyes on you.'

'No,' she replied, grimacing, 'stop it, I don't want this.'

'And,' he continued, 'I told you the truth at Nuffield Place the other night. I pulled rank to be your escort, though Mar had told me about you. Now I don't care how long this takes, though I'd prefer not to hang around, but I will not give up on you.'

'You make me sound like a project,' she said quietly.

'Well that's because you've made yourself into a project. It doesn't have to be this way, but if you insist then that's how it must be. But I will not go away.'

'Peter, I think you're insane, but try to understand that I don't want the whole domestic thing. I don't want to get married and become a housewife and mother.'

'Why not?'

'Because I don't, it's my choice.'

'I don't believe you,' he smiled. 'Something or someone has scared you, but we'll get over it.'

'Look, there was someone, he died in the war,' she whispered.

'Yes, I know,' he said.

'How do you know?' she asked, shocked.

'Mar told me.'

'How does Mar know?'

'Mar knows a great deal, don't ever underestimate her. She said there was a sadness about you and she guessed there was a man involved.'

'But I didn't tell anyone, not ever!'

'Maybe you're not as dark as you like to think. Look, Daisy, I loved someone once as well – my wife.'

'Yes, Mar told *me* that, too,' she said wryly.

'So I know what it's like to lose someone, but that made me determined not to waste a minute of what was left of my life, because it can be snuffed out very easily and quickly. You know that as well as anyone. Not that I expected to meet someone else, but there we are, you came along.'

'Stop saying that!' He touched her hand and she pulled it away. 'I mean it, Peter, you have to stop this. I can't deal with it. I don't like people touching me.'

'It'll get easier, Daisy,' he said gently. 'It'll get easier.'

When Peter left Rose Cottage that afternoon it was with the firm intention of returning as soon as possible, and he didn't care who knew it. He had told Mar and Par that he was going to marry Daisy as soon as she saw sense, and Daisy said he was the one who needed to see sense, and they grinned at her as though she were a moody child. She felt uncomfortable, besieged, yet she had to admit to herself that there was nothing threatening about him. Peter's bullying was of the most gentle and affectionate kind, and he was the most gentle, kind and affectionate man she had ever met; not as loud and booming as the Bentleys but every bit as open with his feelings. He wasn't like younger men she had encountered, he was a man from another generation with manners that fitted a different age, even if he was peculiar. And he was that, too, he could be disconcertingly odd, but he looked her in the eye, she realised with a start. Right from the beginning he'd looked her in the eye, and she couldn't remember that happening since she was thirteen years old.

Yes, she did. Calli. Eileen's lovely boy had always looked her in the eye. She could close her eyes and see him still, those serious dark eyes looking at her from a distance and his lips saying 'Poor Daisy'.

Peter had never laid a hand on her either, except when they were dancing at the cocktail party, and, looking back, there had been nothing objectionable about it, apart from the fact that she hadn't wanted to dance with him. In the car during their chat, he had briefly touched her hand and she had pulled it away and said she didn't like to be touched. So, when he was leaving Rose Cottage he obviously remembered and made no attempt to embrace her. She had noticed that. Instead he had blown her kiss, which reminded her of Bruiser and made her run to her room and lie on the bed for a long time crying. All those ghosts, so many ghosts in her life, and she was so young.

Peter returned to Rose Cottage three days later and continued to woo Daisy — if behaving as if he owned her was a form of wooing, Daisy thought. Wherever she was he was by her side, as though their being together was an established fact, and somehow she couldn't shake him off. Not that she tried, because he had her at a complete disadvantage. She was a guest in Mar and Par's home and he was an old friend who was being pleasant and attentive towards her.

There wasn't the slightest feeling that he was coercing her or trying to force a relationship on her, yet that was what he was doing. In times past she would have delivered a mouthful that would have stripped that easy smile from his face, but she couldn't do it in these surroundings, in the home of their friends; and, curiouser still, she found that she didn't want to. In some ways, she thought with a start, it was like being with Bruiser again, and he reminded her of Frank, too, and his refusal to believe that she wanted no contact with him.

When Peter left again the next day she felt oddly out of sorts and thought she was coming down with a cold, then suddenly she realised that the coldness she felt was the empty space beside her that he had somehow made his own. Not only was this strange man wearing down her resolve, but he was doing so in such a gentle way that she didn't object any longer, didn't want to object either. It made her feel out of her own control when she had prided herself on being the one always in control.

And Mar watched in kind delight. Mar, who she had deceived and lied to, watched Daisy being worn down and smiled at the scene.

'Why don't you phone him?' Mar asked one bright, warm June evening.

'Who?' Daisy asked, looking out of the front window of Rose Cottage, her arms crossed around her waist.

'You know perfectly well who!' Mar chuckled, only being Mar it seemed to reverberate through the entire house.

'Oh, I don't know, Mar,' Daisy replied. 'I've been thinking it was time I moved on, went to London for a while, maybe go abroad now that I'm rested up.'

'Oh, stuff and nonsense! You're missing Peter Bradley!'

'I am not!'

'Daisy,' Mar said, advancing on her, taking hold of her by the elbows and shaking her, 'you are such a bright girl, but you can also be incredibly stupid. Phone the man!'

'But what should I say?' Daisy asked helplessly. 'I'm not good at these things, I'm far better at shooting them down!'

'You won't have to say a lot,' Mar said, hugging her. 'At the sound of your voice he'll jump into that ridiculous little car and be on the doorstep in a second.'

So she picked up the phone, dialled the number, and when someone answered she said it was Miss Sheridan for Mr Bradley.

There was a pause then the voice came on again.

'Mr Bradley will be right with you, miss.'

'Oh, right. Fine.'

'You can hang up now, miss.'

'But you said he'd be right with me . . .'

'He will, miss,' the voice said, and she was sure she could detect a hint of amusement. 'He's in the car and he'll be right with you, miss.'

'Oh. Thank you . . .' She replaced the receiver.

'Didn't I tell you?' Mar boomed. 'Mar knows everything!'

And as they hugged, Daisy thought, *not quite everything*, and decided she would have to talk to her, but not till after she'd talked to Peter.

By the time Peter arrived at Rose Cottage, the Bentleys who were at home had whipped themselves and everyone else within reach into such a frenzy of excitement that Daisy could hardly find a way through the throng. It was just how they were: cheerful, happy, loud people who conspired to banish the most fleeting moment of silence and involved themselves fully in the lives of their friends. They were hopelessly noisy and outgoing and without the slightest inkling that other people might wish things done differently. Indeed, it was very hard to believe Par had been involved in war work so secret that he would never talk about it to anyone. It simply didn't occur to them that whatever was or was not happening between Daisy and Peter, they might welcome some privacy in order to discuss it. It was part of their charm that once an event was in full swing it was accorded a life of its own and the stars were relegated to merely being supporting acts.

Knowing this was one of the secrets of coping with the

family, Peter, as an old friend, was aware that the party would swing without him and Daisy. He motioned to her with his head to meet him outside and whisked her away in the MG to where they had had their last outdoor conversation. It was a beautiful night, as balmy and warm as the best June nights should be, and he produced a ring in a small box.

'Put it away, Peter,' Daisy said. 'This time we really do need to sort this out.'

He put the box into his pocket and sat, hands resting on the steering wheel, looking at her.

'So this is it?' he smiled. 'Make or break time. I'm ready for a speedy getaway, as you can see.'

She nodded. 'I have some things to tell you.'

So she told him about her life in Newcastle, about her father and his hopeless need to be Irish, even though he wasn't, and about the family before him who were. Then about her mother who had been a well-known singer, until she'd married and had children, ending any real chance of a career, but she had been sick from then on anyway, so it didn't really matter. When Kay was born it was obvious she had inherited her mother's musical talent, and she was beautiful, and strange in a way, but was going to make her mother's dreams come true. She explained how she had cared for her mother, run the house and looked after Kay all her life, because Kay had the voice of an angel and was going to be a star. She hadn't minded then, but had begun to as she got older and understood that her dreams, ambitions – her life – were to be sacrificed for the greater good of the family.

Daisy left out certain bits, Dessie mainly, but told Peter her sister had married and had a family, and that 'her people', as Mar called the Sheridans, weren't abroad for the duration, but had all been wiped out in a German air raid. He reached out and took her hand and this time she didn't flinch.

'There's something more you have to know,' she said quietly. 'You'll have heard from Mar and probably others, too, that I had a high old time at parties during the war.'

'You don't have to tell me any of this,' he said quietly.

'Yes, I do,' she replied. 'People will say I'm a good-time girl who married you for your money. You have to know if that's true.'

'Oh, no,' he pleaded. 'Don't spoil the illusion! I just *love* the idea that I've been seduced by a sexy young thing! Think of the sympathy I'll get! No, please, Daisy, leave it at that!'

She glared at him and he laughed. 'The thing is, you silly goose, that the advantage here is on one side – mine. You're young, beautiful, and that body – what? You think I hadn't noticed? I shall parade you for all to see and every male will be eaten up with jealousy and think me a helluva stud!'

'You will *not* parade me about!'

'I bloody well *will*,' Peter said. 'You forget, you'll be marrying me for my money, you'll be bought and paid for, my girl. I shall have my money's worth!' He leaned over and pulled her to him, kissing her hair and laughing.

'Wait, I have to tell you something important. The number of times I've had sexual intercourse –'

'No, I don't want to know that.'

'You have to,' she chided him. 'I have to tell you. Peter, the answer is *once*. I was at the parties, I was on the arms of all sorts of men, but that's as far as it ever went, not that they told their friends that, I imagine.' She pulled away and looked out over the green fields. 'I was raped when I was eighteen years old, Peter, by someone who had known my family for many years. That was it. The one and only time and, the next morning I signed on. I never went home again. I quite understand if it disgusts you. There's nothing to hold you to me yet, you've made no commitment to me.'

Peter put his arm gently round Daisy's shoulders, and when she looked at him, instead of disgust he was smiling at her.

'I suppose that's why I don't like people touching me – men, anyway. But if you think it's too much to take on, that's fine, honestly. I won't think any less of you and neither would anyone else.'

'Well, actually, what I was thinking, Daisy, is that you're so upset about this that I can't see you enjoying your wedding day with the thought of your wedding night hanging over you. I think we should go off now, find a nice little hotel and get it over with. What do you say?'

'You mean none of this – the rape – it doesn't bother you?'

'Oh, it bothers me. I wish I'd been there to stop whoever did it, but it's over, Daisy. Life goes on. Now, try on your ring and we'll get going.'

'Is there nothing that will put you off?' she asked in surprise.

'Well, there is one thing,' he said seriously.

'What?'

'How can I put it delicately?' he mused.

'What is it?'

'You will tell me the absolute truth if I ask this one question, won't you, Daisy?'

'Of course.'

'Well, you're not a man, are you?'

She stared at him.

'I think that would really put me off, you see, so if you come clean now there won't be any nasty shocks later.'

Daisy was terrified, but Peter took her as gently and carefully as if she were a virgin, and she knew instinctively that in his eyes she was. The burden of shame and the feelings she had carried since Dessie, of being soiled and dirty, just evaporated. He was patient and gentle with her, taking his time for her sake, making her feel so safe that she understood for the first time what caring meant. Afterwards she lay across his chest, his arms surrounding her, and wept.

He chuckled sleepily.

'Why are you laughing?' she asked.

'You're not a man,' he said.

She slapped him lightly.

'I'm so relieved,' he said. 'If you were I'd have had to pretend the ring was for myself, so I'd have had to wear it to save face and it would look bloody silly on me.'

21

The first decision Daisy took was not to go away on honeymoon. When she met Peter's two daughters, who were, as everyone told her, lovely girls, she thought about how they must be feeling. They had lost their mother a few years before and that had changed their lives dramatically. Now they must have felt that they were losing their father too.

Laura was nineteen and Libby seventeen, though they looked more like twins, both tall, slim girls, dark-haired with porcelain skin and blue eyes. At twenty-five Daisy wasn't that much older than them, and she remembered being their age, with all the fears and worries that meant so little to other people. Instead of going off with Peter, it seemed more sensible to get to know them, to prove to them that she wasn't a threat, that she wasn't taking their father away from them.

A few weeks before the wedding there had been a dinner party at the family home in Oxford to introduce Daisy to Peter's other friends. She noticed that Laura had been very quiet and had been watching her all evening, so when the girl got up from the table Daisy had followed her to her room upstairs and found her crying. Daisy had put her arms around her and asked what was wrong and, very apologetically,

Laura said she had been thinking of her mother.

'Want to know something, Laura?' Daisy said quietly. 'I've been thinking about mine. She died in a raid, too, along with the rest of my family.'

'It feels so, I don't know, *wrong* somehow that you and Pop are getting married,' the girl wept. 'I don't mean you shouldn't or anything, but it's hard, you know?'

'Of course it is, Laura, and if your mother had still been here, do you think your Pop would've given me a second glance? She was his first wife, she always will be. I can't ever take her place, I can only make a place for myself, but it will be second place you know. Nothing will change where you and Libby are concerned, this is still your home and he's still your Pop.'

'But . . . but I don't think I can call you Mother,' Laura sobbed.

'You do and I'll give you such a slap!' Daisy said tartly.

Laura laughed and cried at the same time. 'And her photos, do we have to put them away?'

'Why ever would you do that?' Daisy asked, shocked.

'Well, Libby and I were talking and we wondered if you'd rather not see her photos. They're all over the house.'

'And that's where they'll stay,' Daisy said gently. 'Look, she's still your mother, you've had all those happy years in this house with her, and so has your Pop. That won't just disappear because he's marrying me, it will last for the rest of your life. And when you're married you'll come back and her photos will still be here so that you can show your children what she was like. We'll be friends, Laura, but she'll always be your mother.' She looked at a photo of Peter's first wife by Laura's bed. 'Look at her, she was so beautiful, who could replace her?'

The girl stayed within Daisy's embrace. 'So you won't want us to move out, then?' she asked in a tiny voice.

'Dear God, where do you get these ideas, you little idiot?' she laughed. 'You know what your Pop's like; how am I supposed to cope with him on my own? You two know more about him than I ever will, I'll be relying on you to help me sort him out. Now go into your bathroom, wash your face and put on fresh make-up.'

Laura blew her nose. 'Pop doesn't like us to wear too much make-up,' she laughed. 'If he sees a tiny bit he pulls a horrid face.'

'Oh,' Daisy said dismissively, 'he's a man, what does he know? Now come down when you're ready, and I want you and Libby to sit by me. I feel as though I'm an exhibit in a zoo with all those people I don't know looking at me, I need some allies.'

When she left Laura's bedroom she found Peter outside, smiling down at her.

'Have you been listening?' she said sternly.

'You're a wonderful woman, Daisy Sheridan,' he murmured, holding her close and stroking her hair.

'I know,' she whispered, pushing him, 'now get downstairs, we don't want Laura to know you were nosey-parkering outside her door, do we?'

'But you are wonderful. I do adore you, you know.'

'Well of course you do, I'm wonderful, remember, you large, tipsy oaf, now move!'

He held her tightly. 'I mean it, though. I've been trying to say all that to the girls for ages, but I couldn't find the words, and you just went in there and said them. You're wonderful. I could just stand here and hold you all night,' he beamed.

'Take my word for it, you couldn't stand here another ten seconds, the champagne has affected your head and sure as hell it'll get your legs any moment now,' Daisy said, force-marching him back downstairs.

★　★　★

The wedding was set for as soon as it could be arranged, which realistically was September, and the reception would be a come-one, come-all celebration at Rose Cottage, where Daisy would remain until her wedding day. Rationing was still in force and clothing was only available with government-issued coupons, but Mar came up with a solution. She appeared at Daisy's room holding a large amount of ivory raw silk.

'Brought it back from India many moons ago,' she said. 'Never had the chance to use it. I'm sure we could have it made up into something stunning for you, what do you think?'

'Have you got a sewing machine?' Daisy asked.

'Upstairs in the attic,' Mar replied. 'You can't work the thing, can you?'

'Yes!'

'I say, Daisy, you are clever! By the way, I've been wondering about your people. I do hope they won't object to me being such a bossy boots, will they? I mean, I promise I'll step back and give them their place when they arrive. When are they arriving, by the way? Do you know?'

Daisy side-stepped the question. 'I didn't know you'd been to India, you dark horse!' she said.

Mar sat on Daisy's bed. 'Oh, it was many moons ago,' she told her. 'My father worked there, he was a civil servant, part of the Raj, I suppose, and we all went out, my mother, my older brother Frederick, and myself. Pretty rough time, actually. We're not built for that kind of heat, the humidity was awful, and there we were all bound up in our layers of English clothes, but still, it was an adventure. We were sent home in the hot season, young Freddy and I. I didn't want to go, I was so cross that as the ship left Bombay I refused to wave to my mother, then when we arrived home we were told the poor thing had died of typhus. Terrible thing, Daisy,' she said very quietly, 'I'd been so angry with her and never had a chance to make up. I don't even know to this day where she's buried. Can't get my head round why that matters, but it does.'

Daisy was silent for a moment and then she took Mar's hand. 'So Freddy's called after your brother?'

'Yes, Frederick was killed in the war, the first one, I mean. My father didn't come home again except for the odd hol. I suspect he had an Indian woman out there, they usually did. Beautiful women they were, quite beautiful. So I was looked after by a succession of governesses who didn't really care, they just took the money and were around, knowing he wasn't, which probably explains why I go about shouting. Never did have any real graces knocked into me.' She looked up and laughed. 'It probably explains why Par and I hit it off, he's just the same, a noisy beggar. We all are, as I suppose you've noticed, but it's so much better than silence, don't you think?'

'I can't imagine this family any other way,' Daisy replied. 'I've never come across a family so openly affectionate with each other.'

'Or so noisy, I'll be bound! Well that was me, too,' Mar explained. 'My poor mother was the only one who ever hugged me. After she died I missed that, so I made sure we all smothered each other to death with affection. I would watch Freddy and Dotty when they were young sprogs, attacking Par when he came home, dragging him to the floor and slobbering over him like great big noisy puppies, and I'd think that was pretty damned fine!'

Daisy decided it was the perfect time to come clean about 'her people'. 'I've got something to tell you, Mar,' she said quietly. 'Remember the first time I came here with Dotty?'

Mar nodded.

'Well, my family, I said they were abroad. It wasn't true. My father, mother, sister and her two children were killed in a raid the week before.'

Mar drew in a shocked breath. 'Why didn't you say?'

'That was me running, Mar. I decided to cope with it by ignoring it and doing something else. I ran to Rose Cottage. They're all buried in a mass grave, the bits and pieces that were found anyway, it took five days to dig them all out. I didn't go home, there was nothing to go home for. I made my officer promise no one would know and said I'd feel better if I kept working. Dotty and I were posted to Langar the next day. I've never told her either. So you see, I do understand exactly how you feel, you lost your family, too.'

'I knew we had something in common, you know,' Mar smiled. 'Right from the start I felt we were drawn together by something, isn't that strange? I said to Peter that there was a sadness deep within you. I guessed it was a man, but you were carrying all that grief, my darling girl, and you went on working.' She shook her head. 'I really do admire you, Daisy.'

'For lying to you, Mar?'

'For being such a brave girl.'

'I think I was more scared than brave. I didn't know what would happen if I faced it, so I didn't.'

'Well, that's something you have to take your time with. I don't know if I've ever faced it, not fully. You leak from the eyes sometimes when something sets you off, feel a bit sad, you know, but it's too hard to face it all at once.' Mar looked at her. 'We're your family, Daisy, you do know that, don't you?'

'Yes, Mar, I know it,' Daisy said, 'and I'm so grateful.'

'Tish!' Mar yelled, her normal volume returning. 'And what's more — *tosh*!' She jumped to her feet, swathed in raw silk. 'To the sewing machine!' she shouted, leading the way to the attic.

22

The week before Daisy and Peter married that September, Daisy had thought of Eileen and, on impulse, tried to contact her by calling the family firm. But before the voice at the other end could take a message, she thought better of it and rang off. Servicemen were returning in big numbers in 1946. For all she knew, Eileen's husband had, too, and she didn't want to interrupt the family as they were trying to get to know each other. The little girl, Calli's daughter, would now be nearly three, and anyway, if Eileen had wanted contact with her, she would have been in touch before now.

Daisy had an address for Edith, though there was no knowing if it was current, but she sent an invitation, just in case. As for the others, she had lost touch with them. In those final dying weeks and months of their WAAF days they had wavered from longing to get out and not believing it would actually happen, and then it had, with a swiftness that took them by surprise. Still, she wished she'd taken Pearl's address, it would have been nice to have some old mates with her. Even Dotty wouldn't be there, she was still overseas, and there was no one else to invite, no family or friends that weren't already Peter's friends.

★ ★ ★

On the day before the wedding Peter had presented her with a gift. It would be her 'something new', he said, a necklace, earring and bracelet set of small linked daisies, each with a yellow diamond at the centre, with white diamond petals.

'It's beautiful!' she said breathlessly. 'But it gives me a problem, Peter.'

'You've got one already!' he cried, slapping his head theatrically.

'Almost,' she said. 'The thing is, Peter, that Mar has set her heart on me wearing the ones I wore when you and I first met. They're family pieces, she had always expected that Dotty would wear them on her wedding day, then Dotty ruined that notion. Mar just assumed I'd wear them instead and I'd feel terrible if I let her down.'

'So, you'd rather let me down?' he said sternly.

'Peter!'

He put his arms around her and laughed. 'I'm joking, you silly woman,' he chuckled into her hair. 'Of course you mustn't disappoint Mar. If she hadn't told me I had to look out for you at Nuffield's party, I wouldn't have gone. I have a lot to thank her for.'

'I have more,' she said softly, 'much more. And listen to me – Daisy Sheridan worried about which set of diamonds to wear!' She thought for a moment. 'I know what my "something new" will be,' she said triumphantly. 'My two step-daughters.'

'They'll be your new *daughters*, surely?' he asked, sounding slightly hurt.

'Men,' Daisy smiled, 'you know nothing! Weren't you listening at our party? They'll always be Elizabeth's daughters, she'll always be there as far as they're concerned, and quite right too. I don't intend ever trying to replace her.'

Peter didn't say anything, but his arms tightened around her in reply.

Daisy walked down the aisle on Par's arm to where Peter waited with Laura and Libby, her bridesmaids. The bride wore a gown she had made herself as Mar watched, fascinated, making frequent loud exclamations of praise for her skills. When it was finished it had a sweetheart neckline, cap sleeves, a fitted bodice that emphasised her small waist, and a very full floor-length skirt, a gown made for her hourglass shape. She had come a long way from the girl who desperately hid from male attention. Now she was happy to show off her figure in a gown that drew gasps, even though Mar had pre-warned everyone by loudly predicting that she would 'knock 'em dead!'

A few months later, French designer Christian Dior brought out what became known as The New Look and was attacked and worshipped in equal measure for his lavish use of material, but Daisy had got there first. All women who had lived through the austerity of the war now wanted a bit of glamour and felt they had earned it, even if their clothing coupons stopped them having it. Daisy was no exception, but she did have all the material she needed, so she had created her own bit of glamour in a style that suited her. When Dior's creations were unveiled, Daisy smugly noted that they needed boning, the modern equivalent of a light corset, to achieve the desired effect, whereas she hadn't needed any such help.

In her hair she wore a band of lily of the valley and carried a small matching bouquet. Mar's family jewels were her 'something borrowed' and 'something blue' was the cushion-shaped sapphire between the two brilliant diamonds of her engagement ring.

'So where's the "something old"?' Peter whispered at the altar.

'Oh, I've had that for a while now,' she smiled, nudging him with her elbow. 'You!'

He smiled widely throughout the service and Daisy was too enchanted by what was happening to be overcome. Then, to complete the day, as they left the church she saw Edith waving at her.

The day had been perfect, or nearly perfect. If only Kathleen had lived to see her married to this lovely man, and Joan Johnstone, and maybe even Kay, though she doubted if her sister would have fully understood what was happening. And there was Eileen. She missed her good friend Eileen, the only really close female friend she had ever had, the only one who had ever truly known her.

The reception at Rose Cottage was as simple as the Bentleys were able to comprehend, with everyone within shouting distance in attendance and as much of the farm's produce as the various tables could hold. It was far too noisy, there were too many people crammed in and it was hot, but it was a lovely wedding. Peter was friendly and attentive to everyone and even in the rush of people he was never less than polite to each guest who wanted to congratulate him, whether he knew them or not, but every now and again he would look up to locate her in the crowd and he would smile such a sweet smile at her that she blushed with happiness. Edith rushed towards Daisy and hugged her, the two friends spinning round with delight.

'He seems wonderful!' Edith shouted above the noise.

'He is,' Daisy smiled.

'But I'm amazed, I never thought you'd ever get married.'

'Neither did I,' Daisy giggled, 'but there's just something about him.'

'I've got a secret, too,' Edith laughed, taking Daisy's hand and placing it on her stomach.

Daisy's eyes opened wide and her mouth formed a silent 'Ooh!'

Edith held up her hand to show off a gold band. 'Married Doug in May. He's back home now, I'm joining him next week! The baby's due in February.'

'You didn't say a word!' Daisy accused her.

'You should talk!' Edith replied.

'How's your cousin?'

'Oh, she's fine. Her lot were about the first to be demobbed, doesn't know what to do now. Not much call for Balloon Operators in peace-time.'

'Look, it's too noisy here, can you stay here tonight and we can catch up tomorrow?'

'But aren't you going off on your honeymoon?'

'No,' Daisy said, 'I want to settle in first. We might have a holiday later.'

A little shadow had crossed her heart for a moment, though she didn't let it show. Edith had married her Aussie and was going to live there. In that split second it was if Frank stood before her. 'Did you know Dotty had got married as well? She's not here, she's still overseas.'

'Did she marry that Aussie Spitfire pilot she used to write to?' Edith asked innocently.

'No,' Daisy said, trying to keep her voice even, 'he was shot down and killed.'

'Oh God, poor Dotty!' Edith exclaimed.

'Yes, poor Dotty,' Daisy murmured.

'So who did she marry, then?'

'Some doctor she met at her unit. Did Mar out of a wedding, too, as she's never stopped hinting.'

'Well, she's had one now,' Edith smiled.

23

In the following years, Peter and Daisy were happy. He clearly adored her and she was so grateful that she adored him back, even if their definitions of adoring were different.

Dotty and her husband returned in 1947, then went straight off again to America, and Frank Moran's name wasn't mentioned, much to Daisy's relief. Although it did prove to her that he had been more significant to her than he ever had been to Dotty, which disturbed her a little. This was a different Dotty: she had lost her dottiness almost completely and was every inch the physician's wife, and the physician, Bertie by name, was a nice chap, which pleased Mar, especially now that she'd finally met 'the blighter'. There was a dinner at Rose Cottage as bois-terous as any of the others, and Daisy told Bertie of her mother's illness and asked what he thought it could have been.

'Simple,' he grinned, lighting his pipe. 'Rheumatic heart disease.'

'Really?' Daisy said. 'My father could never understand why the doctors said it was her heart when it seemed like some-thing to do with her lungs.'

'Well, it was to do with her lungs, the two are linked. She'd had rheumatic fever as a child, it's a condition prevalent in cold, wet climates and where nourishment and living conditions are poor. Sometimes the symptoms are so minor people don't know they've had it, but usually there's high fever, painful joints, then it's gone, but only underground. With women the trouble comes during the advanced stages of pregnancy. At first your mother would've bloomed, but at around seven months the child would start putting on serious weight in preparation for birth, and that would've put a huge strain on a heart already under pressure. The valves wouldn't have been working properly, you see, not controlling the blood-flow to the lungs and back again, so her blood wouldn't have had enough oxygen either, and she'd have had trouble breathing.'

'Could anyone have done anything?' Daisy asked, remembering the sound of her mother's breathing.

'Shouldn't think so,' Bertie said philosophically. 'Wasn't the medical expertise around, I'm afraid, nor the medical care for that matter.'

Before Dotty left for America the two women had a short conversation without Mar, and Dotty thanked Daisy for allowing her mother to dominate her wedding.

'I did her out of one, I'm so glad you gave her yours, Daisy, though it must have been hell!'

'Well, if I hadn't given it to her she'd only have taken it,' Daisy replied. 'But I didn't mind at all, it was lovely to be part of the family.'

'I must say, though, I was pretty shocked when I heard you'd married Peter, but seeing you together I know it's right,' Dotty giggled.

'*You* were shocked?' Daisy said. 'Think how *I* felt!'

Daisy enjoyed her new life, even if she found it difficult to cope with staff. It seemed almost sinful to have a housekeeper, people to clean and open the door, but she adjusted.

The only moment of real pain was the arrival of an unwelcome visitor a year after they had married. The maid had said there was a man at the door asking to see Mrs Bradley. He said he was a relative.

Instantly Daisy knew who it was.

'Show him in, Alice, thanks,' she said, 'then get Peter.'

As he walked into her drawing room all she could think was, Dessie Doyle in *my* house!

She was amazed to see that same smug smirk on his face. 'Well, now, Daisy,' he grinned, 'haven't you done well for yourself?'

'How did you find me?' she asked coldly.

'The neighbours at Guildford Place told me you'd been traced to the WAAFs after the bombing, so I went to the police when I was demobbed and told them we were related.'

'We aren't,' she said, 'we never were. You only married my sister.'

He laughed. 'You never did accept that, did you, Daisy?'

'So what do you want here?' she asked.

'Well, I think I must be due some compensation,' he said.

She didn't understand what he was talking about. 'Compensation? What do you mean?'

'From the bombing,' he said. 'There must have been something.'

Her head was spinning but she managed to project a calm manner. 'As far as I know there was some government grant to help people replace their furniture.'

'That'll be it, then,' he grinned.

'And, as far as I know again, it came in the form of vouchers.'

'Better than nothing,' he said, though he was obviously disappointed. 'It should've been shared between the two of us.'

Daisy was aghast. It took all of her self-control not to fly across the floor at him, nails flailing. 'I think you'll find that the house was in the name of Sheridan, and every piece of furniture, too.'

'My wife and children lived there, I must have some rights,' he said angrily.

'I have no idea what rights you have. I've never been back to claim anything, if you want to try that's up to you. Now, is there anything else before you go?'

'Oh, very hoity-toity,' he smiled. 'Mind if I smoke?'

'Yes, I do.'

Just then Peter arrived, smiling and friendly as usual, looking from Dessie to Daisy for an introduction.

'This is my sister Kay's husband,' Daisy said, without taking her eyes off Dessie.

'Her brother-in-law,' Dessie grinned at her.

Peter stepped forward, his arm outstretched to shake Dessie's hand. Without taking her eyes from Dessie's face, Daisy gently caught Peter's arm and put it down.

He looked at her, confused.

'Peter, do you remember I told you I'd been raped?' she said quietly. 'Well, this is who did it, my brother-in-law, as he likes to call himself.' She moved her hand down Peter's arm and grasped his hand. 'My father was working night shift at the pit, my mother was ill and bed-ridden, and my sister, his wife, was upstairs with a four-month-old baby and already three months pregnant with another. That's when he raped me. I sat up all night then signed on the next day. I never saw my family again.'

'It wasn't rape,' Dessie said smugly. 'If she hadn't wanted it she could've found a way to stop it.'

'I was bruised for weeks,' Daisy said quietly.

'Some women like it rough.' He made to light a cigarette.

Peter freed himself from Daisy's grip and said very quietly. 'Mr . . . ?'

'Doyle, Dessie Doyle,' Dessie said.

'Well, I'm sure I can give you something to help you on your way, Mr Doyle.'

'Don't you dare!' Daisy cried.

'Daisy, be quiet!' Peter said sharply, then he turned Dessie towards the front door. Daisy could hear the sound of their footsteps growing more distant on the gravel outside, and she was bereft. Peter didn't understand men like Dessie. If he gave him ten shillings Dessie would just keep coming back for more. Peter should've let her handle this.

Then Peter came back.

'Daisy, do we have such a thing in the house as some TCP? Something like that, and perhaps a dressing or two?'

'What has he done to you?' she asked, running towards him.

'I rather think it was the other way round,' Peter said cheerfully, 'at least I damned well hope so!' He held up his hands to show her his grazed and bleeding knuckles. 'Felt rather good, actually,' he beamed. 'Didn't think I still had it in me, to be honest.'

'So you were a bare-knuckle fighter in your youth, were you?' she asked, binding his hands with a hankie and calling Alice to bring in the first-aid box.

'Well, I was actually, but I didn't tell you because I thought my debonair side had attracted you. Didn't you notice my nose?' he asked, pulling it to one side. 'I've been turning away from you all this time so that you wouldn't see it.' Then he pulled her to him and held her tightly. 'He's gone,' he said, 'and he won't be back. I told him I'd kill him if he ever comes near us again, and I meant it.'

It was only then that Daisy realised Dessie had been there

in the back of her mind, or rather the fear that he would find her again. Now he was gone and she had this lovely man to thank for making her feel secure, for looking after her, when the pattern of her life had been that she cared for other people. She chuckled into his chest.

'You're laughing!' he accused her. 'I'm standing here in agony, bleeding all over the back of your blouse, may I say, and you're laughing!'

'I was just thinking,' she said, 'of you as Saint George!'

'He had armour and, more to the point, metal gauntlets, and a big pointy thing as well, may I remind you!'

'I love you,' she said, without thinking.

'You've never said that before,' he said quietly. 'It was worth it. Even if I die this moment from blood loss, it was worth it.'

24

Five years on Laura and Libby were both married with children, making Peter a grandfather, then Daisy was shocked to discover that she was pregnant. They had never tried or not tried to have children, but for some reason she thought it was one of those things that happened to other people.

Peter was so ecstatic that he told everyone he knew the moment he did, and instead of calling Mar and Par he jumped into his beloved MG and drove all the way to Rose Cottage with the news. He called Daisy to tell her Mar and Par were happy too, though she could hear that quite plainly from the screeching in the background, and that he'd be driving straight back again as soon as they'd all had some champagne.

What surprised Daisy even more was that she gave birth to a son. Once again she had it in her mind that Sheridan women only had girls, probably because she never actually saw her sister's son, she thought sadly. When she'd been informed that she had been safely delivered of a healthy boy she had almost asked, 'Are you sure?'

Peter was mesmerised by the child and by the change in his life. He had been married to Elizabeth for twenty years and they had considered their family complete with the arrival of

Libby. If anything they were thinking of the years in the not-too-far distant future when their daughters would be off their hands and they could please themselves once again. When Elizabeth was killed he'd thought his life was over. He had only just managed to keep going because of the girls, and then he had spotted 'this comely young wench', and here he was, living a new and happy life – and with a son!

He blustered a bit when it was suggested by his now married daughters that he had always secretly wanted a son. Certainly not, and how could they say such a thing, he had adored his daughters and there hadn't been the slightest thought in his mind that a son would have been nice. He was lying of course, and everyone knew it; all men wanted sons, even when they lied and denied it.

The child was called David, after Peter's father, and he was the handsomest child ever seen. And not just because Peter said so, for everyone he asked told him so, and his daughters and his wife laughed.

David was golden-haired and blue-eyed, as both his father and grandfather had been, and he laughed a lot, mainly because his father made it his business to make him laugh a lot. Peter took David with him as often as he was allowed, and on any excuse: to give his mother a rest, to show him some unfor-gettable sight that he would remember for the rest of his life, to show him off, really. Being an older father he had made his fortune, he wasn't striving to establish himself as he had been when Laura and Libby were children, and so he had more time to spend with his second family. Daisy would watch them together, endlessly talking about some treasure the little boy had discovered, a nicely patterned stone, a branch, a bird flying overhead, and feel incredibly happy that she had been able to give this man, who was so full of love and good humour, the one thing he lacked: a son.

Three years after that, when Peter was sixty years old, Daisy had a daughter. All Peter's male friends teased him and he loved it, telling them that it really was nothing to do with him this time, he had been cuckolded as they had all once told him he would be, because the little girl had red hair and no one in his family had ever had red hair. Daisy was shocked when she saw the baby for the first time. There was red hair in her family, but again, for some inexplicable reason it hadn't occurred to her that any child of hers could inherit the gene.

When Peter came to see his daughter he found Daisy holding her, looking into her tiny face and crying.

'She looks like my mother,' she said, 'and my sister, Kay.'

'And that's what she shall be called,' he said, putting his arm around Daisy and kissing her hair. 'Hello, little Kathleen,' he said to his daughter.

'And Elizabeth?' Daisy suggested.

'Kathleen Elizabeth,' Peter agreed.

In a very short time Katie proved to be a musical child. Peter didn't notice it, but Daisy did; Daisy had been here before. Any instrument Katie picked up she could quickly learn to play, fast outgrowing musical toys and throwing them at the walls in frustration. At school she was given a recorder, and after exhausting its abilities in a few minutes was deeply insulted at being offered something so silly. She had a beautiful voice, but was plagued by having perfect pitch, which meant she was never satisfied with any sound she made, though she was worse with any sound anyone else made. If her father whistled or her mother sang she would hold her ears and beg them to stop, because they were out of tune, which just made her father whistle even louder and considerably less in tune. As a teacher at her school struggled to get the choir to reach a note, Kathleen could bear it no more and ran to the music room, hit the right note on the piano repeatedly and shouted at the children, 'Listen! Listen!'

So it became clear that though she had inherited the ability of her grandmother and her aunt, she had a very different personality from either. Katie Bradley was strong-willed; she knew her own mind and would argue with her own shadow, and she had a temper as red as her hair. David, on the other hand, was a good-natured, easy-going boy, and he was the only one who could handle his sister when she was in one of her prima-donna strops, and he did it by making her laugh, just as his father did.

Unlike his father, though, David was very clever academically, and scored so highly on his IQ tests at school that they did them twice more to make sure, then they brought in student teachers to witness the third series of tests. The only thing that impressed David about the exercise was that he was loaded with sweets for his troubles.

Peter was delighted, but bemused. Compared to him David was a genius.

'But I mean,' he said to Daisy, 'where does he get it from?'

'Well, sometimes a musical gift goes with maths, sometimes it's art,' Daisy explained, teasing him. 'So even though he's missed my family's musical gift, he's got the maths that can go with it.'

'So what you're saying,' he said archly, 'is that they get nothing at all from me?'

She put her arms around his neck and pulled his head down level with hers. 'Wanna try again?' she asked seductively.

'Why, Daisy Bradley!' he said in mock shocked tones. 'You

hussy! But seriously, Daisy, what are we going to do with them?'

'What do you mean – "do with them"?'

'Well, they're both bright in different ways. What do we do about schools?'

'I think schools are pretty well set up to cope with academically bright children,' Daisy said. 'It's the ones who aren't bright they have trouble with. David will be fine, it's Katie who's the problem.'

'I don't see that she has a problem at all. It's David I'm thinking about really. I don't want him to grow into one of those serious-minded eggheads who can't laugh or enjoy life.'

'Peter, he hasn't a chance of that, even if it's what he wants. He can be clever at school, but he comes home to this idiot father who was born minus a serious muscle in his body!'

'Well, I wouldn't agree with that, though we'll leave it till later, but surely all we have to do with Katie is make sure she has the music lessons she needs,' Peter replied.

'No, that's what we don't do, Peter. We have to let her decide.'

Daisy was remembering her sister, Kay, who had a voice like an angel, as everyone always said, and who spent her life going to one class after another, as long as the family could afford it. She'd had singing lessons, dancing lessons, piano lessons, but she'd had no real life of her own. Just because she'd had that wonderful voice, Daisy used to think, was no reason why she shouldn't have a choice about whether she should use it. The family, her mother mainly, made the decision that Kay could sing, so she had to sing, and there was never the slightest sign that Daisy ever saw that Kay got any enjoyment from it. There wasn't enough money to help her to use all of her musical talent, something that wouldn't trouble Katie.

Perhaps that was the root of Kay's problems, that she wasn't able to explore all of her gifts fully, but only skimmed across each one. Her singing was settled on because it was the cheapest, there were no expensive instruments to buy, and maybe dancing co-ordination was beyond her but all she had to do with her voice was let it out. She had never developed in any other way that Daisy could see, though. She was just a voice all her life, no opinions, no happiness or sadness, except when it came to childbirth, of course.

Maybe that was what Kay's childhood of being trained to continue her mother's aborted ambitions had done to her. It made her only able to react to basic things, like pain, or hot and cold. It had troubled Daisy all her life. She had never known if there had been something wrong with Kay since before birth, some mental defect, or if she had been conditioned to be the way she was by their mother's failed ambitions. She just stood where she was told to and sang as instructed, but whose fault was that, if anyone's?

It really made Daisy think. All her sister had lacked were the funds to help her reach whatever musical goal she had, but there had to be many thousands of children out there like Kay, who had ability but would never get the chance to follow their dreams.

So Daisy used Peter's business contacts, bled them dry, he said, to raise funds to help musically gifted children, and she called it Kay's Musical Trust. It became her third baby, though she had to keep repeating the argument that they weren't aiming to churn out superbly trained musicians, geniuses and stars who were emotionally stunted, but individuals who could take their gift wherever they wanted to take it. If they didn't want to become household names, well that was fine, too. It was all about letting them stretch and develop a talent they had been born with, and then they could make their own decisions about what they did next.

Meanwhile, it was agreed that Katie would have whatever music lessons she wanted, as long as she stopped throwing things at the walls, and would be allowed to make her own choices, too. Daisy, Peter and David lived through the piano period, the violin, viola, cello and harp octaves, followed by the trumpet, saxophone and bassoon experiments, before Katie took up art and that was that. She was by far the most bois- terous of the two children all through their lives, so when she left home for Art School it was natural that the house seemed very quiet.

David withstood it all with his usual good humour, went to Cambridge, studied the classics, got a very good honours degree and immediately took off to see the world as if he was going two stops on the tube.

Peter never got over his bemusement. His younger children both amazed and delighted him, but they were a puzzle to him also.

'They're so beautiful, aren't they?' he asked, every inch the proud father. 'David's handsome and clever and I really like him; he's a fine chap, you know? And as for that daughter of yours –'

'Mine?'

'Yours and the milkman's,' Peter said. 'No one in my family had red hair or was ever that . . . that . . . I don't know –'

'Argumentative, highly strung, annoying?'

'Well yes, all of that, but she is such a beauty, isn't she? I can get drunk on her faster than I can on champagne. But those clothes she wears!' he grimaced.

'She's an art student,' Daisy said. 'It's the uniform.'

'Would be nice to see her in a dress, though, wouldn't it?'

'My advice is never to say that to her,' Daisy laughed. 'She'd organise one of her Women's Lib demos against you outside the gates.'

'I suppose I just don't understand them. Must be old age,' he sighed.

'You don't have to understand them,' Daisy teased him, 'you only have to accept them as they are.'

'But do *you* understand them?'

'Of course I do,' she teased him, 'but I'm from a different generation!'

25

So with both their children off their hands, Daisy for the first and Peter for the second time, they began to think about retiring to warmer climes. Mainly for Peter's sake because he was feeling the cold more and more, though Daisy didn't say that. He was still odd; age hadn't brought a great deal of sense to his character.

One day he announced that he was going out to buy a coat.

'But you've got a coat,' Daisy said.

'No I haven't, not a warm one anyway.'

'You have,' she insisted, 'you only bought that nice cashmere one a couple of weeks ago.'

'Oh, that's gone,' he said dismissively, 'which is why I need a new coat. You never listen to a word I say, Daisy.'

'That's my problem, I *do*!' she replied. 'If I didn't life would be much easier. So what happened to your coat?'

'What coat? I haven't got one.'

In anyone else she would have suspected senility, but Peter had always been like this, exasperating.

'The cashmere one.'

'Oh, I told you, it's gone.'

She felt she had been trapped in this conversation forever. 'Where has it gone?' she shouted at him.

'Well, I came across this little man in the street playing an accordion,' he explained, 'and he looked terribly cold, Daisy, so I gave him my coat.'

'You couldn't just have given him a couple of bob?' she asked.

'Well, a couple of bob wouldn't have kept him warm, now, would it?'

Daisy shook her head. 'So now you're going out to buy another one?'

'It's that or freeze,' he replied. 'Thought I might have a look in that second-hand place in town.'

'You can't buy a second-hand coat, Peter!'

'Well I'm not buying a new one! What if I meet another little man in the street playing an accordion and I have to give it to him? I mean, you obviously disapprove of my giving him a new one. You have no logic, Daisy, I've always said it, women have no logic.'

'I swear to God,' she said to Mar later, 'living with him is sometimes like living in a music-hall double-act.'

'He's been like that as long as I've known him,' Mar said admiringly. 'Has he told you about Professor Theodore Quibbe?'

Daisy looked at her, puzzled.

'And the local Flower Show?' Par joined in, then he and Mar laughed loud enough to burst a normal person's eardrums. 'Can't believe you don't know about that!'

'Well, tell me!'

'You do know he enters the Flower Show every year, don't you?' Mar giggled.

'Yes, in the summer our life revolves around it. He's always sneaking about, having sly looks at other gardens.'

Mar and Par looked at each other and the usual peal of laughter rang out. Daisy waited.

'Started years ago, during the war. He said he was worried

that the show was dying off, so he'd snoop around gardens and pick out plants he reckoned should be entered, then he'd sneak back again when there was no one about and nick them.'

'He'd steal from other people's gardens?' Daisy asked.

'He still does!' Mar shrieked.

'But that's terrible; what if he's caught?'

'Well he doesn't actually steal them,' Par explained. 'He enters them under the name of Professor Theodore Quibbe, an old and dear friend.'

'Who doesn't actually exist!' Mar yelled, clapping her hands.

'The trouble started,' Par continued, 'when Professor Quibbe's entries began winning and Peter was forced to accept the prizes on his behalf, because, unfortunately, Professor Quibbe couldn't be there.'

'The Flower Show people have been dying to meet Professor Quibbe ever since, but so far he's failed to turn up. Work of national importance, Peter tells them, a particularly painful attack of gout, that sort of thing. I gather they took to sending him Get Well cards via Peter. God alone knows how he'll ever get out of that one!'

Mar and Par fell about in a mutual paroxysm of mirth. 'Wonderful man, Peter,' Mar boomed. 'You couldn't have done better, Daisy darling!'

When Daisy got home that evening she asked after Peter's good friend the Professor.

'Why?' he asked suspiciously. 'What's wrong with him?'

'Oh, I don't know, he's *your* friend. One of the Flower Show organisers asked me today if I thought he'd be well enough to attend the next show.' Daisy looked at him steadily. 'I said I'd ask you.'

'Well, he may be,' he said shiftily. 'Time will tell.'

'Peter! I know all about Professor Quibbe and his floral

347

triumphs!' she shouted at him. 'You can't go on stealing flowers from gardens!'

'Keep your voice down, you'll frighten the dog,' he reproved her.

'Bugger the dog!'

He leaned forward and covered Buster's ears with his hands, tutting at her. 'I'm sorry, Daisy,' he said loftily, 'if you're going to use that kind of language in front of Buster I'll have to take him out. We'll have to continue this conversation at a later date.'

With that he got up and departed, Buster at his heels.

'And if you should see the odd bloom on your walk,' she shouted after him, '*don't* bring it home!'

Then one day came news that would finally set Daisy free. It was a tiny piece in a newspaper about a fire in a Newcastle pub that had killed three people, one of them Mr Desmond Doyle, whose wife and two children had died in a raid during the war. Apparently no relatives could be found and the authorities were using the newspaper to appeal for someone to claim the body – and pay for the funeral, of course.

Daisy stared at the paragraph, reading it over and over again. Dessie dead, now there was something, and no one to do the honours. As far as she could remember there had only been him and his mother, but there must be other relatives. He was Irish, for heaven's sake, a fact that had doubtless prompted the newspaper appeal. She showed it to Peter.

'Good riddance, I say,' Peter said quietly.

'I agree,' Daisy replied.

'And you're thinking what, exactly?'

'That I'd like to be sure, I suppose.'

'Yes, well, I can see your point, after that big disappointment over Father Christmas not being true one always questions everything.'

'Could we pay for his funeral?' she asked.

Peter looked at her. 'Have you gone mad, Daisy?' he whispered. 'Do you want to dress up as chief mourner as well?'

'I was just thinking,' she said earnestly. 'I'd like to be absolutely sure, that's all.'

'I should think being burned alive would do it, Daisy, you should know that better than anyone, surely?'

'Yes, but . . . well I can't explain it really. I know he's dead, but dead and buried has a more final ring to it.'

'Ah, I see,' he smiled, hugging her. 'Dead and gone and all that?'

'Something like that.'

'I'll see to it,' he smiled. 'But I think cremation rather than burial. What do you think? Do the job properly?'

'Yes, that would do the job properly,' she said quietly.

So now she was free, finally free, and as Dessie could no longer appear on her doorstep he stopped appearing in her dreams, too.

When he was eighty years old, Peter let it be known he wasn't getting old, it was the weather that was changing. He had read somewhere that Oxford was entering into another ice age. Maybe Spain after all, he told the family at the christening of Peter, his first great-grandchild. They were letting all sorts of criminals into Spain in the 1970s, he said, and he'd always fancied himself as a master safe-blower.

Not all of the family were there. David was in Brazil and Katie was in London, from where she had called the day before to say she would not be coming home. Christenings were bourgeois and she would have nothing to do with such antiquated notions and obvious social strictures, and anyway, there was a demo about something, and though she didn't know what, it was her duty to support her comrades. Oh, and tell Pop thanks for the cash.

Daisy had told him when he came in from playing golf the day before.

He nodded. 'Still a Communist, then?' he asked, taking his jacket off.

'Seems so,' Daisy smiled.

'Your one, that one,' he grinned. 'I've always said it and I always will – your one, that one.'

'That's unfair!'

'It's true, though!' he retorted. 'Never been any red hair in my family.'

'That comes from my family.'

'There you are, then, told you. Yours that one,' Peter said, adding, as he always did, 'yours and the milkman's.'

One day Mar called Daisy, yelling cheerfully down the phone. She needed to see Daisy and now. Everything was like that with Mar, it had to be now. Par had died the year before and Mar had been devastated. She had never thought of it happening, apparently. 'I mean, he wasn't like other people, was he?' she'd demanded at the funeral. 'Par wasn't one to die, the thing ain't right.' Then she had looked around and bellowed, 'The place is so quiet now, ain't it?' which made everyone turn away to hide their laughter.

Ever since she had been preparing to go herself, as though Par had gone on a journey leaving her behind and now she was getting ready to catch up with him.

'Been thinking about Granny's diamonds, Daisy, darling,' she said when Daisy arrived. 'You know, the ones you wore at your wedding.'

Daisy nodded. How could she ever forget them?

'Decided you must have them.'

Daisy almost choked on her tea. 'You can't do that!' she said, shocked. 'Apart from anything else, there's Dotty to consider. She'd be very hurt, don't you think?'

'Well that's the thing, you see. I know she and Bertie are doing so much good work that they're assured of sainthoods already – they're with the UN now, did I tell you?'

Daisy nodded.

'Wherever there's someone suffering a bit, there you'll find our Dotty suffering along with them,' she sighed.

'Mar! That's awful!'

'True, though, ain't it? I blame myself, you know, I think I overwhelmed her with the good things, turned her the other way.'

'I think that was the war,' Daisy said, 'and we've had this conversation before, Mar. The war changed all of us. With Dotty it was finding a talent she didn't know she had and meeting all those different people and finding out how unequal the world is. She just decided to try to even things up a bit, that's all.'

'But I never see her and when she does come home she seems ashamed of me in some way, as though I'm to blame for all that inequality. Surely I can only have contributed a little bit?' and her laughter rang out around the room. Mar was right, though, without Par duetting with her the place did seem strangely quiet. 'She would only sell Granny's diamonds to help the suffering if I left them to her. Even if she had children I know she wouldn't pass them on.' She glanced at Daisy. 'Yes, I know, all that good work,' she grimaced, 'wonderful thing to do and all that, but someone somewhere would still be wearing them and she wouldn't be family, that's my point. So I've decided you must have them. Every time I look at them I see you on your wedding day.'

'But what about Freddy's wife? And they have children.'

'Oh, bugger them, they're all boys anyway, and these things should go to the female side, that's the tradition, and I'm a traditional old mare, as you know. The estate will go to Freddy, and Granny's diamonds to my other daughter, to you, Daisy,' Mar said.

Daisy didn't know what to say. 'But shouldn't you at least ask Dotty?' she suggested.

'Already have, darling. She wrote back telling me I could do whatever I wanted with them, that she didn't want them, all but suggested where I could put them, which I thought was a bit rum for a saint!'

Mar died that Christmas. 'Just like Mar to go when there's a party looming,' Peter said. 'She had style, the old mare.'

Dotty came home for the funeral while Bertie worked on, and Daisy took her to one side.

'Dotty, she made me take Granny's diamonds a while back, did you know that?'

'Yes,' Dotty said, 'she wrote to me.'

'But they're really yours,' Daisy said. 'I took them because she wanted me to, but I decided to hold on to them to please her. I always intended giving them to you.'

'But I don't want them!' Dotty said, aghast. 'Didn't she tell you that?'

'Yes, but now that she's finally gone I thought you'd change your mind. They really belong with you.'

'Daisy,' Dotty said gently, 'you have no idea how you've lifted my guilt all these years. If you hadn't been here as the daughter she wished she'd had I wouldn't have been able to live the way

I wanted. You freed me, do you realise that? I'm so grateful to you for being Mar's daughter, for caring for her the way I should have, and she was right, Granny's baubles are yours. I'd only sell them.'

'She said that!' Daisy laughed.

'I'll bet she did! You keep them, Daisy, hand them on to your daughter, that's what Mar would've wanted.'

'My girl is a revolutionary,' Daisy giggled, thinking of Katie in diamonds. 'She'd have me arrested for betraying whichever cause she currently believes in!'

'Yes, well, we were all like that, Daisy,' Dotty replied. 'We all change as we get older, look at us!'

Two weeks later, just after New Year, with the family — minus Katie — still with them, Peter died.

He had insisted on taking everyone outside to see the snowdrops that he was always boasting came through earlier in his garden than anywhere else. And he just dropped to the ground. Not a sound, no cry or sigh. A stroke, the doctor said, he hadn't felt a thing, and he'd died with most of his family around him.

Katie came home for her father's funeral, wearing a dress and torturing herself for not being there when he died. She knew he was old, but she'd expected him to go on forever, she said, and she wished she hadn't argued with him so much and that she'd come home oftener, unaware, as the young always are, that she was saying what every generation has always said and always will on similar occasions.

David had received the message sent to him and made it home in time, looking taller, broader and more grown-up than Daisy expected; she wished his father could have seen him. She was surprised by how weak she felt. She knew Peter had been

353

getting on, she had been almost nursing him for the last ten years and had thought ahead to this moment more than once, but now it had come she felt so much older than her fifty-four years. And alone; very alone.

Even so, she insisted that they all went back to their lives to leave her to come to terms with her new status. It had sounded so convincing, too. Not for the first time in her life she surprised herself, but it was so hard to take in, so hard not to keep looking for him, listening for him, and the feeling in the night when she stretched her arm out and found that empty cold space in their bed was too much to bear. She had refused to wash the pillowcase his head had lain on, so that she could have the smell of him still, and she could hug the pillow for the rest of the night, crying and wondering if it was possible to go on with this pain.

The children were wonderful, of course, but there were things, shared little and big things between husband and wife, that children couldn't and shouldn't share. Things that didn't need words, only a glance, memories that were theirs alone. The nonsense when they had first met and she thought he was insane; their first time in the inn before they were married, when they'd escaped from Mar and Par's huge, noisy party; the moments immediately after David and Katie were born . . . and now there was no one to share them with. He had made her into her own person, she had worked that out long ago. He had brought 'the real Daisy' back to life and allowed her to blossom under his care. She had so much to feel grateful for, so much to miss.

It was a letter from Edith in reply to hers telling her of Peter's death that saved her. They had kept in touch, meeting up on Edith's three or four visits home in the last thirty years, and they wrote, not weekly, not even monthly sometimes, but every now and again. Edith invited her to come out to Brisbane, saying the sun would do her much more good than a winter in England.

At first she dismissed the idea. She didn't think she could make such a long journey without Peter, and part of her didn't want to leave him lying in the cemetery for so long on his own, though she knew he would tell her that was illogical. It would also have made him laugh, she thought, and that's what decided her to go.

She had done a lot of thinking in these last few months, events like this did that. She supposed it was a kind of filing system in the head, and now that something else had to be filed, too, other thoughts were being jostled to the surface. Thoughts about the war years occupied her mind, and how they had all joined the WAAFs because of the flying, the idea of getting up, up and away, escaping from their normal lives. A few of the girls did get into the air, though every WAAF and every pilot who took them up would've been on a charge if they'd been found out. There was that one girl who'd persuaded a Fly Boy to take her for a spin in a fighter, if she remembered correctly, and it had crashed, killing both of them. Funny the things you had barely registered originally that came into your mind at a time like this.

The day before Daisy was due to fly out she was reading a newspaper when her eye was caught by a single paragraph down in the corner. She almost dropped the paper on the floor. The RAF Air Historical Branch was appealing for friends or relatives of two gunners who had served on a Lancaster Bomber in the war. The plane had been shot down over Normandy on the way back from a raid on Italy in August 1943, and had recently been recovered during road-works. The remains of several of the crew had been identified, among them the skipper,

Flying Officer Calum R MacDonald of the RCAF – *Calli*! – and Flt Engineer Graeme Shaw, also of the RCAF – *Bruiser*! She had just been thinking back on those years, so the appearance of that tiny piece of newspaper almost made her collapse.

The boys had been found after all these years and would be buried in Normandy where they had died. Once she had gathered her thoughts she wondered what to do. Should she cancel her trip to Australia and go to Normandy instead? Did she have any right to go there? What would the boys' relatives think and what was she to say to them? And she wondered if Eileen knew, and, if she did, how she was coping. Daisy had just lost Peter, and for Eileen this news must feel like losing Calli all over again.

In a strange way she still thought of them as she had last seen them. What was it that poem from World War One had said? '*They shall not grow old*,' and it was true. She imagined going to Normandy and meeting them again, all of them as they were, jumping about and teasing each other, and saying, 'Daisy, how come you're so old?'

Eileen's lovely boy with the dark, serious eyes. Calli. She had kissed him on the cheek before they left on that last mission because he said he was spooked, and he looked it. And Bruiser had leaped to his feet in his usual mad way, proclaiming that he was the most spooked of all, so where was his kiss? She could still hear their voices in her head, see the two replacement gunners watching them rolling about the NAAFI floor, wrestling over Bruiser's missed kiss. The two new gunners had just arrived, she remembered them standing back and laughing, feeling not enough part of the crew yet to join in. They never did reach that stage, she thought, they died a matter of hours later, and, though she never got to know them, she still had a snapshot of their faces, their young, young faces, in her mind.

She should have given Bruiser his kiss, but to have relented then would have spooked Calli more because it would have been so out of the ordinary. Although the kiss she had given him was, too, wasn't it? Bruiser would look at her with those big, soft eyes and that silly smile, and he always blew her a kiss. It had been one of Peter's habits, too.

It was too much, she thought, crying again, after going through losing and burying Peter she couldn't watch the boys being buried, too, even after all this time. She would send flowers, she decided, and now she would definitely find Eileen when she came home.

On the flight to Australia, Daisy slept a lot of the time, and being able to afford to fly First Class helped considerably. She told the stewardesses she was taking a sleeping pill and not to wake her, then wondered if they might think she was about to commit a very expensive suicide.

Every time she closed her eyes she found a jumble of images waiting for her in her dreams, with Peter and Frank, Calli and Bruiser, and all the shot-up, crashed planes she had ever encountered, and the voices of the pilots crystal-clear, asking for permission to land or to die. On the few occasions when she woke during the long journey, she wondered if she had made the right decision. Perhaps she should have gone to Normandy; after all, Brisbane would still be there another day. Then she thought again about the reason for the gathering in France and knew she couldn't have handled it at the moment.

Brisbane was hot, too hot really, though it was famed for its balmy climate and it was the end of summer there. Edith was used to it, she even spoke with an Australian accent, and she and Doug had four huge, sun-bronzed men they claimed were

357

their sons, and a whole host of grandchildren. It was good to be with a family again, and they were a friendly lot, demanding to know if it was true their mother had run the entire RAF throughout the war, as she claimed, or had she made the whole thing up? Though they were teasing Edith they were more impressed than they had expected when Daisy told them some of the old stories.

Even though everyone was welcoming, Daisy felt odd being on her own and only stayed for a full month so as not to offend Edith. She longed to be at home in Oxford, though, where the summers were kinder and cooler than Brisbane winters, and she was glad when a respectable four weeks had passed and she could make plans for her return.

She was packing one day, ready for the off, the TV playing in the background, and though she was only half-listening she heard something about World War Two. Like all of those who took part in the war, to Daisy those years were the most intense and productive of her life. It was something to do with the close relationships and the kind of responsibilities they knew they would never have again, a feeling that they were doing something of supreme importance and the lives of others depended on them. So, hearing the commentator talking about those days, she shouted to Edith who was baking in the kitchen, stopped packing and sat on the arm of a chair to listen and watch.

Films of D-Day were being replayed. Would anyone of her generation ever forget those pictures of young boys with anxious expressions jumping from landing craft into the water, with those French houses in the background? The boys fighting ashore or dying in the water and on the beaches were, the commentator said, supported by *planes from all over the world, including the only all-Australian Spitfire Squadron based in the UK*, and Daisy's heart was in her mouth. *They were stationed in the remote Orkney and Shetland Islands to the far north of Scotland,'* he was saying, as she desperately examined the faces on screen for the one she knew.

They were all so impossibly young, you knew that at the time, but looking back at them now brought a lump to the throat, especially when you had a son of a similar age. *'One pilot, who had previously survived the Battle of Britain, and also lasted almost to the end of Operation Overlord before being shot down and badly burned, was Queensland man, Frank Moran, from Dalby in the Darling Downs,'* said the commentator. Daisy watched the old film footage on the screen, hardly able to breathe, then a voice came over the images, before the camera picked up the owner of the voice.

It was Frank. He was much older and the scarring from the burns had rendered him only barely recognisable as the boy he once was. As if to reassure the viewer that it was him, a picture was shown of him as he was before he was shot down.

But it couldn't be him: Frank had died in 1944, she knew that.

Daisy's heart was beating in an odd way. She couldn't focus her eyes properly, and, simultaneously, the words coming from the TV seemed to be echoing in a cave. Then her legs fell away from her body and she was on the floor, with Edith's voice coming from a long way off, telling her it was just the heat, she wasn't used to it and not to worry, everything was OK.

But it wasn't OK. She'd just seen a man who had died thirty-one years ago, and he was talking on TV in the present day. And not just any man, but Frank. *Frank!* She got up and sat on the chair.

'Did you see him?' she asked Edith.

'Who? Oh, the Spit pilot? Yes, I saw him. What terrible burns, but then the Spit guys always got the worst burns, didn't they?'

'But did you see Frank?' Daisy asked desperately, then remembered that Edith had never met him.

'Was that his name?' Edith asked, applying an ice-cold compress to the back of Daisy's neck. 'I didn't hear that. Look, I think you ought to lie down.'

'But it was Frank,' she kept murmuring, 'and Frank's dead, but he was alive.'

'I take it you knew him?' Edith asked, and Daisy nodded.

'It was Frank,' she repeated, allowing herself to be led to her room to lie down.

So what was she supposed to do now? she wondered, lying in the blessedly air-conditioned room. Within a few months she had buried Peter, then heard that Calli, Bruiser and the others had been found in their Lanc, over thirty years after they had died, and were about to be buried in Normandy. And here she was in Australia, watching a man she was sure was dead talking on TV. Was there some sort of etiquette that covered these situations?

She lay in the bedroom for a long time, she had no idea how long, and when Edith popped her head round the door to check on her, she asked, 'Where are the Darling Downs? Are they far?'

'Do you want to go there?' Edith asked. 'I don't know why I didn't think of it before, it's where everyone in this area goes to escape the heat. It's the very place for you.'

'So it's near?'

'A couple of hours away, maybe. It's an agricultural area.'

Daisy nodded. 'Yes, I know,' she said quietly.

'Been reading up on it, have you?'

'Yes, something like that.'

'It's that pilot, isn't it?' Edith asked quietly. 'The one on the TV?'

'Yes,' Daisy smiled. 'That's where he lives, or did. But even if he's not there any longer, someone there must know where he is.'

'We could try the phone book.'

Daisy shook her head. 'I want to go there.'

'Do you want me to go with you?' Edith asked, perplexed by how serious and determined Daisy sounded.

'No,' she laughed, 'just point me in the right direction.'

Edith sat on the bed beside her. 'I'll drive you there, Daisy,' she said. 'If we find this, er, Frank?'

Daisy nodded.

'If we find him there I'll drop you off and come back for you. Don't argue, you don't know the way or the area, I'll drive you there.'

Dalby looked like anyone's idea of a farming town, the kind of place that moved slowly, and everyone seemed to know everyone else. Daisy and Edith stopped at what looked like a general store and Daisy got out of the car and bought some soft drinks that were, thankfully, ice-cold. The man behind the counter, about her own age, fair hair going grey, blue eyes, stocky build, was friendly, wanted to know where she came from and how she was enjoying her stay.

She said she was looking for Frank Moran and the man became slightly more suspicious.

'You're not one of those damned reporters or TV people, are you?' he asked.

'No, I'm not,' Daisy replied, opening a bottle of juice and drinking it.

'It's just that we've had quite a few of them here since Frank did that TV thing a while back. Can't think why he did it, he was always a bit shy after he came back, with the scars and that, didn't like people staring at him. Then he goes and does that TV thing, never did understand that.' He shook his head. 'Now it's been repeated and it'll all start up again,' he said peevishly.

'But they must spend money when they come here, so what's the problem?'

'No problem, really, I don't suppose,' he said grudgingly. 'Just don't like them taking their photos and making him look like a freak.' He looked at her, still not sure about her.

'I was a WAAF during the war,' she explained. 'I worked in the tower at an RAF station. I knew Frank then. I thought he'd died when he was shot down, but I saw him on TV and realised he was alive. Couldn't believe it, it was quite a shock.'

'Nearly was dead,' the shopkeeper said. 'Even after he came home it was a long time before he looked like he might live. Broke his mother's heart. I remember him from when we were kids, he was always so good-looking. I almost cried myself when I saw what they'd done to him. I was in the army, came through without a scratch. But he got married, a local girl, had kids. He's widowed now, still living on the farm, but his son works it now.'

'Is there somewhere I can call him from?' Daisy asked, opening the other bottle. 'I don't want to just walk in on him after all these years.'

The man nodded to a phone. 'I'll give you his number. Tell him you're at Isaac's.' He put out a hand. 'I'm his cousin.'

She smiled; they'd crossed some sort of barrier. 'Thanks, Isaac.'

The phone was answered after what seemed like hours. 'Can I speak to Frank?' she asked.

'This is Frank,' the voice replied, but she didn't recognise it.

She turned to Isaac. 'This doesn't sound like him!' she whispered.

He smiled as he took the receiver from her. 'Hi, Frank, it's Isaac. Got a lady here looking for the old man, not you. Yeah,' he chuckled, 'that's right, an old flame, but this one's from England.'

Daisy glared at Isaac as he returned the receiver, then she heard a voice. 'Hello?'

'Frank?' she asked.

There was a long silence. 'Frank?' she said again. 'Frank, it's –'

'I know who it is,' he said quietly. 'How are you, Daisy?'

'I'm fine, Frank,' she replied. 'How did you guess who it was?'

'Remembered the voice,' he said, and she pictured him smiling, not as he was now, but as he had been.

Her mouth was dry. She motioned to Isaac for another drink. 'Would you believe I was just passing and –'

Frank laughed. '– thought you'd stop off for a chat with an old friend?' he asked.

When she put down the receiver she stood with a hand over her mouth, trying to compose herself. Isaac handed her a drink.

'Did you know him well, then?' he asked, grinning.

'Any more of your cheek,' she told him, 'and I'll pull out my secret camera and take a snap of you!'

Edith dropped her off at the farm on the way out of town and arranged to call when she was on her way back.

'I feel terrible having you hang around like this,' Daisy said.

'Well don't. I've never been able to look around here without a pile of kids screaming and fighting. Enjoy yourself, and,' she said firmly, 'I'll expect a full explanation later.'

He had been standing just inside the porch and came out on to the grass to meet her when the car pulled away, arms outstretched to hold her hand in both of his. She didn't even notice that they were badly scarred; she was looking at his face, trying to find the man she remembered. The scarring was on the lower half of his face so the smile she remembered wasn't there any more. She imagined his chest was badly affected too, but from the nose upwards she saw him again. It was Frank.

'Pretty bad, huh?' he asked, rubbing his chin. Once it had been a discernible chin; now it was rounded, like a piece of melted plastic that had reset, but not in its original shape. 'But at least I don't have to worry about shaving, that's saved me a fortune over the years.'

'I was looking at your eyes,' she said, still holding one hand. 'They haven't changed, you're still in there.'

He took her inside the house, having obviously noticed that she was finding the heat hard to bear. There was no sign of his family apart from photos everywhere, so they must have staged a diplomatic withdrawal after her call, making her feel like a teenager on a date. She imagined them watching from every nook and cranny in the farmhouse as she sat down.

'So, how have you been?' he asked. 'You haven't changed in, what is it now? Thirty years?'

'Yes, sure, I haven't changed,' she said wryly.

He looked at her ring finger. 'Married, I see,' he smiled.

'Widowed,' she said quietly, 'a few months ago.'

'Oh, I'm sorry.'

'Me, too,' she sighed. 'Your cousin says you're widowed too?'

'Yes, there's a lot of it about,' he said, trying to sound glib. He looked at her for a few moments. 'You've no idea how often I've thought of seeing you again,' he laughed. 'Never thought I would, but I've had this little speech all ready all these years just in case, and now I can't get it out.'

'A speech? Why?' she asked.

'To apologise,' he said shyly. 'I remember what I called you the last time we met. It was just jealousy, you know, I didn't mean it. I went round to the flat the next day, but you'd gone.'

She nodded. 'We went back to Rose Cottage then I went back to Langar – I was on duty that night. The Yank, Hal, he wasn't a lover, not even a date, he was one of Dotty's waifs and strays. He'd been shot down and was really ill. Mar asked me to show him the sights.'

'Ah,' he said.

'Anyway, it wasn't the last time we met,' she said. 'When I heard you'd been shot down I hitched to the hospital and sat by your bed for weeks, then a weekend, till the doctor told me to stop. Said I was wasting my time because you weren't going to make it.'

'They told me there had been a WAAF. I thought it was Dotty,' he said quietly.

'No, Dotty had transferred her affections to a doctor in her unit by then, married him before they were posted to France.' She stopped and looked down at her hands. 'The doctor promised to call me if you survived. When he hadn't after two weeks I called the hospital and they said they had no one there of your name. I thought you were dead, I've thought that all these years, till I saw you on TV the other day.' She looked up at him. 'I just had to make sure it really was you.'

His eyes looked moist, but burns often did that to people. 'They shipped me home as soon as I'd turned the corner,' he said. 'My mother got the brunt of it. I was a real bastard to everyone for a long time, her especially because she was nearest. Then Kitty took me on, which was a real surprise, given how I looked.' He paused. 'Your husband,' he said eventually, 'you were happy?'

'Yes. He was much older than me, but he was a wonderful man, you'd have liked him. I think he saved my life, to be honest, he just grabbed me and took me on. I told him about you, and he didn't blink an eye.'

'About me?'

'That there had been someone else and he'd been killed.'

'I was your someone else?' he asked.

'Mad, isn't it?' she laughed. 'I wouldn't admit it till you were too ill to be bothered. Life can be really strange.'

She thought of his final letter, the one that had arrived after his 'death'. 'And your Uncle Kevin,' she said brightly, 'the ice man. How is he?'

He laughed. 'Been gone a long time now,' he said, 'but I did see him again.' He shook his head, obviously recalling the last letter he had written to her. 'I had the feeling I was for the chop,' he said quietly. 'I really thought it was my last chance to write to you, and I wrote about my Uncle Kevin! Jeez! And I was a real romantic, wasn't I? Promised you your own ice chest! No wonder you didn't come running!'

Daisy laughed. Here they were, she thought wryly, all these years later, and Uncle Kevin and his services to ice chests was still the topic of conversation.

'After the war kerosene fridges came in, so he was out of a job,' Frank said. 'He bought the local store, made a good living, easier on him too. His son, Isaac, runs it now, you met him.'

'Ah.' Daisy nodded.

'Old Kevin missed doing his rounds, though, didn't like being stuck in the shop, so he did all the grocery deliveries himself. Isaac was like me, only too grateful to be home, so he ran the shop and gave his father some freedom and they were both happy.'

'But the local children missed out on handfuls of ice chips,' she laughed. Another silence.

'And you have children?' she asked.

'A son and two daughters.'

366

'I have a son and a daughter, and two step-daughters.'

There was a long silence.

'This isn't easy, is it?' he smiled.

'No, it isn't. You can't help thinking and wondering what life would've been like, you know? It seems unfair,' she replied.

'I thought about you from time to time.'

'Really? Same here. I'm so glad you've had a good life,' she said.

'So why was it so difficult to admit back then?' he asked.

'Oh, that would take too long, Frank. Things in my life, I was pretty mixed up. There were reasons.'

'You seemed so calm and in control,' he smiled.

'But I wasn't. I wasn't a whore either,' she laughed, 'but that's how it seemed to you!'

'God, don't!' he said, putting up a hand.

So they sat there, talking about the old days, about Rose Cottage and the now late Mar and Par, thinking more than they were talking, and feeling strange. What do you say to the love of your life after thirty years, especially when other partnerships have been forged during those years? If our experiences make us who we are, then in that time and after those partnerships, is it possible for anything of who we once were to remain unchanged?

After a time, Edith phoned, and Daisy told her to come and collect her.

Frank went to the door with her, and as she was about to turn to leave he reached out and held her for a long moment that made him shake and brought tears to her eyes. They promised to write and that was that, but sitting in the car she felt a strange feeling that something was wrong. At first she couldn't work out what it was, then she realised that she felt she shouldn't be leaving him.

'So?' Edith asked. 'Details, please!'

She told Edith the whole story and almost laughed aloud at the wide range of expressions that crossed her face.

'Well, you kept that close to your chest!' Edith said at last.

'That was the point, Edith, no one was getting close to my chest in those days, if you remember!'

'We all wondered what went on during your trips to London,' Edith hinted. 'You never gave the lads at Langar the time of day, so we all assumed you were living it up down there.'

'I did some of the time, went to parties, had a good time, but mostly I went to Rose Cottage to be looked after and pampered by Mar and Par. That's where the wedding reception was, if you remember.'

'And you really thought this Spit guy was dead? Amazing! What are you going to do now?'

'What is there to do?' Daisy smiled quietly. 'Thirty years have passed, he has his life and family here, I have mine over there, and tomorrow I go back to my life.' She shrugged. 'But you, Edith, you're one of the success stories, you and your Aussie!' They laughed together.

'I remember the night he finally became Doug,' Edith said. 'The ENSA show.'

'And the Great Walendo, poor sod.'

'And Tony Hancock in a tutu and army boots!' Edith laughed. 'When he became a big star after the war I could never look at him without seeing him in that tutu and army boots!' There was a silence as the two old friends remembered their youth.

'But you've been happy, Edith? You and Doug?'

Edith nodded. 'We had a bad patch after the war, turned out he was addicted to those damned tablets they gave bomber crews to keep them awake. Amphetamines, struth!'

Daisy smiled. Edith sounded very Australian at times.

'It was my father who worked it out,' Edith said. 'He didn't approve of us getting married of course, but after the war he had heard of lots of former aircrew who were addicted to the tablets. He got Doug help and it was OK after that. You wonder how many went undiagnosed, though, poor sods. And yes, we've been happy, very happy. I feel very sad for you and your Frank and how things could've been different.'

'Don't be,' Daisy smiled. 'I was very happy with Peter, and Frank was with his Kitty. Maybe there's a reason for the things that happen, after all.'

26

The feeling that there was something wrong stayed with Daisy on the journey home, and when she arrived back in Oxford she felt as though the universe had changed, tilted in some way she couldn't define. Jet lag, probably, she thought, half-heartedly going through the pile of mail that was waiting for her, though the bills had been taken care of in her absence. There was one from the florist who had dealt with the flowers for Calli, Bruiser and the boys, and she wondered why that one hadn't been paid, until she saw 'Personal' written in the left-hand corner. Inside was a letter and note from the florist saying a woman had asked for the letter to be forwarded, as, naturally, they didn't want to hand out her address.

Daisy turned it over in her hand, then her eyes settled on the Glasgow postmark and she felt her heart give a leap. Eileen! It was from Eileen, and there was a phone number, so she called it without even reading the letter.

'I can't believe it's you!' they both said, then giggled.

'You sound exactly the same!' Daisy said.

'That's what I was going to say!'

'I've got so much to tell you, Eileen.'

'Me, too.'

'Look, I'm just back from Australia, shall I come up or will you come down here?'

'I spend all my time travelling these days, too! It's a wonder we didn't bump into each other at Heathrow!'

'I'll come up. When? Tomorrow?'

'Well, you've left it a bit late today!'

Afterwards Daisy couldn't settle. She kept thinking of how much had happened in such a short time, and now she was going to see Eileen again. She thought about Newcastle and, as she was heading northwards anyway, was suddenly caught by the notion of going back to Guildford Place, if there was anything of it still standing. It had been a long time since she'd been there, 1944 to be exact, and she'd kept her eyes fixed in the middle distance until she was safely out of it again.

It was when she had conned the little American Major into providing transport to take her to Glasgow and back to see Eileen and her new baby. He'd thought he looked like Clark Gable, she smiled to herself, and she had played a dirty trick on the little man by letting him think he was in with a chance. Then she'd put on a wonderfully wounded performance to get rid of him. At least she should have asked him what his name was, but maybe he had already told her; she tended not to take note in those days unless their usefulness was likely to be extended, and his wasn't, poor little man. He probably went around telling everyone he'd had her in the back of the staff car he had purloined for the occasion. At his age the fantasy was probably as good as reality anyway. Having a gorgeous young sex-pot on his arm told the world – and his friends – that he was all man. He had doubtless collected the nudge-nudge, wink-wink kudos then returned to his wife in the States, so no one was harmed.

* * *

Eileen was waiting at the airport. They recognised each other straight off and hugged and cried for ages before setting off for Eileen's home.

'I've got such a lot to tell you,' Eileen smiled. 'Wait till we get inside.'

And once inside the house Eileen had brought her up-to-date. Her marriage had been awful; she had been unhappy the whole time but had kept quiet because she didn't want to upset the apple-cart. Her husband, the dreaded childhood sweetheart, had never doubted that Annie was his, but he gave Eileen a hard time because he sensed she didn't love him.

'He could be mentally very cruel,' she said, 'but I blame myself in a way. He was right, I never did love him, and that was all he wanted. When he died I was relieved. I know that's terrible, but it's true.' She sighed. 'But so much has happened recently. I went to Normandy for the funerals of the boys. I met Calli's family there, but I didn't tell them the truth about us, or about Annie, made out I had worked at Langar and had known the crew. It was awful. I just cried and cried afterwards. I kept thinking that I'd kept Annie from them and them from Annie, if you see what I mean. They were so desperate to hear about him. You remember how the families always were when we wrote to them after their boys had died? I could've told them so much but I didn't. They're such nice people, too, I felt like a criminal.'

'You did what you had to do,' Daisy said, putting her hand over Eileen's.

'I know, but it was wrong, wasn't it? When I came home, things happened, it's all very strange and sounds even stranger. Calli had the second sight, did I ever tell you that?'

Daisy shook her head. 'You knew better in those days, I'd have laughed.'

'But not now?'

'Not now. I really liked him, did you know that?'

'Well, it was hard to tell at times, Daisy. All Fly Boys were treated with contempt on principle!'

'He was a lovely boy in every sense, though, I knew that back then. He was decent and good. Once I turned round and he was staring at me and his lips were moving. As far as I could tell he was saying, "Poor Daisy." I had no idea why.'

Eileen nodded. 'He asked me once about your family. I said they were abroad, and he said "No, they're dead. She only says they're abroad," and he said something terrible had happened to you before they died. He didn't explain what, but it troubled him.'

'It would have,' Daisy said, 'and he was right. Our house had taken a direct hit and there were no survivors. I couldn't have coped with the sympathy, so I said they were abroad, and something bad did happen to me before I joined up. It was why I joined up.'

'He said you'd eventually have what you wanted all along, though, that you'd be all right. I said you were already and he said you weren't, you just made it look that way. I never mentioned it, I didn't want to upset you, but he really was quite fond of you, Daisy.'

'I always gave him hell, but I was fond of him, too,' Daisy said. 'I knew he didn't see me the way the others did. Before they went on that last mission I saw them in the NAAFI and Calli didn't look too good. He said he was OK, apart from feeling spooked, because he didn't just have his family to think of, but you, too. I don't know what I was thinking, but I kissed him on the cheek – me! Bruiser went wild, you know what he was like. The last I saw they were all rolling about the floor wrestling, with the two new gunners watching. I've thought about it so often. They didn't join in because they didn't feel part of the crew, yet they died together a few hours later. How intimate a connection was that? I didn't go over to Normandy for the funerals. I'd just buried my husband, you see, I didn't think I could cope.'

'The flowers were lovely,' Eileen said. 'Pearl was there, she told me you were married.'

'Pearl?' Daisy said, eyes wide. 'Little Pearl with the head to one side?'

'She still does that,' Eileen laughed. 'She had made a date with one of those new gunners, so she went to Normandy to see him buried. Said she hadn't told you about the date because she was scared you'd round on her.'

'I would have! I remember she sat up in the tower that night, and she did seem a bit anxious. I thought it was because of you. Did she tell you about the boots?'

Eileen shook her head.

'Before we had it confirmed that Lady Groundhog was lost we heard the sound of flying boots outside and thought they'd made it back. When we opened the door there was no one there. We all looked at each other and shivered a bit! There were about six of us still waiting, we all heard it, and you couldn't mistake the sound of flying boots. I've never understood it.' She looked up. 'And all the time Pearl was keeping a secret, was she? Wish I'd known!' she laughed.

'Well, you'll get your chance to tell her off – she's arriving tomorrow! So tell me about your husband. Were you happy?'

'Very. He was quite a man, just what I needed. He was a lot older than me, so I knew he would go sooner, but it's still hard. I'm still a bit confused, to be honest. Something happened to me, too. It was when I was in Australia. Do you remember the Australian Spitfire pilot? The one who kept writing to me?'

'I had to write "Gone away" on his letters and send them back!' Eileen recalled.

'Well, he was Mr Right, I was just too scared to admit it then. He was shot down in 1944, a few months after I saw you and Annie, and I was told he was dead, but he wasn't. I saw him on TV in Australia and looked him up.'

'Really? That must've been a helluva shock!'

'You have no idea! Oh, hell, let's not talk about it yet, I'm feeling so confused about it. Tell me about Annie.'

'Well, this is where it gets very strange, as I said,' Eileen said, glancing at Daisy. 'You know I said Calli had the second sight? Annie has, too. When she was little she saw a man in the corner of her room, never questioned it. He was always there, she thought other people saw him too, and when she understood they didn't she was too confused to say anything. It was Calli.'

'My God, another shiver's just gone up my spine!'

'Think how I felt! It came out recently when her son – Gavin's four, by the way – got annoyed because the man he saw had disappeared.'

'The little boy saw him, too?' Daisy was aghast.

'The man had disappeared completely after the boys were buried, and Gavin was really angry, kept demanding to know where he'd gone, and bit by bit it came out. Annie eventually owned up, said all sorts of strange things had happened throughout her life, but she hadn't mentioned any of them because she was scared it might cause a fuss. That's the saddest thing. I was trying to give her a normal family life, but all those years she knew things weren't right between Alex and me, she said she felt she had to watch what she said and did. Made me feel such a failure.'

'Oh, stop it!'

Then the photos came out, with much Aahing and Oohing.

'Katie's a redhead, full of life, a bit too full to be honest; built like me, too, or as I used to be.'

'You don't look that different.'

'Oh, it's true, old friends are the best friends!' Daisy teased. 'The thing I admire about her, though, is that she handles it so well. I hated all the leering that went on. I had to put on a show every time I walked into the NAAFI.'

'Mae West!' Eileen laughed.

'Yes, that's who it was – you guessed! But it doesn't bother Katie, she just takes it all in her stride and gives them a look that would wither any man to a prune if they sidle up to her.'

'You did exactly the same!'

'Yes, but it honestly doesn't bother her. I was terrified and mortified, I used to cringe inside.'

'I think I guessed that, Daisy. A lot of us did, but we knew if we suggested you might be a sensitive soul you'd be annoyed.'

'It was that obvious? And I thought I was carrying Mae off so well that she'd soon be out of a job! So where's your Annie then?'

'They're on holiday; they live in the flat above. You'll meet her some other time, she'll be so eager to hear someone else tell her stories of her father.'

'So what are you doing about his family, then?' Daisy asked.

'I have no idea,' Eileen sighed. 'Annie says to leave it for now, something will turn up. She's like that – very intuitive. She's Calli's daughter all right.'

Pearl arrived the next evening and they spent the rest of the night talking about their days in the WAAFs, and how their lives had gone since then. Daisy told them about Frank, the whole story this time, about finding him again.

'To tell the truth,' she said, 'I don't know whether he was glad I'd found him or not.'

'And what about you?' Pearl asked.

'I'm confused,' she laughed. 'Did I go looking for him because I wanted to see an old friend, or because Peter had died and I was lonely?'

'You said he was Mr Right,' Eileen said.

'Yes, but things have happened, we've changed, all of us, haven't we?'

'You don't seem happy to have left him in Australia, though,' Pearl remarked. 'Why is that?'

'That's what I don't know. Besides, I'm not the gorgeous creature I once was, am I? Things have moved about a bit, gravity has set in, there are wrinkles in places I can't even see.'

'Tell me something,' Eileen said. 'When you looked at him, what did you see?'

'The scars at first, you can't really miss them, but after a few minutes I didn't notice them, strangely enough.'

'And now, when you think of him,' Pearl said quietly, 'how do you see him?'

Daisy thought for a moment and then looked at them. 'I see him as he was!' she replied with a shrug.

'Do you know what strikes me as really funny?' Eileen asked. 'Here's this woman who hated being judged on her looks, and here she sits, thinking this man can't want anything to do with her because she thinks her looks have gone off a bit.'

'Do you mind?' Daisy said sharply, and they all laughed.

'But think of it, Daisy. He's probably thinking you wouldn't be interested in him because of his looks,' Eileen suggested, 'yet even with the scarring you still picture him as he was.'

'And?' she asked.

'And he probably sees you as you were – not that you've changed one iota, of course!'

After three days the old friends parted, each with their own thoughts on their shared memories, and promising to be in touch again soon. All that time had passed, Daisy thought, yet it had been as if they had last met six weeks ago. They had changed, yet they were the same. She remembered seeing Eileen and feeling sad that their friendship was now over, but it had been there waiting to be picked up again.

Daisy flew down to Newcastle, determined to see again the city where she had grown up as an unwelcome incomer, the place where so much had happened that had led her to where she now was. Fenwicks was still there, a different enterprise but still a quality store, she noted. The basic layout of the city centre was still recognisable, and then she made her way to Guildford Place and was surprised so many of the old houses were still standing. There was a gap, though, between numbers 6 and 25, and somewhere in that gap was where she had once lived and where her family had died. Newish flats had been built over the crater, sometime during the 1950s she guessed, and they were three-storeys high, one above the old houses on either side.

The strange thing was, though, that standing there looking at the flats, she could still see her old home, and, in a strange way, it was as if her family were still there. She could almost hear her mother's tortured breathing, could hear Kay's beautiful voice soaring, and could see her father coming out of a door that wasn't there to go on his nightshift at the pit. She blotted Dessie out of her mind, he wasn't part of her family, but apart from him and the horror he brought into her life, they were all there still. She could feel it.

She wandered round the area, surprised that so much was still recognisable. Robinson's Pork Shop was there, and Clough's Sweet Shop; even the Ice Cream Parlour was still going strong. In her head she could hear as clear as day the voices she knew from when she was young. And when she turned round she could trace the route she had taken home from the shops, and almost see herself walking it and turning in where her door used to be, watching the ghost of herself as a young girl.

She had been to the library and seen a picture of the devastation of that terrifying night in 1941, and she reassembled it in her head. Smoke mingled with steam from the fire crews' hoses as the water fell on the burning remains of the houses. The voices of the rescuers trying to save those buried underneath intermingled with the sobs of the waiting relatives. And hanging in the air was the stench she knew so well and could never forget from her days in the tower, as metals, wood, material and human flesh burned together.

She went to Heaton Cemetery and placed flowers on the mass grave where the unidentified pieces of the dead were buried. It didn't seem enough, but there was nothing else she could do, so she turned to go and then thought for a moment.

There was one more thing she could do. She could say goodbye to them. When she left Guildford Place in 1939 she hadn't said goodbye to any of them, so she could at least do it now. Standing with her hand on the headstone, she broke down in tears and it was a long time before she could get the words out.

She wouldn't come back here again, she knew that now. The Newcastle Hand had long lost its power, and she was leaving for the last time so much that had pained her and shaped her. She had spent only eighteen years here, hardly a lifetime. She no longer belonged to Newcastle, not even reluctantly, and it was time to break whatever vestiges of the hold it had ever had over her. So, after saying her goodbyes to those she cared about, she left without looking back.

27

Back home in Oxford she tried to go on with the life she had had there for the past thirty years. The family came to visit and went back to their own homes again, all of them trying to keep the traditions they had grown up with, each of these painful for being the first ones without Peter. There were birthdays, Easter, the Flower Show where Professor Theodore Quibbe no longer exhibited, Christmas, New Year, and the first snowdrops that, as if to mock them, were even earlier than in past years, so that they all heard his voice say 'I told you so!' and stood in a group weeping.

Daisy spoke on the phone to Eileen and Pearl and paid a visit to Glasgow to meet Annie. There she told her as many stories about Calli as she could, watching the eagerness in eyes that were so like the lovely boy's. Annie's little boy, Gavin, a miniature of his grandfather, asked her if she knew a man who flew planes and asked her why she was so sad, when she thought she was putting on a very good show of being happy.

Frank wrote from Australia, formal letters that gradually became gentler and more personal, then he stopped writing and she panicked in case he might be dead – again. When she phoned his home she was relieved to hear his voice, but he said he was finding it too hard to keep up the correspondence with her.

'What do you mean?' she gasped, feeling afraid for some reason.

'Daisy, I sometimes feel that it was cruel of you to contact me again,' he said wearily.

'But why?'

'So many things I had buried deep in the past came up again. My wife, she was a good woman, she cared for me and gave me children, but since your visit I've been feeling guilty about her, wondering if I ever gave her as much as she gave me, because the feelings I had for you all those years ago are still there. I keep wondering what might have been, and that's disrespectful to my wife. I feel as though you've churned up my life for nothing. It might be easier if you left me to find out if I can settle down again.'

Daisy was sick to her stomach when she replaced the receiver, but she knew what he meant. She had been wrestling with similar feelings. Why had she looked him up and told him he was her 'someone' and that she had sat by his bed as he lay on the brink of death? To absolve herself of blame for hurting him all those years ago? And if that was the case, she had hurt him all over again. And she had all the same feelings as he had, that was the truth of the matter.

She had loved Peter, but it was a different kind of love from what she had felt for Frank: not less, but different, and she had agonised over what that said about their life together. Had she fooled Peter or had she fooled herself, not that there was any difference, because whoever was being fooled it debased the last thirty or more years of their life together. So, unable to make up her mind, she had kept in touch with Frank, for old time's sake, she told herself, but the friendship was kept at a distance. She was safe, and it struck her that she had done that so many times in her life, put a distance between herself and anyone who threatened to get near. She had done it to Frank before, too.

On the outside she seemed to be coping well. Everyone said she was looking better now that the first anniversary of Peter's death had passed, but inside her the turmoil Peter had saved her from was raging again. She had always thought of herself as a strong woman – not as strong as others thought her, but strong enough – but she no longer felt like that and wasn't sure what to do about anything.

David came home that April, providing a welcome diversion and bringing with him a wife, a beautiful blonde Danish girl called Mette whom he'd met on his travels. Daisy wondered what Peter would have made of it, his easy-going, laidback, good-chap son arriving home already married, so when she paid her usual visit to his grave she told him, imagining his reaction.

When she came back, David was waiting for her.

'Why do you do that?' he asked.

'What?' she asked, perplexed.

'Go down to that cemetery.'

'Because your father's buried there!' she replied.

'Yes, that's the point, Mum, he's buried there because he's dead. You're a young woman, why are you tying yourself to a piece of ground instead of living?'

Daisy didn't have an answer apart from the one she had already given.

'You must be about the same age as Pop was when he married you,' David said gently. 'He had lost his wife, but he didn't sit around talking to a headstone. He went out there and got himself a new woman and another family.'

'Well, that's the potted version,' Daisy said defensively. 'And it's only been just over a year, David.'

'That's long enough,' he said firmly. 'Or were you thinking of going on like this for five years? Ten? The rest of your life?'

Daisy couldn't believe her own son was rounding on her when she hadn't done anything wrong, as she told Eileen later on the phone. She was even more stunned when Eileen agreed with him.

'Ask yourself, what would Peter say if he knew you were trotting up and down to his grave with bits of family news? And be honest, Daisy!'

'He'd be annoyed, I suppose.'

'You suppose?'

'Well, yes, all right, he would be annoyed,' she admitted. 'What am I supposed to do? Register with a marriage bureau?'

There was a long silence.

'Eileen?'

'I'm here.'

Another silence. 'Well what are you waiting for?'

'For the penny to drop, Daisy, you clot!'

'What penny?'

'What,' Eileen asked in an innocent voice, 'ever happened to Mr Right, the Spit guy?'

'Oh, him! He asked me not to write to him any more,' Daisy shrugged.

'I can hear you shrugging. The same shrug as when you made me post his letters back to him marked "Gone Away".'

'Dear God, Eileen Reilly, are *you* by any chance running a marriage bureau these days?'

'Go away and think, woman, and don't disturb me unless you have something to tell me. I'm packing. Annie, Gavin and I are going to see Calli's family in Canada,' Eileen laughed.

'What? Tell me more!'

'His brother turned up, saw Annie and Gavin and thought

he was seeing his mother and Calli. I was going to explain anyway, but I didn't need to, he worked it out as soon as he set eyes on them. We're going to Nova Scotia to give his mother what he calls "A couple of surprises".'

'Oh, Eileen, that's just so wonderful!' Daisy said, then cried down the phone as Eileen cried back to her. 'I'm a sucker for a happy ending these days!'

'Would you listen to yourself? And not a hint of irony, either! Now go and think, Daisy. Don't mess up again. We're not getting any younger, you know!'

Daisy couldn't do it, though. She didn't even know what it was she was supposed to do. It wasn't a fear of leaving the house. The house would always be there and David and Mette would be staying for a while at least, while they both did post-graduate degrees. The musical charity she had set up in honour of her sister was running itself without her, so it wasn't that she was desperately needed. The problem was how to go about something that was possibly a figment of her – and other people's – imagination. The whole thing was silly. She was being pushed into something she didn't want to do at a time when she was still vulnerable after Peter.

Seeking support, she called Pearl, who proceeded to tear her off a strip for being timid and lacking backbone.

'When I think of how you bullied us, Daisy Sheridan, and now you're behaving like some shy virgin, it just makes my blood boil!'

'I didn't bully you!' Daisy protested.

'Yes you did!' Pearl almost shouted. 'I was so scared of you I didn't tell you I'd made a date with one of the Lanc's new gunners.'

'I was protecting you, trying to save you from being hurt!'

'Well I'm returning the compliment, Daisy,' Pearl said sternly. 'Have some bloody guts, woman, take a chance. What's the worst that can happen?'

'He can tell me to get lost,' Daisy said quietly.

'So? You're lost already, you silly woman! Spend a little of the large amount of cash that you've got, and buy a plane ticket. *Now*!'

Attacked from all sides Daisy began to feel that the rest of the world had it in for her. It seemed that she'd gone from a happy, sedate family life to complete turmoil, and everyone was telling her off and informing her that she was wasting her life. And furthermore, they were doing so in very angry tones she didn't think she deserved.

Then she woke up one morning and everything seemed clear for the first time in years. She'd often dreamed of being on a road with many turnings, and the more she looked, the less sure she felt about which one to take. That night she'd had it again, and the road she took led to a hot place, where Isaac, Frank's shopkeeper cousin, was waiting to hand her two ice-cold bottles of juice. He was smiling and pointing further down the road, so she took the juice, thanked him and walked down the road she obviously knew she had to take, and furthermore she was happy.

There was one thing left to do before she could go, though: she had to talk to Peter.

She had made many visits to his grave. At one time she had thought talking to him, bringing him up to date with family news, would make her feel better, a device to get her over the raw time after his death, but it hadn't worked like that and each time she got up to go she felt more bereft, more alone. This time, she knew, would be different, this time she really would be leaving without him. It was early May, the time of his precious snowdrops was over and there were daffodils everywhere. At this time of year he would have been looking out for Professor Quibbe's entries in the next local flower show, she thought with a smile, not a plant in the area would have been safe, and she wondered what he would have done with the red roses she had brought to lay on his grave.

Looking at the headstone she cringed, as she always did, at the words. 'Peter, beloved husband of Daisy.' Words had to be used, she mused, but they were always the same, always so formal and they never said anything meaningful. She had often looked around this tiny place and read almost identical inscriptions with nothing but the names and dates changed, wondering if there wasn't a way of saying something true about the people lying below. But what words were there to describe Peter? A man who, at a party long ago, had dragged her about the floor forcing her to dance with him, who good-naturedly refused to be refused, she thought with a smile, who presented her with the engagement ring she still wore and, by way of a romantic proposal, asked her please to confirm that she wasn't a man. She twisted the ring on her finger, remembering how she had closed the box with the ring still inside and pushed it back at him. And when she had given into Mar's bullying and phoned him to surrender, instead of taking the call he had instantly jumped into that ridiculous two-seater sports car and driven to her side. And just how could any words on his headstone describe the nonsense of Professor Quibbe or the business of the cold accordion player who ended up with an expensive cashmere coat? He had been quite the silliest man she had ever met, and that was saying something, during the war she had met a few. There was more to Peter than that, though, much more. She cleared a space beside the stone and sat down.

'Peter,' she said quietly, 'I have something I have to tell you, well, things, actually, and I have to tell you now because I'm going away and I don't know when I'll be back, or even if, which is funny really, I fully expected one day to be lying right here beside you.' She stopped, listening to the breeze rustling through the new foliage on the trees. He had once said to her, 'Ever wondered why the trees in graveyards are so magnificent? It's all that natural nourishment,' and he had chuckled wickedly. 'Peter!' she had chided. 'Do you have to be so graphic?' 'I think it's wonderful,' he had replied cheerfully. 'I'll be more than happy if my old bones can help a tree to bloom, won't you? A nice, sweeping willow for me, I think.' What had she said? Ah, yes. 'In your case it would have to be a monkey puzzle tree!'

'Peter,' Daisy said, 'you saved my life. I think you know that, but I want you to know that I know it, too. When you took me on I was a mass of fear, shoulder chips and confusion, I think you were the only one who could see that.' She looked across the immaculate grass to where Mar and Par lay. 'Though dear old Mar suspected something,' she said with a smile. 'You let me be myself, Peter, you gave me safety and freed me, I know that, and I never did say how grateful I am for that. I would have been a very different person if you hadn't come along – with a push from Mar, of course. I always tried to be my own person, but I couldn't have done it without you. No one had ever loved me unconditionally, I always had to earn it in some way, provide a service of some kind, be what they wanted me to be. It took me a while to understand that you just loved me. You gave me happiness and peace, as well as a great deal of laughter and exasperation, it must be said, and my life is empty without all of that, all of you, I suppose. I loved you, too, I hope I said that often enough. I still do, you'll never

388

leave me, but I think I have to go now, to move on with my life. I've met someone, well, re-met someone, the pilot I thought had been killed during the war. Remember? He didn't die after all. I found him by chance and I've decided to take that chance, if he wants me, that is. If it hadn't been for you I wouldn't be the kind of woman who could try, and I suppose I'm asking for your blessing.'

Around her the wind whispered again in the trees and she laughed. 'I don't know if that came from a willow or a monkey puzzle, but it'll do,' she said. 'Thank you, Peter, my love,' and placing a kiss on the headstone she got up and left, and this time she felt calm and optimistic.

When she got back to the house, she called Edith and asked her to meet her at the airport, and two days later, like the friend she was, Edith was waiting for her.

'Same place?' she asked.

Daisy nodded. 'Same place.'

When Edith dropped her off outside the farmhouse, Daisy told her not to wait. As the car moved away, she stood outside the house and gathered her confidence. 'What's the worst he can do, Daisy?' she repeated to herself. 'Tell you to get lost? Go on, take a chance, have some bloody guts, woman.'

Then the door opened, and as he came down the path he was holding his open arms out to her.

Acknowledgements

As usual there are many people to thank, especially Pip Brimson who, as Pip Beck, was a serving WAAF with Bomber Command during WW2. Her story of those years was invaluable and I thank her for the generosity and patience she showed in dealing with the endless questions I fired at her. Daisy isn't Pip, but Pip gave me a valuable framework for Daisy's working life and an understanding of that time. If we don't give enough honour to the men of WW2, and we don't, we certainly give considerably less to the women who served with them and, being women, they rarely draw attention to themselves or what they did during those years. They gave up their teens and early twenties and, having mastered every trade from Intelligence Officer through Lorry Driver and Mechanic to Pigeon Handler, they were demobbed at the end of the war and effectively sent back in to Civvy Street to become housewives and mothers. They were the women who gave birth to the Women's Lib generation and, though there's still a long way to go, I don't believe women today would be where they are without that wartime generation's efforts and influence. Thanks also to Frances Mahonney of the WAAF Association for supplying back editions of the WAAF News, a goldmine for anyone interested in learning more about that time from the women themselves.

I also have to thank my son, Euan, once again, for his military knowledge, his endless supply of books and videos and his advice on which ones to read and watch! And Marion McMeekin and John Sheen for their knowledge of Newcastle life and history, and the staff of Newcastle Central Library's Local History Unit, who provided many of their own publications and were always happy to help, no matter how obscure the information requested. Others I'll never be able to repay for their patience include Peter and Janine Watters of Dalby in the Darling Downs in Queensland, Australia, James W. Irvine of Lerwick in Shetland and everyone else who found themselves being bombarded with questions they couldn't understand why they were being asked. Oh, and Raymond Murphy, who sat beside me at primary school, purloining erasers, rulers and pencils on a daily basis and who still thinks he should be paid for being sent off to *properly research* the snippets of information he passes on to me at various stages. Also, my friend Kath Hickey in Australia. And lastly, a lady who doesn't even know she provided the ending for the book. Rene Callaghan of Ardross in Australia told an anecdote in the WAAF Association News of May 1997 that I had to have for Daisy. I haven't been able to trace her, but Rene, wherever you are, I thank you for your wonderful story.

SOURCES

A WAAF in Bomber Command, Pip Beck (Goodall Publications, 1989)

Buckinghamshire at War, Pip (Beck) Brimson (The Book Castle, 2004)

There Shall Be Wings, Max Arthur (Coronet Books, 1993)

Women in Airforce Blue, Squadron Leader Beryl E. Escott (Patrick Stephens, 1989)

Tyneside Irish, John Sheen (Pen and Sword, 1998)

Fashions in the Twenties and Thirties, Jane Dorner (Ian Allan, 1973)